THE
LAND
OF MY
BIRTH

THE LAND OF MY BIRTH

ABRAHAM NNADI

PARTRIDGE

A Penguin Random House Company

To order additional copies of this book, contact
Toll Free 0800 990 914 (South Africa)
+44 20 3014 3997 (outside South Africa)
orders.africa@partridgepublishing.com

www.partridgepublishing.com/africa

DEDICATION

Nnadiegbu and Onne Ibezimako
Onyema and Chituru Nwachukwu
Appollus and Grace Ihuegbu
—*For birth and upbringing*—

CONTENTS

BOOK ONE

THE SEARCH FOR HEROES:
SOWING THE SEED

BOOK TWO

THE RULE OF MONEY:
A PAINFUL HARVEST

BOOK ONE

THE SEARCH FOR HEROES: SOWING THE SEED

1.

Ozurumba worked at the raffia palms plantation, clearing it of unwanted plants blocking the sunshine. Much of his task was getting rid of the creeping plants that wrapped themselves around the palms. The creepers assimilated energy from the sunrays, making them lush and green at the expense of the evergreen trees. The trees that failed to take advantage of the sunshine looked sickly—many midribs of the lance-shaped fronds were broken which left them drooping while their tattered blades were at different stages of discoloration. Some turned yellow or brown and a good number of them were riddled with darkish or whitish spots. The spots he attributed to covering moulds as a result of fungal infection. Having cut the plants off from their roots, he expected the leaves to wilt and dry up eventually. It would open up the plantation to much sunshine and probably restore health to the raffia palms.

He was pleased to complete the task without accident. The riverine swamp was not an easy place to work. Lots of crab holes in the treacherous wetland punished careless movement with dislocated or even broken ankle. His toes gripped the wet and slippery clay soil to guard against sudden slide. Stems of the creeping plants threatened to snatch the machete from him at different times. He remembered what happened to Uwandu in such terrain. The man had lost his footing while swinging machete to clear similar foliage. He lost grip when it failed to slice through the cluster of stems. Momentarily, the stems entangled the machete and by the time the blade started a free fall, it met him on the floor. The pointed tip pierced his chest and the resulting injury proved fatal.

Ozurumba stopped by his pond to throw some barks into the water at different points, hoping they would serve the purpose of providing a haven for migrating fish. He returned to where some glossy fruits with imbricate scales littered the base of a raffia palm. Sprouting bunches of such brownish or reddish fruits signalled an end to the life of the tree. It meant that the tree would wither in a little while. He picked some of them into his work bag. His son Okwudiri and his friends would scoop out the seeds inside before fashioning them into slides for their Boy Scout neckerchiefs. He went on to untangle some *utaziri* leaves from the severed clumps of vegetation. Biting into one, he screwed up his face at the bitter taste, but he relished it knowing that its sharpness would soon give way to a lingering sweetness. The plant's medicinal properties were good for the stomach. His children disliked it, but his insistence on using it as a sauce for their meals paid dividends.

Hunger gnawed at him as he made his way home but he completed his work early when he could not be sure of finding any food waiting for him in the house. Anybody who came back hungry in the afternoon was expected to make do with whatever scraps that could be found until the evening meal was ready. Nobody was in sight as he removed the *utaziri* from his workbag, which he placed on the thatched awning that covered the open kitchen. A billy goat came scampering from the outer room. 'Imagine, everywhere was left open,' he muttered, going in to make sure there was no other goat. He came out to meet Ijuolachi emptying water into a big plastic container. 'Who left everywhere open?'

'But I shut the door before I left for the stream,' Ijuolachi said.

'Anyway, what are we having for lunch?'

'Nothing. No food has been prepared for lunch.'

For a minute, he stood at the same spot, hands on hips, sighing with disappointment, wondering what to do. His farm shorts, a cut-off pair of trousers, were threadbare and dirty, patched at different points to cover gaping holes. They stopped at his knees, revealing sturdy well-formed calves. He wore no shirt and his muscular chest was lightly dusted with hair. A fairly tall man, he had a masculine and athletic physique.

Nwakego, his first daughter, came into the yard carrying a load of firewood on her head. She threw her burden down in the open space then stood for a while waiting for her stiff neck to relax, before gradually turning her chin in either direction. Her faded gown, a wax print, clung to her perspiring torso, bringing out the contours of her young unconstrained breasts. Picking up the wrapper that was rolled into a head pad, she towelled her face with it before gulping down the cup of water that Ijuolachi brought for her. Ozurumba praised her for the good job before suggesting that she boil some yam for their lunch. 'Papa, I don't have the strength to boil any yam now,' Nwakego protested. 'Nobody will kill me in this house with work.'

'Did I say *now*?' he retorted. 'You can rest for a while if you like. Anyway, am I the only one who is hungry?'

'No moment of respite in this house,' she murmured, moving away to put a safe distance between them. 'If it is not "do this", it is "do that". Am I a slave?'

'Children don't respect their parents anymore. Talking back to your father, is that not lack of etiquette? *Allrigh ooo!* Surely anyone who is hungry can roast plantain,' he scowled before walking away with a self-retracting measuring tape.

'Ijuo,' Nwakego called, shortening and cooing her younger sister's name, expecting her to cooperate with her. 'Please fetch some burning coals for us to make fire.'

Ijuolachi had already picked up her size thirty-two metal pail ready to make another trip to the stream. Quickly, she relayed their mother's instruction. 'I have to fill this plastic container. That is what mama said. Otherwise, no food will touch my mouth today,' she answered, her feet swiftly walking away. It would take her four trips to the stream to fill the container. Going about looking for where to fetch some glowing embers was an unwelcome distraction. From experience, she could not tell how long it would take to get such fire at that time of the day. She would have to walk around the neighbourhood, looking for houses where smoke was rising through the roofs. Sometimes, the fire in the first or second house had just been made. If the flame had not burnt long enough, it would not produce the hot coals to be taken away. In such a case, owners of the kitchen would not allow her disturb the fire. At times, there was no good firewood burning in the hearth. It could be tiny tinder sticks from shrubs or epical parts of tree branches that enkindled fire easily, burn out quickly before turning to ashes. Perhaps, it was petioles of palm trees and their leaves or anything at all that flames up easily was keeping the fire burning, however unsteadily, just to get the food cooked. They did not produce burning coals. Such scenarios were not uncommon in homes lacking masculine presence or virile youth strong enough to fetch more robust firewood. It was more likely to happen at that time of the day when most homes had not settled down to prepare supper for the night.

Nwakego could not stop her or she would have her mother to contend with. She got up tiredly and went into the inner room. It was dark except for lights peeping through the tiny slits in the thatched roof and the eaves brightened by daylight. She paused to allow her eyes adjust to the darkness. She moved cautiously along a narrow walkway of uncluttered space, her hand stretched out, groping in the darkness to avoid bumping into anything. Both rooms were crowded with household items, a number of them acquired during the family's sojourn in different cities. She got hold of the plantain stem after her hand groped under her mother's bed briefly. She took it to the outer room and plucked five fingers, two of them were green.

At the oil mill, a woman needed more hands to mash her cooked palm fruits. She asked Nwakego to help. Three women were at the oil well pounding with little coordination. But the exercise required the combined effort of six or more persons pounding vigorously to achieve good result. It was in such cases that having teenagers proved to be an advantage as they could easily invite their friends to help. Nwakego told her how tired she was but Iroagalachi pleaded with her all the more. 'You'll live long, my child. Your children will not die untimely.' Disarmed, Nwakego reluctantly agreed to help.

There was no fire in the hearth when Ozurumba came back. Shortly after, he was shouting Nwakego's name. Her answer came from a distance away. 'You're a temptation to me in this house,' he rebuked. 'If I open my mouth now, your mother, the renowned judge advocate that argues the dead back to life, will rise to your defence. How can you. . .'

'I know it. They won't let me drink water and keep cup down. Everything is on my head, even things I know nothing about. What is my offence now, if I may ask?' Kperechi demanded, unexpectedly emerging from the footpath behind the house. She was carrying a basin containing fresh and dried okra and a handful of *ugu* leaves. She snapped when nobody volunteered an answer. 'You may all ignore me but let nobody disturb my peace.'

Ozurumba turned on Nwakego. 'Won't you bring back the plantain you went to roast? Or you want my hand to touch you this afternoon?'

'They are not ready,' Nwakego answered.

'Ready or not, get them as they are if that will buy peace,' Kperechi ordered. She noticed that Nwakego was still rooted on the same spot, she raised her voice. 'Won't you check them or do you want him to call me more names?' When Nwakego returned to the inner compound with the plantain, her mother was still tidying up and arranging the firewood in a corner. 'What was all the shouting about?' Nwakego told her what happened. 'What is the difference? Since you got to the oil mill, wouldn't you have fetched the live coals, bring them home to cook? I have told you time and again, taking the easy route hardly solves a problem.'

'But *daa* Iroagalachi would have seen me all the same.'

Kperechi relented, knowing that she had a good argument. 'Anyway, did he expect you to refuse that childless woman a helping hand? That is unheard of. Ozurumba Mbachu and hunger,' she heaved her shoulders. 'I have not seen anything like him. Nothing makes sense to him whenever he is starving. I know him like the back of my hand.'

Turning the handle, Ozurumba unfastened the wooden latch of the picket gate to enter the *obu*—the sitting room where Mbachu, his late father used to receive guests. He sat down to get some rest while waiting for the food. The wall of the *obu* leading to the inner compound had given way but the thatched roof was held in place by wooden pillars. The *obu* had suffered neglect as neither Ozurumba nor Uwakwe, his elder brother, adopted it as personal sitting room. A number of slabs and hand stones used in cracking palm kernels littered the floor, making it untidy. Obviously, the children who worked there did not clean up after their task.

It occurred to him that *obu* had lost its significance in their time. Domestic activities that took place at the *osokwu* were carried out in the *obu* without inhibition. In a compound, the *osokwu* was the structure built behind the *obu* where women and children slept and where other household activities took place. At the times of his ancestors when actual *osokwu*—sudden attack and invasion—was not unheard of, the *obu* equally served as the householder's military outpost. Whenever such internecine war broke upon his community, retreating behind the *osokwu* was the immediate line of defence. The various clusters of plantain and banana stalks and other trees became his momentary fortress that attackers were quite wary of. Such military strategies did not occupy the mind of householders in modern times.

With more than one hour to go before their kindred meeting, Ozurumba decided to thresh some of the palm fruit bunches heaped together at their frontage. 'Is the food not ready yet?' he asked, standing up, walking towards the wall of his two-room building. He removed the new hand axe from the bag hanging on the wall. With his left thumb he felt the edge.

'Are you not done?' Kperechi asked Nwakego, leaving the firewood she was arranging to help her in making the sauce. On top of the mud oven in her open kitchen was a basket tray containing fresh red and green pepper which were spread out to dry. She took some and plucked off their peduncles, adding them to those in the *oku*—the clay bowl used for such meals. Taking hold of the wooden ladle, her hand moved back and forth, crushing and grinding the pepper and salt into a paste before plucking some of the *utaziri* leaves to blend them together. She noticed her husband open the gate. 'Where are you going to again? The food is ready to be served any moment from now.'

'Take your time,' he answered, closing the gate. He needed to occupy himself with something instead of sitting there waiting for food to be served. He was pleasantly surprised at the result the hand axe produced after threshing a head bunch. Unlike machetes, the new axe did not split the palm nuts, making it a better tool for the job. Ozurumba was good at taking to new tools that made his tasks less difficult. Life in Mboha was changing gradually but steadily. The villagers eagerly acquired modern tools and utensils which were easily affordable. At the gathering of *umunna*—kindred meeting—it was no longer necessary to fashion *ogirishi* leaves into cups for scooping hot pepper-soup cooked with yam and the entrails of the sacrificed animal. At such peace or fellowship offerings, spoons of various sizes did the job better than cupped leaves or *akukonko*—clam shells. Enamel or plastic plates, basins and cups displaced earthenware utensils such as *oku* and *udu* for different uses in the house. They were lighter to carry about and some of them looked more presentable. Every house could boast of at least a hurricane lantern imported from Germany. It took over from *tunja* and *mpalaka*—the locally improvised lanterns with no globe to shield their naked flames. Inevitably, they became relegated as inferior sources of light. Homes that boasted the presence of men did not lack radio transistors. The villagers even knew what a gramophones looked like when a kinsman brought one back from the city. It did not take the village long to assimilate the new technologies, and to forget that the world had ever been any different.

Akwakanti, walking barefooted, stopped as he came close to Ozurumba. He held a machete with the blunt edge resting on his arm and a dead beaver dangling in his left hand. His kinky hair was growing thin, unevenly tufted unlike his robust chest, which he bared down to the waist because of the enervating heat. 'What a neat job,' Akwakanti remarked, dropping the beaver to the ground with a thud.

'Yes, it is quite good for threshing,' Ozurumba agreed, straightening up. At Akwakanti's request, he passed the axe.

'This is super-light!' cried Akwakanti, admiring and swinging the axe with absolute ease as he visualised himself harvesting or threshing a bunch of palm fruits with it. 'How much did you buy this for?'

'Four naira.'

Akwakanti grinned, giving Ozurumba a doubtful look, his smallish head angled to the right. '*Haaa,* agile soldier, you have seen a gullible kid who will believe that, isn't it?' Who will shell out two pounds for a small axe like this?' he asked, his voice low as usual. Mechanically, he converted the four naira into two pounds, the original exchange rate when the currency supplanted the pounds sterling.

'Delicious soup costs money,' Ozurumba countered. 'This beaver is such a good catch. Which of your traps caught it, the one in Achiaghara?'

'It is yours. Your trap in Okata caught it.'

'*Owoworom ooo!*' he rejoiced, his face brightening with smile. 'Imagine, today that I was too tired to pass there.'

'I passed through Okata on my way from Imo.'

'I heard there were so much fish floating on Imo River today.'

Akwakanti confirmed it, telling him how it caused another rough and tumble between their village boys and those of Abadaba. The situation had been arrested by the time he got there. Adindu, another villager that was led by his son, stopped to hear more gist about the fight. There was fear in his voice as he asked what happened?

'Ohia, the dredger, ordered our boys out of the river claiming that the Ovoro beach belonged to Abadaba. He got into a fight with Umevu, and as you can imagine, everybody took sides. He is lucky I did not get there in good time. I would have smashed his face to teach him a lesson he won't forget in a hurry.'

'It is a good thing it did not escalate. There is nothing to gain by making trouble,' Ozurumba said.

'What is the need of fighting over such mundane things?' asked Adindu, his voice was quite shrill. 'It makes no sense at all.'

'Papa, Mama asked me to call you,' Ijuolachi announced from the entrance. She went to meet Okwudiri when she saw him lifting the beaver from the ground. 'Is it ours?' she asked, beaming with delight.

Ozurumba was surprised to hear that the 'Gamalin 20' poured into the river by Ofeimo people could cause such trouble. He could only imagine what would happen if it was Abadaba people that poured it. Fishermen poured the insecticide into the river during dry season and as the poison flowed downstream, it affected most of the fish swimming close to the water surface. They all knew that if officials of the ministry of agriculture and water resources became aware of it, there would be grave consequences. The practice became less frequent as officials of the ministry sustained a campaign against it. They harped on the health hazards and the adverse impact on the fish population and stock. On one occasion, policemen arrested some men from a community that poured the insecticide. It became quite clear that the ministry could bark as well as bite. To the best of his recollection, it was more than five years since such insecticide was poured into the river.

The plantain was served when he got into the inner compound. He sat on the low kitchen stool and his children joined him, surrounding the *oku*, some of them squatting or sitting. Ozurumba asked Akudo, Uwakwe's youngest daughter, to join them. Hands bumped into one another, each eating as fast as possible before the bowl was emptied. The smacking of lips as they licked their fingers attested to how hungry they were. He uncovered his aluminium cup to drink from it but Akachi went to him for water also. 'Woman, do we have to bring a keg of palm wine to appease you before you join us?' Ozurumba asked.

'Don't worry about me,' replied Kperechi, keeping herself busy with chores. 'I'm not you who cannot stand hunger for a moment.'

'Well, if the moon rejects food, the stars feed fat.' But Ozurumba ate only three pieces and watched his children devour the rest. 'Sit like a woman,' he told Ijuolachi. She adjusted her clothes to cover herself properly. The plantain was too hot for Akachi and each time it burnt his fingers, he attempted using his left hand but Ozurumba would not let him. 'Do you want to become left-handed?' he asked, a little peevishly. 'One more piece for each of you,' he told Okwudiri and Nwakego. He reserved three pieces for his wife before getting up to prepare for the kindred meeting. He was barely inside when the alarm clock went off, the clacker going back and forth with rapid intensity, striking the bells on the handle, the metal casing vibrating, sending it dancing across the table. He had mistakenly set the alarm to go off at twenty-four minutes past five in the afternoon.

The outer room doubled as the parlour. A big table and a twelve-spring metal bed took most of the floor space. A storage cupboard shared the remaining space with two iron cushion chairs. These household items told the story of his life: the bits and pieces acquired in different towns at different times all of which followed him home.

Rummaging through the clothes hanging over the rope, he took a top to the door for closer inspection. 'If I say I'm not amazed at the type of people I have in this house; I would be telling a lie. Ordinary clothes, they can't wash. Whether they expect me to personally do my laundry, I, Ozurumba the son of Mbachu, cannot tell,' he muttered. Yet he pulled on the creased and dirty top. 'Who's interested in what I wear anyway? Am I scouting for a new wife?' He took up a hardcover notebook, made sure a biro pen was inside it, and left the house.

'Please, my husband, is that top not dirty?' Kperechi asked as he came to the frontage.

'Did I threaten you with a lawsuit if it was washed?' he countered.

'Don't be angry!' she said, making a mealy-mouthed apology while carrying on with her chores. 'I know that's not the only shirt you have in this house. There must be one or two clean ones you can wear.'

Ozurumba ignored her. 'Do you need to buy anything? I don't want to hear "I bought this or that on credit". I won't pay if you pledge my credit.' He did not wait for Kperechi to list all the condiments needed for preparing soup before he called on Okwudiri. 'Give your mother one shilling from where I keep money. You know where I mean?'

'Under the radio?'

'Did I ask you to announce it to the whole world? Foolish idiot, I don't know when you'll get wiser. Make sure that beaver is properly gutted. We shall take Akwakanti's portion to him when I come back.'

Kperechi noticed that the heap of palm nuts that Okwudiri was meant to pick was still remaining. She turned on him for failing to do any tangible thing all day. 'You did not complete your task. What happened?'

'I have picked the good ones before I left for the river. The remainder are bad.'

'You know I won't buy that. Before the blink of an eyelid, make sure that task is completed. You want to tell me that all you did today is attending Boy

Scout meeting and going to the river to have a wash, isn't it? You know what to do if you want dinner to touch your mouth tonight.'

'They will soil my hands,' he protested. 'I have taken my bath already.'

'Story! Who will listen to all that? I know you are the incarnation of *Nwa DC* that dirt never touches. But as you know, soiled hands bring about oily mouths. You have to do your bit. Otherwise, how do you expect any food to touch that your mouth? You can return to the river for another bath if you want.'

*   *   *

Waking up at five in the morning was a regular part of Ozurumba's life. He noticed it was three minutes past the hour as he flashed his torchlight on the table clock. He stretched his hand to turn on the radio. The morning devotion was still airing; he lay in bed, drifting between slumber and consciousness. At six, the news programme *Panorama* started with an account of the previous day's proceedings at the state's legislative assembly. Determined to attract the presence of the Federal Government to the state, the governor broke down in tears while listing the pressing and urgent needs of his people. Alleging neglect, he pointed out that the only significant presence of the Federal Government in Imo State was the prisons. The world news followed, and the assassination of Muhammad Anwar El Sadat jolted Ozurumba. He imagined what a serious setback it could be in the search for peace in the Middle East.

Keeping abreast with current affairs was a passion he developed in the city, where ignorance was often greeted with scorn. As a staunch supporter of the Great Zik of Africa, he did not only follow the events leading to independence but was a volunteer, helping to arrange the grounds and tables for the rallies held by the political party, NCNC. He could not afford to look lost while anything about their charismatic leader was being discussed.

He believed in the visions articulated by the political leaders. As a result, he turned up at rallies to join others remonstrate against colonial rule. The right to self-determination was their singsong and they looked forward to the time when the British colonial administration would depart from them. They dreamed of the future when their own flesh and blood would govern their country. All the abundant human and material resources would be channelled into building one nation, one people, one destiny. Development would not only be rapid, but the opportunity to involve everyone in the pursuit of happiness would be easier to realise. Like many others, he read newspapers, magazines, listened to radio, making sure he was up to date.

Those were the halcyon days, when city life held so much promise. He left the village, hoping to amass enough wealth for a pleasant retirement. A mud house with thatched roof was the last thing he expected to retire to. Anything less than the house modelled on the district commissioner's residence roofed with zinc—the corrugated roofing sheets—would not be good enough. But the civil war that forced him to flee the city destroyed that dream. Fed up with the arduous task of re-thatching his house every other year, he was determined to roof it with zinc even if he could not put enough money together to build a more elegant house.

Mboha, his village, was situated on fairly even terrain made of loamy soil and surrounded by dense and verdant foliage. Trees bearing essential fruits—oranges, mangoes, lemon, guava, coconut—were regular features of many compounds. The leafy trees such as calabash trees, *ube* trees—the local equivalent of pears, *udara* trees—the local equivalent of apple provided shades from sun, adding to the dense flora of their ecosystem. Every family owned *oha* tree from which sprigs of vegetable leaves could be plucked off for making soup during dry season when the soil was too dry to grow *ugu*. In addition, virtually every compound in Mboha grew the much cherished plantain and banana of different variety which were regarded as *ozuru umu mbia*—the food that sustained orphans and the needy. *Akum shut-up*, the tree that produced the bitter herb for combating malaria were not common. The deep green leaves of *ogirishi* with its brilliant white and purple flowers were more likely to be found in compounds of those regarded as idol worshippers. They were planted closely together to surround the shrines and screen off inquisitive eyes. It also produced the eerie ambience to make it an awesome holy land which commanded the reverence of worshippers while keeping at bay others with incompatible belief.

Few houses roofed with corrugated and galvanised iron sheets interspersed the landscape of regular thatched roofs of mud houses. Along with the new houses came a new habit of growing flowers. It became unfashionable to cultivate every available space for food. Instead, a vegetable garden or small orchard was usually cultivated behind the house so as to leave the frontage beautified and presentable.

The village owed much of those changes to her dissatisfied indigenes who left home in search of wealth. As children, most of them attended the school run by St John's Anglican Church. Day by day, they sat in the thatched shed learning the basics of life. Those who endured to the end came out equipped to lead a lifestyle different from what the village could offer. Determined to live life above subsistence, they charted a different course. With the coming of the railway, they followed their hearts to the cities.

Mbachu had sent his two sons to the school. Uwakwe, the first of his five children, dropped out before completing standard two. In his view, it was not only a waste of time to study another man's language but a distraction to anyone who was ambitious. He could not come to terms with the idea of compelling students to fetch water and firewood for teachers or work in their farms. Any pupil who failed to do so risked punishment. Though helping others was not strange in the culture of his upbringing but a volunteer was different from a paid hand. He concluded that school would not make much difference to his life. Farming yam and tapping wine from palm trees were the tasks and skills expected of a strong and prudent man in his community. He decided to focus on those.

Contrary to all expectations, Ozurumba, his impulsive younger brother, continued schooling. After standard six, he became qualified to get work in the townships. Before he left the village, Mbachu found a suitable wife for him, collapsed the *mkpokoro* fence to the left to add another three-room structure to the two that existed in the rectangular-shaped compound. Their mother, Ehichanya, was still alive and was occupying Mbachu's room adjoining the *obu*. The third room in that structure served as her kitchen and pantry. Ozurumba fled the North before the pogrom, returning to the village with three children to occupy his portion of the family house. Uwakwe's household was already making use of one of the rooms in his three-room structure, leaving him and his household to make do with the remaining two rooms. Like other returnees, Ozurumba's family had been traumatised by war and were in a state of chronic starvation. Uwakwe noticed that most of the crops and fruits he and Ozurumba held in common were wantonly harvested. He protested this in strong terms. 'Is plantain more important than my starving family?' Ozurumba snapped back when the issue was raised.

'Is that a reason for wasting them while they are still tender and green?' retorted Uwakwe.

'Tender or not, we have to stave off hunger.'

'Is it not better when it is mature and ripe?' Uwakwe sighed, walking away.

Kperechi sensed trouble. 'My good husband, please it is enough,' she appealed to Uwakwe. 'Surely, this can be sorted out.'

'Do I have to beg him? Our father planted them,' Ozurumba maintained.

'Does he tend them from the grave or did you mulch them while you were in the cities?' Uwakwe replied, gathering his tapping kits.

Ozurumba lost his temper and lashed out angrily. 'What do you take me for? A fool, isn't it? All because I have not asked for an account of all you did while I was away? Were you not harvesting and using them while I was away?'

Uwakwe could not believe his ears. 'Does it include the crops I personally planted that were harvested? Tell me.'

'I did not touch your crops. Count me out.'

'So Mbachu rose from his grave to harvest them. Isn't it?'

'What are you implying?' Ozurumba queried, walking towards his brother. But neighbours intervened to stop the altercation getting out of hand. Ozurumba would not accept being called a thief. He was ready to fight anyone who dared to bring such allegation against him. He denied having anything to do with such losses. Uwakwe was not the only victim, and Ozurumba was not the only returnee who fled the city.

Ozurumba was vindicated the day Onwuka was caught uprooting cassava from another man's farm. It provided a good opportunity for Kperechi to berate those who had slandered her husband. 'Speak up let them hear it. Heaven and earth hear it ooo! Today, the dead and the living have heard it. It is not Ozurumba that was caught uprooting another person's crops! All the haters, what do you have to say?' she raised her hands heavenwards in thanksgiving. 'This God in heaven, how can I thank you enough? Yes, a cow without tail, you are the one that drives away flies from him.'

Jenny was on her way to the stream when she came upon Kperechi in her hysterical state. 'What is the problem my fellow woman?'

'The person who has been reaping where he did not sow has been caught today. Imagine, dogs have been eating faeces while sheep have been suffering the tooth decay? So it is not Ozurumba that is harvesting other people's crops after all? Is that not why soldiers were instigated to conscript an innocent man? They sent him to the warfront to die but. . .'

'Calm down, Kperechi. God has already fought your battles. He went to the warfront but is he not the one who walks about full of life and zest?'

Kperechi thanked her for the concern she showed. She spoke to her in Efik, a language both of them understood as persons who lived in Calabar at a point in their lives. 'I couldn't help myself. I don't know what Ozurumba did to them. Is our family the only one struggling to survive these hard times?' she asked, using the end of her wrapper to dab tears from her young face before picking up the child crying for her attention.

Uwakwe was at the whetstone sharpening his machete when he heard the news. 'What do you expect of men who left the farms they should cultivate in search of adventure in the cities? What about the school and learning that puff their heads? Of what use is it to them in times like this?'

Ozurumba's conscription as an auxiliary soldier during the war did not help matters. Soldiers from Afougiri training ground had swooped on him and Daniel early one morning as troublesome fellows who had to be at the warfront. Though Uwakwe was ready to swear to the contrary, his brother did not believe that he knew nothing about the compulsory recruitment. Ehichanya, their aged mother, hated the growing feud between her sons. She blamed it on gossips and feared it could end in a disaster if left unchecked. She told them a story to drive her point home.

A man took three days to sharpen his machete. With it, he followed his brother to the *oforo*—the public toilet in the neighbourhood—where he stealthily crept up to assassinate him. Why? He had been shown the thigh of a goat as the price paid by his brother to have him murdered. Because of blind hatred, he believed the story without asking his brother. By the time he realised that it was not true, it was too late. 'When brothers are at each other's throats, it is strangers that reap the fruit of their labour,' Ehichanya warned.

'Blood feud is a terrible thing,' Nwugo agreed. 'Anyway, advice is effective only when it is heeded.'

'Anger, has it ever produced anything of good report?' Kperechi asked, knowing it was her husband's weakness. It was Uwakwe who always walked away from most of their arguments, giving peace a chance. In a fit of rage, Ozurumba had drawn his machete once, threatening bloodshed. Astounded by the contrast between the brothers, she concluded ruefully that the same mother gave birth to them, but the same Creator did not make them.

2.

On leaving the Ohuhu Motor Park, Ozurumba stood by the roadside, waving down a cab. At his third attempt, one of the township taxis stopped and the passengers in the back seat adjusted their sitting to make space for him. The taxi was quite neat and clean, a brand new Peugeot 504SR saloon car. As the cab drove through the township, they passed a number of roadworks. Streets were blocked with MCC barriers and marked with diversion signs. This forced the driver to take a longer and tortuous route. Still, Ozurumba was delighted to see how rapidly changes were taking place. Improving the drainage system was an integral part of the construction work. The workers were laying down a mixture of sand and gravel to stabilise the soil, then reinforcement for the drains. Excavators were busy digging out what would become a big carnal in the middle of the town for channelling floodwaters.

The smooth surfaces of the tarred streets made up for the detour. The cab operator drove carefully, slowing down before crossing or completely stopping at several intersections that was a feature of the gridiron plan on which Umuahia was built. The front seat passenger got out, and moments later, the driver stopped for another passenger at Queen Elizabeth Hospital. 'If other passengers alight, can I book you as my personal driver for two hours?' asked the genteel elderly passenger, exhibiting the sophistication in his speech and manners common to those educated outside the country during the colonial era.

'Yes sir,' the cabman answered with joyful haste, his manners becoming obsequious as he reckoned that the gentleman must be a distinguished senior civil servant. His podgy face that was hitherto bland became animated and his manners, more pleasant. He quoted the hourly rate cab drivers charged for their services in the township and to his obvious delight, the new passenger accepted to pay without haggling. Without further delay, the cabman told the passengers to wind up their windows before turning on the air conditioner, a courtesy exclusively reserved for very important personages.

'*Eleooo*, the road is so smooth that one could be tempted to lie down on it,' the female passenger declared, beaming with delight.

'Oh, it's definitely a good job,' the gentleman agreed, bringing out his white handkerchief to clean his face.

'It will save our cabs from frequent breakdowns,' said the cabman.

'If the roads had been like this before now, the Queen of England would surely have officiated in person at the opening ceremony for the Queen Elizabeth II Hospital,' said the gentleman. Ozurumba did not hesitate to contest the statement. He had not forgotten a fact that was much celebrated in his youth that their native land hosted the queen when she performed the opening ceremony of the hospital. 'HRM visited quite alright, but our roads were in such a deplorable condition she could not risk getting stuck in the mud. She had to commission the hospital while she was airborne.'

'*Ooho*, is that what happened?' asked the cabman, astonished that such information had eluded him all the while. 'Can you imagine it? And it is our church that built it.'

'What church?' asked the gentleman.

'Methodist.'

The gentleman smiled. 'I'm also a Methodist, but our church alone did not build it. The amount of money required was quite significant. So the Church Council provided the funds to ensure it was built like one of the best hospitals in England. Indeed, it has turned out to be the best hospital in Eastern Nigeria.'

'I'll be stopping,' the female passenger spoke up. Pulling off the road, the cabman made sure it was safe before he allowed the door to be opened.

'Mbakwe has done well. God will bless him,' the cabman commented, as he pulled back unto the road.

'I'm not surprised by his achievements,' the gentleman agreed, adding that Mbakwe who was a lawyer must have studied the works of Jeremy Bentham, John Stuart Mill, and other great philosophers whose work centred on the common good and the greatest happiness of the greatest number. He believed that Mbakwe must do more to extend the frontiers of public service in their part of the world. 'I'm sure he saw things for himself when he studied abroad.'

'I see!' Ozurumba exclaimed reflectively, a smile breaking forth on his oval face. 'Maybe that is why he was weeping the other day while listing the needs in our Imo State.' Following the incident, journalists were swift to tag him as the weeping governor.

'Democracy is good,' declared the gentleman. 'He knows that nobody will vote for him for a second term if he doesn't perform. So, he has to do whatever he can to attract development.'

'That is very true,' Ozurumba agreed. Reaching his stop, he handed a fifty-kobo note to the cabman and received thirty kobo change before bidding farewell to the driver and passengers. He had arrived at the Timber Shed market where building materials were sold. He stopped at a cement dealer's shop and inquired about the current prices of cement. There had been a fifty-kobo increase. A bundle of zinc, twenty-four sheets, sold for thirteen naira. He checked some other shops.

'Star Brand is the best,' a trader argued as he tried to persuade Ozurumba to buy from him. 'Year after year, it will still be shining. It doesn't rust like others.'

'What about Horse Brand?'

'I'll give it to you for twelve-fifty.'

Ozurumba started bargaining from ten naira before stating that twelve naira was the last price he could afford. He needed to buy metal pillars too. Reluctantly, the shopkeeper agreed to let him have it at that price. The trader claimed he was doing Ozurumba a favour since he was practically making no profit from it. Ozurumba bought two packets of roofing nails from him before the trader asked his trainee to take him to a shed where he could buy metal pillars. The wooden cart pusher was still unloading the twelve pillars he bought when a pickup truck driver came to negotiate with Ozurumba. 'I can't pay four naira,' he protested. 'Am I chartering the vehicle?'

'Where will I get more passengers to Mboha?' asked the driver.

'You can pick some up on the way!' Ozurumba was used to haulage men and their habit of picking up passengers and their goods until there was no room left to cram in another bean. The trader cut into the conversation and tried to persuade the haulage man, Jonah, to reduce his price, arguing that the load was not much. Jonah was unyielding and engaged the trader in a back-and-forth argument. '*Oga* Silas, have you considered the distance I will cover from here all the way to Mboha, that faraway village in Umuhu? If it is their *afor* market day, when I load my vehicle with passengers, I make more than five naira for one-way trip.'

Silas argued that it was unreasonable to make Ozurumba pay the sum of four naira which several passengers would have paid him. This did not seem to sway him as he came up with a ready counter. His vehicle would consume the same amount of fuel to cover the distance and the same length of time would be required to get there. On a second thought, he reduced the fare to three naira. Silas was encouraged by the change of mind and he turned to Ozurumba. 'He's not one of those that quote arbitrary figures; that I know too well. I can vouch for him on that. Sometimes I give him goods to deliver to my customers unaccompanied. Three naira is a fair deal.'

'I don't have that much. I can add fifty kobo on the two naira that I offered to pay.'

Jonah started to load the goods after he was persuaded to accept. Two female volunteers wearing *ANC* polo shirts adorned with the silhouettes of Nelson Mandela and Walter Sisulu approached them asking for freewill donations. 'Whatever you have, please give. Nothing is too small or too big,' one of them announced, thrusting the lidded can forward. When the trader demanded to know why he had to make such contribution, the second volunteer had a ready-made answer. 'We have to liberate our brothers in apartheid South Africa,' she announced, her mood bubbly and carefree. 'You have heard what is happening to them, haven't you? They need our help to dismantle apartheid.'

The trader dropped two ten-kobo coins into each can.

'Dee, what about you? Nothing is too small,' the first volunteer repeated.

'I've spent all my money,' Ozurumba answered, dipping hand into his pocket. He had more than one naira in excess of what he would pay Jonah. He squeezed a fifty-kobo note through the hole. The girls thanked them profusely and cheerily. The sight of the fifty-kobo note made them glad since they were not expecting such generosity from such undistinguished member of the public. They crossed the road to join other volunteers.

'You were the person crying you have no money,' Jonah challenged as they drove off. 'But you have a whole fifty kobo to give away.'

'I wish I had more to spare. Have you asked yourself how we survived the war? It is such kind donations that got us all the Formula-II, the stock fish, the corned beef, and all the other relief materials.'

Jonah pouted his lips thoughtfully. 'That is quite true,' he said finally, nodding his head. 'I will give something when I come back.' That seemed to ease his pricked conscience before he resumed chattering about the giant strides the governor was making in developing their state. 'What you have just seen is happening in Aba, Okigwe, Orlu, and Owerri as well, right now,' he said. His tone was combative; his shaggy moustache and beard accentuated his unkempt look. His keen eyes were on the road but he stole quick looks at Ozurumba to make sure he was listening.

As they paused at a junction, Ozurumba beckoned to a newspaper vendor and bought *The Nigerian Statesman* with the picture of Mbakwe splashed on the front page. He looked ebullient in the ash-coloured silky suit. 'Is that not why we voted him in? He must have the interests of people at heart,' he said, more as a matter of fact than singing his praises.

'You are not wrong,' Jonah agreed, nodding. He dropped into low gear as he queued behind the other vehicles; his brow creased with concern at the grinding noise of metal against metal. 'My gearbox is threatening to go wrong again,' he muttered, strenuously turning the steering wheel as the traffic warden beckoned them to move on. 'What about other governors? How many of them have done half of what he's doing? I hail from Etiti Local Government Area just like the governor.' His face lit up as he forgot his momentary worries. 'You have to visit the power station he's building at Amaraku. If the whole country is in darkness, power will not fail in Imo State,' he boasted. 'The same thing goes for the poultry in Ndudu-Avutu-Obowo. Soon, everybody can afford chicken like crayfish.'

'But what industry will he site in Umuahia?' Ozurumba asked, alluding to the uneven spread of development, a point that the governor's critics harped on.

'Don't worry, development will get to everywhere. Charity begins at home, isn't it?' asked the driver. Clearly, it was not the first time that he was coming up against such objection. 'We're blessed to have him. See, he's building our Imo Airport. Is that in his village?'

'How many times have we been taxed for it? I paid airport levy for each of my child that is schooling.'

'I equally paid but I'm not complaining,' he said, beating his chest in self-acclamation. 'It is something we're doing for ourselves. *Ibu anyi ndanda*—the dung beetle is never defeated by the size of his load—that is what we are,' he enthused, easily mouthing a local cliché.

Like those growing up in his time, Ozurumba knew how tenacious the dung beetle could be. He employed every tactic to conquer the task of moving the load that was far bigger than his size. Watching him scramble atop the load or go round it, looking for what was impeding the dung from rolling forward could amuse a keen observer. His activities never failed to drive home an important lesson: where there is a will, there is a way for the unyielding dung beetle. 'Why should we toil and labour to build what the government build for others? Why must the rule change when it is our turn? Why should our case be different? What makes us different from others?'

'Don't let that bother you. You may think they are hurting us but if we continue like this, with our *kobo, kobo, afu, afu,* we'll be like London and America.'

'And when will that be?' asked Ozurumba, amused by his extreme optimism. Given the realities on ground such optimism was a big dream. However, they could not deny that there was something remarkable about Mbakwe. He did not preoccupy himself with only managing monies accruing to Imo State from the Federal revenue allocation. As a visionary leader, he set a number of targets for the State and despite limited resources, tried to achieve the goals with unstinting zeal. The airport project was a glowing testimony. In addition to taxes, he mobilised people of Imo State to freely and wilfully give towards the project. Knowing that most of the well-to-do indigenes of the State resided in different parts of the country, he had to set up an appeal fund for the project. They bought into the vision and came together under different umbrellas to pool resources together to realise the project.

As a governor, he decried the situation where governance was increasingly more about the governor and a little or nothing about the governed. Looking at how public service and administration was collapsing in the country, Mbakwe wept. He could not help but remember what it was before the departure of the British. Completely disenchanted, he wished that the British could come back. It was as if he knew what the state of affairs in the country would be more than thirty years after he supposedly made the comment. Perhaps, it qualified him as another man who saw tomorrow.

*   *   *

In the village square that evening, a number of Ozurumba's kinsmen congratulated him. One of them was Akobundu who was making thatched sheets for the renewal of his own roof. The rainy season that year did not make his task easier. Bowls and every kind of container were placed at different points to collect the steady drips of water. The back wall that was sodden with rainwater caved in. 'You don't know the huge favour you have done to yourself by escaping this thatch-clipping chore.'

'You must have made a fortune from the building contract you handled for Sunday,' Akwakanti thought aloud.

'Is it a question of how much I made?' asked Ozurumba. 'Almost every year I find myself clipping thatches. I really got fed up and decided to do something about it.' Without knowing it, he expressed the deep yearning of many who desired to escape the drudgery. Like other villages, most men in Mboha became involved in making thatched sheets before the age of fifteen. As a boy, he followed older men to the plantation to fell one or two raffia palm trees, cut off the long stalks and then pluck out the fronds from their extremely spiny bases. Carrying the fronds and stalks home was another arduous task before preparing the stalks for the clipping exercise. Each clipped frond must overlap the other in regular sequence.

Such a boy must learn to endure the sting of the tiny spikes that pricked his skin at every turn, leaving small lacerations all over his hands and other parts of the body. Spurts or trickles of blood from the body must be ignored or endured whenever the barbs poked the skin deep enough to cause such bleeding. Since they were not life threatening, he must learn to put up with the momentary pain and inconvenience. Each pinch, laceration, or cut played a role. Collectively, they taught him how to perform such task as safely as he could despite the innumerable hazards.

Living under a zinc roof no longer required the long planning and savings needed to build *mgbidi* or brick houses. Roofing the existing mud house with zinc roofing sheets was a welcome innovation that many were eager to embrace. 'I had to race down to town when I realised the lump sum Sunday paid me could buy two bundles of zinc. As you know, money is not good company.'

'As far as I am concerned, Sunday has really made a success of his Cameroon stay,' Akobundu noted, putting away the thatched sheet he had just completed.

'It's not a lie,' Josiah concurred but having heard about the risk involved in crossing the Atlantic Ocean to get to Cameroon, he heaved his shoulders, shuddering at the thought. 'It takes a lot of guts to cross that water by any kind of boat!'

As the biggest waterbody around them, the villagers were in awe of the Imo River. A boatman could paddle across it in less than thirty minutes except when it was in spate with the current becoming quite rapid. At such times, the skilled boatman did not paddle straight across the river but must paddle up a bit against the tidal flow to make room for the rapid currents working against linear movement. With such technique, the boat did not overshoot the landing on the other side. All the same, it did not take the skilled boatman up to one hour to row and manoeuvre his boat across the river.

But they had heard about different waterbodies including the River Niger and the River Benue that were far bigger than Imo River. The size of each was like multiplying Imo River into several places. Yet, it would not take an hour for an engine boat to cross any of such rivers. Hearing that it took an engine-powered boat several hours to cross the Atlantic Ocean before getting to Cameroon, it was left to the infinite conjecture of their minds to fathom the size. 'Life is all about *agba ekperechi*—prayerfully journeying along. The water that takes hours to cross by engine boat cannot be a small waterbody,' Ozurumba agreed. 'Is it once or twice that speed boats have capsized in that ocean?'

'Merciful God,' Anosike exclaimed, heaving his shoulders. 'Even if you offer me millions of naira, it won't tempt me to risk my life like that. No sane person can embark on such a journey.'

'Are you saying that Sunday is not sane?' Akwakanti challenged. 'Whoever wants to embark on such a journey must swallow the heart and liver of a tiger. The courage required is not a little thing.'

'There are certain wealth that cannot be acquired with sane mind,' Josiah reasoned. 'Anyway, Ozurumba, all you need now is to buy wood from Bernard, the sawyer, and your thatched roof will change into zinc,' he said, going back to the topic they were discussing earlier. 'What is the current price of a bundle of zinc?'

'Star brand is thirteen naira while horse brand is twelf naira fifty kobo. But I was able to get it for twelve naira,' Ozurumba told them.

'The sky and the gathering clouds may threaten rain as much as they want. Your heart won't skip a beat and you won't lose sleep,' Akobundu stated.

'Hmm, hhmmm. . .' Akwakanti hemmed and hawed as George got closer to them. 'Today's cash has entered the till and the pockets that are heavily lined cannot allow some walk freely.' The suggestion was a reference to the perceived corruption going on at the local tax office.

George stopped to exchange greetings with his kinsmen. 'What pocket has been lined?' he asked, pulling out an empty pocket to rubbish Akwakanti's implication and deflect attention away from himself. 'If you're looking for those with loaded pockets, you should be talking to cash crop merchants like JJ,' he said. At that point in time, cash crops like cocoa commanded good prices in the produce market. 'Where will ordinary civil servant find the money to line his pocket? Is it the coins or severely squashed fifty kobo notes that will line my pockets? That tax office? We merely use it to while away time.' He took notice of the newspaper in Anosike's hand. It was not one of the crumpled, sullied, torn, or dog-eared old newspapers which had passed from hand to hand in the village. Anosike allowed him to have a look.

'It's today's paper! JMJ, did you go to town?' George knew only few of them made a point of buying a newspaper whenever they went to the town.

'When the moon shines so brightly, even the cripple craves for a walk. I was terribly bored so I decided to go for a bit of sightseeing,' Ozurumba answered.

'That's the understatement of the century,' Josiah declared, a fleeting smile creasing his face before the few strands of moustache on his fair-complexioned face went back to the usual serious mien. 'If buying bundles of zinc is sightseeing, it's an excellent form of recreation.'

'I can sniff JMJ from afar. I know when he is loaded,' George announced, looking at the headlines on the front page. 'It must be time for our tongues to taste spices,' he said, leafing through some pages. 'Let me glance through. I'll bring it back.'

'But I'm still reading it,' Anosike protested.

'Do you mean looking at the pictures?' George inquired sneeringly.

'King Solomon, the wise man,' Anosike grinned sarcastically. 'All the books you read made today's headline. For all the battles Okeke claims he fought, we are still waiting to see his boots!' It was a deft verbal punch, but he laughed to make light of it. Courtesy forbade him from openly insulting his elders, but nothing could stop him from taking a sly dig at them.

'Are you being rude?' Akwakanti asked, trying to call Anosike to order. However, his voice lacked the hostility of a reprimand. His mouth twitched in an effort to hide the veiled smile of approval. Knowing that George had somehow called for it, he could not be overly harsh on Anosike. 'Do you realise who you are talking to? That's King George!'

'Will a person be dragged out and shot for speaking the truth?' Josiah challenged, agreeing with George. He was one of those who disapproved of the laziness in reading news articles. It was common knowledge that most of them only looked at the pictures without taking the pain to read it. They relied on the conversations at the village square to make sense of the pictures they saw. 'How many of us truly take the trouble to read the stories?'

'Don't blame him, it's not his fault,' George said, clearly avoiding an argument. He picked up his oversized black portmanteau, the uneven surface and alloyed chrome defaced by patches of caked dirt. There was a thin layer of dust on his coarse leather shoes, and his socks had lost their elastic strength and were bunched at his ankles. As he walked away, he drew out a hanky to wipe his mouth after spitting out phlegm.

George liked to walk at a slow, deliberate pace to fit the image of a super clerical officer, which he portrayed. The red and blue *BIC* biros were never absent from his breast pocket. His hair was cut into a wedge with a parting despite the early signs of bald spot. His faded blue polyester jacket, bought second hand, was a little too big for his slender frame and clashed with his maroon trousers, which were held tightly above his navel with a worn-out belt. The villagers thought he dressed like a typical English gentleman because of the suit he was usually dressed in regardless the weather. The women in the village were quick to describe anyone who was attired in suit as a person who dressed up like George, the king.

Ozurumba snuffed the pinch of tobacco he had shoved into his second nostril. 'This tobacco is grade one. It was well-blended,' he declared pleasurably, handing the snuff box back to Akwakanti. He blew his nose after a loud sneeze and used his hand to clean up the dark mucus.

'Mercy has no rival when it comes to tobacco blending,' Akwakanti agreed, tucking the box into the pocket of his khaki shorts, which were tied up with a piece of rope.

Anosike was surprised to see Ozurumba snuffing tobacco again. 'Is it up to two weeks ago you said you were giving up tobacco?' he asked, remembering how Ozurumba had denounced it as a dirty habit.

'I have been fighting the cravings,' Ozurumba admitted. 'Cutting it off abruptly has not been easy. Do you see me with any snuff box or handkerchief?'

Their conversation was interrupted when Amalambu cycled into the village square on his new bicycle, ringing the bell repeatedly to draw attention to its mint condition. He dismounted with a swagger, slapping the padded saddle before flipping the kickstand. The bicycle had been fancifully decorated with two mirrors mounted on the stem and ribbons dangling off the handlebars.

'Your bicycle is *igba*, excellent,' Anosike congratulated him. 'You must have spent a fortune on it.'

'You know it,' Amalambu beamed. 'Good things have guzzled my money; kinsmen can carry on with the blame game.' He was obviously happy with himself for what he must have considered a great achievement. The time was past when buying a new bicycle was a bold statement of enterprise. So much thrift and self-denial was required for putting together the money required to buy it. For his generation, it was simply a tool for performing their tasks quicker and easier. At that point in their lifetime, there was a bicycle revolution in Mboha and other villages and nobody wanted to be left behind.

Ajuzie rode to the village square with David sitting on the carrier behind him. As David hopped off, Ajuzie challenged Amalambu to a race to test the speed and reliability of his new bicycle.

'This bicycle can beat aeroplane in a speed race,' Amalambu boasted, accepting the challenge. Pedalling off vigorously, he tried to catch up with Ajuzie.

Their exuberance reminded Ozurumba of his exploits with the Raleigh bicycle he used to own. He rode all the way from Aba to Mboha, covering a distance of close to fifty miles in less than five hours. 'Can any of these bicycles withstand such rigours? They are no bicycle when compared to Raleigh.'

'Or White Horse,' Josiah added.

'You will live long,' Ozurumba thanked him, stretching out his hand to shake him. 'The bicycles in those days were completely in a different class,' he said, naming certain features like derailleur, sprocket wheels, and generators that were absent in the available cheaper models.

'Raleigh bicycle, is it a motor-car that can travel all the way from Aba to Mboha, our village?' Anosike queried, his mouth pouting in disbelief, doubting the possibility of a bicycle covering such distance. His thumb and forefinger stroked the scanty goatee on his chin, searching for non-existent bumps.

'It looks like an impossible exercise now but back in the days when motor-cars were few and scanty, people actually covered such distance on bicycle,' Josiah clarified.

'Motor-cars have made people lazy,' Akobundu added. 'In those days, people trekked to Umuahia carrying tin of palm oil. My mother did so on a few occasions.'

'Why did you have to ride all the way?' Akwakanti asked.

'I got a message from my father that the person he wanted to see at the blink of the eyes is me,' Ozurumba explained. 'Whatever could warrant such a message must be a matter of life and death. Although it was late in the evening, I wasted no time at all. I strapped my pistol, mounted my bicycle, and headed home. Wherever the road was smooth, I simply pulled the shifter to let the bicycle cruise—*Zziiiii!*—like aeroplane.'

'Radio-without-battery,' Anosike hailed in mock admiration, knowing that most of Ozurumba's stories were embellished to delight his listeners.

Ozurumba continued with zest, ignoring the distraction. 'Listen, let me give you story! I sensed something untoward as I approached Ugba junction. My headlight picked out the roadblock quickly enough. On hearing some rustling in the nearby bush, I pulled the trigger and it exploded: *kpooooh!* The next thing I heard was the muffled scream of *"anwuolamu ooo!"'*

'You must have shot one of the robbers?' Akwakanti surmised.

'I didn't stop to find out. I was fleeing for my life,' Ozurumba admitted, provoking boisterous laughter.

'It's a case of run when I'm running,' Josiah believed, calling to mind a well-known fable about the tiger. A startled tiger would take off upon an unexpected encounter. Whatever he was running from must turn and run in a different direction. On regaining composure, the tiger would stop to ask why he must run from a fellow creature. He would return to the scene as a ferocious animal to see who it was that sprang the surprise on him. If, against good counsel, the person had not departed the scene, the tiger must pounce to tear him into pieces to reassert his supremacy in the jungle, his domain. 'They could have come to fight you.'

'Didn't they know that anyone who had the guts to be on the road by that time of the night cannot be empty handed?' Akobundu asked.

'I just cannot understand it. How can anyone leave the comfort of his house to waylay others on the road at night?' Akwakanti wondered.

Ozurumba became even more voluble. At the next roadblock, several other travellers had just been robbed and he was ordered to join them in lying prostrate by the roadside. After appearing to obey them, he struck when they least expected. His first target was the robber with the automatic rifle. He shot the second as he was going to pick up the gun. He gunned down the third man before the last member of the robbery gang fled into the bush. 'The way I was shooting; you would think I was a cowboy. The other travellers celebrated me as a hero and showered me with money!' His face beamed with pleasure, his hands moving now and again to give life to his story.

'Okoko Ndem himself!' cried Akwakanti, calling him by the name of the Biafran broadcaster renowned for his knack for propaganda.

'I salute the person that invented revolver gun,' Akobundu enthused.

'Truly, those who made revolver knew what they were doing!' Ozurumba was completely animated. 'If the cylinder did not rotate automatically, the second robber would have finished me off. Nothing happened again until I got to Mboha Bridge where I was overwhelmed with inexplicable fear. "Whoever stands on my way is a dead man," I declared, my voice was quite loud before I released another bullet—*kpooooh*!' As soon as I got home, my father strangled a cockerel, making sure that the blood dripping from the beak entered my eyes.'

'If he had not done so, you could have continued to kill,' Ikpo nodded. He was sitting on the bare floor, resting his frail frame against the log of wood that served as their bench. Again, he was picking his tobacco-stained teeth; his grey hair was pale and the patches of vitiligo on his face and hands contrasted sharply to give him a hideous appearance to those who were not used to him. His shortened or missing finger showed that he must have been attacked by leprosy at a point in his life.

'Agile soldier, your bravery did not start today. You were a warrior long before the war,' Bartholomew noted.

'It is not today that I started facing the challenges of life,' Ozurumba said.

'So you are another James Bond,' George sneered. He had returned to the square and had followed the second story. He knew this must be one of Ozurumba's fictitious tales—or possibly a story he had heard or read about a different person but adapted it to make himself the lead character. He was wearing short sleeves blue cotton shirt, with trousers and leather flip-flops. His Quartz watch with the silver chain was on his wrist. 'Have you read about what happened to Joshua Nkomo?'

'I've not really read the paper,' Ozurumba confessed. 'But I heard he has fled Zimbabwe. He's in South Africa.'

'Didn't I say it would come to that?' George felt vindicated by the turn of events. He had been predicting a bad outcome to the political impasse ever since the North Korean-trained Fifth Brigade turned their guns on innocent civilians.

'How can that be?' Josiah was shocked. Like most of them, he had followed the post-independence political debacles with genuine apprehension, sympathising with Joshua Nkomo when it looked like he was being schemed out of power. They remembered his role in Zimbabwe's struggle for independence and called him Father Zimbabwe.

'It was in the news last night,' Ozurumba told George.

'I didn't realise. . .' he snapped his fingers in disgust. 'I've only just read about it.' He was pained that Zimbabwe was not learning from the mistakes of other African nations. 'History is repeating itself, isn't it?'

Ijuolachi called her father from a distance but Ozurumba called back to ask what it was. 'Mama wants you!' she announced from the distance.

'Do I owe her?' he retorted. 'Tell her I'm coming.'

'Despite all the concessions he made?' Josiah was still bewildered, knowing that Nkomo had tried to act in the best interests of his people. 'I have to read this story.'

'Sometimes I wonder why people behave so irrationally,' George brooded. 'How can those who know nothing about leadership insist on being leaders?'

'Escaping with his life, is it not better than getting killed?' Anosike wondered.

'Ian Smith, or what do you call him, will be having a good laugh wherever he is,' Ozurumba mused, standing up and slapping dirt from his buttocks. 'I'll be back.'

3.

The sermon of village evangelists interrupted the quietude in the neighbourhood early that morning. A metal cone was improvised as public address system to amplify their voices. The preacher vigorously attacked various traditional beliefs and practices. In condemning idolatry, he referred his listeners to the twentieth chapter of Exodus, itemising things forbidden by the Ten Commandments. 'You shall have no other god beside God. . .' he iterated. 'For those in adultery or fornication, don't you know you are defiling your body, the temple of the Holy Spirit?' He charged thieves to steal no more. 'Some stealthily go to harvest other people's crops thinking that nobody is watching but forget that the Eye that watches the universe is watching.'

He flayed churchgoers that gave themselves to hatred. 'How can you call yourself a Christian when you kill and maim others with witchcraft and sorcery? Can it ever be well with the wicked? It is time to accept Jesus Christ and depart from such evil. He who sins is of the devil, for the devil has sinned from the beginning. For this purpose, was the Son of Man made manifest, that he may destroy all the works of darkness. Christ is the light and the entrance of the Word brings that light which darkness cannot comprehend,' he proclaimed. He urged his listeners to repeat some prayers after him to lead them to Christ. Anyone who had said the prayer and had faith in Christ was born again and a new creation. He concluded by announcing his denomination and inviting his listeners to join his church to experience the new life in Christ. He started a song as they moved to another location.

'Oga chochi n'ezu ori
Chegharia!
M'ezi ihe!
Matakwa n'onye nmehie g'akwa akwa!
M' emesia.

'Oga chochi nakw' iko
Chegharia!
M'ezi ihe!
Matakwa n'onye nmehie g'akwa akwa!
M' emesia.

Like his preaching, the song subtly berated the non-evangelical churches. Members of the new-generation churches denounced virtually everything done by the older, more orthodox churches. But the established churches knew that their creed were incompatible with much of the customs and tradition of the natives. Rather than turning their less conforming members away, the orthodox ones gently and patiently continued to persuade them to abandon their old ways for the 'unsearchable riches' in Christ Jesus. They entreated the natives and tolerated their backsliding, giving them chance after chance, hoping they would grow in maturity and unto all good works by putting to death all the sins that easily enslaved them. This was seen as weakness by the more radical evangelicals. The new puritans insisted on complete holiness and conformity to the image of Christ. As far as they were concerned, anything less rigorous was regarded as a compromise. Environmental influences were not acceptable excuses for deviating from the high standard of righteousness and holiness. That was the only sure way to experience the presence of God as it was in the early church. Some worshippers, won over by the new crusade, subscribed to the argument and insisted that all who names the name of Christ must depart from iniquity.

They made the decision not to walk in the counsel of the ungodly, nor walk in the way of sinners, nor sit in the seat of the scornful. Their option was leaving the church that brought Christianity to them to join one of the Pentecostal fellowships. The orthodox churches disapproved of the zealots' habit of poaching their more devout members on the pretext of being born again. It was particularly so when little or nothing was done to persuade those who were still steeped in fetish practices to give up their ways. As long as the idol worshippers continued with their divination, enchantment, and medium consultation, it was difficult for many members of the orthodox churches to credit the new churches with advancing the frontiers of the gospel in their various communities.

Ozurumba heard a knock coming from the entrance door at the *obu*. Wondering who could be visiting at such early hours of the morning, he opened his door to walk up to the *obu*. 'Who is there?'

'It's me,' answered the visitor, clearly expecting to be identified by his voice. Ozurumba made sure it was Ikwuako before unbolting the door to see him standing there with a lantern. They exchanged greetings as Ozurumba unsecured the picket gate to let him in. He expressed surprise at seeing him that early. 'I want to see your brother before he leaves for palm wine tapping.' He went to Uwakwe's part of the compound that used to be the *osokwu*.

Uwakwe opened the door. He assumed that whatever brought his guest so early must be important. The room was still smoky from the *ogbe*, which had burnt throughout the night as mosquito repellent. 'If antelope takes a dangerous flight you let out a dangerous bullet,' Ikwuako remarked, sitting down as they exchanged pleasantries.

'What do I offer you as kola?' Uwakwe thought aloud, groping under the *okpoko*, his bed made of raffia palm stalks. Ikwuako told him not to bother as it was too early in the morning, but Uwakwe found the wooden kola disk. 'As you unlock the door, you unlock the mouth,' Uwakwe said, passing the wooden disc to him.

Ikwuako merely touched it. 'The king's kola is in his hand,' he said, pushing it back.

Uwakwe sneezed loudly for the second time as he took the disk. 'Who is after me?' he queried and began to mouth some mantra. Whoever was trying to invoke him cannot succeed. He was not available. The person must answer the call.

'*Iiiha!*' Ikwuako pronounced his affirmation to the prayer, joining to mouth more mantra to ward off any form of evil directed at Uwakwe. 'Anyone whose life demands a sacrifice of human head must use his own head.'

'*Gbam!*' Uwakwe concurred and took over the prayer. 'Whatever evil that is going after anyone shall not see me!'

'*Iiiiha!*'

'It shall not see my kith and kin!'

'*Iiiiha!*'

'Whatever wrong anyone has done; the repercussion shall be on his head!'

'*Nnam*—my father—that is exactly what happens!' Ikwuako affirmed every prayer wholeheartedly, making it clear that he was no harbinger of evil.

If he had come with evil in his bosom, he would not join in calling the wrath of the gods on himself.

'A mind preoccupied with goodness shall experience goodness.'

'*Gbam*, it is a fundamental truth!'

'The one obsessed with evil devices shall not escape evil.'

'*Iiiiha!*'

'Goodness shall follow the one who does good.'

'*Iiiiha!*'

'There is a just recompense for the upright and the righteous.'

'*Gbam*, it is the law of our land. It is not contestable.'

'Evil shall dot the heels of evildoers.'

'*Omereme!*—It happens!'

'Can evil overwhelm him whose hands are clean?'

'Never! Have our dead ancestors gone blind?'

Uwakwe threw the particles he pinched from the kola nut on the floor as he continued to pray. 'Our ancestors, here is kola, take, eat, it is the dawn of a new day.'

'That is very true.'

'Keep us this day as you have always kept us.'

'*Iiiha!*'

'Do not let evil overrun us.'

'*Iiiha!*'

'Live and let others live.'

'*Gbam!* That is the law,' Ikwuako continued to voice his agreement at every pause. They dipped the kola in the peppery sauce, chewing crunchily, the sting awakening their senses. Uwakwe gave him *nkuku*—a calabash cup—and poured palm wine into it.

Ikwuako tabled the matters that brought him without much ado. He was not happy with the passes Umevu was making at his wife. 'He has failed to heed my warning. Maybe I had water in my mouth when I spoke to him or he is simply hard of hearing. Please give him this stick as a warning. The next time I see him around my wife, I will tell him that scorpion stings.' He gave Uwakwe a twig.

'But what does he want with your wife? He can take a second wife if his wife is not coping with his libido?' Uwakwe was bewildered. Umevu was notorious for his extramarital affairs and escapades. The affair he had with Okoma's wife resulted in triplets, but none of them survived.

'If he defies me, I'll cut off his testicles and show them to his face,' Ikwuako threatened, touching his tongue and raising his finger up as a sign of swearing an oath. 'It may be too rash if I deal with him without warning.'

'A war that is foretold does not consume the cripple. Well, I will pass your message across and hear his side of the story,' Uwakwe promised. 'As you know, judgment cannot be passed after hearing only one side to a matter.'

'That is true. Let me ask, you know the iroko tree in my Okata farm, how much do you think it can fetch?'

'Three pounds or thereabout,' Uwakwe guessed. 'Did anyone make you an offer?'

'Bernard, the sawyer, offered me two and five. I thought that would amount to a giveaway if I accept.'

'It's not far off the mark. He must have added the cost of his labour and the little profit he expects to make.'

Ikwuako was conscious of time. He thanked his host as he stood up to go.

Uwakwe left home shortly after for his routine wine-tapping. Arriving at the cocoa plantation in the neighbourhood, he plucked a tender leaf from a shrub. Cupping his left palm, he tucked the leaf in before slapping it with his right palm. It produced the desired sharp echo. He repeated it two more times before he began his morning invocation.

'*Eke kere igwe kekwa ala* hear me,' he started, calling on the Creator of the heavens and the earth. 'Our ancestors listen. *Umuagbara, umuagbara*, listen also. The sky, listen, and the earth, listen too. My prayer is that it shall be well with the strong and it shall be well with the weakling. Let it be well with man and let it be well with woman. Life of the water and life of the fish. The water should not dry up and the fish should not die. Let the eagle perch and let the kite perch too. If one does not want the other to perch, may its wings break! Whoever holds aloft what rightly belongs to a child will bring it down when he gets tired. The spirit child should not oppress the human child and the human child should never cheat the spirit child. Nothing is comparable to peaceful coexistence. Do not spare the cheats and troublemakers. Hunt such people down in the morning, noon, and at night. It is those that desecrate the land that flee from its presence. Anyone whose hands are clean has nothing to fear. Whoever does not like what I do, I also do not like what he does.

'Who can lay a charge against me? Whom have I wronged in any way? For those who seek my life when I have done nothing wrong, do not spare them. Go after them in the daytime and at night. Give them no respite until they kiss the dust. Anybody whose life demands a sacrifice of human head must use his own head. Why am I labouring if it is not to feed my family and keep the homestead going? I hold *ofo*. I hold *ogu*. That is why I call on you to uphold the cause of justice and vindicate the righteous. Men of ill-will will overrun my homestead if you turn a blind eye.'

He slung the twine over his shoulder and picked up the empty calabash to move on, ready to start his daily routine. In pleading *ofo na ogu*, Uwakwe had declared his uprightness. *Oji ofo ga ala*—the righteous shall escape harm—was a saying that expressed one of the fundamental ethos which his people strongly believed in. He had done his bit by committing himself into the hands of his Maker. This did not exempt him from the challenges of life, but all in all, he was confident that they would maintain the fair balance that sustained their cosmos.

As the symbol of truth, justice, and fairness, *Ofo na Ogu* required conscientious observance of all the abiding tenets. Their Creator and ancestors were ever ready to defend and advance the cause of the righteous. Their only handicap was usually the tainted hands of a supplicant. They did not only have to take delight in the actions and omissions of the supplicant but his thoughts and intents of the heart must equally be pleasing.

Uwakwe had five surviving daughters out of Nwugo's twelve pregnancies. The only boy was a stillborn. It was rumoured that that particular pregnancy was the result of an extramarital affair. His mind was afflicted with the thought of having no son to succeed him. The implication was obvious. His brother's sons would inherit their common property at his death, and his name would be forgotten. He had expected Nwugo to give him at least a son from so many pregnancies, but his last hope was dashed when Akudo, the youngest girl, was born. Ironically, he had fathered two sons with his concubine, who was a widow. The boys did not belong to him. A widow who did not remarry could continue to have children in the name of her late husband.

He had made up his mind to take another wife in his old age. A number of spinsters were suggested. Olejuru told him about Nwulari, a lady from her village. Her first marriage had failed due to the man's bad character, or so Uwakwe was made to believe. She had not given birth. That was as good as marrying a maiden. Olejuru persuaded Uwakwe that Nwulari was the most eligible bride in the circumstance.

Uwakwe agreed to visit Umuacham with her and asked Ozurumba and Onyenwe to come with them. They were well received. Nwulari was charming and smart and appeared to have everything under control during the visit. They enjoyed the meal she had prepared—although Ozurumba kept stealing glances at her ankles to assess her childbearing age.

Olejuru was delighted at the turn of events. Everyone seemed happy with her pick of bride. She sought their views as they walked home.

'You don't lick hot soup in a hurry,' Ozurumba remarked, sounding grumpy.

'What's the problem?' Onyenwe asked. 'I'm impressed by what I saw. She is smart and sharp. She will make a good wife, if you ask me.'

'Her food was nice,' Uwakwe agreed.

'Umuacham women are known to take good care of their husbands,' Olejuru boasted, happy with the general reaction so far.

'But we're looking for a wife to bear male children, not one that cooks good food or has shimmering skin,' Ozurumba tactlessly bared his mind.

'Are you suggesting she is beyond childbearing age?' Olejuru queried.

'I know she's not in her prime,' Ozurumba maintained.

'In my opinion, she is not past childbearing age,' Onyenwe stated.

'Can she be older than Leriakawa who is still having children?' Olejuru asked. They left the subject to discuss other issues until they got home.

Three days later, the rumour circulating in the village was that Ozurumba was against his brother taking another wife to bear him male children. He was scheming to keep their common inheritance to himself. When Kperechi got to the source of the rumour, she picked a quarrel with Olejuru. Kperechi demanded to hear from her husband when she got home 'What did you say at the bride's place?'

'What did you hear?' Ozurumba retorted peevishly.

'That you don't want your brother to take a bride that will bear him male children. That is the gossip making the rounds.'

'Is it because I expressed my candid opinion?' he rasped. Realising that his wife had taken the trouble to defend him, he relented. 'The world does not like to hear the truth. Of course, some people may claim to have his interest at heart more than I do. But it won't stop me from saying the truth as I see it.'

'You could have waited to hear what your brother had to say about the bride. Was he not the one that invited you to accompany him? If he says that is what he wanted, would it make any sense to oppose him?' It was obvious that her husband was sincere in the opinion he expressed even if he had been tactless about it. 'If she does not bear children tomorrow, they will accuse you of tying her womb.'

Uwakwe went ahead to take Nwulari as his second wife.

*   *   *

Work was at an advanced stage for the construction of a soak-away toilet, which Chief Ogbudu had contracted Ozurumba to build. The six layers of blocks required for the inner chamber was completed the previous day. 'Who took my pliers?' Ozurumba asked, looking around. He was completing work on the rods for the reinforcement. David returned the pliers and went back to continue work, using the shovel to mix sand, cement, and gravel. Spreading the cement bags on the floor, Ozurumba arranged the wooden formwork and reinforcement on top of them. At his instruction, David shovelled the concrete mixture into the formwork. At intervals, Ozurumba used his trowel to ensure an even spread, pushing the mixture to all corners. 'This corner,' he directed as David brought a pan of the concrete mixture.

'The skill you acquired is not one or two,' Joshua complimented, dropping the empty carton of Golden Guinea he had brought with him. Ikwuako was happy to hear another person express the same view. He had also paused to chit-chat and admire the work.

'You can't work with Cappa and D'Alberto or Borini Prono without learning such basics,' Ozurumba told them. 'Italians have no equal when it comes to civil engineering and constructions.'

'If I may ask, all this trouble is just for where people will defecate, isn't it?' Ikwuako voiced his thought. At a time when even a pit latrine was not common, the idea of putting in an actual flush toilet was quite spectacular. Yet Chief Ogbudu had a circle of important friends and felt it was demeaning to ask them to use the pit latrine when they come visiting.

'The white man's lifestyle is not cheap,' Joshua agreed, his right hand crossed behind his back, holding his left elbow. Flush toilets were not new to him. He had worked as a cook and housekeeper for expatriates at the teaching hospital in Zaria before his retirement. 'Is this Armitage Shanks or Twyford?'

he asked, name-dropping toilet manufacturers. He went close to the ceramics to check. 'Yes, it is Twyford, the type in Dr Kishor's quarters!' Joshua's face brightened at the memory.

'The Indian doctor, isn't it?' Ozurumba asked, knowing the fond memories Joshua had of the doctor.

'*Chei!*' he exclaimed, clasping his hand and his head tilting momentarily to the left. 'I tell you, since I was born I've not come across a doctor as good as him. He is so good that the hospitals in Kaduna, Kano, even as far as Sokoto called him to handle difficult cases of childbirth. But if you saw him sitting with me on the bench, talking like a friend to friend, you won't believe he was a chief consultant gynaecologist.'

'Whoever tells you that learning is not profitable, tell the person he told a big lie,' Ozurumba nodded, straightening up from his labour. 'Okwudiri, gather up the tools and put them away,' he directed. 'It's a sunny and dry day. It is the right weather for me to burn the farmland I cleared to make it ready for tilling.'

'This will definitely add to the prestige of this house,' Ikwuako said as he was taking his leave.

'Definitely so,' Joshua concurred.

Undoubtedly, Chief Ogbudu's compound was the most modern structure in the village. The uncommon roofing pattern added to the fairly complex architecture to make it outstanding. An improvised gutter channelled rainwater into a cistern made of big metal tank positioned in the compound. The cistern spared members of his household many trips to the stream, particularly in the rainy season. White pebbles were poured in both the outer compound and the backyard of his compound to stabilise the soil. The tumbled pebbles were as hard as granite and a number of them were ovoid and smooth like pheasant eggs. Others were either flattened or possessed irregular shapes but all of them were the perfect stone for boys testing the distance of their throwing shots. No one had to be told that the stones must have cost a lot of money. Pouring more than a tipper load to pave both the frontage and the backyard added to the visual enhancement of the compound in no little measure. Whenever it rained, the feet or footwear stepping on them did not have to worry about muck or muddy stains. The small red flowers contrasted with the deep green leaves of the ixora used to hedge the driveway. The young leafy ebelebo tree stretching out its horizontal branches was laden with large leaves and fruits. It was planted at the centre of the compound to provide shade. A wooden signpost tucked away in a corner declared the premises as Chief Ogbudu's Royal Palace. His initials were also framed in the wrought iron gate. To crown it all, he was the first son of Mboha to own a car—a Morris Minor, before he replaced it with Peugeot 504SR.

Chief Ogbudu succeeded Asagwara as the village head even though it was not the turn of his lineage to produce the village head. During Asagwara's tenure, the village had started sending delegates to attend functions where English was spoken. To keep up with the changing times, Mboha needed an educated village head who could speak the language used in corridors of power so as to attract development to the community.

Chief Ogbudu was a dignitary who could be trusted to hold his own at any gathering. He had a successful business as dealer and distributor of alcohol beverages and soft drinks in Umuahia Town, and the grocery store ran by his wife was also thriving. A well-known philanthropist, he donated extensively to charity and was the patron of many societies and clubs. Imo Broadcasting Service often broadcast grateful thank-you messages to him at the request of his beneficiaries. He was one of the few village leaders who had name recognition.

Ozurumba and Joshua were walking home when the rumbling sound of an approaching motorcycle assailed their hearing. Iroegbulem drew up beside them, on his well-decorated Honda Road-Master CD 175. He looked distinguished in his smart khaki top and short, well-polished boots with long socks drawn up to the calf. He still wore his constabulary uniform whenever he was on the road. His headgear, which was more like a captain's hat, combined with his aiguillettes to give him the look of a man who had power and authority. 'Welcome!' they greeted him.

'Welcome too,' he returned their greetings, bringing his motorbike to a stop. 'Ozurumba, I thought we agreed to meet?'

'I will see you this evening,' Ozurumba promised.

Armed with a potshard wreathed in smoke, Kperechi eventually joined Ozurumba at the farmland he had cleared. 'What took you so long?' Ozurumba asked, a bit curtly. He knew that the sunshine wouldn't last, and that the land must be burned, tidied, and made ready for tilling before the rain came.

She chose to ignore his impatience by refusing to whimper or give timid answers to gratify his machismo. Instead, she praised him. 'You've done a lot of work. That was fast.' She had become thoroughly secured in her marriage and was not threatened by his moods. Usually, she found that the best way was to ignore them altogether, although occasionally she was provoked into answering back without caring if it resulted in a row. Those who understood such mood swings advised her to be more patient with him. Though he was ordinarily impetuous but some knew he was battling with the trauma of the war which made him more irascible. In accommodating such moods, she often told herself that two persons cannot be mad at the same time.

'I would have been out of here by now,' he muttered, continuing to rake the dry leaves and sticks away from his boundary to make sure the fire did not spread to neighbouring farms. Kperechi gathered some of the dried leaves and sticks together to start the fire. A flaming tongue sprang up, spreading, crackling, hissing, and consuming everything on its path. Ozurumba carried burning materials to different corners of the land. Plumes of smoke billowed from the fire, tossing weightless debris up far into space before they floated gracefully down again. Attracted by the fire, kites flocked, hovering above the raging flames until they were reduced to glowing embers or hot ashes. Ozurumba had done a good job of preparing the land for burning. It was the difference between the work of a true native and that of hired farmhands that were notorious for their hasty and untidy jobs. 'I really need to soak myself in cool water. It has been terribly hot today.'

A short walk brought them to the path leading to different beaches. To the dismay of many farmers, the tyres of tipper-trucks widened the rough and crooked footpath, flattening the mounds of earth painfully cultivated by the farmers and destroying crops along the way. Ruffled *oguoka* grasses still grew, defiantly refusing to die not minding how many times they were crushed by the tyres. Patiently, the feeble but persistent grasses waited for the rainy season, when the bullying tyres would have to stay away or risk getting stuck.

Kperechi paused as Ozurumba stopped to rub soap on his head. Then he continued beyond the Ovoro beach, the more secluded spot where the eyes of young children and women would not see him. Kperechi turned left towards the more popular beach. It was a bedlam at the river. Many were busy with family laundry, spreading the washed clothes out on shrubs. Frolicking children rolled in the sand, or gleefully dived into the shallow part of the water at the banks, pretending to swim. Anglers perched on tree trunks that fell into the river ages ago, waiting to feel the tug on their hooks and lines. A fisherman stretched to cast his net while his partner paddled, steering the boat away from the many obstructions littering the water surface.

Further down the river were dredgers and a sand-laden boat moored to a stake, discharging the sand into head pans for labourers who took them to the loading bay. Two women washed breadfruit nearby. A pile of dirty plates at the edge of the water caught Kperechi's attention. They came from her house. As she was asking after Ijuolachi, she was interrupted by a scream. A little boy was swimming deeper into the river, forcing Ochiabuto to scream at him. 'You want to make me miserable this afternoon, isn't it? Whoever sent you, tell him you did not find me, do you hear me?'

'All of you children leave that water, now. It's enough,' Kperechi ordered, spotting Akachi in their midst.

'I have not seen a thing like this. They have kept me screaming all day.'

'*Chei, mama muo,*' wailed a girl, as an aluminium basket flew out of her hand. Water rushed into the basket, making it sink out of sight. Ejituru asked what happened. Serechi was swinging it back and forth to shake all the water out it when it slipped from her hand. She dissolved into tears, her hands clasped over her head. Kperechi comforted the girl who bore a variant of her name. It was a mistake which could happen to anyone. 'But my mother borrowed it. She promised to return it in one piece,' she lamented. 'She will tell me how worthless I am today. *Eleooo!* I'm lost.'

'Stop crying. It was an accident, wasn't it?' Kperechi cajoled. 'Is it worth a human head?'

'It's not your fault, my daughter,' Ochiabuto added.

'So you left my plates by the riverbank to search for wild *udara nwa enwe*, isn't it?' Kperechi berated Ijuolachi when she returned with sprigs laden with fruits. 'If any of them gets missing, you will deny ever bringing them to the river.'

Ijuolachi told the boys and girls tugging at the epical branches to stop. They wanted to have a taste of the *udara*. Kperechi plucked some of them before going into the river for a bathe. Splashing water over herself, she used *sapo*— the native sponge—and *ncha-ogbe*—the locally made soap—to sponge herself thoroughly. Once more, the acrid whiff from the rich leather of the *ncha-ogbe* was so welcome. It was reassuring that no dirt and grease would be on the skin after scrubbing the body with it. 'I feel fresh,' she murmured, hiding behind a shrub to change into a clean wrapper. She went back to wash the dirty wrapper. 'Ochiabuto, you are not yet done. You have to meet us at home.'

'Oooooo, my fellow woman,' Ochiabuto responded as Kperechi walked up the sandy banks to join her children and Ejituru, who was equally ready to go home.

4.

Waning daylight succumbed to the encroaching darkness. But the village of Mboha was far from being sleepy. Darkness overtook a family at the oil mill. Their flickering *tunja* glowed waveringly but withstood the mild breeze. Three women returning from a neighbouring village market cried greetings as they passed by. Four drums of palm fruits were positioned on engine blocks and stones; a fire raged beneath two of them. They crackled, sizzled, hissing now and again as the boiling water bubbled over into the fire. Hearing his name, Ozurumba turned as Jenny walked up to him.

'Please my good husband, may I make use of your pestles? My palm fruits will be mashed first thing in the morning.'

'I promised I will not lend them out anymore. A number of them have gone missing,' he told her, but he changed his mind when she promised to be careful with them.

Ozurumba got home just as his family was settling down for supper. *Gwam-gwam-gwam*, a favourite programme for the children, full of jokes and riddles in Igbo language was airing on the radio. He went inside to get metal chair with the cushions before returning for the radio and torch. Kperechi rose from her meal to dish his food. 'Okwudiri, get the centre table,' she instructed, putting soup into the smaller of the two enamel bowls normally used to set his food. 'Nwakego, get the food for your father.'

Ozurumba did not see his torch under his pillow. 'Who removed the torch from here?' he asked, his impatient voice was loud enough to be heard.

'Nobody has touched your torch today ooo!' Kperechi countered.

'Is it my dead ancestors or creditors that came to confiscate it?' he fired back.

Nwakego remembered suddenly. 'Oh hooo!' she exclaimed. 'I used it to search for my scarf in the inner room!' She hurried into the house for the torch.

'Don't touch it next time if you cannot return it after using it. Do you hear me? I will be forced to repeat it tomorrow. Nobody takes me seriously in this house because I have not used it to break someone's head. Imagine, your mother did not let me speak before she dismissed me as if I didn't know what I was saying!'

'Don't be angry, please.' Kperechi attempted to mollify him without showing remorse. 'It is Nwakego who refused to listen with the ears God gave her. If she is a goat, I won't eat her ears. How many times have I warned each of them to keep away from things that annoy you but they won't listen?' She knew how crossed he could get if she opposed him. It did not matter if subsequent events proved her right. In his determination to exert maximum control in his household, Ozurumba was not ready to brook any form of opposition.

The familiar IBC signature tune filled the air, its rhythmic percussion reminding everyone that it was time for the news broadcast. It was a welcome distraction to the momentary hostility. Ignoring his wife's perfunctory apology, Ozurumba changed the position of the plates. He asked for salt after the first mouthful. Kperechi knew it was a subtle reproof; once again she had failed to present his food properly.

'You really washed your hands to prepare this soup,' he added. 'Whoever prepared this *utara*—pounded cassava—equally did a good job. Did you give some to my mother?'

'Why not give her what you have,' Kperechi suggested in a tone that showed she was still smarting from his reproof.

'Is that an answer to my question?' he fired back, ready to deal with the affront. On a second thought, he calmed down. 'Lack of etiquette is a terrible thing, have I not always said so?' he lectured. 'Love your neighbour as you love yourself, is it not what the Holy Bible teaches? It's not a matter of hurrying off to church every Sunday.' Raising his voice, he called his mother to join him for supper.

'Your wife already gave me food,' Ehichanya replied, massaging herself with some soothing balms, *okwuma* and *ori*.

Part of the news programme was devoted to the life and times of the legendary Steve Biko, the anti-apartheid martyr who died in custody. In a tribute, the analyst described in detail Biko's role in organising the 1976 Soweto uprising, which brought the evils of apartheid to the attention of the international community. His writings provided the intellectual basis for black consciousness, giving the natives the true self-worth to assert themselves.

'How time flies,' Ozurumba muttered, realising it had been five years since Biko died. Like many others, he had followed the events leading to Biko's arrest with genuine concern. That fateful night, while everyone was anxiously awaiting his release from custody, a newscaster instead broke the news of his death and this was attributed to hunger strike. Ozurumba remembered his agony at the news. He had cried out: 'How can people be this wicked?'

'What is the matter?' Kperechi had asked at the time, perplexed.

'Somebody died in the radio,' Igboajuchi had answered.

Kperechi could not understand how things happening in distant land could impact her husband that much. 'If I ask that the radio be turned off, nobody will listen to me,' she had muttered. 'It gives news that upset people.'

'*O nuru ube nwanne agbaloso!*' Ozurumba had intoned, calling to mind one of the time-hallowed communal ethos: no one ignores the distressed call of a kinsman. 'That is what saved us during the civil war, am I lying?'

'That's true,' Kperechi had agreed. She had even wailed in pain when she eventually saw a magazine picture of Hector Pieterson's body, the twelve year old shot dead by the police as students protested the compulsory use of Afrikaans in black schools. 'These children were born by fellow women,' she had lamented at the time. That was about five years back.

'I greet the people in this homestead!' A guest spoke from the entrance to the compound. It was Nathaniel. He greeted each household before sitting down to join Ozurumba. Kperechi added more food and soup to the plate. Ozurumba told him about the news commentary. 'JMJ, so you are still keeping tab with current affairs? Well, our country is one of the frontline nations spearheading the war against apartheid,' he added confidently, telling him about Joe Garba, their permanent representative at the United Nations, who was held in high esteem for the nation's commitment to the cause.

'Their cries have gone up to God,' Kperechi said.

'There has been a lot of progress,' said Nathaniel with much optimism as a result of recent positive developments. 'They are ready to release Mandela on the condition he renounces violence, but he told them that prisoners cannot enter into contract. Only free men can negotiate.'

'You don't mean it!' Ozurumba was delighted at that piece of good news. That was the difference life in the city could make in terms of depth of knowledge. They had access to *Drums*, *Headlines*, and other news magazines that carried in-depth reports and analyses of news items. All the same, the radio and the newspapers, which they bought occasionally, had drummed the world's trouble-spots into their consciousness—from the FRELIMO freedom fighters in Mozambique and the UNITA rebels in neighbouring Angola, to the Palestinian question with the seemingly intractable Arab-Israeli conflict, the disputed West Bank and the Golan Heights. The bloodletting in the UK as a result of the activities of the IRA which was declared a terrorist organisation was a common feature of the news. The name of Jerry Adams was frequently mentioned. The cold war between the Eastern and Western blocs, the espionage and the counter intelligence networks of the CIA, KGB, and MOSAD all continued to pop up as frequent news items. His radio made sure he was not ignorant of these global events shaping his distant world. 'If I were him, I would secure my release first. He has been there too long.'

'The man is really stout-hearted,' Kperechi was surprised that he refused to jump at the offer to be released.

'It's a question of integrity,' Nathaniel told them. 'He has suffered much already. If he comes out without dismantling the racial barriers, his years of incarceration would have been in vain. From what is happening, they will release him soon and peace will return to the country.'

'Let it be,' Ozurumba affirmed. 'I hope we'll live to see it. Thanks be to God that lives in heaven,' he said, belching satisfactorily after drinking water. He drew the wash-hand basin closer to wash his hands. 'Albert said he saw you three days ago but I have not caught sight of you since then.'

He confirmed his return three days earlier but he hurried off to Uboma as soon as he dropped his bag. His good friend was one of the candidates for the *Iwa Akwa* ceremony which took place during the customary *Mbomu Uzo* festival. It was one of the major reasons for his return. Ozurumba was surprised to hear that he travelled all the way from the north for the *Iwa Akwa* of a friend in Uboma. They asked him about their people in the north. 'They are fine. They sent their greetings,' Nathaniel answered. Nwakego was quick to ask after Igboajuchi, her elder brother. 'We met at our Bende Town Union meeting on Sunday. He came from Kachia.'

'When did he move to Kachia?' Ozurumba was surprised.

'About two months ago,' answered Nathaniel. 'The company he works with has a contract there.'

'Where is Kachia and how safe is it?' Kperechi could not mask her apprehension. Like everyone in the village, the fear of another pogrom was never distant in her mind. For the survivors of the war that returned to the northern cities, living in close proximity to one another was an important lesson. It was common to find their people in the Sabon Gari—new city—of the different cities of the north. News could travel more quickly that way to enable them know what was happening in times of crises and to flee when others were in flight.

Nathaniel tried to calm her down, saying that such fears were unfounded. Nothing would happen to him. War could not come upon them without initial turmoil. Since they were never far from their radio and read the newspapers dutifully, they would know when there was such turmoil. 'At the slightest hint of trouble, we shall run like Pheidippedes,' he said. He told them that Igboajuchi sent some things home. 'I brought the letter and waybill.'

'You see?' Ozurumba was quite elated.

Kperechi could not dispute with her husband openly on that point but merely murmured her disagreement. She did not want to cause a row in the presence of a guest. 'My good husband, how long are you with us?' she asked, her mood was pensive. She could put some foodstuffs like *garri*, *ukwa*, plantain, palm oil together as parcel for him. It would spare him the costs of buying such items that were known to be quite expensive in the northern markets when compared to what they cost at home. Nathaniel told her he would go back on Thursday, one week from that day.

'That is quite brief,' Ehichanya observed, her fingers busy shelling *egusi*. It was rare for those returning from distant cities to make such brief visits at that time. It took three days to complete a leg of the journey by rail. Usually, the purpose of homecoming was to farm. That was another lesson of the war. It was a grave error to neglect farming because one was living in the city. Nobody wanted to face starvation again if another war broke out. For many years that followed the end of the war, many of them living in the north took out time to return to the village to cultivate their farms. For those whose wives remained in the village for fear of the unknown, it was a good opportunity for family reunion.

'If I may ask, what is keeping you in the village when people are earning handsome wages in the city?' Nathaniel asked.

'I have had my fair share of city life. One has to know when to retire from all that adventure,' Ozurumba told him. Although he was not ready to admit it, he was surprised to hear that unskilled labourers earned as much as one naira a day. He imagined what a semi-skilled worker like him could earn but he resisted the temptation of going back to the north. They parted company at the oil mill. He was about to lock the compound door when Nwugo reminded him that his brother was not back. 'A known fact does not amuse,' he muttered. 'All this night crawling, *Allrigh ooo!* One day na one day. Monkey go go market e no go return,' he spoke in Pidgin. 'The day all these adventures will boomerang is fast approaching. Even if anybody cries so loud as to wake Mbachu my father, Ozurumba will not do *tu tu tu*. What a man with two wives is still looking for in another man's home, I, Ozurumba cannot tell.'

He heard some rustling as the picket gate opened shortly after he had locked the door. The door failed to yield as Uwakwe pushed it. He knocked at it petulantly. 'Who locked the door this early?' Uwakwe demanded boldly.

Ozurumba turned back to unbolt it. He did not bother to answer Uwakwe's question. Uwakwe took his twine and cutlass into the *obu* before returning to wheel his bicycle into the yard.

*   *   *

Early the next morning, Kperechi prepared to join other women to visit Ezeoma, their former vicar. Members of the church in Mboha still had fond memories of him. His new station was a smaller church with fewer converts. To help him, Mboha women organised themselves to work in his farm. 'Please, my husband, can I trust you to keep any message I have until I come back?' Kperechi asked Ozurumba as he was leaving for Nathaniel's house.

'Why not come with me to collect all the millions sent to you?' Ozurumba retorted, stepping out of the house.

'You dare not tamper with any money sent to me this time around. I took it from you the last time, but I won't do so again,' she threatened, raising her voice loud enough for Ozurumba to hear. 'Who has seen my brassiere?' she called from the inner room, where she was getting dressed. Nobody volunteered an answer. 'Am I not talking to human beings in this house?'

'What do you need brassiere for?' Nwakego asked, joining her to look for it.

'Do I have to flap my breasts about all the way to Ofeimo? I have to look decent before changing into work clothes at the farm.'

Kperechi had left by the time Ozurumba returned. He was in high spirits. When Nwakego offered to serve the food she had warmed for him, he told her not to bother. There were more pressing issues for him to attend to. Okwudiri tried to know where he was going to. He was going to the railway station to claim goods. From the look on his face, Ozurumba could tell Okwudiri wanted to come with him. 'You can come if you want,' he offered. Okwudiri gleefully jumped at the offer.

The Kano-bound train was pulling into the station when they got there. The ground was vibrating. Passengers lined up at the edge of the platform, ready to jump in to grab seats once the train stopped. At the same time, they kept vigilant eyes on their luggage. It was common knowledge that it was not everyone in the crowd jostling for space was truly a passenger.

Ozurumba checked the warehouse, but the storekeeper was not there. The train's horn blared again and again, warning people to stay off the tracks. Announcements spewed from the loudspeakers, warning everyone to keep clear until the train had come to a complete stop. 'Passengers please keep away. This is the Limited Express train travelling to Kano via Kafanchan, Kaduna, and Zaria. This is the Limited Express train travelling to Kano via Kafanchan, Kaduna, and Zaria. Lafia and Jos passengers must keep away. The Jos Limited Express train will arrive later. This train. . .'

The announcements continued as the would-be passengers pushed and shoved, trying to enter the coaches before allowing those inside to disembark. Securing a seat and luggage space depended on being fast and smart. Ozurumba noticed that a heated argument was developing between a new passenger and another that was already seated. In a flash, a punch was thrown and the next moment they were entangled in a brawl. Other passengers intervened to quickly separate them.

'Imagine, he won't let me sit down! He only paid for one ticket like me. Did he hire the whole coach?' fumed the new passenger.

'Where does he want me to move my bag to? There's palm oil in it, and if he spills it, all I will get is "sorry",' complained the other passenger.

'There's no sense fighting because of such things,' Ozurumba noted wryly. He knew some passengers could be troublesome. Some left their bags on seats to stop people from sitting beside them, claiming the occupant went to use the toilet or to buy something. Some did it so they could choose who sat beside them, others so they could have extra space. From experience, he knew these two passengers could eventually get along and possibly become friends.

'*Dee*, please help my wife pass that luggage,' another passenger called. His wife was struggling to lift the sack of *garri*. Ozurumba helped her to lift it and pass it through the window.

There was relative calm after everyone had secured seats or at least a space to stand in. After a while, the deafening sound of horn was blared again—a warning to all familiar with rail travel that the train was about to take off and the track must be cleared. One of the railway staff walked past them ringing a bell. The horn went off again. Some exuberant boys remained on the embankment waiting for the opportunity to chase after the coaches and hang from the doors. The staff in the control tower received a signal and the traffic light changed from red to amber before going green. The horn blew briefly once more, before an unsettling tug was followed by a clatter and the train pulled slowly out of the station. Ozurumba momentarily wished he was travelling. The horn blared intermittently and more furiously. Even the deaf was supposed to hear it. One coach was almost empty except for few students in white and green checker uniforms, with a few adults who must be their teachers.

'Papa, see, that coach is almost empty while passengers were fighting each other for space,' said Okwudiri.

'It must have been reserved for students of the Federal Government Colleges in the north,' Ozurumba told him. He was sure that more students would be waiting to board the train in Enugu. The few passengers that arrived from Port Harcourt continued to make their way out of the station. Goods train carrying cattle and other livestock had pulled into the station on a track far away from the embankment. The commotion that attended the passenger train was absent in the case of the goods train. They returned to the warehouse, believing the storekeeper must have resumed his seat, but the door was still locked. As they turned away, a man strolled past them. 'Are you the storekeeper?' Ozurumba asked.

'Any problem?' asked the man gruffly. Ozurumba told him he had goods to claim. 'Let's see your waybill, then.' They entered the store. Ozurumba handed over the waybills, and the storekeeper scrutinised it and opened a big notebook. 'It has incurred demurrage.'

'When did the goods arrive?' Ozurumba asked, nonplussed.

'This is the ninth day. You have four days to claim them and three days of grace. After that it starts incurring demurrage.'

'But I just got the papers this morning,' he explained. 'Why would I leave what was sent to me to incur demurrage?' he asked. The storekeeper ignored him as he searched for something in his drawers. 'What do I do?' Ozurumba asked.

'Pay the demurrage,' replied the storekeeper indifferently, turning to a messenger from the stationmaster's office who had arrived at the desk with some waybills.

'So there's no way you can help me?' Ozurumba pleaded.

'*Dee*, please help us,' Okwudiri added innocently as the storekeeper was entering the new waybills into the logbook. They waited a while for him to say something. The music filtering from the transistor on the table stopped as the programme changed from Igbo language to English. The signature tune drummed stridently, stopping abruptly to announce the time. It was twelve noon. Finally, the storekeeper spoke to them. 'Time is fast spent. The only thing I can do is to take you to the station manager, an Indian man. If he waives it for you, it's your luck.' He stood up. As they left with him, two more people arrived seeking his attention. 'You just have to wait,' he told them nonchalantly. 'I have to see the manager.' He locked the storehouse door after him.

*   *   *

Ozurumba alighted from the pickup truck that brought them home with all the goods. Children joyfully cavorted around, each claiming ownership of any property his or her hand touched first. There were two iron beds, two foam mattresses, a bicycle, and a bundle of zinc. Ijuolachi noticed that Okwudiri was feeling quite pleased with himself. 'You really enjoyed the ride in that motor? You are quite lucky papa took you along.'

'Don't you know I'm a man?'

'Are you the only man? What about Akachi? Next time, I will make sure he takes me along.'

'My money, I have to go,' the driver called. Ozurumba handed two naira to him. 'One naira more,' he demanded but they haggled until Ozurumba agreed to add fifty kobo note.

The neighbourhood was abuzz with the news of the goods. A pickup truck was not the usual passenger-carrying taxi and cabs seen in the village at different intervals. It was usually hired by someone with goods to carry. Words went around that Igboajuchi had sent goods to his family from Kaduna. Neighbours and passers-by flocked to catch a sight of all the exotica. It called for celebration, and in the absence of Kperechi, Ulu started a song and they did justice to it in their dance steps. 'Whoever prays for a child should ask for a resourceful one,' Ashivuka declared.

'That is very true, my fellow woman,' Egobeke agreed. 'It is not just about having a child. The question is, how resourceful is he?' Their joyous celebration expressed their deep longing for modern lifestyle. Each experience further convinced the villagers that technology had the power to rescue them from the drudgery they all wanted to escape from. The manufactured goods, unlike most products made by the natives, did not wear out in a hurry. It saved them from having to repeat the same task over and over again. There was every reason to rejoice as civilisation crept towards them. Anyone that hurried its approach was a hero worthy to be celebrated.

Ozurumba handed a loaf of bread to his visiting younger sister, Ulu, for everyone to share in. The beds and bicycle were taken into the yard. The bamboo bed in the inner room was brought out and replaced with the old iron bed in the outer room. While Ehichanya got the eight-spring iron bed, the new twelve-spring bed and mattress was placed in the parlour. 'Vono Bed' was printed on its metal frame, in black against a yellow background. Ozurumba bounced gently on it, testing out the difference in comfort level.

5.

Kperechi spat out particles of chewing-stick she was using to clean her teeth. She adjusted the wrapper tied above her breasts for better grip and tucked it just below her armpit. The dusting powder she used in the night to combat the swathe of heat rashes on her dark-complexioned body left visible streaks on her nape and chest. Typical of a Christian mother, her upper arm was fleshy and in equal proportion to her bosom. Her *some-gaps* threaded hairdos, which Nwakego plaited the previous night, kept her face tidy. She was sorting out the goats' feed when a shout of joy caught her attention. It came from Iroegbulem's homestead. Wondering what could call for such celebration that early in the day, she took down a blouse to cover the upper part of her body, adjusted her wrapper down to the waist before making her way out of the compound.

Many neighbours had gathered in Iroegbulem's compound before she got there. Leo, Iroegbulem's first son, had achieved grade one at college. The significance of such academic excellence was not lost on anyone in the village. It meant he could get a scholarship for further studies outside their shores, and this was the surest passport to success and fame.

'*Owoworo muooo Owoworo muo*,' Kperechi joined in making a joyful noise. 'Jemima, my fellow woman, God has done great things!'

'It's not a small thing ooo, Kperechi *nnem*. In the Lord my horn is lifted high. My mouth is enlarged to make boasts in the Lord of my salvation. . .' Jemima repeated in a singsong, quoting a portion of Hannah's thanksgiving in her Owerri accent.

'With this, you have become *nne dokinta*,' Leriakawa predicted, implying that Leo could qualify as medical doctor with such a good grade. Kperechi shared the view. It was the good fortune which they all craved for. While receiving four cabin biscuits from Jemima, Jenny prayed for such heart desires to be pleasing and acceptable to God. The crate of soft drinks that Iroegbuelem ordered arrived in good time for her to get a bottle. She asked to see Leo, the person they were celebrating.

'He's still in school,' Jemima answered. 'His father brought back the good news.'

'Where are you off to?' Kperechi asked Leriakawa as they took their leave at the end of the celebrations.

'The men from the ministry are coming today,' Leriakawa answered. 'Have your crops been enumerated?'

'Yes, it was done before the palm tree accident,' Kperechi said. A team of workers from Feugerrol, the French construction company, and the Federal Ministry of Works had arrived in Mboha with rough-terrain vehicles, to map and survey lands for the proposed Enugu-Port Harcourt Express Road. A few white men had been directing the exercise while the counting of the crops and orchards was under way. The exercise was suspended when an uprooted palm tree fell on the white man operating the caterpillar and killed him. 'Didn't I hear they are coming tomorrow?'

'We shall find out when we get there,' Leriakawa said with less certainty.

Kperechi was certain it would take quite a while to enumerate the cocoa trees in Josiah's cocoa plantation. 'You will have much to do if it is today,' she said as Leriakawa set off down the footpath leading to the farm.

She was at the frontage of the compound when Ofeimo women passed by in quick strides, carrying their wares. They were a regular feature in major markets. No market could be considered complete without their fermented cassava and *ugbakala*—the African oil bean. Kperechi raised her voice in greeting, which they returned without breaking pace. She stood at the entrance of the compound for a while. 'I won't be at the market today,' she mused. 'The market can buy and sell whatever it likes but it won't see me today,' she said, spitting out chewing stick debris.

Being the eight day of the week of the Igbo calendar, that *afo* day was the *afo nta* and therefore the *afo nso* – holy *afo*. Originally, it was a day of complete rest when nobody was expected to engage in labour. But with time, what was considered less strenuous activities such as trading in the market became permissible. Even in their days, villagers did not go to distant farms notwithstanding the liberties they were wont to take. Eerie silence was known to descend on such farmlands. Those who defied that day of rest told stories of scary encounters.

Kperechi made up her mind to do some general clean up that day. She had been battling with the niggling feeling that the house had accumulated much dirt. It was an exercise she undertook at intervals, albeit irregularly, to take care of places outside the immediate areas routinely swept on daily basis. Her sensitivity came with the ill foreboding feelings that the dirt could invite and harbour stinging arthropods like centipedes and scorpion. '*Chaaa!*' she shouted, chasing away a billy goat attempting to eat the *egusi* inside a basin. 'Why eat my *egusi* when your fodder is there?' she wondered aloud. On entering the inner room, Kperechi saw Akachi moving pillows as he anxiously searched for something. He hunted through the bedclothes that were wet with his urine but it did not produce the desired result. He was sniffling with frustration. 'What are you looking for?' she asked, turning the lever of the sprocket a little to make the lantern glow more brightly.

He was startled. 'My money, I can't find my money,' he answered, ready to dissolve into tears.

'What money?' Kperechi was surprised.

He was looking at his open palm with bleary eyes, wondering if the coin had slipped through his fingers. 'My money. . .'

'It must have been a dream,' she concluded, picking him up and cuddling him. '*Nna dim*, my father-in-law,' she murmured soothingly. 'Did you wet my bed again? Why?' she asked, stepping out into the open compound. She turned to greet Ehichanya, who had just walked into the yard with her walking stick. 'You stayed too long in the *oforo* this morning. I hope all is well.'

'I went to see Ahudiya from there,' Ehichanya replied, her demeanour calm as usual. She held on to her walking stick to stabilise her. Ahudiya suffered a terrible accident. She was returning from the farm carrying a number of palm fruit bunches on her head. When she slipped, the load fell on her with the spikes piercing her chest at different points. 'She is hurting terribly.'

'That is true. She was in terrible agony when I saw her yesterday. It means her condition has not improved?'

'I doubt.'

'*Ewooo!* How sad. Are they waiting for my fellow woman to die of pain before they act?' Kperechi asked, sighing with disappointment. 'What do they mean by "there is no money" to take her to hospital. Can't they take drastic actions? Or is her life not important enough? If nothing else, they can take her to the hospital in Umuagu?'

'Who can foot *igebuli*'s bills?' she asked. *Igebuli*—can you carry? It was the question many villagers asked at the mention of the private clinic in the neighbouring village. This alias became the name they preferred to call the health centre that was notorious for its outrageous charges. The villagers welcomed the idea of bringing healthcare services closer to their rural community. With time, the management made it no secret what their priority was. They took account of the psychology of the rural poor and their tendency to always plead for bills to be discounted or waived. The bills were designed to ensure costs were covered by all means in addition to reasonable margin. The medical director realised that the rural folks panicked whenever the cure for any sickness involved abdominal hernia surgery. This was seen as a matter of life and death and relatives of patients readily went the extra mile to raise the money even if it was disposing landed property by pledges or outright sale. For the hospital, any form of sickness outside common cold became a reason to carry out a surgery for hernia or appendectomy. 'Whatever will take my kith and kin to that hospital, may the God of heaven keep it far away from us.'

'Who will say she did not give birth?' Kperechi queried, her tone reflective and melancholic. Her question mirrored the crucial importance of having children in their land. She was not expected to endure such severe pain when she gave birth to grown up children. One's flesh and blood were the surest protection against such vicissitude of life. But the four sons that Ahudiya gave birth to were all struggling to make it. Two lived in the North but rarely visited home. They were not as enterprising as other young men of their time. Many did not believe this was ordinary and had concluded that a spell must have been cast on them. 'Poor widow. It's a terrible thing to languish in such want when a person is surrounded by people.'

'Isn't it?' Ehichanya asked, sighing in agreement. '*Enwere madu, madu ako*—to be surrounded by people but lack a helper: isn't it a terrible thing? Chinedu went to meet the one in Elugwu. They want to take her to Amachara or Queen Elizabeth.'

'*Ehee*! They have to take her to hospital to receive treatment first before running around to raise the money.'

'That is what we told them this morning. Ekeleme was there. But the question is: won't they deposit some money before she can be admitted in any hospital? I heard that Iroegbulem agreed to loan them the money that would cover what may be demanded as deposit. They got Okoro to drive them to hospital before I left,' she stated. 'Anyway, how are you fellows today?'

'We are all well my good mother except that your husband is guilty of wetting my bed again,' Kperechi replied with a sigh, looking genuinely worried. Ehichanya had always called Akachi her husband as he was believed to be the reincarnation of Mbachu. Ijuolachi overheard this and threatened to make Akachi eat wall gecko to stop him from bedwetting. Akachi, really scared by the threat, raised his head, looking into his mother's face, voicelessly asking if she would allow such thing.

'When I'm here? Nobody will do such thing to you,' Ehichanya reassured him, walking towards the entrance door into her inner compound. *Mkpokoro*— fence made of palm stalks and fronds—was used to carve out a small but inner compound for her. Nwulari equally had such inner compound.

'Nwakego lee!' Kperechi called some moments later.

'Oowee!' Nwakego answered from a distance.

'Come ooo! We have a lot to do today!' She bundled up the wet clothes on the mackintosh sheet. The stink of urine stung her nose. 'Akachi, it's high time I spanked your little buttocks. You have to stop this bedwetting.' It occurred to her there was nothing to eat that morning and afternoon. She decided to cook rice for brunch.

Meanwhile, Ijuolachi and her friends were at the *obu* working energetically to crack the heaps of palm nuts before the various stone slabs. They had declared a contest of who would be the first person to fill the can of milk cup. As usual, it tested their work rate, the speed and efficiency of each person's skills. Both hands were quite busy—the left fingers nimbly positioning each nut on the stone slab for the right hand to swiftly hit it with the hand stone. If the single stroke did the job, the left fingers quickly retrieved the ovoid kernels before positioning another nut. The left palm held onto the kernels until it was full before pouring them into the cup, the immediate measuring unit. Unable to slow down while waiting for another nut, the hand stone kept knocking on the stone slab to sustain the high tempo. Experience was needed to differentiate between the *osukwu* nuts with softshell from the *okpuruka* with hard shells. It determined the amount of force to be applied when hitting the nuts. A person did not do a neat job where remnants of nutshells were left clinging to so many of the kernels. Ijuolachi noticed Ogbonna pour a handful of kernels which almost brought the cup to the brim. She quickened pace to ensure she was not outdone.

Nwakego noticed the high level of concentration on their faces as she turned the latch to secure the wooden picket gate. She could easily tell that they were competing. From experience, she knew that such drills were the best way of developing skill by the village children. Since nobody wanted to be outdone, everyone worked as hard as possible to keep pace. Although some finish ahead of others, their emulous spirit ensured that the difference was only marginal. By so doing, they imbibed the culture of working hard and training their hands to become adept at such task. Indeed, they were not just taught how to work but to enjoy and love whatever they worked at. They equally learnt to put up with the inconvenience and strain of sitting for a long stretch. Any sign of incipient laziness was stoutly resisted by the family by frequent talking to. 'Keep it up,' she urged them in greeting as she made her way to the yard.

Akachi came to the *obu* holding a ball of white *ochicho*. The crunchy fruit looked like the albumen of boiled egg. He wanted to tell Ijuolachi something but she would not let him distract her. 'Go away, Akachi. We are in a contest,' she told him. As she poured what she had in her palm, the milk cup was almost filled to the brim. At that point, Ekwuzu declared victory. By the time Ogbonna poured what was in his hand, the cup overflowed with kernels. Ekwuzu demanded to know why he did not declare victory before her.

'Are you sure there were no kernels in the plate before we started?' Chinenye asked.

'Didn't you see when I turned the plate face-down?' he asked, rebuffing the insinuation of cheating. 'It was just at the brim when I poured the last handful.'

Nobody contested it further. They all knew he was quite good and faster than most of them. He was usually the person to beat in such competition. They described him as machine or engine that cracked palm nuts, but what surprised them most was the effortless ease with which he did such tasks. At different times, his speed had been attributed to his good hand stone and the slab but even when he used different work tools, his mates were not his match. 'Akachi, please get that kernel for me,' he said, pointing at the kernel that bolted away from the nut he had just cracked. Akachi readily picked it and handed it to him.

'Your *ochicho* is so white,' Obinna said as he spat out the crushed residue of the kernel he chewed. 'Is it as sweet as the yellow one our *ochicho* tree. . . ?'

'Do you know that mama is about to cook rice?' Akachi asked his sister, announcing the question to the hearing of all.

'It's a lie. Today is not Sunday,' Ijuolachi doubted him.

'Can't you see the smile on his face? He's joking,' Akudo said, looking at Akachi for the faintest sign of hoax.

'It must be April fool,' Ekwuzu added.

'It's true,' Akachi maintained.

'True to. . .' Ijuolachi prompted, expecting him to swear an oath to show he was serious.

'True to God!' Akachi affirmed, touching his forefinger on his tongue, the floor before raising it skywards. Ijuolachi went inside pretending she wanted to drink water. She returned, beaming with excitement, confirming what Akachi had told them.

'*Chai!*' Chinenye exclaimed longingly. 'Untold riches—that is what you are enjoying.' Rice was the special delicacy of their time, which most families cooked on festive days or other special occasions. With time, some families cooked rice fairly regularly on Sundays. It was not like other staple crops grown by the villagers themselves. Even the podgy short grains with bran residue known as Abakaliki rice was also cherished notwithstanding the inner husk visibly clinging to the kernel. They were ready to put up with the boring task of carefully picking out the tiny stones common to Abakaliki rice. It was to avoid the sensitivity and trauma which happened when the teeth unexpectedly gnashed against stone.

As a special delicacy, rice was not known to die a solitary death. When a family was cash-strapped, salt and pepper and perhaps crayfish could be used to make other basic dishes which could be eaten to keep the stomach going. But rice demanded condiments that many families in the village did not grow. They had to buy onions, vegetable oil, *azu gbamgbam*—tinned fish—and other seasonings to prepare and bring it to taste. So rice was not a common food for everyday. After the distraction, Chinenye started a song to help them focus and control their excitement. Everyone joined her to sing.

> *Onye kpo nkita bia chochi*
> *Chupu ya O na eri nsi*
> *Obia mo tagbuore anyi agenti*
> *Agenti onye isi chochi anyioo!*

It had the desired effect of energising them once again. The tempo and rhythm at which the hand stones cracked the nuts for the retrieval of the kernels became much faster as they sang the song again and again. Then Ogbonna changed it to *Egom Egomoo!* This was particularly popular with the boys. They sang it heartily, while working as hard as they could. Without breaking rhythm, Ijuolachi came up with *Jordan mmiri Jordan!* It was cheerfully received and saw everyone singing with gusto.

> *'Jordan mmiri Jordan*
> *Jordan mmiri Jordan*
> *Akwadi Chukwu kere mmiri*
> *Kere el'igwe n'uwa*
> *Akwadi Chukwu kere mmiri*
> *Kere el'igwe n'uwa*
> *Osimiri Jordan bilie*
> *Umu Chukwu abiala*
> *Osimiri Jordan bilie*
> *Umu Chukwu abiala.'*

The River Jordan standing before them that day was the heaps of nuts each of them had to crack. Their songs were the war cry rallying the inspiration needed to conquer. Ekwuzu had barely changed the song to *St Steven bu onye amuma* when the sound of onions frying in hot oil assailed their hearing. Having ran out of groundnut oil, Kperechi bleached the red palm oil as a substitute. The aroma of the stew pervaded the air, making the children salivate. Distracted, they prattled for a while, talking about the most delicious stews they had tasted in the past. They did not see Kperechi or her children pick stones from the rice, which meant it must be foreign rice. The rice in the foodstuff Igboajuchi parcelled through Nathaniel was foreign rice, which did not require such a task. Kperechi dished up the food when she finished cooking, giving her children a plate each and one plate for the other children. When she noticed this was going to cause a fight, she shared the food out properly among them, making them cup their palms together before dishing three spoonsful out to each.

She continued with the clean-up after the meal—retrieving dusty old shoes, clothes, and other household utensils which had fallen into hidden places, and items of food that had been hidden out of the reach of other family members and then forgotten. Like her mother, Nwakego kept sneezing as the dust went up her nose. Kperechi was still sorting out all the items she had recovered when Ure, who was visibly pregnant, made her way to the inner compound.

'Aaaa aaa aaaaaa?' Ure babbled, gesticulating, trying to convey a message.

'Yes, we're cleaning,' Kperechi nodded, raising her voice as if it would make her hear.

Ure equally nodded in approval, suggesting it was a task worth doing once in a while. 'Aaaa aaaaaaaa?' she pointed to the small door leading to Ehichanya's part of the compound. With her fingers, she made signs of breaking *egusi*, an indication that she wanted to buy soup ingredients.

'Yes, she is in,' Nwakego signalled.

Kperechi asked after the child in her womb. She replied with a smile, making signs that the child was healthy and kicking.

'It shall not be well with the devil. Imagine, such a beautiful woman, deaf and dumb,' Kperechi sighed as she went to the barn with *akpankpa*—the long strong broom. Hearing Okwudiri's voice, she called him to climb the orange tree. Wilted banana leaves had been fashioned into a pad which she needed Okwudiri to use to cushion a pumpkin pod up in one of the branches. She swept the barn clean, condemning a number of things for the refuse dump.

'Papa wants to use those as ladder rungs,' Okwudiri told her, making Kperechi change her mind about throwing away a handful of short sticks. His father had carved each at both ends, making them taper to a rounded tip. Ozurumba could not be rated as a successful farmer as his barn did not measure up to standard. Since his return, he had engaged in farming like other villagers and nobody could deny it that he worked very hard. He however lacked the restraint required of a disciplined farmer. He was not able to save yams for the next planting season and so had to buy new seedlings year after year. He could not resist the temptation of opening the barn to pick a tuber whenever hunger tortured him and family. Why should the yam remain in the barn when they could get shrivelled or rotten before they were planted? It was better to eat it to fend off hunger. A truly good farmer would not entertain such reasoning and would endure some measure of hunger in order to sustain good farming practice.

Kperechi was distracted by the raucous singing of those making a public show of a young man caught stealing. The live goat he had stolen was draped over his shoulders. Some booed and others sang for him to dance and jump around with the goat. He was sweating and begging his tormentors to stop flogging him. He fell to the ground, exhausted. Noticing that the hold on his limbs had been relaxed, the goat leapt nimbly, bleating furiously as he scampered away. Some boys gave a chase to catch the billy-goat. 'I won't do it again, please I'm sorry. It is my first time,' the young man avowed.

Some elders pleaded on his behalf after he had promised that he would never do it again. 'It's enough. He has promised he won't do it again,' Amos told Bartholomew who was leading the pack.

'What do you expect of a thief? Any time you catch him, he'll say it is his first time,' Anosike countered.

Okpukpukaraka thought otherwise. 'Can't you see that he has collapsed? What happens if he passes out? We shall not be talking about shaming a wrongdoer but would be grappling with the murder of our own kinsman.'

They followed him to take the goat back to the owner before he was allowed to remove the snail shells and grass tied around his waist and neck.

*   *   *

Kperechi and her family were glad to receive Cecilia, her elder sister and her daughter, Ekwutosi. The two were in Aguebi to inform their relations that Ekwutosi was about to get married and, as a mark of courtesy, they stopped in Mboha to spend a night with the family of her younger sister. Ozurumba was on his best behaviour, making sure they were lavishly entertained. Cecilia thanked them after what could be considered an excellent meal of rice and chicken stew in the village. Ozurumba wished they knew they would be entertaining such important guests that day, they would have made better preparation and have more dishes available for their enjoyment. Kperechi was equally apologetic. 'I'm afraid you have to take us as you find us. As our people say, even a warrior can be beaten when taken by surprise.'

'What else could you have done that you didn't do?' Cecilia queried. 'Even *Nwa DC* would be delighted with such a meal.'

Kperechi was delighted to hear that. Cecilia, her troublesome sister, was not one to give praise if she did not mean it. Whatever could please the District Commissioner, the colonial administrator, would certainly pass the test of any reasonable man. *Nwa DC*'s standards were often too high for their liking. 'We didn't see you at the burial of Dr Okpara,' she said.

'I was there,' Cecilia told them. She arrived after the burial had started. When she asked after them, she learnt that they had joined a car heading to Mboha. Kperechi confirmed it. A number of them decided to join Okoro when he was returning to Mboha to save them the long walk from Umuegwu. They all spoke about how grand an event the burial ceremony turned out to be. Uwakwe came in and exchanged pleasantries with Cecilia. He stood for a while listening to the conversation.

'Since I was born, I've not witnessed such a grand burial ceremony,' Ozurumba confessed. 'I'm sure nothing less than twenty cows was slaughtered for the guests.'

'If I say I am not pained by the death of that man, I would be lying,' Uwakwe said.

'His death is a big lesson. Death fears and respects nobody, whether rich or poor, big or small. How it could boldly consume such an illustrious son is beyond comprehension,' Ozurumba added.

'There is no gainsaying that,' Uwakwe agreed. 'Death, is it not the only thing that has defied *nwa beke?*' he asked, once again expressing the generally held belief that even the white man could not defeat death. In their estimation, the white man had successfully answered several of life's questions. As a result, his people held them in awe for the various breakthroughs made possible by science and technology. Such inventions did not cease to mesmerise them. Cries of *Ogbara Igbo gharii*—the thing that puzzled the Igbos—easily captured such admiration. But death remained the only thing that confused the white man, or so they believed. 'Did I hear we were given a cow, as his maternal kinsmen?'

'That was in addition to how many goats?' Ozurumba answered. Umuegwu and the surrounding villages were very proud of Dr Okpara and had benefited from his visionary leadership as the premier of their region. Mboha and other communities had been granted the rare privilege of enjoying pipe-borne water in their villages when he was the premier. That experience had become a distant memory. For over ten years after he left office, not even a single drop came from the public taps.

'We have really lost a gem in that man, true,' said Kperechi.

'You are talking about running water pipes, what about the farm settlements he established everywhere?' Uwakwe asked. 'We shall feel his loss for many, many years to come.' Agreeing with him, Ozurumba talked about the new factory he was attracting to Umuegwu. They saw the metal skeleton of the factory structure. It was the talking point for many that attended his funeral. They blamed death for failing to discern the right time to strike. If death had allowed him to complete the good works he started, they would have been better off as a people.

'You should have seen the number of dignitaries that turned up from all walks of life for his burial,' Kperechi enthused. 'Nobody needs to be told that he was well-known.'

'There is no doubt about that,' Uwakwe was not surprised. 'If they don't turn up for his burial, is it at my burial that they will turn up?'

'*Sikky*, two *sikky* and five,' Okwudiri announced, his jubilant cries rising above other voices in the compound with every roll of the dice. He was facing Ekwutosi after Nkechi and Nwakego were eliminated in the ludo game.

'This boy, are you using charm to throw this dice?' Ekwutosi asked, taking her captured piece back to her starting area. Nwakego told her to watch him carefully before he pulled a fast one on her. He could play *ojoro*.

'Say whatever you like, you have been sacked,' Okwudiri retorted, slamming the cup on the board, getting another six and two. 'My luck is shining, *mmeee*,' he said, sticking out his tongue.

'*Ndi Igbo lee O biara ije ya anwula. . .*' the signature tune of *Ije Uwa*, the popular radio drama series, filled the air. It created much excitement in the compound—having followed every tense moment in Ego's romantic epic, everyone was eager to find out what happened next. 'So you have been following the drama also?' asked Cecilia, with pleasant surprise.

'*Daa*, we follow it closely,' Nwakego answered, sitting on a mat with others. 'Some of us would rather go without dinner than miss an episode,' she added, pointing to Okwudiri who was happily mimicking the familiar whistling of Ego's beau.

Ozurumba raised the volume of the radio while placing a pineapple-shaped plastic jug on the table. 'Do you like palm wine?' he offered, pouring out the palm wine Uwakwe gave them into a glass.

Cecilia made a pleasurable smacking sound as she relished the undiluted palm wine. 'This is *okpokiri*.'

Ozurumba's family and their visitors continued to enjoy one another's company as the moonlit night wore on. The rushing clouds made the moon fly in the sky at great speed. After looking away and then back again, it was always a surprise to find that the moon had remained in the same place. Nwakego noticed Ekwutosi yawning. She went to Ehichanya's room to make the bed where both of them would be sleeping that night.

Ozurumba was still in a generous mood when Cecilia and her daughter got ready to leave the following day. He saw them as far as the primary school before pressing something into Cecilia's hand. 'Add this to your transport fare.'

'*Ogo*, isn't it too much?' Cecilia asked, surprised at the two naira notes in her hand.

'What is too much?' Nwakego asked, her mood carefree. 'Papa owes it to you. We don't want anyone leading Aguebi to our house to ask for another bride price.'

The suggestion got Ozurumba protesting before a smile caressed his face. 'Keep that mouth shut and go away,' he said before bidding farewell to their departing guests.

Later that evening, Ozurumba retired to the village square to relax with his kinsmen. He had barely sat down when Anosike asked whether he heard about the riot in the north. Fear immediately crept into his voice as he asked for details of the attack. Anosike confirmed he heard it from the radio. George doubted him when no other person was corroborating the news report. They became more sceptical when he told them it was in the afternoon broadcast of IBS news program which was normally in English language. There was a strong chance that he misinterpreted what he heard. When he was asked for more details about where it happened and the name of the group, Anosike exclaimed in self-pity. '*Chai* Anosike, I'm so sorry for you! Whatever I say has to be thoroughly cross-examined just because I am not Nnamdi Azikiwe? Anyway, they said the sect was called Masine and it was in the north,' he insisted, not ready to lose face.

'That must be the Maitatsine sect that struck in Yola some time ago,' George concluded. 'Surely they cannot strike again so soon after the first attack?'

They were still debating the possibility when Udogu rode up on his rickety bicycle. He hopped down off the saddle to exchange greetings with his kinsmen. He was dressed in knickerbockers that stopped just after his knock knees. Instead of a long sleeve shirt folded at the forearms with suspenders to keep his knickers in place, he was wearing a flowing pinstripe top, light brown in colour with the three big buttons. It was clearly designed as a chieftaincy top. His black sandals and white stockings with green hoops were pulled up to cover his robust calf. This combined with his low haircut and thick nose on his oblong face to cut the picture of a self-conscious popinjay. 'Where are you coming from?' Ozurumba asked.

'From the council meeting,' he replied, his voice deep and throaty due to his regular intake of *ogogoro*—the local gin.

'*Okpoka! Igidi Igidi* that never dies!' Anosike hailed him mischievously as a prelude to prying information out of him. 'You've been enjoying yourself all day. What remnants have you brought for us?'

'Well, if marathon deliberations amount to enjoyment, then. . .' he said, his voice drawling and trailing off while positioning his bicycle. He fiddled with the locally made kickstand of his bicycle for some time before it came on. 'All premises must be clean henceforth. Sanitary inspectors will be paying us a visit very soon.'

'Not again,' Anosike protested. 'Anyway, whoever fails to keep his place clean will pay the fine themselves this time.'

'Wrong!' Udogu disagreed. 'The whole community will be liable.'

George had no problem with that. 'It is simple. The community will recover the money from the defaulter.'

'*Gbam*,' Ozurumba agreed. 'It is the head that knocks the honeycomb that gets stung.'

'That is not all,' Udogu continued. 'Open toilets have been banned. Every compound must have a pit latrine at the very least and as soon as possible. It was in a proposal made by the health committee.'

'They must allow us some time to dig it,' said Ogbuka, an elderly man. His body was bare like Ikpo, except for a wrapper fashioned into a thong to cover his genitals. He sat on the floor with his trunk resting on the timber log. Now and again he picked his teeth with a broomstick.

'We have up to six months to do it.'

'Fair enough,' George remarked, with his usual air of civility, his legs crossed and his clasped hands resting on his right knee. 'The colonial masters banned open toilets, but nobody enforced the bye-law after they left. Apart from being unhygienic, they are the source of most communicable diseases.' He was critical of the post-colonial public administration—the failure of the regulatory authorities to implement the rules was fast resulting in the collapse of public services. 'It appears the incumbent chairman is waking up to the task of steering the council in the right course.'

'Adiele knows what he's doing,' Udogu agreed.

'A war that is foretold does not consume the cripple,' Ofoegbu quipped.

'Many who parade themselves as public servants don't know their left from their right anymore,' Ozurumba pointed out.

'Exactly the point I'm making,' George concurred. 'For instance, have you noticed that the veterinary offices at the local government is no longer functional?' He went on to analyse the wider implications. 'Abattoirs now operate without veterinary doctors to certify animals fit for consumption before they are slaughtered. Can such a thing happen when the British. . .'

'Someone in the public health office would have lost his job,' Ozurumba was certain. 'No one was allowed to sell meat that was unfit for human consumption.'

Ofoegbu recalled: 'In the old days, butchers wore white overalls and their stalls were impeccably clean.'

'I've done my bit,' Udogu said. 'The crier will disseminate the news tonight.'

'*Okpoka, Enyimmiri* the indestructible!' Anosike hailed Udogu as he mounted his bicycle to continue his homebound ride.

Somehow Udogu did not wobble as he rode away although he looked soaked in alcohol. With four wives and many children, he was the only man whose family was comparable to Agbakuru's in size. He was also the butcher that sold dog meat as special delicacy.

'If Murtala Mohammed had not been killed, he would have restored complete sanity to the public service,' said George, bemoaning the death of the man who had done so much to halt the pervasive rot in the civil service.

'His death was a serious setback to this country,' Ozurumba's voice conveyed the pain of losing him. Murtala Mohammed had served a short but remarkable period as head of state. They did not forget how he had sent an aircraft with military despatch to Fernando Po to evacuate their countrymen who were being subjected to dehumanising treatment in the cash crop plantations. But they remembered him most for his efforts to repair the quality of the civil service.

Joshua was happy to tell one of the stories that made him a national hero. Pretending to be critically ill, Murtala had dragged himself into the accident and emergency unit of a general hospital, disguised. A number of doctors and nurses had refused to attend to him before he eventually disclosed his identity and ordered the retrenchment of all the doctors and nurses who failed in their duty to uphold the Hippocratic Oath to save life. This sent shivers down the spine of many, prompting ultra-efficient service delivery for some time to come. The storyteller did not fail to add a clincher: Murtala had recruited the secret police in every state to check on the service providers and ensure they were diligent in their duties.

'Wicked people are everywhere,' George stated with resignation. 'They don't allow good leaders to last. Is it not why they assassinated John Kennedy, the American president?'

'It is terrible. I don't know when we shall get another head of state like Murtala,' Ozurumba lamented.

Their attention was arrested by the grinding sound of an approaching water tanker driving into the village square. Nwokocha, their kinsman, jumped down from the head of the purring Steyr water truck to exchange greetings with them. Young children hurried off to get containers. Villagers on their way to the stream with buckets and basins were the first to join the queue, waiting for Nwokocha to fix the hosepipe to the tank. This was a favour that Nwokocha, an employee of the Ministry of Works, did for the village every now and then. Whenever he detoured to visit his family in the village, he made sure his tanker was full and distributed water freely to everybody. No matter the number of containers that were brought out, his tanker, which held about two thousand gallons, had more than enough to go round.

6.

George was sitting on the six-spring bed in the room that served as his parlour when Ozurumba came in. He poured hot water into a porcelain cup placed on a small but carefully planed wooden coffee table commonly called centre table. The remainder of an Alaoma Special Loaf stood next to a blue packet of sugar adorned with the picture of a lion, the brand logo of St Louis, and a tin of Peak evaporated milk. These were imports from France and Holland. George could not tell why, but something within him kept insisting on the best he could afford. The children present were on the floor, each with a plastic cup half-filled and a chunk of bread in their hand, dipping morsels into their tea, chewing eagerly and noisily or slowly in a deliberate effort to prolong the pleasure.

In addition to the almanac on the wall, a black and white picture of George taken in the 60s hung above the bed. His posture and carriage was that of a man in authority. The flowing top he wore must have been sparkling white. With his brimless black hat and finely rimmed eyeglasses, he must have shared some ideals with the iconic Mahatma Ghandi or Obafemi Awolowo that he wanted to look like them. His urbane appearance reflected the elitist culture of that time. The photograph was evidence of George's glorious past, when his closeness to Zik ought to have placed him on the path of success. But, so the story went, Zik grew weary of George's incessant hedonism, debauchery, and failure to seize new opportunities.

'King George, you're having a good time with your subjects,' Ozurumba humoured him, taking care to keep his sharp machete out of the way. The international news was on the radio as he took a seat. 'Do you know that there is truth in what Anosike said about the riot?'

'I really don't know what they expect of us,' George shook his head, munching his bread before taking a sip of chocolate. He asked Ozurumba to help himself. 'What do you want?' he asked, transferring the pack of Lipton teabags and Ovaltine can on to the small table. 'Can you hear that?' he asked triumphantly. Israel had completed their withdrawal from the Sinai Peninsula. 'I know they will keep the pact.'

'Why won't they when it led to the death of Anwar Sadat?' Ozurumba agreed. They had followed the Arab-Israeli conflict with much concern and were relieved that Sadat, the 'Hero of the Crossing', was committed to the peace cause to the point of visiting the Israeli Knesset. The words of Sadat, 'Let us put an end to wars, let us reshape life on the solid basis of equity and truth' had struck a chord with resounding impact across the globe.

'I'm sure they can come to some agreement if only they are willing,' George nodded, his optimism buoyed by the pace at which events were unfolding.

Relentlessly, IBS continued to feed them with news of important developments in the armed conflicts, often using reports sourced from or monitored by the News Agency of Nigeria, Associated Press, Reuters, and the International News Wire and many others. The Golan Heights, the occupied West Bank and the Gaza Strip, Yasser Arafat and the Palestine Liberation Organisation, Hamas and Hezbollah, the various ceasefire agreements reached and breached, the botched peace treaties—all these became part of their concerns. The attacks and reprisals, rocket launchers, suicide attacks and air raids, the casualties—most of them civilians—were no longer faraway happenings to which they could close their minds to but were part of their own life story.

They associated what they heard with blood and life, things they held sacrosanct; and found it difficult to insulate themselves from the pain of these distant lands. They shared in the trauma; they cringed at the horrendous loss of lives and wanton destruction. Shuddering at the idea of displacement, they imagined a whole people exposed to the elements, pitching makeshift tents for shelter. It became difficult not to ask the question: the belligerents and the victims, were they not fellow human beings? It was difficult to understand the refusal of each recognising one another's right to existence. It was the elusive pre-requisite for negotiation. 'But they can live together on the land if they choose,' sighed Ozurumba.

'Of course they can,' George agreed. 'Originally, they all belong together. Isn't it?' That much he could tell from his knowledge of the Bible.

Work had barely started when they got to the site. Akwakanti threw thatched sheets on to the roof where Chikwendu and several others were working at the front roof, tying each sheet to the rows of bamboo purlins. James worked on the far side of the roof with others. It was the second time they were working on the project.

Adindu had asked his kinsmen to help him build a new house. He could no longer do most of the things a man ordinarily did for himself. His kinsmen willingly came to his aid. Nobody could refuse him, for they knew he had shown great strength of character since his wife died shortly after the birth of their second son. He had carried on so well before his failing sight worsened. At one of the kindred meetings, a member had called for a resolution banning him from climbing. 'He can't see any longer,' Ekeleme urged.

'That is quite true,' Akwakanti supported. 'The last time I saw him trying to climb a palm tree, he was groping for the trunk.' They were surprised to hear that. Akobundu asked how he was able to identify the ripe bunches. Uwakwe told his kinsmen it would be a communal shame if they remain quiet only for him to climb and fall off a palm tree. Anyone who heard it would query the kind of kinsmen he had. They noticed that he was not at the meeting that day. They all agreed it was a reasonable thing to do. The crier had to announce it, anybody that engaged him to harvest palm fruits was undertaking to foot his bill in the event of any accident. And if he fell off and die, the person would not only take care of his burial but pay damages to his children and obligated to raise them. Akwakanti suggested that they took his twine from him. Agbakuru agreed it was not a bad idea but thought it was not necessary. 'I don't see Adindu defying his kinsmen on such issue.'

After clearing the site on the first day, they laid out the skeletal framework—the pillars, the ridge beam, rafters, and other roofing trusses were put in place before sticking in the rods and working on the reinforcements. It was a great result for collective effort and everyone worked hard despite the banter and jokes. They were quite satisfied at what had been accomplished within a day. Such building project usually took some time to complete but they achieved that much due to the number of hands available to work. 'Joint urines bubble very well, is it a lie?' Okezie asked.

'Take it easy, Jack,' Ikwuako protested when he got spattered with wet mud. It served as the brick and mortar. Jack apologised but noted there was too much water in the mud. Akwakanti guessed that it must be the handwork of Amos. He remembered he had been told to stop overwatering the mud.

'Ask a child to name the person he knows; his mother's paramour is the first name that comes to his mouth,' Amos delivered a riposte.

'*Dee* Amos, are you making a true life confession?' Anosike cackled with laughter.

'Carry on with your work, nobody has mentioned your name,' Amos retorted. 'Can't you see you are lagging behind?'

'I'm doing a thorough job, you know me,' Anosike boasted.

'Well, only wind and rain will tell whose work is best,' Obike countered.

'Are you surprised? What do you expect when your balls hang too low to allow you keep pace with others?' Akwakanti teased.

'*Eh eh hmmm!*' Anosike hemmed and hawed. 'I know it. Some voyeurs won't keep their eyes off me!' His hand went to his private parts, adjusting their position. 'When you see a man, you see his big nose, isn't it? I'm sure some secretly covet my rich. . .'

'*Tufiakwa!* Who wants the testicles of *osompi*?' Akwakanti taunted, provoking more boisterous laughter. *Osompi* was the big old ram consecrated to the shrine of Igwekala that roamed the village freely. Anosike's laugh rang out the loudest at the joke, showing he was not offended.

Uwakwe greeted them on his arrival and praised their effort. 'You have done a great job.' Work was progressing reasonably well at the time on his arrival. Nobody complained about his late arrival at such events due to the nature of his job. He handed up roofing sheets to Ekeleme who passed them to those roofing the house. As a gesture of goodwill, he had added a demijohn of palm wine to the one ordered for their refreshment.

'You finished quite early?' Adindu spoke up as he heard Uwakwe's voice.

'I had to start early,' Uwakwe answered. 'I saw Ahamba on my way here.'

'Did he come home?' Albert was surprised to hear that.

'No, he went away,' Ozoemelam cut in, considering the question unnecessary.

Albert's saturnine face did not welcome his interference. 'Won't you keep that mouth shut for once? Was the question directed at you?' In mock alarm, Ozoemelam asked if it was Albert that he interrupted. He carried on with the work without taking offence.

'Another crisis is brewing in the north, that is what he said,' Uwakwe announced, a little casually.

'Not again. . .' Adindu whimpered. 'Our people must hurry back before another massacre.'

'*Eehe!*' Anosike exclaimed, there was triumph in his voice. 'Have you heard it now? Nobody believed me yesterday all because I did not study in Cambridge.'

The news troubled them and it led to different questions. George was bemused at what was a confirmation of the bad news. It left him wondering what kind of crisis it could be again and the cause. Anosike asked whether the northerners would ever get tired of making trouble. He feared the frequent killings could result in another war. Uwakwe added his voice to their fears of another war. He could not imagine his people fighting another war. His brother, Ozurumba, equally dreaded the thought of war but Akwakanti who was a Biafran enthusiast did not share such sentiment. 'So you are afraid of another war breaking out?' he asked. There was a tinge of mockery in his voice. 'Do you think they will defeat us if the war is fought all over again?'

'Who has ever survived a war that asks for more?' Ozurumba asked, disagreeing with Akwakanti. 'It is only a person who has not been to a warfront that fantasises about war. When you hear the deafening sound of mortar alone, nobody needs to tell you that life has no duplicate. What about the machine guns singing *tatatatata* like song? All those *tatatatata* are bullets aiming to kill human beings,' he said. He knew that Akwakanti was not old enough to be enlisted in the army during the war. Recce was the highest level of involvement for boys of his age. As a combatant, the gory sights he witnessed at the warfront would last him more than a lifetime.

'What happened during the war was not a child's play,' Agbakuru said, agreeing with Ozurumba. 'Oriaku of Abadaba lost his hearing due to such heavy bombshells. Whoever calls for the drumbeat of war does not realise that war means nothing but death.'

'*Oji oso agbakwuru ogu amaghi si ogu bu onwu* – whoever rushes into war does not realise that war means death. Is it not what Sir Warrior sang?' Bartholomew asked, re-echoing a native aphorism that was captured in the music of Oriental Brothers International Band.

'Agile soldier, are you the one speaking?' Akwakanti asked, disappointed to hear Ozurumba speak strongly against war.

Ozurumba's exploits during the war easily established him as the most accomplished combatant soldier from Mboha. He was not only a member of a battalion that captured an armoured tanker known as the Red Devil but fired the all-important shot that slayed the driver. As he told his kinsmen, there was a long pause after heavy shelling at the warfront. His battalion could not return fire with their Mark IV Rifles when they realised they were up against an armoured tanker. Believing the task in that warfront was done, the driver of the armoured tanker opened the hatch to survey the whole area. It coincided with the time when Ozurumba raised his head to peep from the trenches. 'Swiftly, with my Mark IV, I took a quick aim. The bullet rang out *kpooooh!*' His right palm slapped his fisted left palm, giving action and life to his storytelling.

'Agile soldier!' Onyinye hailed him, completely enthused by the story.

'Mgboatu quickly took control of the armoured tanker and began to shell the Federal forces. It brought no little joy to the whole of Biafra when the news of the capture was broadcast throughout the land. Ojukwu visited our base to congratulate us. He promoted Mgboatu to a major while I became a sergeant major.'

'Does the fear of death deter men from war?' asked Akwakanti, refusing to give up his argument. 'Such thinking makes sense only when there is no cause for war. Would you stay away from the warfront if they come to overrun us again?' he asked, equally enamoured by the war story. Unwilling to yield to any argument to the contrary, he burst into some of his favourite war songs.

Ole ebe k'unu si
Biafra!
Ole ebe k'unu si
Biafra!
Agaghim ahapu Biafra gawa ebe ozo ga biri
Agaghim ahapu Biafra gawa ebe ozo ga biri
Biafra ga di ndu!

Umu nwoke ibem
Jikirewe nu na ehemehe
Umu nwanyi ibem
Jikirewe nu na ehemehe
Biafra gadi ndu!

Biafra win the war!
Armoured car
Shelling machine
Heavy artillery
Commandos
Enweghi ike imeri Biafra!!!

Most of the young men joined him in singing the songs. The deep throaty sound of their vocals charged the atmosphere with positive energy. The last line was sung with the index finger wagging in front of the singer, strongly affirming that Biafra could not be defeated. It was Bartholomew that changed it to another favourite.

Nuru olu anyi
Chukwu nuru olu anyi
Nuru olu anyi
Chukwu nuru olu anyi
Odighi mgbe ike nmadu ga akari ike Chukwu
Odighi mgbe ike Gowon ga akari ike Ojukwu
Chukwu nuru, Onye Kere Uwa nuru olu anyi
Chukwu nuru, Odum Ebo Juda nuru olu anyi

Soulfully, prayerfully, they sang it, passionately pleading with their Creator to hear them. The stirring effect of such songs and dirges effectively mobilised and sustained their will to fight. In singing the heroic exploits of the fighting men, it was an encouragement that the whole land would hear about them for laying down their lives to ensure that never again shall their people be massacred for little or no reason. For the ill-equipped soldiers fighting under extremely harsh conditions, it was a psychological weapon, giving them the determination to attack and advance not minding different obstacles at the warfronts.

He introduced *Sheri's* song. The exchange between the two lovers was a romantic epic that captured the height of their patriotism. Implicitly, it denigrated those sabotaging the war effort by discouraging their men from fighting. The male character was about to join other fighting men but his lover repeatedly begged him to stay away from the warfront. Suggesting that he went into hiding, his retort was not only musical but captured the reality of their situation and the courage to face the challenges of the war squarely. If he ran away, who would fight the war when the enemies come? 'In one of our recce missions, our boy's company cheated death by the skin of our teeth,' Bartholomew told them when the song came to an end.

'That I didn't die during that war is a miracle,' said Ekeleme, narrating how he narrowly escaped death. His platoon had attacked the Federal forces one evening during their dinner. As he was escaping, one of the soldiers that survived the attack shot at him. A bullet nearly severed his ulna bone but running in a zigzag pattern, he dived into a river, submerging himself for a while. By the time he came back up, he was on the other side, putting a safe distance between them. It was at the Red Cross camp in Obowo that a doctor sutured the wound. 'That is how my tongue can still taste spices till date. How I mustered the strength to run with the gunshot still amazes me.'

'Does one get tired when running the race of life?' asked Uwakwe. Most of them knew that his deformed hand was as a result of war injury.

'But why did you leave the army after the war?' Onyinye asked. 'By now your rank would have been quite high.'

'In which army?' asked Ekeleme.

'It appears you did not hear about what happened to Onwuatuegwu,' Ozurumba asked. Addressing him by his 'agile soldier' nickname, Chikwendu asked who was Onwuatuegwu. 'He was the soldier that was asked to renounce his allegiance to Biafra but he stubbornly declared 'Long live Biafra'. At the order of the commandant, he was shot and buried. It was too risky.'

'There was indiscriminate killing of those identified as soldiers even after the end of the war. Who wanted to be killed after surviving the war?' Ekeleme asked.

Ozurumba told them about Mgboatu, the commander of his infantry brigade. 'He was so brutal and never called a retreat. Bullets were flying left, right and centre but he insisted that we returned fire. He turned his gun on anyone who tried to desert the warfront.'

'Ah ah,' Obike marvelled. 'The bullets were not getting to him or what?'

'Why do you think he was called Mgboatu?' asked Onyinye. 'Of course he must be wearing protective charm.'

'One day, the battle was so fierce that I decided to escape. As he turned his gun on me, I tumbled quickly to dodge his shot. With the muzzle of my

Mark IV Rifle, I scooped up sand and was about blasting his head but the idiot dropped his gun and raised his hands in surrender.'

'JMJ, give us story,' Anosike hailed, urging Ozurumba to continue. 'Why did he surrender suddenly?'

'Whatever amulet he was wearing came from the earth, one way or the other. That sand was enough to neutralise it. If I had pulled the trigger, the bastard would have kissed the dust.'

Many of them reeled with laughter. 'Radio-without-battery!' Akwakanti hailed him. 'So he loved his own life but was trifling with the lives of others? Did he let you go?'

'Immediately, of course. He signed my pass without thinking twice,' Ozurumba answered. 'That was how I escaped from the warfront.'

'Truly, your father gave birth to you,' Agbakuru paid him compliments. 'Our people really fought that war with fierce determination.' They were familiar with the major success recorded at different warfronts. The most outstanding of such stories remained the exploits of Major Jonathan Uchendu who led the attack on the military convoy at the Abagana sector.

'But why didn't he call retreat when it was absolutely necessary?' George asked. It was not the first time he heard about a senior officer easily maiming or killing subordinates for no good reason or by sheer hubris. Just like the Mgboatu story, the senior officer, a Major, also had protective charms to make him impervious to bullets. Thinking he was a tin god, he expected everybody to revere him. He shot a young soldier at a roadblock because of the attempt to search his vehicle. The officer eventually died from the gunshot of his fellow Biafra soldier.

George believed that the blockade was the only reason why they lost that war. It proved the most effective strategy against them. They did not take delivery of the military supplies Ikemba bought from France. But the *ogbunigwe* developed by their scientists was used with maximum impact at the Awka sector. Also, the Federal forces would have been further frustrated and driven behind the Oji River if the scorched earth strategy was successful in Awka.

The *ogbunigwe* was, perhaps, the most significant invention of the Biafran scientists during the war. After the low flying Russian MIG 15 Jet was used to demobilise the B.26 bomber, the air force commander assembled scientists to discuss how to stop the fighter jet. It was agreed that making the aircraft suck in debris, pebbles and dust would affect its propulsion and eventually bring it down. William Achukwu, an agricultural engineer, took time to fabricate a metal bucket device that was improved upon, tested and perfected. When it was deployed in Awka, the impact was so devastating. An elderly man that saw the number of soldiers killed said that *ogbuefa n'igwe* – a confirmation that the dust mine killed the soldiers massively.

'No mouth can tell what it did to soldiers in Uzoakoli,' Albert remembered.

'The war made our people inventive,' Akwakanti said, brightening up. In all the sad story of the war, they were comforted by the fact that their people gave a good account of themselves. The assailing Federal forces did not overrun them without a fight. An operation that was meant to last one week stretched to thirty months.

'*Dee* George, I remember how people used to cluster around your radio to listen to Okoko Ndem!' Onyinye recalled. The war blockade made it difficult to get batteries to power their radio. They needed the news of what was happening in different warfronts to keep hope alive. George eventually learnt the trick of improvising power for the radio by putting a small piece of zinc sheet in brine water, tying a wire to it and using the lead from the worn-out batteries. He connected it to the radio and it worked perfectly.

'Is there anything the war did not teach us?' Ozurumba asked.

But the memory of extreme deprivation had clouded George's shining face. 'What we went through during that war is difficult to put in words.'

'Do I talk about the mangled bodies of fellow human beings that littered everywhere whenever they bombed us?' asked Ozurumba, his mood completely downcast. 'Indeed, what do you say about the bodies of dead soldiers that were roasted and eaten just to stave off hunger? No, the horrors of the war are difficult to put in words,' he said, heaving his shoulders. 'It can be quite traumatic when I remember what happened at the warfront.'

'The best thing is for our people to leave their cities and return home,' Jack spoke up. 'If our people are not there to be killed all the recurrent mayhem will come to an end.'

'You have just re-echoed my thought,' Adindu agreed. 'If township life is becoming this unpredictable, they should come back. Who does not have a place to lay his head or a farm to grow what to eat?'

Their conversation was interrupted by a feminine wail. '*Onye puta ibe ya puta oooooo!*' Everyone knew what it meant—a goat had strayed outside the owner's compound. The command that no goat was free to roam around because of the crops planted in nearby farms was still in force. Any woman who sighted an errant goat had to issue a call to arms. Any woman that heard the call was bound to join forces to club the animal to death.

'*Chai*, who is about to lose a goat?' Adindu bemoaned, knowing that women would be running out of various compounds, carrying their clubs. 'I hope the poor thing is pregnant.' That was the only time the women spared their victim and would return it back to the owner's compound with a warning and a fine. The billy goat fled towards home, dodging blows until one finally felled him. All the women gathered around, clubbing the animal until he showed no further sign of life.

'It is your goat, Ofoegbu,' Agaranna announced, as he returned to work.

'It must be that stubborn billy goat I was keeping for Christmas,' Ofoegbu said, trying to mask his pain.

On completing the task, they snacked on the tapioca and coconut prepared by Mboha women, in addition to the heavy meal of *utara* they had consumed during their break. Smoothening the mud wall and painting it with *shimmanu*—a by-product of palm oil—was all that was remaining. This, the women had gladly undertaken to do.

7.

News of the religious riot in the north horrified Mboha. More details of the havoc wrought by the Maitatsine followers filtered into the village. Alarmed residents in Kaduna, Kano, and surrounding cities fled the northern cities. Mboha witnessed the mass return of her indigenes from the north. Mere sight of a lizard's head was enough to scare anyone who had once suffered snakebite. Kperechi was not herself when Igboajuchi failed to return after the first four days. 'If only I could set my eyes on him,' she lamented, hands clasped over her head, looking languid. 'Sleep did not cross these eyes last night,' she said, after Emma narrated the story of the carnage.

'It's not everybody that is back,' Leriakawa tried to calm her down, mentioning a number of other indigenes dwelling in northern cities. 'Are they back? The riot did not spread everywhere. It depends on the city.'

'All I want is to set my two eyes on him,' Kperechi despaired. 'You know what happened before the war. Those who doubted that the crisis would escalate did not live to tell the story.'

'Emma, *Sarkin Geri*,' Ahamba called from the gate. 'Where are you?'

'He has just stepped out to greet our kith and kin,' Leriakawa replied.

Noticing Kperechi's gloomy countenance, Ahamba turned to her. 'You don't have to kill yourself before Igboajuchi comes back,' he advised. 'We are not even sure the riot got to Kachia.'

'Is that not what I just told her?' Leriakawa was happy to hear it from another person.

'That is what I heard,' added Ashivuka, again reciting the names of others who had not come back.

Suddenly, the picket gate swung open and their conversation was interrupted by the speed at which Ijuolachi was bursting into Josiah's compound. Brimming with excitement which she could hardly contain, she quickly came within hearing distance to announce to her mother. 'Mama, mama, *dee* Igboajuchi is back.' She turned back to run even before the elders could chide her for leaving the gate open. In a dashing speed, she hurried back to the gate to secure it before any goat could escape. Kperechi went down on her knees, raising her hands skywards in joyous celebration and thanksgiving.

A handful of curious villagers had gathered to welcome Igboajuchi and listen to his account of events by the time Kperechi arrived. 'I know you have been terribly worried but didn't you know I would be on my way,' Igboajuchi asked. 'As you can see, nothing happened to me.'

Kperechi took a deep breath and exhaled loudly. 'I was dead before but now I can truly breathe again. *Chei, Abasi Etubom mi sosong!*' She lapsed into her habit of thanking God in Efik, the language she spoke as a child raised in Calabar.

'*Alhaji ba Mecca,*' Emma called Igboajuchi by his Hausa nickname. 'The whole village has been waiting for your arrival.'

'We did not hear about the riot until three days ago,' Igboajuchi told them. 'Kachia is some distance away from Kaduna and the population, largely Christians. So the riot did not get there. I would not have come back but for the uncertainty of what might happen later.' 'You would have heard that a dead body was waiting for you,' Kperechi said.

Igboajuchi shook hands with his father as he came back to meet the crowd in the compound. Ozurumba's face beamed with smiles. 'My ears can now have some respite. Your mother was driving me crazy with her fretting. I told myself, if I don't see you today, I will take the next available train to look for you.'

'What have you been waiting for?' Kperechi reproofed, her tone a bit acerbic.

Igboajuchi joined others to sit on one of the benches as curious villagers came round to hear more account of the riot. On hearing it was about the Maitatsine again, Albert asked if it was not the same sect that killed people in Yola and Kano. Emma confirmed it was but described the extremists as a different species of human beings. They were not the flesh and blood that bullets and machetes could pierce. The returnees told story after story of how the fanatics went on the prowl, killing, maiming and forcibly converting everyone to their religion. On hearing how they ripped the womb of a pregnant woman, tearing the unborn child from the expectant mother, Jenny could not take it anymore.

'*Eleooo!*' Jenny exclaimed. 'Don't they have women in their place?'

'What about those who jumped into wells to escape their sickles and cudgels?' Ahamba asked.

'*Cheeeiiiii!*' Jenny wailed again. 'What the Bible says is true: weep sore for the traveller ooo!' she lamented, '. . .for he shall not return again, nor see the land of his birth! For how long shall they continue to slay us?' The village knew her story. Jenny's husband did not escape the pogrom. Her husband was a senior staff working at an oil palm estate in Calabar. She took to frying and selling *akara*—beans ball cakes—to augment the family income. Out of kindness she habitually gave some *akara* to the children of her neighbours. When a plan was hatched to attack Igbo families working in the estate, one of the local families and neighbours looked for how to warn her family. Their daughter came to tell her that her father would be visiting them that evening.

Like other natives, it was obvious he had been sworn to an oath of secrecy. Realising that informing them in plain language would amount to breaching the oath, he approached a coconut tree in front of their house that evening. He spoke to the tree in his native language which Jenny understood perfectly. "This cocoanut tree, listen to me carefully. You know you have many fruits. You just have to take your fruits and run away. If you remain here in another few days, you will be cut down."

She interpreted all he said to Peter, her husband. He did not hesitate about the evacuation of his family to Aba. However, like other men, he waited to see how events would unfold. That was the last she saw Peter. Her first son, Maduabuchi, was the first son of Mboha to be admitted in University of Nigeria, Nsukka to study engineering. He was involved in the war effort and never returned. The tragic story was unfolding once again. Believing she had heard it all, she turned to go away looking distraught and dejected. 'Ehichanya, disaster has struck again. How long can this go on?'

'It's terrible,' was all Ehichanya could say, shrugging her shoulders and looking comical in her old and crumpled organza gown that stopped after her knees. Her grey hair, which she did not bother to plait regularly, had lost volume and length. Her right hand clutched the long walking stick that supported her frame. Her bowlegs, which had thinned out with age, displayed different stages of varicose veins and an inflammation of her kneecap. She made her way slowly to one of the benches to take a seat and hear more accounts of the riot. Turning her face from one point to another, she tried to make her one eye see those who had gathered there. Her second eye had become blind with glaucoma, turning it to *anya ezego*—the cowrie eye. 'Does human life mean nothing to them?'

'Is it not why I relocated back to the village?' Joshua asked, walking away unhurriedly. 'How can one reside in a place where his mind can never be at rest?'

'If truly they loathe us this much, why was the war fought?' Onyinye asked.

'I have asked myself that question again and again but can't seem to find the answer,' George replied. In addition to their people killed during the war, several soldiers from different parts of the country paid the supreme sacrifice. But the continued killing was undoing the very reason for which the war was fought. It left him wondering what was the nature of the war. Was it a war of conquest in which the conquered lived in subjugation? Or was it merely an effort to preserve the geographical entity left by the colonial masters? They were all troubling questions he could not answer.

As Emma told them, just the sight of their scarified faces and stomachs could frighten daylights out of anyone. Policemen in the north could not stand them. Anosike was not the only one who was astonished to hear this. The thought of a people who could stand up to policemen and their brutality surprise them and brought fleeting smile to some faces. It was good to hear that the same policemen that make people cow at the sight of their guns could be defied. It was not every day they heard that gun—the very instrument of subjugation and oppression—could become effete in the hands of policemen especially in the face of challenge. 'What sort of magical power did they possess?' asked Anosike.

Igboajuchi attempted a more detailed account of the people they were talking about. 'They are always bedecked in amulets. You need to see when they are demonstrating the potency of their charm,' he said, standing up and slicing himself with an imaginary butcher's knife. The blades were known to be razor-sharp and long. 'But it never rips their flesh because metal cannot pierce their body.'

'What type of charm defies such sharp metal?' asked Albert.

'Does it mean they have not heard the gospel at all?' asked Anosike, looking bemused. In his part of the world, such arcane practices had been consigned to the dustbin of history. He thought that the gospel had been preached in equal measure in every part of the country, including the north. 'Don't you preach to them?'

Emma responded with a quick riposte. 'Perhaps we shall send you as a missionary to preach to them.' He believed that Anosike was making light the gravity of their tale.

'You don't have to blame him too much. He does not understand the people we are talking about,' Igboajuchi said. 'What mouth will you use to preach to a people who force others to accept their own religion?'

'Please don't be mad at me,' Anosike apologised. 'What one does not know is beyond him.'

'I thought the age of such savagery was long past,' Ehichanya brooded, placing her walking stick by her side. 'The brutality that ancient people gave up is what another people is proud of in this generation? Does it mean that white men did not get to their place or what?'

'*Oohoooo*, my good mother,' Anosike exclaimed, happy to receive support to his view. 'That is what I was asking but they won't let me.'

'If it is whether the white man got to their place, of course they did,' answered George. 'Lord Lugard, where did he build his headquarters? Is it not Lokoja?'

'Maybe they did not learn how to live peaceably with others,' Ehichanya concluded.

Ahamba told the story of the Igbo boy who lived as one of the northern nomads and wanted to take a wife like any one of them. 'He readily presented himself for the caning exercise which was one of their eligibility test.' It got his listeners worried. Akwakanti thought it was a strange test with a mischievous smile on his face as he imagined the scene. Onyinye could not believe that anyone would foolishly want to get himself into such trouble. Ozurumba knew that such test must have been designed to test their magical prowess since they were always on the go and exposed to various forms of attack. Ahamba agreed with him, confirming it was exactly the reason. Continuing the story, he told them how the boy yelled out in pain after two strokes of the cane. Some of them could not help but laugh despite the pervasive gloom. 'He thought that by speaking their language and acting like them, he became one of them.'

'He could have asked them to teach him the secrets of their manhood?' Bartholomew said.

'Anyway, those charms and spells are nothing when it comes to military weaponry,' Ozurumba disputed, trying to dismiss the notion of invincibility about the magical powers of the sect. 'If they were that powerful, why did they run when soldiers were brought out from the barracks?' he asked.

Ahamba told the story of the Igbo woman rescued from the sect's enclave. As he heard, one of the taxi drivers on their payroll hypnotised her and took her to their den. '*Chaiii*, my fellow woman,' Kperechi recoiled, her palms clasped over her head in shock. 'She must have gone through hell.'

Akwakanti agreed with her. 'Certainly, they must have turned her into a sex slave.'

George was surprised to know that the man who started the whole trouble was a foreigner. 'How did he attract such fanatical followers in this country?'

'When the *almajiris* are there?' Ozurumba asked. Having lived in north, he knew much about the *almajiris*. Following the tradition of the early Muslims that sent their children to major learning centres, many Muslim parents from the north sent their young and vulnerable boys to Quranic schools in distant lands. Knowing nobody at the place of such religious education, the children were forced to live on alms and the kindness of others. Often, the boys supped on rancid foods rejected by households in the areas in which they found themselves. Such leftovers that were fit for the *bola*—the rubbish heap—ended up in the *almajiris'* bowl. In their bid to escape starvation, food poisoning made little or no meaning to them. Only the lucky ones survived the resulting scabies that eventually covered the skin of most of them.

As protégés of their religious instructors, the boys were bound to take orders. Having been turned away from home, they could not muster up the guts to question the instructions of their benefactors. For those who never developed strong bond and attachment towards others, they did not understand the pains of those that survived the victims of their mayhem and slaughter. Readily available to be used, the *almajiris* were easily turned into pawns in the hands of religious and political schemers.

*   *   *

Uwakwe was still arranging tubers of yam in the barn that evening when Akudo came to get him. There was an emergency that needed his attention. A boy was clutching his left leg in agony, writhing in pain. 'What happened, Ikechi?'

Kperechi wailed empathetically, kneeling with his mother, Onyenankeya, to take a closer look.

Onyenankeya, who looked distraught, answered her. 'I just came from farm and found him like this. Do I know the deuce that made him jump down from an orange tree?'

Uwakwe had built a reputation as a bonesetter, a practice he inherited from Ehichanya. He tried to inspect the boy's leg, but Ikechi pushed his hand away. 'Ikechi, if you don't know the rules, I'll tell you. You must not stop me when I am tending your bones. Otherwise you'll neutralise the potency of my medicine. Is that clear?' Ikechi nodded, weeping.

'Children hardly allow one peace of mind?' Ehichanya mumbled, spitting out tobacco.

Tenderly, Uwakwe inspected Ikechi's right knee and shinbone. The swollen ankle was limp and his veins throbbed. He moved the foot a little but Ikechi screamed in agony and tried to push away his hand again. 'It's a serious dislocation.'

It was bad but not beyond his skills. Uwakwe had successfully handled cases referred to him by other bonesetters. In one case, he had set and splinted a fractured bone before breaking the leg of a cock. The patient's recovery depended on how quickly the cock's leg mended. The present case was not as bad. Two or three manipulations might do it, followed by a massage of the ligaments. Ikechi wept louder as Chikwendu and James held him still. Uwakwe spat into his palms and mumbled incantations to invoke the healing powers.

'Abadaba eee! Mother, are you silent?' yelled Ikechi. 'See what they're doing to your son ooo! I'm dead! I'm dead ooo! I'm dead ooo! *Chineke leeeeee*!'

Uwakwe did not hesitate. He moved and twisted the boy's ankle until he heard the soft pop of the joint returning to its rightful position. He massaged the ligaments firmly, then shook the boy's leg to ensure the joint was no longer loose. Ikechi entreated his captors to let go. His mother, unable to withstand his agony any longer, rushed to hold him, cuddling and cooing, her own tears running down her cheek.

He was bathed in his tears, sweat, and snot. 'Mama *muooo*, mama *muooo*, it aches terribly ooo! My heart is broken. *Daa* Kperechi, you allowed them to do this to me? Beg *dee* to take it easy.'

Uwakwe mumbled something briefly as he touched the ground and touched the leg a number of times to signify the end of treatment. Ikechi dragged himself away as quickly as he could. '*Chei* mama *muo ooo*! My eyes have seen my ears!'

'The pain did not stop your mouth,' James observed, to general amusement.

'Water must not touch it,' Uwakwe instructed. 'Come again in two days' time and make sure you bring my fee.'

*   *   *

As the villagers heard, normalcy returned to the affected cities of the north after police and military personnel were brought in to quell the mayhem. By the third and fourth week, a number of the returnees had gone back. Like fish out of water, they were not comfortable with the happenings in the village. If it was not a dispute over land, it was about the harvesting of cash crops. Some went too far, with the protagonists using spells to fight their rivals. It was a culture which most of the city dwellers had left behind, in preference to urban life. Most of them wanted to live a simple life that was consistent with their Christian faith.

The reward of keeping the tenets of that faith was self-evident. With the money earned, it was possible to return to the village to build any kind of house which could last from one generation to another. Food would no longer be an issue. Above all, they could live in peace with themselves and fellow men.

But Kperechi was not enthusiastic about Igboajuchi returning to the north. She pleaded with him to explore job opportunities in nearby towns. Reluctantly, he went to visit Jerry in Aba. For over one hour, he waited at the 7UP depot in Ogbor Hill before Jerry eventually turned up, beaming as he approached him. 'Mmm. . .my co. . .co. . .colleague just told me som. . .someone is waiting for me,' Jerry stammered, welcoming him with a handshake.

'I heard you were out on distribution and deliveries,' Igboajuchi said, picking up his bag as they walked to the restaurant.

'I'm just co . . . co . . . coming back with that . . . that 911,' he said, pointing to a Mercedes-Benz truck specially fitted to carry crates of 7UP. The company's jingle—*7UP, the difference is clear*—and the skinny *Fido-dido*, the indefatigable cartoon character with bag of tricks and stunts sang and danced in Igboajuchi's mind.

The two men chatted for thirty minutes over plates of rice, with Jerry expressing shock at the gory tales of the riots. He fully agreed with Igboajuchi about leaving the north entirely and asked him if he could drive. He wanted to put a word across to his boss to see if there was a way he could be absorbed. Igboajuchi shook his head. The thought of driving a vehicle had not crossed his mind before. For the first time, he realised it was an important skill to acquire.

It did not take him long to realise that the construction industry in Aba was too backwards and over-saturated. In the absence of the construction giants, the local contractors who were bent on maximising profit paid far too little when compared to the going rates in other big cities. 'Jerry, things are not like this in the north,' Igboajuchi said, munching a cob of corn with *ube*—the local pears—his Adam's apple bobbing up and down each time he swallowed.

'Thi . . . thi . . . things a . . . a . . . are getting bb. . .bad every day,' Jerry responded, taking a bite of coconut to make the corn juicier. Tall and hairy, his enlarged lower lip seemed outlandish on his otherwise handsome face. His brow and mouth twitched each time he made effort to speak. He told Igboajuchi how people were struggling to afford both rent and food, in addition to school fees. Aba, like other cities, was visibly reeling under the yoke of austerity measures. The poverty worsened as more and more workers lost their jobs. Modern goods became luxuries, forcing many to make do with cheap locally produced imitations. 'Iiiif the. . .the. . .the. . .situation is. . .is. . .not arrested soon, there. . .would be. . .be...be troooo . . .trouble ooo.'

'That is why *abali di egwu*—the night is fearful—is rampant in the east,' Igboajuchi agreed, using one of the euphemisms for armed robbers.

According to Jerry, it would have been a lot easier if it was two years earlier when he was in CFAO. But the company had downsized its operations in Aba, laying off most of its workers. Now those displaced by the riot had swelled the ranks of the unemployed. 'Ma. . .many workers ff. . .frr. . .from the north are looking for jobs here.'

Igboajuchi knew a number of others who also considered the idea of remaining in the east. 'Who wants to face continual setbacks?' he pondered. As far as he could tell, the writing on the wall was clear. Their northern hosts were becoming less accommodating of all the people of different ethnic origin that often offended them. If the foreigners insisted on remaining with them, they must be ready to dance to any tune that was played.

When Jerry closed up and ready to leave, Igboajuchi followed him to his apartment where he would be spending the night. Jerry and his family lived in one room, divided by a long curtain. The inner space served as the bedroom and the outer space, the parlour. Among other things, two chairs and a centre table were crammed into the space. Underneath the centre table was a pile of newspapers, the oldest on top, some pages torn or halved, used as toilet paper for the pit latrine in the yard. That was all he could afford with a wife, two young children, and the girl living with them. It was not particularly different from what he and others had in the North, except for the fan and turntable, which Igboajuchi owned.

'Your bathwater is ready,' Irochi announced from the door. Jerry ducked past the curtain that divided the room to get his soap dish and towel then left for the common bathroom shared with other tenants in the compound. Igboajuchi went to have his bath when Jerry returned to the room.

At twenty-seven, Igboajuchi, like his mother, was dark in complexion but sturdily built. After his primary school, which was interrupted by the war, he followed his fellow villagers to the north to seek employment. Like many others, he was ready to give all his skills and labour, expecting in return what he needed to pursue his dream of success. But this was the second time he had fled the north to escape the onslaught of religious extremists. Completely disillusioned, he could not tell when the incessant loss of lives and properties would cease. For how long would the northerners continue to dictate the heights they could aspire? When would they be free to live and work wherever they chose without let or hindrance?

On the fourth night of his visit, they were at *ama awusa*—a section of the town with high concentration of the northerners—and watched one of the Hausa men serve them with *suya*, barbecued beef on stick. Jerry noticed that they were happily and freely doing their business with nobody molesting or disturbing them. Jerry was eating suya where he stood, enjoying the tingling taste of onions and spices.

'That is true,' Igboajuchi agreed, munching with much appetite. The irony of someone whose ethnic group forced him to flee the north, the place of his business, freely and peacefully doing his business in the east did not escape him. Jerry told him that they had to head home while crumpling the piece of cement bag in which the suya was served. The police would be patrolling about shortly looking for whom to pick up and throw into their cell. 'For doing what?'

Jerry assured him that policemen would not hesitate to charge him for one offence or the other. They could even charge the person for roaming and malingering.

Igboajuchi was surprised to hear what Jerry told him but wished they could stay longer until when he would be feeling quite sleepy. He would get to bed and sleep off more easily. Given his small apartment, Jerry had approached Reuben, a young man in the compound who lived by himself, to allow Igboajuchi spend the night with him. Without knowing how many nights Igboajuchi could spend, Reuben had agreed and allowed him to spend the night. The eight-spring bed was not too comfortable for them to share but he could not be heard to complain especially when a complete stranger had agreed to take him in. Besides, Reuben snored loudly. The first night, it took him a long while before he slept off. 'If it is so, how come people still complain of armed robbery in Aba since policemen are working very hard here?'

'What kind of ha . . . ha . . . hard work?' Jerry spilt out the words hastily. 'They . . . they are only loo . . . looking for who to fleece. They catch as many as they can an . . . an . . . and make mo . . . money from the bail. When they see armed robbers, they flee.'

Igboajuchi could not help but laugh at the ironic situation. He believed that the policemen were not taking up the robbers seriously. But Jerry disagreed with him on that point. Policemen were always serious but the robbers were becoming more daring. He remembered how armed robbers robbed a bank in broad daylight and killed the police escort. What bothered him was how they got the weapons with which to challenge police men to gun duel. Igboajuchi was equally surprised at what was turning out to be an alarming crime rate in other parts of the country. Lagos was not the only place suffering from such violent crime. He heaved his shoulders as he sat on the bench placed close to their entrance. 'If only the big companies are here, it would have been a lot easier. I would have approached the foreman and I'm sure he would have absorbed me. You know they value skill and experience.'

Emma and Ahamba had returned to the north by the time Igboajuchi came back to the village. With much bravado, Igboajuchi made up his mind to return to the north. 'The fear of death does not stop men from going to war,' he said, mustering up courage to travel.

'Well, we'll continue to pray. Life and death are in the hands of God,' said Kperechi, accepting his decision with resignation.

'Have you not seen people who die in the comfort of their homes?' Nwugo said to encourage them. 'Yet a person may go to warfront and still come back unhurt.'

'That is true, my fellow woman,' she agreed.

All these worries weighed heavily on Ozurumba the day he saw Igboajuchi off to the railway station. But the voice of his fathers, sharing his concern, spoke up within him. Reluctantly, he must cast his bread upon the waters, knowing that when the time was right it would return to him. He was not the only father ever to say goodbye to his son. Others in distant lands endured the same pain, allowing their loved ones to embark on perilous journeys for the glory of fatherland. At departure, there was only a faintest hope of another earthly meeting and in many cases it was almost certain they would not behold the faces of their loved ones in their lifetime again. The reason for hymns such as *God Be With You Till We Meet Again* dawned on him. Another meeting could be at the feet of their Maker, yet they must not despair. Such loss was not without reward. Even generations which did not witness their agony, nations of the earth both far and near, all rose to call them blessed. Truly, their land did not fail to flow with milk and honey, becoming a sanctuary where the violated or those fleeing violation sought refuge. Again, the voice assured him. It predicted a future time when the years of the locusts and vermin would be past, giving way to a time of unsurpassed glory. That would put an end to their suffering and their reproaches would be no more.

8.

Ehichanya sat close to her wares displayed on a nylon sheet for sale. Soup thickeners like *ogbono*, *egusi*, *achi*, and *oruruo* were her main articles of trade. She added *maggi*, *urupiri*, and crayfish for seasoning at the requests of customers. Her fingers worked steadily, shelling *egusi* to be displayed for sale. This was better than sitting at home all day doing nothing while time crawled by. It gave her a sense of gainful employment, equally allowing her to keep a tab on the happenings in the village.

The village was dreary and calm as time crept by. It was not the happiest thing waiting for life and activity to return. She was dozing when her friend came around. 'You're sleeping,' Chilaka teased, giving her a nudge as she sat down.

Ehichanya sighed. 'There's no market.'

'One can easily walk away with something without your knowledge.'

'That is, if I'm owing the person, isn't it?' she asked absent-mindedly. 'Was I really sleeping? I was actually lost in thought.'

'About the child you will suckle at night or what?'

'Let me be, Chilaka. You're such a bother,' she protested, then lapsed into momentary silence before saying, 'Didn't you go to the farm today?'

'I was in Upata briefly. I don't want that sun to beat me today when I don't have much to do,' Chilaka answered. Fishing out a snuffbox from her undergarment, she shoved a pinch into her mouth, massaging her gums with it. The initial sting gave way to a soothing relief from toothache. 'My teeth hurt terribly,' she said, the tobacco in her mouth slurring her speech.

'Toothache is such a nasty thing,' Ehichanya said, empathising with her friend.

Chilaka spat out the tobacco before addressing Ashivuka, who had come to sit with them. 'You look pale. What is the problem?'

'My stomach,' she complained. 'My eyes have seen the dead since yesterday.'

'What did you eat?' Ehichanya's concern was masked by her stolid disposition.

Ashivuka could not remember eating anything outside the ordinary. 'Nothing unusual,' she answered slowly, searching her mind to recollect if there was anything unusual. 'It has been disturbing me for some time now but it was terrible yesterday.'

'Could it be venereal disease?' Chilaka wondered aloud. Ashivuka looked surprised and her brow creased with disbelief. 'Don't be naive. If you didn't do anything to contract it, your husband could have. Such things affect the womb and the ability of a woman to conceive.'

Ashivuka became more concerned. 'But I don't know my husband to keep concubines.'

'Can you swear to that?' asked Ehichanya. 'You may die if you do.'

'You know what the mother monkey said when she was asked to swear that the infant on her back did not pluck *utu*—wild berries?' Chilaka asked. She was using a well-known fable to illustrate her point. Just like everyone who knew the story previously, Ashivuka was aware that the mother monkey had refused to swear the oath. She was only prepared to vouch for her foetus, the unborn baby in her womb and not the infant on her back. It was not impossible for the infant on her back to stretch out a hand to pluck *utu* while they jumped from tree to tree without her knowledge. Ashivuka, who until then trusted her husband's fidelity, looked shaken. Realising the damage they could have done; Chilaka tried to manage it. 'It could be a mere fling and the body incubates the disease for a while.'

A boy that was approaching them caught their attention. He was driving a big toy car made of *afiri*—the woody fibres making up the xylem and phloem of raffia palm stalks. Empty milk cans served as the tyres. A white and purplish frangipani flower, held in place by a broomstick, oscillated whenever he was in motion like the fan on the dashboard of Chief Ogbudu's car. With his mouth, he provided the sound of the motor engine. His limping younger brother caught up with him, holding the ends of the rope that served as the imaginary cabin of the car. '*Vroooommmm vroom vroom vroom!*' his mouth uttered the sound of a revving car engine before bringing it to a stop. '*Pipipiii!*' Given the sophistication of the toy car, it was obvious he was not the one that cobbled it together. Uchechukwu, his elder brother, built it. Older boys in the village had taken time off *boress* cruising to build vehicles of different descriptions. For more than two months, cruising on *boress* was the craze of the moment. In their desire to take jolly rides, many of them made wooden trolleys which worked like skateboards. A wooden bar served as the rear axle. Two disused car or motorcycle bearings were fitted to provide the back wheels. The metal balls of the bearings were clearly visible. One of such bearings was fitted as front wheel. Some added handles that enabled them steer the *boress* to different directions. Each board was wide enough for just a joyrider to sit on while a friend gave a push to get it rolling forward on hard smooth surface of unpaved roads. When it went down a slope, the cruise was such a delight that it was repeated again and again.

For more than two weeks, they had pursued their imagination further by competing with one another on who would build the best of vehicles using *afiri*. Okwudiri built a big *gwongworo*—the lorry normally used for long distance haulage. He fitted it with his own version of whatever could be found in such lorry that he remembered. In demonstrating how the *gwongworo* was sturdily built, a plastic can of water—not more than five litres—was placed in it. Although it lacked self-propulsion, it was driven to a considerable distance without the vehicle coming apart. Chukwudum's car built by Uchechukwu and Akachi's *gwongworo* were the most outstanding in the village.

He asked Ehichanya for four cubes of Maggi. Ehichanya expected ten kobo in return but when he searched his pocket, there was no coin. 'Have you lost your money, Chukwudum? Retrace your steps fast, you will find it,' Ashivuka instructed. He left them with a gloomy face that was gradually dissolving into tears. His younger brother hobbled after him. 'Wait for your brother!' she called. The boy's struggle to catch up with his brother twisted her heart. 'It will not be well with the devil. How could an ordinary measles vaccination wither his leg like that? It's so annoying.'

'I suggest you ask Ofoegbu to prepare roots and herbs for you,' Ehichanya advised, returning to their earlier conversation. Chukwudum returned with the money, his face brighter.

'Make sure you don't lose the maggi. Stop playing at driving until you have given the cubes to your mother,' Chilaka warned. Obediently, he left the rope with his brother. 'Who believed that Egobeke would ever conceive?' Chilaka carried on. 'No child for four years. It was the roots and herbs Ofoegbu prepared for her that made the difference.'

'Make sure Akwakanti drinks it to flush his system too,' Ehichanya advised.

'Is Kperechi at home?' Ashivuka asked Nwulari, who was passing by and carrying some household compost for mulching plants in the neighbourhood.

'What about her? I don't bother myself with her whereabouts,' Nwulari replied, her voice lacking in friendliness and warmth. Her right heel remained suspended from the ground while her weight rested on the ball of her right foot. She had paused in her springy stride but ready and eager to resume her movement. The swiftness of her movement pointed to how feline she carried herself, a feature that belied her thickset frame. Her fat calves, square face, prominent forehead and the searching deep-set eyes gave her more ogre look than the image of a woman that her bosom, scarf, and earrings suggested. When she spoke, she kept her eyebrows constantly raised, seeming to listen more with her eyes than with her ears. She never laughed and her rare, fleeting smile was always quickly replaced with a frown. 'You're looking pale. Is anything the matter?'

'Nothing,' responded Ashivuka, reluctant to continue the conversation. 'I'm sorry if I had upset you.' The apology was without remorse or warmth, but Nwulari did not appear to notice.

'What a character your daughter-in-law is,' Chilaka said, making sure Nwulari was out of earshot.

'I don't have any comment,' Ehichanya told them, suppressing a mirthless laughter. 'I don't have the strength to withstand her onslaught. She has not been on speaking terms with Kperechi and I don't expect it to end soon.'

Ashivuka was not surprised to hear that. An innocuous incident had led to a minor quarrel between her and Nwulari, which resulted in both of them bearing grudge that lasted for over six months. At a point, it became a question of ego as to who would break the ice first. 'She takes too many things to heart and easily kept record of wrongs. But in fairness to her, she can be loyal to friendship.'

'There is no gainsaying that,' Chilaka agreed with her. 'Even lunatics have friends. I know her type. Ochiabuto, my daughter-in-law, can sometimes gripe about nothing.' Many in the village found it difficult understanding Nwulari and her type of person. She expected others to rigorously observe rules and codes of conduct and would take offence at every breach, however trivial. Indeed, she was always mindful of causing offence to others or being in the wrong. As a result, when she was offended, she found it difficult to take.

'Anyway, those who castigate Nwugo for being meek have seen the embers of a burning faggot,' she joked, obviously referring to the sharp contrast in personality between Nwugo, the first wife, and Nwulari. 'Did I hear that her hut was pulled down a day after she was married to Uwakwe? Is it true?'

'Oh, you also heard it?' Ashivuka asked. 'They must have been happy to get rid of her. This is not her first marriage, I understand.'

'Who is busy carrying all these rumours?' Ehichanya feigned anger.

'What bird flies up in the sky without exposing its belly?' Chilaka was speaking while a heavily pregnant woman stopped by them. '*Eleooo* woman, where are you coming from in this condition?' she asked. Lydia took a seat to rest herself for a while. She told them that she was tired. Ashivuka was surprised that she went to farm at such advanced stage of pregnancy. She must be lucky she did not go into labour. Grimacing as she stood up, Lydia told them that she was already in pains. With much effort, she went away lumbering her heavy frame slowly. 'Hasten to Afugiri as quickly as possible. Where is Anosike? The time to show what makes him a man has come. It's not only by carrying a big sack. . .'

'Chilaka, talk less!' Ehichanya chided. 'Take care, my fellow woman. How I wish Okoro can just drive in at this point.'

'*Daa* can I have two cups of *egusi*? I'll pay you tomorrow,' Ashivuka requested. Ehichanya told her she no longer allowed credit. Too many people were owing her. Chilaka tried to cajole her friend to give Ashivuka the *egusi* especially as she was not feeling fine. But Ehichanya would not budge. She told Chilaka to use her own hand to give out the *egusi*. Ashivuka reminded her that she always paid promptly and was not in the habit of owing her.

Ehichanya acknowledged it to be true before relenting. She drew the basin containing her wares closer, opened the nylon, and began to measure out the *egusi*. 'Don't mind Chilaka. She wants to use me to get into your good books.'

'Have you made the annual contribution to the *Ikpeghe Onyemaechi*—Unknown Tomorrow Fund?' Chilaka asked Ehichanya, ignoring her protest.

'*Aaaa*, that is very true. Do you know what? I forgot it completely,' Ehichanya admitted.

The lay leader had emphasised the need for timely payments into the funeral fund the previous Sunday during the church service. The last synod had put a stop to the practice of making posthumous payments on behalf of deceased members. It was defeating the purpose of having a ready fund. 'You heard the announcement or were you dozing as usual?'

'You think I'm a koala that sleeps all the time?' Ehichanya retorted.

'He said our circuit is always cash-strapped,' Ashivuka stated, collecting the egusi. Ehichanya wondered what happened to all the Sunday takings. Chilaka took the opportunity to needle her with more questions. She was running a big risk if that was where she was pinning her hopes. It was better she paid up. Otherwise, if anything happened to her, the church would not be there. It would amount to the burial of a pagan, as insignificant as that of a day old chick. Ehichanya did not take kindly to the comment. She shot back with her own questions: was death afraid of Chilaka? How was she sure that Ehichanya would die before her? Chilaka admitted that she equally needed to make her own contribution. She was still talking as Nwanyinma approached them in hasty, agitated strides, announcing something at the top of her voice. They paused to listen.

'Nobody should walk Umuobiala road alone *ooo!* Head-hunters are on the prowl again,' she declared, hurriedly telling them how Ojigwe had narrowly escaped death. 'He is still alive because three men came to his rescue.'

'The three men must have been God sent,' Ashivuka quipped. 'Can you imagine that?'

'Of all people, it's Ojigwe they saw? Imagine him trying to escape!' Chilaka visualised how defenceless Ojigwe must have looked, trying to hobble away with his hip wrenched from the socket and his withered left leg unable to move at desirable speed. She laughed and shuddered as she thought about the scenario. 'Sometimes, sheer evil can be amusing.'

Ehichanya could not help herself as she let out a mirthless laughter. 'I'm laughing at my rotten teeth.' It reminded them of Oyiridia's encounter with the marauders who used to lurk around Mboha footpaths.

*   *   *

Oyiridia's victory over a head-hunter made her a legend in the village. News of the death of Amambele's traditional custodian had put various villages on the alert. Everyone knew he would be buried with many heads and so everybody had to take care to avoid lonely paths. But Oyiridia needed to ferment more cassava if they were not to starve. Her husband agreed to escort her to the farm.

Aririegbu walked behind his wife, looking carefully from side to side lest he be taken by surprise. But halfway home, Oyiridia heard a sound that chilled her blood. It was the thumping sound of *akparaja*, the warrior's sword. Instinctively, her neck tilted to the left to let go of the long basket of cassava. The gory sight that accosted her was what she feared most. The *akparaja* had struck her husband and the head-hunter was coming at her. In a split second, she made up her mind not to go down without inflicting some pain on the man. She came at the head-hunter with fearless determination, ready to land some blow before he could decapitate her. Thinking she would be the easier prey, the head-hunter raised his machete, ready to strike. Her long walking stick cracked his wrist and the benumbing pain made the *akparaja* fall from his hand. She rushed at him as he bent to pick it, clubbing with the fiercest determination at his skull; blow after blow until he dropped unconscious. Her husband was lying in a pool of blood by the time she raised the alarm: '*Agu la Diawa unu gbara nkiti eee! Gbatalikwanu oso ooo! Ala aruolani ooo!*' Again and again, she valiantly cried for help, while standing guard over her wounded husband in case another head-hunter tried to attack them.

'What is it?' a man's voice rang out from a distance.

'*Agu la Diawa*, come to our rescue!'

'Who dared to attack you?' asked another warrior-like voice. 'If anybody has hurt you, I say if anybody dares to touch you, I will make mincemeat of him. Nobody pulls the tiger's tail whether the beast is dead or alive!' the approaching voice threatened.

'Cry no more!' the first voice reassured.

Aririegbu lay in his pool of blood and was still breathing when he was taken to the big dispensary in Amaogwugwu. He had lost so much blood and the chemist had to refer them to the hospital for blood transfusion. Aririegbu was discharged five months later with a big scar on his neck.

Mboha decided to honour Oyiridia for her exceptional bravery. A warrior's dance at the Nkwo market was to be the highpoint of the occasion. As expected, the business of buying and selling started early, to allow sufficient time for the celebration. Those who came to witness the dance did not have to be kept waiting for too long. Many from neighbouring villages came to witness the celebration—the first like it in the history of Mboha and of all the surrounding villages. The market had never been more crowded.

The atmosphere overflowed with festivity. The ceremonial symbol of *okonko* fraternity—the brilliant yellow sprouts of palm fronds, which contrasted sharply with the deep green *ogirishi* leaves, festooned the village. Suddenly, the bellowing sound of the *ikoro*—the big wooden gong—tore the air while a group of young men dressed in *okonko* outfits approached the market square, chanting war songs. Various types of feathers graced their multi-coloured hats. Their faces and bodies were decorated with dots and lines, drawn in *nzu* and charcoal, to make them appear more terrifying. The instruments took up a more rhythmic and aggressive percussion. A dancer disengaged from his group and ran up to an elderly man, almost barging into him before stopping abruptly. 'Onyeugwo *dee dee dedededeee!*' he sang, dancing to the percussive rhythm that possessed the air, shaking his hairy, macho chest to the music.

'The dried meat that fills the mouth! The black ant that stings the buttocks! The great iroko that blocks the road!' Onyeugwo, a titled man, eulogised him with many words of praise. 'You're the true son of your father!' The dancer moved away suddenly to join his friends as they advanced towards the arena. They danced briefly, exciting the crowd that encircled them. One or two of them charged at the crowd, forcing them to retreat in fright. Then they broke through the circle of onlookers, as if to return in the direction they came from. But before they were out of sight, they changed direction again and returned leading another troupe of dancers. These new dancers moved more slowly and gracefully. In their midst was a resplendently dressed woman, bedecked in cowry shells and beads of all sizes. An excited elderly man showered her with praises: '*O meka diya! O ji nkpara eme ogu! Aha eji aga mba! Nwanyi mara obi diya! Elewe ukwu egbuo ewu! Etete etete!*' he cried, staring at her waist lasciviously.

The festal procession moved on. The sound of the *ikoro* joined the rising tempo of the drumbeat. And then, the thunderous clap of *nkponala* reverberated in the horizon. The local cannons tore the air three times to welcome them into the market square. Two young men became locked in ceremonial combat, each trying to wrestle out of the other's hold. In a swift move, the shorter of the two lifted his opponent and brought him down on his back. The whole crowd cheered as they disappeared back into the band of cavorting dancers. An older man took centre stage, his body quivering in response to the rhythm. An appreciative member of the crowd came forward to dance with him and pressed a coin to his forehead.

The celebrations continued for some time before three young men re-enacted the scene of Oyiridia's heroism. One of them, dressed like a woman, was wearing fake breasts and the whole crowd cheered when one of these fell off as he clubbed the assailant. He picked it up and disappeared into the crowd to fix it, before returning to give an agonising cry for help, and being joined by other dancers who came to remove the 'victim'. For the moment, Oyiridia was the queen and the dancers flocked around her, ready to escort her home.

9.

The goats bleated eagerly on hearing the dense sound of approaching palm leaves. They kept up the wail until they could no longer hear or see the leaves. The palm leaves tied to their pen were completely scraped to bare sticks. Some resumed their squatting position to either doze or chew cud. The little ones were free to roam the compound looking for what to eat. Ehichanya wanted someone to get them fodder. The goats had suffered since Uwakwe took ill. Nkechi got some feeds growing in the neighbourhood such as *opete* and *oyorohuo*. The latter was the wrong specie of siam weed and the goats refused to eat them. Nwugo managed to get some fronds later in the evening but they were tender shoots from young palm trees. The full-fledged and more luxuriant fronds which made more succulent meal for the goats came from palm trees pruned during wine tapping or fruits' harvest.

They heard another dense sound of leaves coming towards home and started their bleating again.

The bearer did not walk away this time. As the gate opened, Uwakwe came in with the leaves. The unfettered goats ran towards him stretching and craning their necks, their tongues catching and tearing tips off the fronds before he brought them down. The bleating stopped as their mouth got busy tearing and chewing.

Noticing the absence of a billy goat, his mind turned to his barn. The goat was fond of sneaking into it, to eat anything within reach. The gate was open. 'I knew it! Who left this barn open?' The billy goat saw him and fled for the exit but then stopped, keeping a safe distance. Anticipating Uwakwe's next move, the goat ducked quickly enough to escape what was flung at him. Chasing the goat into the corner, Uwakwe lashed at him furiously. Bleating frantically and snorting, the he-goat escaped from the barn. 'I've not seen such a terrible goat all my life. At the slightest blink, it sneaks into the barn. By the way, who left this barn open?' He repeated his question, but there was no one to answer.

'They have all gone out,' Ehichanya spoke from her inner compound. 'Did you have to climb in your poor health?'

'I didn't do much,' he answered, although he had pruned seven palm trees in readiness to resume wine tapping. He was well enough to resume normal activities. 'Does sitting idly in one place help? I have to move around to exercise my limbs. That is the best physiotherapy.'

'Men are stout-hearted,' Ehichanya muttered, as Uwakwe left again. 'You must not trifle with your health; those legs need rest.'

Uwakwe had complained about his right leg for over two years. His productivity had declined with time as he tried to reduce pressure on the leg. The protruding veins were conspicuous, leaving terrible map-like contours on his leg, an advanced sign of varicose veins. The throbbing pain did not stop at the bone but penetrated even the marrow. It was especially swollen at the left knee and a bit at the ankles and he gnashed his teeth due to the pain. He remembered stepping on a spot after coming down a palm tree. It had sent a shockwave through his system. The pain had been intermittent, before his leg swelled up.

Anyanwu, the medicine man from Ofeimo, confirmed his fears. Neither arthritis nor rheumatism was the probable cause, despite the fact that he was soaked by the early morning dews each day as he made the rounds. A diabolical kinsman had cast a spell to incapacitate him. The diviner failed to mention any particular name. He prepared the antidote to be added to herbal balm which had to be rubbed into the leg.

That night, Uwakwe heard the familiar tune from the radio, '*Ndi Igbo le O biara ije ya anwula. . .*' as he opened the gate. It must be Wednesday—the cast of *Ije Uwa* was being listed. As he brought his work tools in, he asked Ozurumba how the *okonko* meeting went. It was the last meeting held to admit prospective candidates who were to be tutored in the secrets and symbols of the society. 'How was the turnout?'

'Nothing impressive,' Ozurumba answered, disappointed. 'Only a few boys turned up today.' More candidates had been expected since the initiation had not taken place for five years. In the past, there would have been too many candidates to contend with. 'Why didn't you come?' he asked Okwudiri.

'I attended choir practice.' Okwudiri answered but failed to disclose the true reason for his absence. The church had banned members from participating in the activities of okonko, having labelled it a cult. Ozurumba asked why he could not miss the practice for just a day. Kperechi prodded Okwudiri to state the vicar's firm instructions about the okonko fraternity. Sensing opposition, Ozurumba took offence at his wife, challenging her repeat whatever the vicar had said since she was a broadcaster. Kperechi stated it simply. He warned the church youth to keep away from all appearances of evil including the okonko fraternity. Her husband would not take it. He hushed her as quickly as he could, asking her what made okonko evil? Nwakego rose to her mother's defence, agreeing with her that whatever women could not see must be evil.

'Ooo please don't kill me!' Kperechi made a pretext at apology. 'I was only repeating what we heard in church. You can take it up with him. You know who the vicar is.'

'One of these days you will all move into his house to feel free to do whatever he says,' Ozurumba lambasted.

'Has the vicar told you there are no traditions in the place where he comes from?' Uwakwe asked with disdain.

'I don't know how people read the Bible these days. If the vicar has not read it, has he not heard Christ's teaching? Give to God what is God's and to Caesar what is Caesar's,' Ozurumba declared. Kperechi would not let it go. As far as she was concerned, he was turning the Bible upside down. 'How much of the Bible do you know?' Ozurumba asked with contempt. She did not hesitate to tell him that it was even worse for him as a person who knew the truth but did not follow it. She knew that he stood in as the pastor of the church they attended when they lived in Fegge, Onitsha.

'Nwulari, haven't you heard my voice? Open this door!' Uwakwe raised his voice impatiently. It took her some time to open it. 'What type of woman are you?' Uwakwe asked on seeing how she swaddled herself with wrapper. 'It was stomach ache two days ago. Yesterday, it was headache. What is it today?'

'I don't blame you,' Nwulari sighed and walked away with a stoop.

'Live, you won't live. Die, you won't die. Are you vegetable?' Uwakwe asked, exasperated.

'You're asking me to die? You worthless man, may my ancestors strike you dead first. You're a disgusting idiot, as you well know,' Nwulari berated. 'You passed all the bad blood you accumulated from your numerous concubines into my body, yet you have the guts to complain that I'm sickly. Did I look sickly when you came to marry me? If you. . .' Her rant was cut short by Uwakwe's slap.

'Will you shut that rotten mouth?' Uwakwe rebuked. Nwulari pushed him, sending him sprawling. Only the quick intervention of Ozurumba stopped her jumping on him furiously.

'What is wrong with both of you? Are you children?' cried Ozurumba.

'Leave me alone! Let me deal with him!' Nwulari struggled. 'What? Nwulari the daughter of Anyakogu has suffered. How dare an old man like him slap me? Does he think I don't know what a real man looks like? Allow me to tell him no one toys with a tiger's tail whether it is dead or alive!'

'Nwulari, it's enough. You're a woman and he's your husband. If he can't slap you, who can? Is it the dead?' Kperechi confronted her, angry that an elderly man had been embarrassed. 'He has every right to slap you.'

'I won't take that from any man,' Nwulari protested. 'Why don't you submit yourself to Ozurumba to pummel you black and blue daily? Such a husband should go to the blazes.'

'That is what he wants,' Nwugo said from a distance.

'If the women of Mboha get to hear this, you know what they will do to you,' Kperechi quarrelled. 'Imagine, pushing a sick man. Don't you feel his pains?'

'It's enough,' Ehichanya said. 'You want the whole village to gather here tonight?'

The commotion had died down before Emevo came in with her sister. 'I'm here to collect my choir music notebook.'

'I'm done with the sol-fa and almost through with copying the lyrics,' Nwakego said. 'Say the rest to me aloud. I'll write faster.' Emevo stooped to dictate to her. She was not comfortable with the *tunja* that was emitting a lot of black smoke. She called on her younger sister, Ajutarachi, to give her the lantern they brought. Emevo loved the song and she started humming it. Nwakego and Nkechi joined her as she sang the lyrics of the first stanza.

When they left, Kperechi began to memorise the portion of the Bible she would recite at her confirmation. 'And seeing the multitudes, he went up on a mountain, and when he was seated his disciples came to him. Then he opened his mouth and taught them, saying: "Blessed are the poor in spirit, for theirs is the kingdom of heaven. Blessed are the meek. . ."'

'No,' Okwudiri corrected. 'Blessed are those who mourn.'

'Blessed are those who mourn for they shall be comforted. Blessed are the meek for they shall inherit the earth. Blessed are those who hunger and thirst for righteousness, for they shall be filled. Blessed are the merciful, for they shall obtain mercy. Blessed are the pure in heart, for they shall be called sons of. . .'

'They shall see God,' Okwudiri interrupted.

'I'm always mixing it up at this point. Blessed are the pure in heart for they shall see God,' she repeated.

'So you have not perfected what you have been learning for over a month? I wonder if you would have done well in school,' Ozurumba teased, proud that he could still remember the things he had learnt as an infant.

'Let it be. Your intelligence was the subject of today's broadcast,' she retorted.

'Must you respond to every taunt from this your husband?' Nwakego chided, while braiding cornrows on her mother's head. They all knew her father's favourite English word and quote. Everything was all about 'etiquette'. At his pleasure he would quote: 'As I was descending the declivity with such ponderous velocity. . .' the words reeled off her tongue. Nwakego always thought the quote came from one of the great explorers, such as Mungo Park, the Lander Brothers or Macgregor Laird. It was not until she came across *Veronica My Daughter*, one of the Onitsha Market Literature titles in the house that she realised it came from Ogali O. Ogali. Her father had corrupted the exchange between the two characters who were expressing themselves in grandiloquent language.

'Don't mind me,' Kperechi said, before continuing. 'Blessed are the peacemakers, for they shall be called sons of God. Blessed are those who are persecuted for righteousness' sake, for theirs is the kingdom of heaven. Blessed are you. . .' Ijuolachi and Akudo rushed in from the outer compound, distracting her.

'Do you want to get hurt?' Ozurumba rebuked.

'A ball of fire was floating towards us,' Ijuolachi cried, scared.

'Eyes-that-see-ghost, what type of fire was coming after you? Akudo, is it true?' Kperechi asked.

'I didn't see it. I saw her running, so I joined her.'

'Children,' Ozurumba sighed, stepping out to see for himself. He saw the approaching light and exchanged greetings with the bearer as he passed by. 'It was Okpukpukaraka's carbide light,' he announced as he got back.

'How does he summon the courage to go hunting at night? One can only imagine what ghosts could do to him if they get hold of him,' said Nkechi fearfully.

'I'm locking the door,' Ozurumba announced after his bath. Nobody raised an objection. The family stayed together while the night wore on. Nwulari was still cursing and quarrelling at intervals, all by herself. After reviewing the programmes for the next day, the announcer ended the broadcast. The station's signature tune was followed by the national anthem, and the radio fell silent. The distant hooting of the owl and the chirping of the cricket jostled to control the airwaves as utter peace and quietude returned to the neighbourhood.

*   *   *

The air buzzed with excitement on the eve of the *okonko* celebration. The initiates had to banish or at least mask their fears—this was not an affair for timorous souls. The roaring sound of *odum*—the ferocious lion—tore the air intermittently, followed by the *ikoro*. The youth cavorted about, devising special dance steps that would be theirs alone. It was time to take the final seclusion flight and to prove how many of the society's secrets they had internalised. The initiates were required to flee from prying eyes. Having gone into hiding, they were trained in the traditional form of communications amongst men. It was a form of fraternity. There were special greetings by which members could make themselves known to each other. As well, virtually every feature of the *okonko* man's appearance was symbolic. Even the positioning of his cap revealed his ranking. An initiate must not fail to decipher *okonko* symbols wherever he might find them. Mistakes such as facing the entrance while making an entry into the *ogba*—the inner sanctum of its members—instead of backing the entrance were not taken lightly. All affairs had to be conducted away from the eyes of the *okpo*, the uninitiated. Women in particular were barred from the society's mysteries. Infertility and even death would be visited on any who pried into its secrets, with the spirits themselves keeping watch to enforce the law.

'*Otitikoriko!*' Okpukpukaraka bellowed.

'*Owei! Ihe amuru amu, ka ihe agworo agwo!*' cried Okezie, taking agile dance steps before bursting into the popular warriors' song:

'Che kpru che kpru che kpru che!
Ana agba nwa nza egbe?
Ihe ana agba nwa nza obu uta
Ana agba nwa nza egbe?'

The initiation was over by dawn. The budding warriors were free to gyrate to the masculine dance. In their excitement, some hacked down plantain and cassava stems with single strokes of machete. Any goat that strayed out of the owner's compound was theirs. Nobody listened to the plaintive voices of those complaining of wanton destruction. It was all part of the ceremony. The celebrations grew in intensity at the approach of noon as the reverberating sound of *ikoro* tore the air again and again. Once again, a salvo of *nkponala* pealed off with many counting up to ten explosions before it came to a stop. Even distant villages had to know something important was happening in Mboha. The sunshine was proof that the *okonko* society had left nothing to chance. A medicine man might want to test the efficiency of a rival by spoiling the day with rain.

The preparations were in full swing as many families prepared to receive visitors. The day was not restricted to the families of the novitiates. By noon, relations, friends, and well-wishers from neighbouring and distant villages were streaming into Mboha. A visitor need not know any of the celebrants personally to join the eating and drinking in his house, and that was beside the food brought to the arena, where anybody could be served.

Okpukpukaraka entered the *ikoro* hut. It was in a good shape. Trickles of fresh but coagulating blood contrasted with the faded blotches obscured by accumulated dust. A white cock had been strangled, its downy feathers strewn all over the big wooden gong, some still stuck in place by the drying blood. He picked up the live cock and weighed it. It was a cockerel in every sense. It would dangle from the waist of *atu*, the fearsome masquerade. His sinewy hands started to beat the *ikoro*, slowly at first, one sound following another at different intervals. With each staccato of sound, he called out the praise names of *okonko* men. Each of them cried out an acknowledgment in a peculiar way. The rhythm gathered momentum, continued at a sustained pace before becoming feverish as the sound rose to a crescendo. It stopped abruptly, giving way to the comparatively dull beat of the drum.

The highpoint of the celebration was following the procession of the new members to the market place. Their white singlets and George wrappers distinguished them. Each had the multi-coloured and well-knitted *okpu okonko* on his head, either blending or contrasting with his attire. They responded to the drum beat with sprightly steps, saluted their elders and danced away to make room for the next novitiate. Finally, the festal procession left for the market as the admiring crowd cheered and waved. *Atu*—the big masquerade—went ahead of them causing gleeful fright amongst the children.

It was great fun, but observers did not fail to notice that the number of initiates presented to the public that year was few. Since it was five years after the last ceremony, the number of initiates expected to participate was far more but many qualified candidates declined the offer because of the vicar's instructions. Light and darkness had nothing in common. The fear of excommunication caused them to keep their distance. Only two members of the church participated freely, daring the vicar to punish them.

*   *   *

Kperechi noticed her husband coming back without his bicycle for the fourth day. She could not withstand the temptation of confronting him again. She asked him for the umpteenth time what happened to their bicycle. Ozurumba took offence and readily countered her by asking if that was the new way of welcoming a husband? Once again, she had displayed lack of etiquette, something he considered as a terrible flaw. Kperechi refused to back down, asking him how the question had anything to do with etiquette. All she merely asked about was the bicycle Igboajuchi sent home. She concluded that he was simply avoiding her question. He fired more questions, asking whether greeting was food or the relaxation a man should get when he arrived his home. 'That is beside the point,' she maintained. 'All I am asking is what happened to the bicycle Igboajuchi toiled and laboured to buy?'

'Haven't I told you it is with the bicycle repairman?' Ozurumba replied rudely.

'What type of repairs is it undergoing?' Kperechi doubted. 'The bicycle was as fit as a fiddle before you took it out, what terrible fault takes four days to fix?'

'If you have the money to pay him for it, let me have it. If I don't bring it back straight away, you can do whatever you like,' said Ozurumba.

'Did you burst the tubes and ruin the tyres? Why do you need my money to get it back?' She remembered some delicacies he bought three days earlier when he went to town. He had been evasive when she asked where he got the money. She suspected her husband of mischief, the more so as he did not do any paid jobs recently.

'Is there no food in this house?' Ozurumba asked, trying to change the subject.

'I will serve your food. My question is: who is the repairman? Don't worry about the money, I will pay the bill.'

'If you have the money, let me have it. All you need to see is the bicycle. Is it not?'

'I don't want to believe what my mind is telling me. I can't even say it out. If anything happens to that bicycle, you will regret it!' Kperechi seethed with anger.

'You have forgotten you are the one living off that boy. Don't say what will annoy me this afternoon,' Ozurumba threatened.

'You want the neighbours to come around?' Nwakego challenged.

'Don't mind her. She just delights in baiting me,' said Ozurumba.

'But Papa, she's right. How could you sell the bicycle someone worked so hard to buy for you?' Nwakego challenged.

'If you don't keep your mouth shut, I will break your head,' Ozurumba threatened. 'That's it. When a goat chews cud, the kids watch.'

'Can you imagine? I was still learning how to ride it. Now we don't have a bicycle anymore.' Okwudiri could not hide his disappointment.

'You see how a woman is misleading her children? Honour your father and mother if you want to enjoy long life on earth!' Ozurumba sermonised.

'That is your favourite quote. What about, "Do not provoke your child to wrath?" Haven't you read that one, Mr Preacher? You are grieving the Holy Spirit in me. You know that is an unpardonable sin,' Kperechi told him.

'But I don't know the type of classroom where you were taught that a woman should challenge her husband all the time,' he sneered, stalking off.

'No, don't run away from this argument. Come back let's continue to pick at each other,' Kperechi called after him. 'You think you know everything because you went to school? Who told you that passing sixth grade is the same as having common sense? Every time you are in the wrong, you ask if I could read the dead back to life. If reincarnation is true, in my next life I will study so well to prove to you I'm not a dullard. You know I'm not dumb. If I had not been born a woman, do you think I would have failed to acquire this education that puffs your head up?'

Kperechi's illiteracy had always been a sore point between her and Ozurumba. Insinuating that she did not see the wall of any classroom let alone to acquire formal education was the easiest way of Ozurumba provoking her and kept her railing at him all day long.

*   *   *

A tremendous clanging announced the tinker's arrival in the village. He came at periodic intervals, when he knew there would be enough leaking pots, plates, buckets, and other metal containers to patch. He took great delight in telling his customers how he brought their utensils back to life instead of throwing them away. But his patched containers were not fit for certain uses, as the pan could colour anything it came in contact with.

'Akatikporo, the profiteer!' Nwakego hailed the tinker in greeting.

'I'm here again,' announced Okosisi, acknowledging her greeting. A slim fellow in his mid-fifties, Okosisi looked scruffy in his work garb. He was hoarse, so he cleared his throat and ended up in a coughing fit, spitting out the phlegm as far as he could before banging his pan again. 'Bring out everything that needs repair—quick, quick! My train is on the move! It wastes no time!' he announced, while removing his tools from his bicycle.

Kperechi heard his cry and remembered she had some items to mend. 'Who is in the house? Nwakego!' she called from the outer compound.

'She's not in,' Ijuolachi answered. 'She's gone to see Emevo.'

'Please bring that leaking pot. Okosisi the tinker is here,' Kperechi instructed.

'Ah, he has to fix my lantern too,' Nwugo spoke up. 'It has been wasting my kerosene.'

'Okosisi, it's quite some time we saw you. I hope we did not offend you?' Kperechi asked as she got to the square.

He stopped the clanging sound to answer her. 'Not at all, good woman. *Ojemba enwe iro*—travellers keep no account of wrongs. Farm work has been quite demanding.'

'I have a few things to mend,' she told him. 'My daughter is bringing them out.'

'No problem, I'm here,' he answered as Kperechi walked away while he laid out his work tools. He started off with changing the base of a bucket. Placing it on the anvil, he knocked out the metal ring before removing the corroded base. He had different metal pans he could use to replace it. He was about cutting aluminium pan but changed his mind and went for the base metal.

Anosike noticed he was double-minded. 'Are you torn between the two pans?'

'It's all about the cost. If I use this aluminium I bought at a great price, when that woman comes here, she would not want to pay what will cover the cost of buying it let alone my labour and workmanship,' he voiced his fear.

'Which one is better?' Amos asked.

'Aluminium is better by far,' he answered. 'If I change it with the base metal, she cannot store water with it for long without a film covering the surface. It colours any clothes that comes in contact with it and it corrodes quicker. But with aluminium, it is as good as new. She can do anything with it.'

'Use the aluminium then,' Amos suggested. 'Even if she does not have the money to pay all at once, she can pay the remainder later.'

'At your instance, I will do so,' he agreed, using a locally fabricated shear to cut out enough pan. Placing the bucket on his anvil, he nimbly knocked out a bit of the bucket, covered it with the aluminium pan, and folded both together before applying putty round it. It was not possible to put the metal ring back as the tapering height of the bucket had been reduced and the new base was wider than the ring. He put the bucket away, counting it as a completed task.

'Nothing compares to acquired skill,' Amaregbu commented, admiring his concentration and the pace at which he worked.

'Nothing,' Okosisi concurred, nodding his head, his hair brownish and a little scrubby. 'Charms may fade but acquired skill never deserts you,' he parroted a time-honoured saying. 'Penny, penny *afu*, *afu*, you will think they are no money until you add them up. You will be amazed at what you can do with them.'

'However poor a skilled man may be, he never lacks food to eat,' said Amos, joining the conversation. He was working to prepare his *akwara*—the raffia palm ropes—for use.

'Who will believe that a tailor is putting up the big structure in Umuochoko?' Amaregbu asked, his jaw working rapidly as his teeth crunched the roasted corn and coconut in his mouth.

'Imagine, ordinary tailor, but that is what Silas of Abadaba does,' Anosike stated, knowing there was no basis for comparing both tailors in terms of success.

'That's the difference the city makes in the lives of people,' Okosisi pointed out, putting aside the bucket. 'Who can make the money to build such a house from villagers?'

'It's not a lie,' agreed Amos, baring the contents of his mouth as his tongue retrieved the corn stuck in his back teeth. 'The *penny* and *toro* we pay can't build it.'

'Anyway, it's not everybody that will own a mansion, that's a fact of life,' Okosisi declared. 'Once I get enough to pay my children's school fees and run the homestead, what more can I ask for?'

'Chikezie, where are you coming from,' Anosike asked a young man who paused in his long clumsy stride as he crossed the square.

'Huuu huuuu huuuuu,' Chikezie spoke indistinctly, pointing at the direction he was coming from. Breadcrumbs mixed with spittle were visible on both sides of his mouth. A lock of hair curled either way above his upper lips as moustache while some strands bunched together below his jaw for his beards, both showing that he had attained full manhood. The shorts he wore exposed long legs and flat feet. They were used to taking long strides. His drooping shoulders and long arms looked oversized for his short trunk. They combined to cut a picture of a person with irregular body frame. His poor carriage and uncontrolled posture robbed him of gait whether standing or in motion. This easily sent a message of abnormality before anyone was told of his mental disability. He was a familiar sight in Mboha when he visited his aunt, Jenny.

'Is it Aguebi?' Anosike asked, offering him a ripe guava. He readily took it.

'*Eii*,' Chike answered, nodding his head, his gaping mouth disclosing dirty teeth.

"Who bought bread for you?' Okosisi asked. Chikezie pointed in the same direction, and as Kperechi came closer, he pointed at her. Since he hailed from Aguebi, Kperechi regarded him as her brother.

'Woman, you have shown kindness to your brother. I can see his bulging cheek. Wherever it came from, may the Creator of the universe replenish in abundance,' Okosisi thanked her.

'What is that? It's just ten-kobo bread? It is nothing,' Kperechi said, trying to be modest and self-effacing.

'Who told you that ten-kobo bread is nothing? What did our Lord say? Even ordinary water given to such as this is not without reward,' Okosisi stated, nodding his head as if persuaded by what he had just said. 'What is happening back there?' he asked. Voices had rung out in jubilation at what must be some good news.

'Emma Nwokocha made grade one,' Kperechi told them, beaming with delight.

'Wonderful!' Okosisi exclaimed, completely enraptured. He dropped the hammer and placed each hand on each thigh, feet spread apart, his goatee jutting to attention, his dark oily face animated. 'Excellent!' his head bobbed like the agama lizard.

'What is good is good, true,' Kperechi affirmed, still delighted. 'What I love, may it be acceptable to the Creator that made the heavens and earth.'

'That is what it should be,' Josiah affirmed, he was equally pleased with the news. 'Show me a father who will not be pleased with such a child? If God keeps him, the whole family has escaped hardship.'

'Wherever good fortune gets to, let it remain. May it get to me,' Kperechi prayed, unfolding the head of her wrapper and undoing the knot to retrieve her money to pay the tinker. They were not ignorant of the vista of opportunities such a good result heralded. Amos repeated what they all knew: it was such academic excellence that took Leo to *alabeke*—the white man's land—where he was training to be a doctor? It meant that Emma Nwokocha could follow in his footsteps. He prayed that *Obasi bi n'elu*—the Creator in heaven—would help them learn and equip them with what they needed to develop their land.

'It will benefit all of us,' Amaregbu said.

'There is no gainsaying that,' Amos agreed. 'When the cock crows, is it only the owner that hears the cry?'

'That truth is self-evident. It does not need further scrutiny,' Okosisi added. '*Ji ghe rughu rughu obara ndada*—when yam cooks properly, even ants participate in the meal. Don't you see the Ikwu waterworks? How did it come about?'

'Who else but Dr Okpara?' answered Amos.

'Who did not benefit from it? Can I remember the number of times I turned the tap on to have a drink of water? I'll surely go to congratulate him when I'm done,' he promised. 'Even if it is only a bottle of soft drink that I can afford, I'll buy it for him. He deserves it.'

Ejituru arrived and began to haggle with him on what to pay for the bucket he had changed with aluminium base. Okosisi was unyielding to all the wheedling and other antics aimed at making her pay the same rate as she would have paid if he used the base metal. 'What is the difference? They are all metal.'

'Is it not what I said?' he asked, expecting those present to lend their voices to the conversation. 'Please have a look at the two, how can they be the same?' he asked, pointing at the two pans.

Anosike confirmed what he had just said, urging the woman to add something reasonable to cover his cost and workmanship. 'It was even *dee* Amos that persuaded him to use the aluminium pan so you can have the best result.'

'*Chei*, Akatikporo the profiteer, the voice that cries for money,' she hailed him, opening the knotted end of her wrapper to get more money.

'Here I am. If you call me, I will answer,' he replied, unfazed. 'How can a hen care for her brood if she stops clucking?' he asked. Okosisi was left with no choice but to drive a hard bargain if he was to get anything from the villagers, who seemed to expect him to render his services free of charge. Ejituru handed a ten kobo coin to him. He looked at it and stretched out his hand again. 'More, please.'

Ejituru hesitated, pondering whether to add another ten kobo coin when the approaching Nelson jangled his bell, before proclaiming on top of his voice: 'Feaaaaaaaar Jehovah! And keep aaaaaaall that he gaaaaaaave as commandments!' The bell clanged once more before he continued. 'This is the whole duty of man on earth!' His voice faded away into a mumble, while reciting what was obviously John the Baptist's call to repentance.

He was skimpily clothed in what used to be a white frock with a piece of white cloth bound round his head to hold something that was meant to remind him about the laws of God on his forehead. Something similar was tied round his left arm. Different marks and writings were on the doorpost of his house to also keep him reminded about these laws. His grey beard was unkempt. His slippers were patched; his calloused toes poked through and there were gaping holes at the heels. His regular missionary work had taken a toll on Nelson: with his bald head and shrunken body, his protruding abdomen and his wizened chest, he was the picture of a pot-bellied man who escaped being a midget.

Nelson was an eccentric. A previous worshipper of the mermaid queen, he had cured people of various ailments by calling on her for help. Ozurumba had gone to him after he ingested poison that was making him cough blood. Taking him to the river at the dead of the night, Nelson instructed him to stand with his back to the water to ensure that he did not sight the goddess. After a sacrifice and invocation, Ozurumba heard splashing as the mermaid made her way to the shore. A female voice asked why she had been disturbed.

'Queen of the coast, I have come to worship,' said Nelson, bowing.

'Who is our guest?' she asked.

'He's a patient, dying slowly from poison. We've come to find solution.'

'Very well, take this. He'll be well again,' she reassured him.

Taking the vial from her, Nelson handed it to Ozurumba, instructing him to drink it and go home without looking back.

Nelson's compound was lined with trees dedicated to the different idols that he once worshipped. He poured *odo* or *uhie* coloured powders at their base and kept small clay bowls by the trees containing different things. Tiny down and powder-down feathers were generously littered around them. The harrowing sound of young hatchlings twittering ceaselessly after they were separated from their mother was not uncommon feature of his compound after a ritual. Passers-by who felt for the chicks could do nothing to help them.

He had given it all up so suddenly, to pick up a bell and a Bible which, however, he never seemed to open to denounce the very idols he had worshipped all his life. He was obsessed only with his evangelism. Any day he woke up and felt like evangelising the earth, he trudged the length of the village and beyond to bring anew the message of straightening every crooked path and filling every valley in readiness of Him the thong of whose sandal he was not worthy to untie.

People were rather sceptical of this sudden transformation, especially as Nelson never attended any church. Yet he was dear to Mboha and her inhabitants, who had learnt to live with him.

10.

Chief Ogbudu was relaxing at his veranda when Ozurumba and Amos arrived for the meeting. Kola was served after they exchanged greetings. The chief turned to a covered dish set before him, removed the antimacassar before lifting up the cover. Inside it was a bowl of sliced paw-paw and pineapple prepared as his dessert. He invited his visitors to join him in eating the fruits. Ozurumba thanked him while declining the offer. Amos was amused. 'The dish looked so elegant, my mouth was watering—I thought you were about to produce a real meal.'

'What meal can be better than this?' smiled Chief Ogbudu, using a fork to help himself to a small plateful. He munched gently; his well-kept beard shimmered with the movement of his jaw. 'Fruit is very good for the body.'

'But it doesn't fill up the stomach,' complained Ozurumba. 'Rather, it aggravates hunger.'

Chief Ogbudu's beamed with a quiet smile. 'But that's what it is meant to do, to help the digestive system.'

Their light-hearted debate was cut short by the arrival of more representatives from other families. 'The king shall live forever!' Okezie cried out his greetings, grovelling with his right knee on the floor while his left elbow rested on his left thigh in outward show of loyalty. He remained in that position momentarily, his gaze fixed on Chief Ogbudu, waiting to hear a comment releasing him. For a people who were fiercely egalitarian, such fawning was regarded as sheer jesting calculated to curry favour from him.

'And those who made him king,' the chief returned heartily, motioning perfunctorily for him to rise to his feet. 'Please make yourselves comfortable,' he said and signalled for more kola.

'Did you hear about the fight between our boys and those of Abadaba?' Albert asked.

'That's true,' Okezie confirmed. 'Today's fight was nasty. It's a miracle there was no casualty.'

'When was that?' Josiah asked in apparent surprise.

'This afternoon,' Ozurumba answered.

'What was it about this time?' Josiah wondered.

'It was about who has the right to dredge sand in Ovoro beach,' Okezie told him.

'We must do something about it before it gets out of hand,' Chief Ogbudu stated. He then moved on to his main reason for calling the meeting. At the proposal of the education secretary, the local government was planning to merge a number of community schools due to inadequate funding. Apparently, the community school in Mboha was in danger of being merged with Umuhu.

'They are at it again,' said Akwakanti, referring to a similar incident in the past. It was the threat to close down schools with thatched sheds and other substandard structures which forced Mboha to levy her indigenes to raise money for building the *mgbidi* structure with three classrooms and an assembly hall. Otherwise, the three teachers taking the children up to primary three would have been withdrawn. That singular effort was rewarded when their community benefited from the Universal Primary Education programme. The federal government built a block of two classrooms for every primary school in the country. After all that, they imagined that their village school was safe and secure.

'So do we know what is going to happen to our school?' Albert queried, doing all he could to suppress the anger in his voice.

'If you ask me, who do I ask?' mused Chief Ogbudu.

'Maybe the people you heard this from in the first place,' Albert suggested, as everyone started butting in with different opinions.

'Can we stop all the bickering?' Josiah demanded, then waited for the babble to die down. 'The man that summoned this meeting must have something in mind that he wants to tell us. Can't we allow him to say it?'

In the ensuing silence, Chief Ogbudu proposed that the village send a delegation to meet with the local government chairman on a fact-finding mission before adding, 'But I suggest we don't go empty-handed.'

'Good idea,' Ogbuka agreed. 'A mouth that tasted spices speaks differently.'

After much debate, they agreed to raise twenty naira. 'Ten pounds for a bribe?' Albert was displeased, almost alarmed. 'I have never heard of such a thing. Maybe we should summon a general assembly of the village before taking such a decision.'

'Does ten pounds compare to what we stand to lose if the school is closed down?' Okezie challenged him.

'We must not forget that this is sensitive information,' Chief Ogbudu reminded them while maintaining his cool. He was used to Albert opposing him. 'I could have done this without letting any of you know, but then there would have been no witnesses and the chairman could have pocketed whatever I give him which you call a bribe and you will hear nothing.'

Two days later, Ozurumba and Josiah were at the local government secretariat waiting for Chief Ogbudu. They kept themselves busy eating cups of boiled groundnuts, which Ozurumba had bought from a hawker. Four heavy duty machines with CAT inscription and other earthmoving equipment were parked in the grounds of the building. Judging by the overgrown weeds all around them, they had not been in use for a long time. Two had no tyres, their frames resting on old engine blocks. 'All these are worth money,' Josiah remarked, throwing groundnuts into his mouth.

'They could be auctioned instead of being left here to rust,' Ozurumba agreed.

A short distance away, three men were busy manually mowing a luxuriant lawn while another man was lopping the ever blooming ixora hedge. A different person was raking together the litters and flowers that fell from the royal Poinciana trees. The dense canopy of brightly red flowers and the large feather-like leaves from the flamboyant trees planted one pole apart from the other provided the much needed shades. In addition to the beautification of the landscape, they were planned to provide calming shelter to those seeking respite from the scorching sun. A pole bearing the national flag stood at the centre of the lawn ringed round with herbaceous border. The arrival of a chauffeur-driven white Peugeot 504SR brought their wait to an end. Chief Ogbudu stepped out, his bearing regal, a walking stick in hand. He turned to face them as they approached.

They made their way through the corridors of a new block of offices. Since independence, architectural standards appeared to be undergoing changes. Keeping costs low seemed to be the main motive. Roofs were no longer steeply pitched, resulting in the disappearance of the gable in most of the new buildings. Why add more than two lines of blocks above the lintel when they were not a nation of giants? Public buildings, like residential buildings, began to look shorter than those built prior to or immediately after independence.

An arrow drawn on a piece of paper stapled to the chairman's door directed them to the next office. A female secretary was cutting a stencil on an Olympia 80 typewriter when they entered. She stopped to attend to them. 'Please, is *oga* expecting you?' she asked, checking her register.

'Tell Mazi Adiele that Chief Ogbudu is here,' said the chief, managing to evade her question.

The secretary's face revealed her dilemma—it was clear that she didn't have his name on her list, yet could she dare to turn away such an important person? She was hesitating when the door opened.

'Ah, Chief Ogbudu!' Mazi Adiele was obviously surprised to see him standing there. He opened the door wider and led them into his office. 'Please make yourselves comfortable. People keep trooping in here, most of them for frivolous requests and favours that are difficult to grant,' he added, by way of explaining the strict new appointment system.

'I didn't know you'd moved to the new building. It's so nice,' Chief Ogbudu complimented him. Batons crisscrossed the low, newly painted asbestos ceiling. The ceiling fan, oscillating furiously, had had its supporting rod shortened to take account of people's height. The slatted blinds were open and the curtains drawn back to let in some air. The wrought iron burglar-proof was shaped like a whorl of maple leaves in-between vertical rods and were coated in black oily paint. Nobody, however skinny, could have slipped through them.

'We are still in the process of moving,' Mazi Adiele told them. Heaps of files were piled on the bare floor close to some wooden shelves. The two black and white checked plastic carpets did not cover the whole floor.

'It is very different to the old building,' Josiah commented.

'Times are changing,' Mazi Adiele agreed. He listened as Chief Ogbudu explained the reason for their visit. 'It was an issue raised at our last council meeting as part of cost-cutting measures, although we have not reached a definite decision yet,' he confirmed. 'We don't have enough funds at our disposal to keep all the schools.' The door swung open as his secretary burst in to answer his buzzer. 'Ask Mr Ojimadu to come over with the school list.' Mboha community school was indeed one of the schools to be merged, but at Chief Ogbudu's request, it was removed from the list. 'But we might have to think again, if the budget remains too tight,' said Mazi Adiele.

'I will be right behind you,' Chief Ogbudu told Ozurumba and Josiah at the end of the meeting, asking them to go ahead of him. Ten minutes later, he emerged from the office and led the way back to the car. 'Drive to Golden Guinea first,' he instructed the chauffer. 'And turn up the fan.' Okey, his driver, pressed a button and the fan affixed to the dashboard spun faster. The three passengers relaxed, delighted with their effort and happy that they had not just left the school situation to drift. At the next junction, a madman stood in the middle of the road controlling the traffic. Ozurumba and Josiah were amazed that the cars obeyed him and he did not misdirect them.

'Are you sure he's really mad?' Ozurumba wondered.

'He's doing a really good job,' said Josiah, equally surprised.

'Ari the War!' one of the motorists called, throwing a ten-kobo coin to the madman. It seemed to energise him as he continued to wave ahead the cars in that line of traffic. Another driver honked his horn, encouraging Ari to beckon on vehicles on their lane while stopping the other, his dazed oily face brightening with smile.

'That is what smoking *weewee* can cause,' Chief Ogbudu sneered. 'That's a man who attended college.'

'*Eleooo!*' Ozurumba groaned. 'What a calamity!'

Josiah snapped his fingers in revulsion. 'God forbid evil.' He could not understand how a student would abandon his studies to indulge in cannabis. 'Did I hear some of them smoke it to help them get higher grades?'

'First they neglect their books in the pursuit of fun. Then the exams draw near, and they take drugs to force the books into their heads!' Chief Ogbudu was not sympathetic.

Okey blurted out, 'Master, I heard he would have made grade one but another student cast a spell on him.'

'Jealous of his scholarship, I suppose. . .' Ozurumba sighed and shrugged his shoulders.

'That must have been it,' Chief Ogbudu agreed sadly.

A lady on moped rode into the road without observing traffic. Okey quickly slammed the brakes, throwing all his passengers violently forward. 'Imagine, the devil wants to work overtime,' Ozurumba said, adjusting himself back on to the seat. None of them was wearing seatbelts. 'I could have hit my head on the windscreen.'

'This is how accidents happen,' said Josiah.

'You remember what I told you about speeding?' Chief Ogbudu remarked sharply. 'I know the lady was at fault but Ozurumba could have gone through the windscreen and that would have been a different story altogether,' he scolded.

'Sorry Sir,' apologised Okey, suppressing his annoyance. He knew arguing back would only make things worse. He checked the side mirrors, glanced over his shoulder to make sure no cyclist was in his blind spot, then turned into the Golden Guinea Breweries. A security man peered into the car, saw Chief Ogbudu, straightened up and saluted in military fashion. They drove to the visitors' parking lot; the chimney towering into space above them was steadily puffing out smoky steam.

'I won't be long,' promised Chief Ogbudu, alighting from the car.

'Dr Okpara did well!' Ozurumba took pride in the size of the brewery built by the late Premier.

'This is nothing compared to what he did in Trans-Amadi in Port Harcourt,' Okey told them, relaxed and chatty now that Chief Ogbudu had left them.

'So, we have saved our school from being merged with another school,' Ozurumba remarked. 'Thank God for that.'

'We must also thank Chief Ogbudu. What if he did not know Mazi Adiele?'

'They belong to the same social circle. Your kinsman is well-known. No important meeting is held in this town in his absence.'

It was almost dark when Ozurumba returned to his busy family. Kperechi was tidying up their part of the compound, which was littered with cassava peels. As Nwakego dished out the food she pounded, Okwudiri assisted Chikwendu to tie up the sack of cassava they grated by hand.

'Who littered my doorway with these sticks?' asked Nwulari, approaching with a bucket of water on her head. Okwudiri made haste to remove them. But it did not placate her. 'You want me to trip over them, is that not so? And if I hurt myself, all I will get from you is a "sorry". All this space is not enough for you, but you have to encroach on the little space I have here?'

'Don't be angry, *nwunyedi m*,' Kperechi apologised, as Nwulari set her water down. 'It was a mistake.'

'And I suppose it was a mistake when I tripped over a bucket carelessly left on my doorstep some time ago. The person who left it never owned up but I was the one who nursed the injury for weeks,' Nwulari continued.

'Sorry, my fellow woman,' Kperechi repeated.

'You should be sorry. I know he's not acting off his own bat. But I'm ready for him and the person that sent him. I will give you more than you bargain for. What. . .'

'That is enough, woman!' Kperechi snarled, losing her cool. 'What has he done that is so terrible? And who sent him?'

'Oh, I knew you would stick up for him because he has done your bidding, isn't it?' Nwulari would not stop. 'Let us know if you want to take over the whole compound because. . .'

'You're raving mad! Do you hear me? What is wrong with you? Every day you keep winding yourself up! Since you came into this compound, you always keep picking quarrels and arguments. How can you get pregnant when your mind is never at rest?' Kperechi fumed.

'You said I won't get pregnant, eh? Everybody listen to Kperechi and be my witness ooo! Kperechi said I won't bear children in my marriage!' Nwulari wailed, attracting attention from all around.

'That is not what she said,' called a neighbour.

'Then what did she say, Egobeke?' Nwulari shot back, angry at being contradicted.

'You can see what I have to put up with,' appealed Kperechi, more miserable than shocked.

'Tell me what she said?' Nwulari challenged again, daring Egobeke to gainsay her.

Neighbours eventually intervened to settle the altercation. Chikwendu was surprised at how a little issue had been blown out of proportion.

*   *   *

Nwakego returned from the stream to meet the one-hour session of rousing and soul-enriching gospel beats. The presenter of Sunday Melodies spoke briefly before allowing the segueing melodies to continue. Most of the songs were compositions combining biblical portions and exhorting canticles in addition to the stirring rhythm and percussions. The melodies were meant to arouse lethargic soul from every form of slumber. Like the winnower, it was another opportunity to sift the beliefs and practices in their local settings, assessing their compatibility with the nobler and universally acceptable thresholds. It was a vital tool for reinforcing the core truth of the gospel deep into the minds of listeners to build character and attain the goals of the crusade for social change and reformation.

Nwakego stepped into the bathroom with half a pail of water as the familiar signature tune of Radio Nigeria network news came on air. Effectively, it brought the music session to an end. She made sure no eyes were watching before untying her wrapper and hanging it over the doorway. The unroofed area was fenced round with palm fronds. The floor, sodden with bathwater, was mucky despite the periwinkle shells heaped on it. She took time to scrub each foot with a pumice stone, to get rid of rough skins, before stepping on to a stone placed in the middle of the bathroom. After washing and towelling her body, she rubbed herself with the well-perfumed cocoa butter cream in her soap dish.

Nwakego touched her plaited hair to straighten them. She had carried a basin of water earlier that morning. The pad of wrapper which she had placed at the centre of her head had flattened some of them. Ebereonu had artistically created a field of lines and shapes from her wavy frizzy hair and plaited them into tightly wound squiggly curls, twists, and ringlets. They were a bit painful but made her face look quite tidy and brought her facial features into prominence. Looking at the piece of broken mirror in her left hand, she carefully ran the eye pencil on her eyelashes and brow to make up. She was part of the growing number of girls that preferred the eye pencil to the tiny pot of local *tiro* and *tanjele*. 'Nkechi, you are ready?' she asked her cousin.

'You are still preening yourself, aren't you?' Nkechi asked as she emerged from Nwugo's room. A hardcover notebook for her choir songs was under her left armpit. 'It appears someone is expecting some suitors today,' she teased, tying a bandana to cover her short kinky hair plaited in the *ukwu ose* style. It was a way of grooming the tightly curled hair. The pleated skirt and blouse made of synthetic cotton covered her lean and slim torso.

'Nigeria is longer than Africa, isn't it?' Nwakego pointed out.

Nkechi looked at her clothes and noticed that her off-white underwear was slightly longer than her skirt. She quickly adjusted it and raised her slender arms for Nwakego to help her zip up. 'Can I have some?' she asked, stretching out her hand for some of the beige loose powder but Nwakego passed her the small plastic compact, along with the powder puff. 'This pancake has a nice scent,' commented Nkechi, examining the compact, which had Avon Cosmetics printed on the underside.

'I got it from Emevo. She bought two of them,' Nwakego told her.

The sound of the church bell echoed throughout the village as they hurried off to the Mboha community school hall. The new church auditorium was still under construction. Though they could not afford a cathedral, a draftsman had drawn up a less complicated plan with the same cruciform layout. They went straight to the old headmaster's office, which served as the vestry. Choir members, robed in cassocks and surplices, joined the procession of officiating ministers to file into the auditorium. The congregation stood up, singing the first hymn.

'*Kelenu!*' Ebereonu intonated to bring the song to a stop.

'*Jehovah, gozienu aha Ya!*' they chorused, annunciating every word to bring the offertory, beats, and dance session to a close. Festus, the lay leader, announced the third congregational hymn: *Abu 160*. As they leafed through the *Ekpere Na Abu*, the Igbo Hymnal, Nkechi, a soprano, sang the lead. '*Nuria onu n'ime Onyenwe anyi. . .*' Walking to the lectern, the visiting Bishop Ibegbu commenced the dialogue between the priest and the congregation:

Priest: The Lord be with you.

Congregation: And also with you.

Priest: Lift up your hearts.

Congregation: We lift them up to the Lord.

Priest: Let us give thanks to the Lord our God.

Congregation: It is right to give him thanks and praise.

Ibegbu commended their efforts in building the new auditorium. He used an inspiring sermon on patriotism to drum more support for the project: 'It has to be home, sweet home. Have you heard the Boy Scouts sing it? *Oh my home, oh my home. . .*' he chanted. Many joined in, jubilantly singing the Boy Scouts' favourite song:

> *Oh my home, oh my home,*
> *When shall I see my home?*
> *When shall I see my beautiful home?*
> *I will never forget my home!*

Urging them to be steadfast in their labour of love, he preached that nostalgia was only possible if there was something special about the home left behind. 'If not, maybe the prodigal son would have been lost forever. What is each of us doing to build a home to which everyone would love to return?

I love the word 'homesick'. It suggests a longing for the comfort, the joy, the stability which cannot be found in any other place but home.

'As a community, it could be the peace of village life, the flora, the fauna, the warmth radiated by people so dear to us. This is what makes us homesick when we are far away. Think of those who have toiled for the sake of their distant homeland, while travelling in different lands and climes. Explorers risked their lives undertaking voyages of discovery, charting their way through dangerous rivers filled with crocodiles and hippopotamus. Mungo Park and the Lander Brothers readily come to mind. What about McGregor Laird? Imagine him enduring the scorching Sokoto heat just because he was trying to outdo others during the scramble for Africa. Why? He had heeded the clarion call to build and extend the British Empire. Successfully, they took treasures from all over the world to build their home. They loved not their lives unto death.

'Hear the vow of the Babylonian captives: "If I forget you, O Jerusalem, may my right hand forget its skill, may my tongue cling to the roof of my mouth. . . If I do not consider Jerusalem my highest joy." Ezra and Nehemiah motivated their people to build. What are we building?' he challenged, his embroidered cotta swaying with each gesture.

'What hearts are we setting aglow to make them miss home when faraway? It could be your cheerful dispositions, your small acts of compassion, your occasional words of encouragement.' He imitated the usual village greeting, his poor mimicry of the dialect provoking laughter. 'You may not know how far these many little acts go to create the common heritage we share. That ten or twenty kobo for the pencils and exercise books you buy for a child who is not from your own womb—they all go a long way in building so strong a bond. Your contribution towards this building, paid even though there are other things you need the money for—this is helping us build a landmark we will all be proud of.'

It was one of the most encouraging sermons Mboha had ever heard. The congregation listened with rapt attention, their eager ears providing fertile soil for his words. At the end of the service, Nwakego emerged from the vestry to sight the photographer some distance away. 'Here he comes, Hero the photographer.'

'I hope he has our snapshots,' Ebereonu said, handing a Hacks sweet to Nwakego as she unwrapped another for herself.

Hero brought the bicycle to a stop, but continued to sit on the saddle. 'You are all looking so gorgeous in your beautiful church dresses. What is special about today's Sunday?'

'*Dee* Herooooo! We know your style,' Emevo winked, making it obvious they were not falling for his chat-up line.

'Don't you know; the bishop is visiting?' Nkechi answered naively.

'Ah, that explains it!' There was triumph in his smooth, deep baritone. 'No suitor can resist you today. I have a hunch that some are on their way.'

'Do you have our pictures?' Adanma interjected in a carefree mood. Her two fingers were on her cheek trying to force out pimple from a particular spot on her oily face.

Ebereonu got hold of her hand to stop her. 'Your fingers are always on your face. What pleasure do you derive in pinching those pimples?'

'There's one there; I need to get it out.'

Ebereonu took a closer look and noticed that the pimple had hardened into a tiny piece. With minimal pressure, she dug the spot with her thumbnails. The hardened fat popped out speedily. Mercy cringed at the stinging pain before putting a finger on it.

Hero unbuckled a small bag in the basket in front of his bicycle. 'I do, here they are.'

'Waoo, the pictures are beautiful!' Ebereonu gasped with delight, studying a photograph of herself. Tall and ebony in complexion, her smile brightened her well-sculptured oblong face; *tanjele* and *tiro* showed off her eyebrows and her powdered skin was flawless.

'I'm happy you like it. That makes my day.' Hero was smiling, revealing white teeth with a gap tooth in his anterior. He had *tomtom* in his mouth, as he often did, the menthol counteracting the acrid smell of cigarettes, which most of his customers did not like. His long sleeves were each folded twice and the top three buttons of his shirt were left open, baring his hairy chest; his hairstyle was modelled after Harry Belafonte. He exuded the sort of successful and important masculinity portrayed in newspaper adverts. 'Show me the man who will not fall in love after seeing your portrait, and. . .'

'. . .propose marriage, of course!' Nwakego predicted in a singsong, swaying her body to and fro.

'I need my portrait taken, please,' Mgbechi declared with a 'notice-me' swagger.

'Each of us will have a personal before we pose as a group,' Nwakego suggested. Hero was pleased with the suggestion and, without a waste of time, started the photoshoot. Mgbechi stood beside Chief Ogbudu's Peugeot 504SR, her height barely above the car. Each angle of a white handkerchief was stuck behind her ear to cover her plaited hair. A red belt with a butterfly head went round her stomach to hold her skirt and blouse. The blue petals of morning glory deliberately placed at different points on her pink top drew a sharp contrast. Her busty chest made it difficult for two buttons to remain in their buttonholes. Taking a cue from Ebereonu, she quickly buttoned them, pulling the tight top together to keep the buttons in place. With the back of her left hand on her hip and the other on the bonnet, she looked confidently into the camera, a smile breaking forth, disclosing a gap tooth. A clicking sound came from Hero's camera, a sign that her image had been captured. Two other girls took their position by the car also.

Nwakego went to the big gmelina tree. She stood on one of exposed roots, leaning on the trunk with her right shoulder. Her hands were folded across her chest but the right hand held a hibiscus flower, her gaze focusing on the stigma and anther.

Ebereonu went to stand by the flower bed planted to hedge the corridors of the mgbidi structure that served as classrooms for primary three, four, five, and six. Stems of the climbing rose were sturdy with age, the branches extending as high as the roof trusses and purlins and on the zinc roof. While she was in primary three, Chikwendu as the head boy was assisted by other boys to improvise trellis with ropes to connect the tender shoots of climbing rose. Leafy trees such as gmelina and African oil bean provided good shades in the school compound. During the dry season when the sun made the classrooms too hot for studies, teachers and their pupils opted to take their lessons under the airy atmosphere of such trees. In addition to the sunflowers, daisy, ixora and tulip, lemongrass was common in the school yard for its utility. Everyone knew that the strong smell kept snakes away. It was quite useful to those preparing herbs for anti-malaria decoction.

Subsequently, Ebereonu brought the hyacinth, calla and gloriosa lilies, forget-me-not, violets, and fairlady that were planted in the school. She got most of the seeds and cuttings from the high school in Ohuhu while visiting her elder sister who was married to one of the teachers. Planting and tending them was a rewarding experience. She remembered the argument that ensued while that particular flowerbed was being cultivated. Anna, the head girl, wanted to do the planting but Emevo confirmed that Ebereonu's hands were good at making plants grow easily. Like other children of her time, she had planted different crops to test how well they responded to her touch. As she was given the chance, she mulched and tended them with the best available manure in the village—the droppings of goats and fowls. The highest test of her commitment to the flowers came during the first harmattan. She sprinkled them with water fetched from the stream three times in a week. The flowers grew and blossomed so well; it was another proof that she had green fingers.

The pink and deep-red roses contrasted with the green leaves, blue morning glory and day lily, creating a beautiful scenery and a nice background. With one of the rose flower tucked to her plaited hair, she posed sideways, a dimple becoming obvious on her oblong face as she smiled to the camera. Looking through the lens with his left eye shut, Hero told her to raise her chin a bit. Her long eyelashes moved with each rapid blink. 'Ready? Steady?' asked Hero, and immediately, the camera clicked.

'Your face is a bit oily. You want some powder?' asked Hero, offering Emevo talcum powder in a white and blue plastic. Emevo rubbed her hands together, clapping gently to get rid of the excess before applying it to her face. Her hair, about two inches long, was straight as a result of running hot comb through it. A mixture of hair cream and a little jell made it shiny and, to some extent, held them together. A yellow and white frangipani flower was on her hair and she held a red hibiscus to her nose, breathing in the fragrance. Her bright chocolate skin was made fairer by the use of Venus Cream occasionally mixed with the gel. 'Ready? Turn your head a little,' he murmured. 'Ooh, what a lovely face. . .' he crooned. 'Give me your best smile. No, not that smile. . . The head-turner!' Emevo beamed effortlessly. The camera clicked. 'Perfect. Next!'

Though photography was gradually gaining ground in villages like Mboha and several others, it was still regarded as a pastime. Anyone who devoted too much time to it must be lazy. However, nobody could deny the growing importance. The fact that their kinsmen who lived in the city took photographs was enough reason why the villagers began to patronise it. It was not uncommon to see different sizes of enlargements hanging on the sitting room walls of those that returned from the cities. Even the elderly in the village put on their best clothing and posed for photographs. At their transition, the crowd of mourners searching for his or her whereabouts had something to show as the identity of the deceased they were searching for.

Hero was even popular with the village girls, as each built up a collection of pictures to be presented to worthy guests. Any dear relation or friend might go away with a copy. The best of the pick would be sent to any eligible suitor living in the city who, tied to his work, might have no time to personally inspect the object of his affection. About her character, they relied on testimonies from neighbours and others who knew her well. This was part of the careful enquiries the groom's family had to make about the bride. Similar investigations had to be carried out on behalf of the bride to ensure she was not sold into a life of slavery and perpetual regret. Hero showed them the black and white postcard-sized group shot he had taken of the choir four weeks earlier. Each of them vied to identify herself first in the picture. '*Dee* Hero, how much is a copy?' Mgbechi asked.

'Five kobo.'

'*Eleooo* that's expensive,' Mgbechi exclaimed. 'Imagine all the profit you will make.'

Hero looked put out, and Nwakego said hastily, 'Don't mind Mgbechi. She is always haggling. She thought you were selling crayfish.'

'Nwakego, if that is a joke, stop it,' said Mgbechi, taking offence.

'Will you kill me for telling the truth?' Nwakego challenged her.

'Don't let me lose my temper,' Mgbechi fumed, pointing at her.

'Stop it,' cried Hero. 'I make little or no profit. I just do this for the pleasure of capturing the faces of beautiful maidens like you. Well, to make everyone happy, each copy will go for four kobo.'

This was greeted with glee. 'Mgbechi has secured a good bargain for us,' Mercy said. 'When will today's snapshots be ready?'

'In two weeks,' Hero promised. When she looked disappointed, he explained, 'I have to use up all the film in my camera before I can print them.'

Mmagwuru was approaching them, reciting to an invisible congregation the Bible passage she had memorised as a catechumen. 'I will lift up my eyes unto the hills. From whence cometh my help? My help cometh from the Lord the Maker of heaven and earth. He will not let your foot slip. He who watches over you will not slumber. Indeed, he who watches over Israel will neither slumber nor sleep. The Lord watches over you. The Lord is your shade at your right hand; the sun will not smite you by day nor the moon by night. The Lord will keep you from all harms. He will watch over your life. The Lord will watch over your coming and going both now and forevermore.'

'Amen,' Nwakego and her friends chorused cheerfully. Mmagwuru had memorised the passage for her confirmation test, and she continued to recite the passage so often that it became part of her identity. For anyone who knew her, the image of Mmagwuru sprang immediately to mind whenever they heard any part of the passage recited.

11.

Mboha sued Abadaba before Ohu Ahia N'Otu over the disputed land in Ovoro and the adjoining beaches of Imo River. It was the best way to put an end to the skirmishes between the two neighbours before it degenerated into full-scale hostilities. In the past, war was used to resolve such issues. In their time, the police had the duty to maintain law and order and would intervene at the slightest sign of unrest to herd the community leaders and their youth off to their cells.

The thought of filing a civil suit in court was quickly dismissed. They simply did not trust the administration of justice in the courts. The Umunwanwa case, which was fresh in their minds, was often cited as one of the many instances where truth could easily be subverted as a result of the clever manipulation of lawyers. Truth was sacred and ranked very high in the communal ethos of the villages. It was not only the living that sought it. Their ancestors and the gods upheld and enforced it. Besides, the risk of a protracted court proceeding which could last over twenty years was not ruled out. It had happened to Umuagu. Quite a number of the litigants had died without the court reaching a decision. To everyone's horror and disgust, the court made an order enjoining the parties to maintain the status quo. It restrained all parties from doing anything on the land until the suit was finally determined. The civil court was part of Western civilisation that filled the villagers with dread.

On the *eke* market day fixed for the hearing, *okonko* title holders from the twenty-one autonomous communities making up Ohu Ahia N'Otu in the Bende Division gathered in Mboha. Robed in full paraphernalia, they carried themselves with the dignity befitting their status, their sober faces betraying the solemnity of the task ahead. As the highest point of arbitration, the tribunal's reputation for upholding the cause of justice remained unparalleled.

Evuleocha called the gathering to order with a resounding cry of greetings. He cleared his throat and launched into his opening remarks, riddled with proverbs. 'Our people say that whoever has to sit in judgment must keep his door open so that any decision he reaches can follow him home. Truth shines brightly like the moon. Whoever turns it upside down is not only running afoul of the laws of man and the Creator in heaven, but is bringing curse unto himself and his generation. There is no other reason for this arbitral proceeding today but to ensure that the kite can perch and for the eagle to also perch. Any one of them that does not want the other to perch, what will happen?'

'The wings will break!' was the resounding response.

'Whoever holds what belongs to a child and raises his hand up, when he is tired won't he bring his hand down?'

'Certainly!' many roared in response.

'That is why we are in favour of the life of the water and the life of the fish. The spirit child must not molest the human child and the human child must not oppress the spirit child. Nothing is like peaceful coexistence. My people, is it not so?'

'That is it!'

'*Cha cha cha* Ohu Ahia N'Otu *kwenu!*'

'Oooeee!'

'*Rienu!*'

'Oooeee!'

'*Nuonu!*'

'Oooeee!'

'*Kwezuenu ooo!*'

'*Iyaaaa!*' was the tumultuous response, a feeling of elation and approval sweeping through the crowd.

The two village heads then took their turns to speak, expressing their intention to cooperate with the tribunal in every way to achieve the peaceful resolution of the dispute and be bound by its decision. Irokogu took the floor to declare the rules of the proceedings; his occasional witty asides sending ripples of laughter sweeping through the crowd. He handed over to Evuleocha who called on Mboha to present their case.

Ikpo, the oldest man in Mboha, opened the case of his community. Instead of wearing his usual loincloth, he looked presentable in cream khaki shorts that stopped at his knees. A rope was threaded through the belt holders to hold the shorts up. His *okonko* cap and the chieftain's top looked well on him. However, his slippers had seen better days; there were gaping holes at the heels. His toenails that were thick, long, and rimmed with dirt poked the slippers, leaving indelible marks. The slippers had been his only footwear for years, and after a very long time, he was wearing them once again. His shrill voice recounted all he knew.

'At the height of every rainy season, Abadaba, threatened by floodwaters, fled their homes to escape drowning. That particular year, Imo River was in a serious spate, claiming two lives and washing away their properties. A number of them went towards Uboma while others with our consent, crossed over to Ovoro, our forest reserve.' This was the account he heard from his father as a young lad when a fight broke out between the two villages for cutting *mbazu*, the wooden rods used for wall beams. Murmurs of approval and dissent welled up in equal measure.

'*Cha, cha, cha, gbrrrrr mmanu!*' Evuleocha roared, calling the audience to order before silence was restored. 'What has happened since then?'

Ikpo did not hear him. It was repeated twice, loudly. 'Nothing,' he answered, looking vacantly into space.

Oleforo was allowed to speak. 'Is *Dee* Ikpo expected to deny that Mboha owns the land? I heard differently. I was never told that we owe Ovoro to the kindness of anybody. Rather, I learnt it was part of Akwuoroko, the former abode of Imo River. Our forefathers were the first to cultivate it after the river ceased to flow there.'

'Truth shines like moon,' Agbakuru spoke. As one of the leaders of Ohu Ahia N'Otu, he was well-respected and had led the tribunal to various dispute resolutions, but today he was a native of Mboha, an interested party. 'Please, do not be offended with my questions: Can all that expanse of land be part of the river? Secondly, do you dispute that your ancestors lived on the other side of the river? They are simple questions that call for determination and. . .' His voice was drowned in angry protests. But Egwuatu of Abadaba, in making a rejoinder, suggested that Mboha swear before any shrine they would nominate.

'Swear by what?' Akwakanti thundered, springing up, his neck veins bulging, his burly chest heaving, all his being itching for a fight. '*Chai!* Treetops are no longer the land of squirrels. But for the injury that the tiger is nursing, how could the antelope ever go to him for debt recovery?'

The gathering turned rowdy once again. It took another round of warnings to bring it under control. 'Tempers are rising, no doubt,' Ojemba said slowly but ominously. 'It does not mean Ohu Ahia N'Otu can be taken for a ride. You all know what it means if we declare a breach of our rules. Anyone who doesn't know can ask.'

Ezeogo of Umukabia was furious with Egwuatu's suggestion, insulting him thoroughly although in veiled language. 'Swearing is a last resort. This is a decision only Ohu Ahia N'Otu can make. Are you the judge? Or do you want to dictate to the tribunal? It is not the day the child pours away oil, the rich extract of the palm fruit, that he is punished. Human beings are prone to errors. But the day he spills *shimmanu*—the watery residue—because he fails to be careful, he must be taught a lesson of how to care for whatever is entrusted in his care. That is the way of our people.'

The village head of Abadaba intervened, apologising profusely and describing it as a genuine human error. The tribunal could decree oath-taking as proof of ownership when it seemed otherwise impossible to tell who had right on their side but it was quite rare. A whole generation might be born and die without witnessing the tribunal resort to such a measure. Ohu Ahia N'Otu was not afraid of handing down any decision, however unhappy either of the parties might be, if they felt certain of the truth.

Yet before long, it appeared that oath-taking was going to be the only way. The tribunal reconvened after a recess to deliver judgment. Mboha had to swear to put their claim beyond doubt. Ikpo stood by what he said and was ready to swear; he trusted his father did not lie to him.

Opinions were divided when the elders of the community met to review the decision. Many believed that Ikpo could not lie in such a sensitive matter. Perjury was a grave offence in which the gods personally execute judgment. But there were a handful that urged caution. According to them, there was nothing so important about the riparian rights Mboha exercised over Ovoro beach and the adjoining forest. Whatever benefit that was accruable, nothing could justify exposing a whole village to the wrath of the gods in the unlikely event that such claim proves untrue. 'If it is oath-taking, count me out,' Albert voiced his strong dissent. The gods must hear it that he neither aided nor abetted any perjury and should not include him and his family in their wrath. 'Is land more important than human heads?'

After the discontent had died down, Ozurumba spoke. 'I agree that land is not more important than human heads but can we live without land?'

They all knew the terrible consequences of false oath. The deity invoked could wipe out the deponent and his entire family. The property of such a family was forfeited to the priest of the deity. The village elders might not be spared for aiding and abetting falsehood. Though Ikpo was ready to swear, Mboha would not allow him. He was old and frail and might not survive another year—the length of time allowed the gods to execute judgment. His death by natural causes could be misinterpreted, giving room for conflicting opinions.

'What is the role of a village head in times like this?' Iroegbulem wondered, he was visibly irritated. 'Is it only for opening doors with. . .' A number of protesting voices stopped him.

'Is he the only head fit for the death sentence?' challenged Okezie.

The hand that Josiah raised remained suspended. The whole community knew that he would not speak until complete silence returned to the gathering. He took a deep breath and exhaled loudly to calm himself. 'In times like this, we should listen to the elders amongst us. *Dee* Agbakuru, Amaregbu, Amos, and even Ikpo himself are here. Let us hear them speak.'

Eventually, the majority agreed that the village head, as their corporate sole, was the proper person to swear the oath. Some of those present followed Chief Ogbudu home, urging him to ignore the decision. 'They are being ridiculous. They want to extinguish our beacon of hope. But we'll not allow them,' insisted Okezie.

'They are not happy because you are not from their lineage, that is what I think,' said Hezekiah, shoving a pinch of snuff into his nostril, sneezing loudly as a result.

'How I wronged Iroegbulem, I can't tell. He is the one leading the charge.' Chief Ogbudu looked tired. 'It is difficult sticking out my neck for what I'm not really sure about.'

The conflict of views between the two men was deep-rooted. Iroegbulem, after passing standard six, enlisted in the colonial constabulary frontier force, rising to the rank of inspector before his retirement. Later, he joined the native court in Alai as an assessor versed in native law and custom. This brought him great fame throughout the Bende Division. His service spanned well over four decades and had been well-rewarded. He was among the first set of successful individuals to build *mgbidi*, the architectural revolution of their time. People lost count of the bicycles he bought when owning one was a status symbol. Then he bought motorcycles—some still remembered his Kawasaki, his Suzuki, and his Honda CD 175 Roadmaster, which many boys simply called 'the monster'. He left several people guessing why he refused to buy a car, the ultimate symbol of wealth.

'Common riffraff, expecting people like me to shy away from the truth,' Iroegbulem remarked condescendingly, as Chief Ogbudu left the gathering. 'The image of Mboha is at stake, yet he is busy chasing rats. Do I look like one of those he can bribe with filthy money that nobody knows the source? I, Iroegbulem, the son of Ogbuagu, cannot be party to such nonsense!'

* * *

The legend of Uwahulamiro's revenge was still retold in Mboha as the reason for the movement of Imo River from its former channel. Without it, the land dispute between Mboha and Abadaba would not have been possible.

The story was that it took Uwahulamiro several years to conceive Ohaekelem. Nweke, her husband, was delighted to have an heir at last. Their effort to have more children failed. They began to live in fear of the fate that could befall them if they lost their only son. It was not impossible for a malevolent kinsman to kill him and leave their homestead desolate. Dreading the thought, Nweke engaged a sorcerer to prepare a protective charm for Ohaekelem. The medicine man was said to have put Ohaekelem in a big pot but while the boy was being boiled, he reappeared from nowhere. At the end of the exercise, the medicine man confirmed that no mortal could harm him.

When Nweke died, Uwahulamiro refused to remarry. Nor did she allow other men to sleep with her. She doted over Ohaekelem, her one hope of realising her husband's dream of continuity. Refusing to let him out of her sight, she took him to weed her farm on that fateful day. They ran out of drinking water before she finished her task. 'Mother, I'm thirsty ooo!' he yelled in anger.

'We'll be on our way soon, let me finish this remaining portion,' she pleaded, scraping at the dry soil with renewed vigour. The greenish ground reminded her of the puddle on that very spot made green by algal growth. She was relieved when the last weed yielded to her small draw hoe. She sifted the weeds quickly from the sand, spreading them atop the heaps to mulch the cassava. 'Ohaekelem, are you through with the melon?' she asked, straightening up. There was no response. It suddenly occurred to her, she had not heard the sound of his stick hitting the melon pods for some time. 'Ohaekelem, come, let's go. I've really worked hard today.'

His long silence irritated her. 'Are you not the one I'm talking to, Ohaekelem? What have I done to offend you? Because I refused to leave my work until it was done? Okay, I'm done, let's go.'

She did not hear his usual protest or cry which would have elicited her apology, a cuddle and a promise to make it up to him. Disturbed, she left the firewood she was gathering to scan the farmland in all directions. She could not spot him. She went to the point where she had left him breaking the pods. The leaves spread on the floor for him to sit on were still there, and so was the stick he had been using. But he was gone. 'I'm not ready for your pranks!' she warned, becoming frustrated. She looked behind trees and in other likely places a child could hide. He was not there.

'Ohaekelem!' she yelled. 'Ohaekelem, come out, let's go home! What type of child is this? Ohaekelem leeeeee!' she called again and again, angrily. All she heard was the echo of her own voice and the sound of fluttering trees by the river abutting their farm. Anger gave way to alarm. She searched both her own farm and the neighbouring farms, looking for him. She hunted for his footprints and found the imprint of his toes on a branch overhanging the river. She noticed the small plastic bowl they used to soak tapioca floating close to some leaves. Her heart leapt into her mouth.

A log floated under the overhanging branches. The log had eyes, and legs and hands. 'Ohaekelem, what are you doing there? Oh ooo is this your plan? *Ooololorom Imomiri aka ete*, what have you done? You have drowned the only apple that the blind man found after groping with his legs? Creator of the universe, you allowed them to do this to me?'

For a while she wandered in despair, but she could not be expected to take such a blow without striking back. She came to herself and went to a palm tree, picking the fruits then sitting down to break and chew them until she piled up a heap of wastes from the kernels and palm nuts. 'What am I living for? It's not Uwahulamiro you will strike and expect her to sit down crying,' she cried aloud, carrying the kernels to the river. She knew it was a taboo to throw such things into the river and did not know what might follow. In her grief, she did not care.

As soon as she threw in an armful, the waters rose and rushed against the banks, foaming and surging, turning the river to a frightful sight. She could hear the voices of beings running around frantically.

'Who is responsible for this sacrilege?' cried one.

'Okoronkwo, you have time to ask questions? The roof over our heads is gone. Hasten up, we must leave immediately,' said Mgbakwa, his wife.

'Nwokorie, where is my ladle?' a woman asked her husband.

'Keep looking. I have my staff, and I'm out of here!'

'Who is blocking my way?' asked an irritated voice. 'Make way! I'm in a hurry.'

'Nkalari, where are you? I'm on my way ooo!' a masculine voice called his friend.

'Okereke, wait for me!' responded his friend. 'Uwalagwuike, I can't find my *akpa-agwu*.'

'Stay back and look for it,' retorted Uwalagwuike, refusing to help him look for the medicine bag. 'I warned you to have nothing to do with that child.'

The scurrying footfalls of invisible beings escaping their violated sanctuary continued to haunt her as she returned to sit and rest her frame against the palm tree. The following dry season, no water flowed in the channel in which Imo River had coursed from time immemorial. The strait, which served as seasonal tributary during the rainy season became the regular course and the water found a new abode.

12.

Iroegbulem was taking a nap in his easy chair. The wrapper he tied around him was knotted at the navel and a handheld fan made of raffia palm rested on his stomach. Globules of sweat trickled down his forehead. His hands were above his head, displaying bushy armpits with greying hairs. The net singlet, which used to be white, was soaked at the chest. His discoloured hair, brown on top and grey beneath, showed that the dye he applied was wearing off. It did little to compliment his bright chocolate complexion. He woke up to the shuffling sound of Ozurumba's footsteps with George in tow. 'This heat is terrible,' he yawned, swiping the sweat from his forehead with his forefinger. The casement windows designed as plantation shutters were held wide open with hooks, but this failed to make much impact as the air was at a standstill.

'If your house is this hot, others must be ovens,' Ozurumba commented, making himself comfortable.

'Inspector-General. . .' George called him by one of his sobriquets. 'You didn't come to witness the oath-taking?'

'I'm on medication,' he answered, pointing to a half-empty glass of decoction which he had been taking to combat malaria. 'I've been drinking and bathing with it.'

'I need something like that,' said George. 'Last night, I ran out of mosquito coil. Mosquitoes fed on me mercilessly.'

'I don't like making that mistake,' Ozurumba declared. 'Nothing annoys me like their droning noise. It can keep me awake all night.'

'So how did the oath-taking go?' Iroegbulem asked.

'Can he wish it away? He had taken it, though reluctantly. . .' George told him.

'Who would be eager to swear an oath?' Ozurumba interjected.

'But that is the job of the village chief, isn't it?' sneered Iroegbulem. Opening the cupboard, he brought out a bottle of Dubonnet red wine and another of Scotch whisky. 'He cannot enjoy power without responsibility.'

A calendar of the Nigerian Police Force, the almanacs of different organisations, and other memorabilia hung on the wall, which was painted with white emulsion. Enlarged photographs, in black and white, adorned the walls. Directly above the entrance door was a picture of him posing with his wife in their city home, followed by two portraits of himself alone—his focused and unsmiling face in official uniform and again as a gentleman in suit and tie. A group photograph of his family of seven children and his wife's portrait hung above the door that led to the backyard.

'But Ohu Ahia N'Otu actually indulged Abadaba. How can they ask for oath-taking and get it like that?' George wondered.

'When I suggested we go to court; did he not overrule me? He thinks he is all-knowing,' Iroegbulem pointed out vindictively. 'It is even good that things turned out this way.'

Ozurumba decided to change the subject. 'Have you noticed? One can't see this type of wooden settee to buy anymore,' he observed airily, while crunching bitter kola. The parlour was richly furnished. The settee, uncomplicated in design, was a masterpiece of woodcraft. The wood, properly treated and perfectly planed, never warped despite several harsh harmattan seasons. Such perfect joints could not be rendered by roadside carpenters working manually with limited skill and tools. The glossy finish had not been totally worn away despite patches of ingrained dirt that had accumulated over the years, particularly on the armrests.

It made George recall his days at Leventis Technical. 'I remember Eluwa, my boss that finished from Yaba Trade Centre. Under his direction, our factory produced the most excellent products like this.'

'Didn't you tell the white man to go?' Iroegbulem asked, his tone clearly accusing him of wrongdoing. 'You want to own and manage everything by yourselves. They've pulled out, leaving us with *adigboroja*—quackery.'

'We were in a hurry to be like others without giving adequate thought to what made us different,' George reasoned.

'It's you fellows in government,' Ozurumba stated, trying to absolve himself of any blame, knowing he had nothing to do with the policy that Iroegbulem was attacking. He recalled one of the arguments in the debate leading to the

1977 law aimed at promoting indigenous ownership of enterprises. In a bid to escape the multinationals' hold on the economy and the capital flight as a result of huge profits repatriated, their country followed a number of emerging economies that came up with the idea of indigenisation. 'That's the danger of the rat joining the lizard to get wet. When the lizard gets dry what about the rat?'

'It is creating a lot of problems already. Do you know, some foreigners nominated our people to hold shares on their behalf?' Iroegbulem asked, putting on his eyeglasses with black ivory chrome. Slowly, he browsed through the newspaper looking for the news item about some court decision relevant to what he had just told them.

The quartz wall clock chimed three times. The pendulum continued to swing to and fro, unperturbed. Various pieces of woodwork—the casing for the clock, the standing mirror frame, the big cupboard with a chest of drawers and compartments for bottles and goblets—all had one thing in common, an exquisite touch of class. There was also a collapsible rack fastened to the wall where sundry items were hung. 'What are shares?' Ozurumba asked uncertainly.

Iroegbulem slowly fixed his gaze on Ozurumba as if surprised to hear the question, his serious mien becoming vacant with uncertainty. 'You don't know what a share is? Ehm, how do I explain it?'

'It's just like sharing things with others. Your shares. . .your portion or. . .ehm. . .or call it the stake or contribution you made to raise money for a company. . .' George laboured with the explanation. 'For instance, if three of us start a business, what you contribute to. . .'

'Oh hoooo,' Ozurumba exclaimed, happy to grasp what had eluded him all the while.

'That is why the white man enterprises are different. Don't you know that a company may have as many as two million shareholders and you, as a shareholder, may contribute only twenty naira to the company's capital,' Iroegbulem explained, standing up.

'Pool the little sums together, the company enjoys robust capital base. Whatever project they point at, they execute it *fiam*. . .' George snapped his finger, suggesting speed. As his reasoning grew more insightful, he became enthusiastic, the black mole on his left cheek adding to his keen look.

'. . .because the money is there,' Ozurumba reasoned along.

Iroegbulem emerged from his room with a document in hand. 'This is a Golden Guinea Breweries shares certificate. With only three hundred naira, I'm a part-owner of that big company. Once they declare profit, I get my dividend warrant.'

'And that explains why they have such big companies like UAC, UTC, CFAO, GB Ollivant, PZ Industries, Challerams, Bata. . .' George continued to reel off the names, nodding his head as if he had just discovered the secret behind their size, the quality of product, and service delivery. 'Imagine if IG has started an enterprise with that one hundred and fifty pounds, what guarantee do you have that it will survive? If it does, how long will it take to grow it to the size of Golden Guinea?'

It made a lot of sense to Ozurumba. Unlike the individual lockup shops, the multinational trading outfits were big and strong. He had not given thought to the ownership structure and what the power of collectivism could do in enterprise promotion. It also explained why they could afford a well-trained and skilled workforce providing an opportunity to the worker to apply himself with diligence. On the contrary, the trader with limited resources first had to ensure he made a living out of his shop. This was followed by the task of growing the money into a substantial figure with every form of cost-cutting and profit-maximising measures.

Josiah paused to greet Iroegbulem as he was passing. A locally fabricated harvesting knife was attached to the long bamboo on his left shoulder and a curved cutlass, at the end, in his right hand. 'You are off to your cocoa plantation?' asked Ozurumba.

'The whole day is almost lost to the oath-taking. Let me see what little time I can salvage before the day runs out,' he said, his slight bowlegs circling as he walked swiftly away.

Ebereonu came in with a tray of sliced cassava laced with *odudu* and *akidi*, two different species of beans. She brought three side plates, knowing that her father did not approve of the practice of dipping hands in the same bowl to eat with others. 'Ogbodiya, this must be one of your Owerri specials,' George complimented, savouring the taste. His voice was loud enough to be heard out in the backyard.

'The way Owerri people prepare certain dishes is exceptional,' Ozurumba agreed, munching and relishing every bit of it. He could tell the taste of crayfish, smoked beef that was diced into pieces, bits and pieces of stockfish, all well-cooked and seasoned. The *utaziri* and *uziza* leaves blended perfectly with the spicy *ehiri*.

'After sampling their dishes, I told myself there's no way one of them will not follow me home,' Iroegbulem spoke haltingly as always, carefully choosing his words and leaving his kinsmen choking with laughter.

'Don't mind Iroegbulem, your brother,' Jemima said. 'He has a bond with good things of life.'

'If you had run a restaurant in the city, the place would have been humming,' Ozurumba imagined.

'Your brother won't hear such a thing,' she replied sweetly.

'Who has not heard the fable of the pussycat and his scat?' Iroegbulem called their minds to a common anecdote. 'Asked why he insists on covering his scat each time he defecates; you know what the pussycat answered? It is no longer difficult for one's property to be the subject of adverse claims. So, if you don't protect what you have. . .' he left it hanging, his head nodding and swaying from side to side and his piercing eyes focusing through his lenses with measured smile brightening his face, challenging his listeners to figure out what he meant. It was not common to see him in such lighter mood, one of the reasons he remained an enigma to many.

'*Olooo nda*. . .' she beamed with smiles, patting him on the knee. 'Iroegbulem, my husband, but you didn't tell me you cherish me that much.' Her voice was full of happy surprise with the covert expression of love. Noticing a woman walking towards her backyard, Jemima excused herself. 'Let me see my fellow woman.'

'Celestine, my son, lost his job in Aba recently because GB Ollivant closed shop,' said Iroegbulem, revisiting their earlier conversation. Although he believed in the country's independence, his view about the indigenisation was different. The policies that forced the foreigners out led to the collapse of the organised private sector. Also, it did not favour people from his part of the country. Still reeling from the effect of the civil war, the implementation of the indigenisation policy came at a time when they lacked the finance to participate effectively in the economy. Forming the bulk of the unemployed, they did not benefit from the largesse doled out to public servants as Udoji award. At the direction of the authorities, banks granted credit facilities to workers to buy up the available shares which the departing foreigners had to sell. Again, this policy did not benefit his people. 'Do you know something?

If oil had been discovered before the British agreed to grant us independence, I'm sure they would still be here. We would have been like South Africa.'

As if on cue, Miriam Makeba's hit album, *Pata Pata*, came on air. 'Ah ah, were they waiting for you to mention South Africa?' Ozurumba asked with a wide grin.

'She is such a great performer,' George beamed in agreement.

'She captured many hearts at Festac '77,' Iroegbulem recalled, equally thrilled by her tongue clicking, her remarkable Xhosa trademark. The anchorman spoke, stopping the music towards the end of the track while welcoming listeners to the one-hour programme of South African music dedicated to the anti-apartheid awareness campaign. The agony in the voice of Ladysmith Black Mambazo as they sang *Homeless* with Paul Simon in their classic, *Graceland*, was irresistible. The voices were soulful and lachrymal but defiant, bold, remonstrative, and unyielding; they evoked a gamut of emotions, striking a strong chord which listeners could not ignore. The hearts and souls unmoved by intellectual speeches and writings were captured by these powerful songs. Successfully, the legion of anti-apartheid music had mobilised an army of sympathisers to decry the injustice that was apartheid and, by so doing, shaped international resolve to dismantle the system.

'Do you know what? We were handed our independence on a platter of gold,' Ozurumba stated, unable to push the picture of South Africa's trauma from his mind.

13.

The kola disk was passed round as Ozurumba joined his kinsmen in a meeting. As he chewed a lobe, the smarting peppery sauce stung his senses to life, giving him sufficient presence of mind for their deliberations. Handing him a tumbler from those arranged in a big tray, Chikwendu poured palm wine from a clear glass jug. Ozurumba downed it to assuage the hot taste of the kola-nut sauce. The monthly stewardship of the oil mill operator was the first item on the agenda. Ugwunna gave an account for five tins of oil and two drums of palm kernel, reflecting the busy milling season.

'After deducting your due, what is left?' Amaregbu asked.

'Twelve pounds, six shillings,' Ugwunna answered, handing it over to Ozurumba. They all understood it to mean twenty-four naira and some remainder.

'What I have here is nine naira and some fraction,' Ozurumba noted, confirming the cash before recording it in the financial register.

'Sunday Ogwo, the produce dealer, has not paid for two tins,' Ugwunna answered before reminding them about the terrible condition of the press. Some woods in the press were broken and the spindle was thin with age. 'The modern all-metal press is the one to get. That is what you'll find in other villages,' he concluded, subtly challenging them to rise to the test. Rather than just fix the old mill by renewing its thatched roof, they had agreed at the previous meeting to modernise it entirely. A number of other neighbouring villages had taken the bold step to put behind them the drudgery of biennial renewal of the thatched roof. Josiah, as the secretary, read out the proposal for a big shed with twelve pillars, a store and zinc roof.

At Ogbuka's instance, Ozurumba read out the financial report. They passed a resolution agreeing to commence work after one week and the subsequent suspension of milling activities until further notice. Those who must mill in the interim could use the mills in the neighbouring villages. The crier took note.

'Amos, what were you saying about Nwaneto?' asked Iroegbulem.

'Before that,' Amaregbu interrupted. He informed them about Uluotuwe's application to join in harvesting the communal palm fruits. 'I could not accept her money until I had your approval to do so.' The subtext of the application did not escape them. As a widow, she was not qualified to join the harvest. It was her way of protesting the practice of allowing women whose husbands lived in the cities to join, while widows were excluded.

It generated ribald jokes and noisy exchanges until Agbakuru called for order. 'It's enough. Women's meeting cannot be this noisy.'

'Why not exclude all the women if that is causing bad blood,' Amos suggested.

'Has any woman been registered?' Onyenwe asked.

'Return their money, simple,' Albert suggested.

Josiah attacked the basis of selection. 'Our kinsmen living in the cities may pay levies, but do they perform other civic duties? No. So why admit their wives but exclude the widows?'

Iroegbulem spoke after another general outburst. 'Why are we bothering our heads? Why not throw it open and allow everyone into the bush.'

'Alternatively, I suggest each lineage take its turn to harvest it,' Ozurumba proposed. 'It will scale down the number of participants and make more economic sense.' They agreed to the idea and decided that the first lineage would take the first turn to harvest it.

'Can we talk about Nwaneto's naturalisation now?' Amos asked. Nwaneto had come to Mboha as a farmhand in his youth but stayed on after that farming season. Though he returned to take a wife, he had raised his family in Mboha and gave his daughters in marriage to suitors in neighbouring villages. His easy-going disposition and honesty endeared him to virtually everyone. A number of the farmlands he acquired from the villagers were on a long lease and he had built a barn through sharecropping.

When he introduced rice farming in the village, many curious villagers wanted to see how rice, the staple food they loved so much, was grown. They found it an arduous task—trekking the distance to the marshy land and dragging their feet bogged in mud around the farm. Having spent half of the day trekking, they were forced to spend some days in the makeshift farmhouse, returning on the third day. Some suffered from rice rashes and never went with him again. He gave it up when he realised that the yield was not worth the trouble.

He brought two young men to assist him tap wine from the palm trees he acquired from the villagers. This gave him time to attend to other matters, including his farm. Some villagers borrowed from him and pledged their land as security. In some cases, the agreement was that he could till the land and harvest the crops for two farming seasons or hold on to the farm as long as the loan remained outstanding. Principled and painstaking, he stretched himself to painful limits to maintain cordial relationship with others. The villagers quickly came to his defence on the few occasions he was forced into altercations. As the saying went, whatever could make the dumb talk must be imperative. He gave his help freely without demanding a ransom. Having participated freely in communal activities, he was entitled to most of the rights accorded every person in the village. The only thing that gave him away as an outsider was his accent. His children spoke like everyone in the village.

However, he was not admitted into the kindred meeting or initiated into *okonko*. They were the exclusive preserve of the freeborn of Mboha. A few were hesitant because of the obvious security implications. A stranger who had little or no stake in the village could be a risk and they continued to advise against any decision they might regret. But many were sympathetic to his cause. They said that he had acquired sufficient stake in the community over time. Everyone knew how infrequently he visited his own village. His children and wealth were all in Mboha. Whatever happened to the village will certainly affect him. He paid every levy, even those meant for the benefit of their kinsmen. They had reciprocated it on two occasions when he gave his two daughters away in marriage. 'Whoever is against his admission to the gathering of our kinsmen should say so now,' Amaregbu announced. 'Otherwise we shall admit him.'

'That does not include the *okonko*. Does it?' Ekwuribe protested.

'Why bother yourself about that? Is every freeborn a member?' Akwakanti asked.

'No objection then,' Anosike agreed.

'Among other things, we have to enter into a blood covenant with him that he would bear true allegiance to our community and would never compromise our security,' Agbakuru spelt out.

'He will give us five jars of palm wine, two cartons of beer, two heads of dried tobacco leaves, two limbs of billy goat,' Kanu added. 'After these we shall give him our laws.'

'He knows most of them already,' Anosike said.

'It doesn't matter. We shall still give him. We must not allow him claim ignorance in the event of a breach,' Agbakuru added.

'That is the practice of our people,' Uwakwe concurred.

'What are we doing with five jars of palm wine? Are we hosting the neighbouring villages?' Iroegbulem asked. 'Three jars should do.'

'He is a man of means. He can afford it,' Anosike said.

'Don't be ridiculous. Are we accepting him because of his wealth?' Agbakuru reproved. 'I have to go now. If there's any other thing, I will hear it later,' he stood up. 'I'm preparing roots and herbs for a patient this evening.'

Uwakwe followed him to complete the second round of tapping which he started earlier in the afternoon. The meeting dispersed shortly after.

*   *   *

Okwudiri saw Uwakwe's unlocked bicycle outside. Knowing he would not be allowed to touch it if he asked for permission, he went in to know what Uwakwe was doing. As Uwakwe was busy in the barn, he mounted the bicycle and rode off. Nwulari returned from the nearby bush where she had gone to dump refuse. She noticed her husband's climbing rope but the bicycle was not there. 'Where has this man gone to?' she wondered. 'We agreed he would help me get that *okpoko*, the bamboo bed, outside before he goes out.' She was surprised to see her husband when she turned to enter the compound. 'Did you allow anyone borrow your bicycle?' she asked.

'Did anyone say I gave him my bicycle?' Uwakwe retorted.

'It's not here. I thought you went out with it?' Nwulari was bemused. As Uwakwe made his way out, she began to wonder who could have taken it. 'Has the devil and his cohorts whisked it away? Or have your creditors come for debt recovery?'

There was no answer to her questions. Uwakwe left her and wandered towards the village square hoping that whoever took it had not disappeared out of sight. 'I'm sure that was Okwudiri riding a bicycle past the school,' Albert was saying, as he drew closer to them.

In the outer compound, Nwulari was raging: 'Whoever removed the bicycle, may *umuagbara umuagbara* break his neck, break his waist, and snuff life out of him. He'll never live to see any good thing in life. Is it not the bicycle this man suffered to repair barely three days ago that a stupid imbecile removed without permission? What upstart, what brat has the guts to remove it? Who is that person? *Kamanu ozuzu, igwekala, ibini ukpabi, amakohia, ogwugwu* and other terrible spirits of this world go after him, lift and break him into bits and pieces. Who is that person? *Ikpechi, ochaere, ukwaranta, akwukwu* consume him! Who is that person in this compound that won't let other people's things be? Who is it that keeps removing them at the blink of eyelids without permission? May all. . .'

'Who are you heaping all those curses on?' Kperechi cried hotly, as she came to the outer compound.

'Whoever it is, I don't care,' Nwulari retorted.

'All the curses shall return to you. You were married into this family to bear children and not to curse those already born,' Kperechi raged. 'The ancestors of this homestead will deal with you even more so severely first,' she lashed out, angry at the incessant curses Nwulari was quick to place on people at the slightest provocation. 'But I don't blame you. It is because you have not carried a child for nine months and suffered the pangs of childbirth. If you had, I'm sure you would have been more considerate in. . .'

'Are you the first to ever have a child? This is not the first place I have seen children. And it's not just a question of having children, it is about bearing useful children. One can't put anything down for a moment before it is gone. If children are what you have here. . .' Nwulari was still ranting when Nwakego stormed out of the inner compound after setting down the bucket of water she had just brought home. She made straight for Nwulari and had delivered some well-placed slaps and a few blows before the neighbours could intervene.

The sudden attack left Nwulari dazed for a while; on regaining control, she walked about looking for what she could fling at Nwakego but other women held her back.

'I have warned you to lay off my mother, but you won't listen!' she stormed. 'Allow me to tell her she must know her limit. The next time you dare raise your voice at her, I say the next time you dare. . .'

Ijuolachi supported her with all the invectives she could muster.

Nkechi was watching from the entrance to the compound, gloating at what was a good lesson to the woman who had been a pain to her mother. 'That is what this woman deserved. I have never seen a person so difficult.'

'Nwakego, don't touch her please!' cried Kperechi. 'She's trying to find some poor innocent person to blame for her murder! Just because she's breathing does not mean she's not dead already! But she won't trick anyone from my house into killing her!' Kperechi was bewildered at the value Nwulari placed on all her property, however insignificant. But her anger turned against Okwudiri who was found with the bicycle; she tongue-lashed him while he kept a safe distance. 'The person I blame for all this is your father! If he had not sold the bicycle Igboajuchi bought, I wouldn't be putting up with this nonsense!'

Ozurumba came in while her harangue was still ongoing and lent his voice to scolding Okwudiri. 'What a badly behaved child! Why can't you keep away from what is not yours?'

'It's entirely your fault!' Kperechi screamed at him. 'If you had not sold our bicycle, this would not be happening in the first place!'

Ozurumba hastily made his way back to the village square. 'I don't have the strength to withstand your onslaught.'

*   *   *

Kperechi tied her wrapper, getting ready to join other women at Agbakuru's compound. The *ozo* title which he had decided to take was causing no little excitement in the community. It was one of the traditions that were in fast decline. In the whole of Ohu Ahia N'Otu that made up the Old Bende, there were only a few such titleholders—except in Abiriba and Item, where such customs and traditions continued to thrive. Mboha women accepted the duty of preparing all the food for the momentous occasion. 'Woman, you're still at home?' Kperechi asked Egobeke.

'I just came back from the river,' she responded, spreading clothes on the thatched roof. 'I've spent the whole day on this laundry. How was the marriage ceremony?'

'Splendid,' Kperechi answered, sounding quite happy. She had been away for two days. 'Whoever says money is not good is not telling the truth,' she stated, narrating the highpoints of the event that took place in Aguebi.

'Nwalayobi, will you stop?' Egobeke screamed at her young son, who was attempting to climb a ladder. They ate the sliced cassava, *ugba*, and *odudu* which she quickly prepared before going out. 'Your food is in the cupboard. The key is behind your radio,' she told Albert. She hurried to catch up with Kperechi. 'Did you hear what happened in Umuochoko yesterday?' she asked.

'What happened?'

'You know Agbazue's nephew that lives with him? I can't remember his name now.'

'Is it the very dark one with marks on his face that moves like Haco fowl?' Haco Farms and Feeds became well-known for the very big birds raised in their poultry farm. However, the native home-grown fowls of similar size were known to weigh more and had more meat after scalding.

'That's him. He slept with Irina.'

'What? You mean Irina opened her legs for that brat?'

'Agbazue was feeling too hot in the night. He went outside to cool off, and didn't realise that the boy had sneaked in to sleep with his wife.'

Kperechi was disgusted. 'What? She must have welcomed him to her bosom thinking it was her husband.'

'Of course, but she quickly noticed the difference,' Egobeke said.

'If he wants a woman, must it be Irina that cooks to feed him? How embarrassing for her. Did he share the same room with them?'

'How can they share room with that Haco fowl? He sleeps in the next room. He must have been lying awake all night listening to them.'

'I sympathise with her. He deserves to be castrated,' Kperechi said. Jenny and Ashivuka joined them as they approached the oil mill. Jenny had a big bowl of *egusi* on her head. It was the contribution made by the women from her neighbourhood.

The *ozo* title was reserved only for a man of means and character. Agbakuru was such a man. He was accomplished in every sense of the word: he was a high priest of Ogwugwu, the god invoked to protect Mboha from a plague that had threatened to wipe out the village. He had the largest homestead, which bustled with children, and he had more wives than any of his kinsmen. With so many hands to cultivate his large tracts of land, food was never a problem for him and family.

As a consummate *okonko* man, he had been called upon to lead his fellow men of stature on important missions. His towering height and charisma were always a great presence in any gathering. Agbakuru was a man of talent and speech, with a great command of the language, he spoke loftily at gatherings of great minds, using riddles and proverbs to communicate at a level above the ordinary. Though he did not lack tact and diplomacy, he used the truth like a knife to prune any overbearing party down to size. It won him many admirers, but a few believed he was acting as one who was indestructible.

The air was full of festival noise. Along the path leading to Agbakuru's homestead, many women danced in celebration. '*Onye ihe oma di nma: Bia kwe anyi iyo, iyo, iyo ooo Bia kwe anyi iyo!*' Okoro had bought a new Peugeot 504SR car for his transport business. Legibly inscribed on both sides of the car was his business name: *Okoro & Sons*.

'May good fortune remain wherever it settles,' Kperechi touched the car for luck. 'Let mine settle on me.'

'That's our prayer too!' chorused other well-wishers.

'Who does not love good things?' asked Ashivuka rhetorically.

'To God be the glory,' Jenny rejoiced as she took some of the cabin biscuits Okoro's wife shared out.

Most of the houses in the neighbourhood were decorated as if it were Christmas. They glowed from the *shimmanu* used to touch them up. Beautiful patterns such as flower petals were drawn on the walls with charcoal and *nzu*—white chalk. The entire place, including the oil mill, was spick-and-span.

Agbakuru's compound looked like new. His quintessential *mgbidi* house shone with the blue emulsion paint. There were two rooms in each wing with a sitting room in the middle. Two of the rooms had a connecting door for the husband and wife, and to fit in with the modern image of the ideal family, the other two were for a son and a daughter—although of course, no man in Mboha would settle for so few children; it was a culture they were not in a hurry to adopt despite their craving for the new civilisation. To complete the display of class, Agbakuru's parlour was arrayed with wooden furniture and collapsible rack for tumblers and spoons; the big metal four-post bed with a canopied frame graced his bedroom.

There was no fear of rain marring the event. Osigwe, the foremost rainmaker, had been wearing his black garment for some days and eating roasted yam without water. So it did not rain those four days preceding the event.

The Honourable Commissioner for Lands and Chieftaincy Titles, Mazi Anyanwu, a son of the Old Bende, was the chief guest of honour. Several members of the state's council of traditional leaders were equally present. After

Chief Ogbudu presented the kola to the august assembly, Elder Asogwa blessed it in accordance with tradition.

The commissioner delivered his keynote address. He was proud of the patriotic men who made up the council of *Nze na Ozo* and high chiefs. As men of integrity, they had helped to maintain social cohesion in their various areas. '. . .I must not fail to salute the effort they make in bringing development to the people. "Mazi Anyanwu, the piped water in our area is no longer running." "Mazi Anyanwu, we have bought electric poles and wire for our rural electrification. Please help us, we need a transformer." "We need a Caterpillar to grade our Okpara Road and its feeder roads." I can go on and on about how our people hunger and thirst for development. Some issues I am not able to address immediately, yet we must keep trying our best. We shall continue to rely on these men as the arrowhead of community development. God bless Imo State! God bless Igbo land! God bless the Federal Republic of Nigeria! *Cha, cha, cha, Igbo bu Igbo kwenu, rienu, nuonu, kwezuenu!*'

The crowd roared in tumultuous response, followed by loud cheering as he handed the microphone over. After the speeches, Eze Ogo I of Ubaha, the oldest *ozo* titleholder, eventually stood up to place a ceremonial hat on Agbakuru's head, graced by peacock and eagle feathers. His neck and wrist were bedecked with beads of different sizes. A twenty-one-gun salute exploded one after another. He shook hands with those who pushed to the front to congratulate him and waved a cow's tail to acknowledge the adulation of those who could not reach him. While the dignitaries were served with refreshments, Chief Ogbudu and the commissioner drove to his palace.

Mboha men gathered in Agbakuru's compound again the following evening to share the cow that was slaughtered for them. It was another round of merriment. 'Make sure it is properly seasoned,' Ozurumba instructed, as he handed a portion of fresh beef wrapped in cocoyam leaves to his wife. He turned down her offer to serve his dinner. 'Nothing else will enter this stomach tonight.'

14.

Uwakwe's heart skipped a beat on noticing his two goats in the outer yard. Quickly he dropped his tools to chase them back into the compound, railing at whoever left the gate open. To protect crops planted in the vicinity, herbivorous livestock were banned from roaming the neighbourhood. They could only graze in the nearby bushes if tethered to a post or tree.

To add to his annoyance, no one had fetched the bucket of water needed to dilute the kegs of *okpokiri*, the undiluted fresh pure palm wine. Nwugo left for the church premises to join other Christian mothers in a weekly activity while the entrance to Nwulari's inner compound was padlocked. 'So, attending the programmes of the church takes precedence over the water needed to dilute this wine isn't it?' he asked Akudo in a surly tone.

'Nkechi went to the river for clean water,' Akudo answered, hoping it would placate him.

Uwakwe sighed crossly. 'My customers will be forced to wait because I live with people who don't know their right hand from their left,' he was still muttering when Nkechi came back.

Okezie came through the gate, 'I greet the people in this compound,' he said, his voice loud enough, hoping that everyone in the compound heard him. 'The snake we killed, how many pieces are they?' he asked, fearing that the order he placed the previous day was already late in coming. The fact that Uwakwe did not expressly decline his order had given him a glimmer of hope but he was noncommittal all the same. He merely promised to address his order as soon as he had dealt with earlier ones.

'You are right on time,' Uwakwe commented. 'With your eyes, you will see if it is enough to take care of your order,' he answered, placing a filter in a funnel. Okezie held it steadily as he sieved four bees and some debris out of the wine. He took a sip after diluting it with the water and offered Okezie a cup. 'Try it.'

Okezie nodded, satisfied. 'This is *igba*, grade one.'

Uwakwe had built a reputation for tapping the best wine around. The amount of water he used to dilute each keg of okpokiri had never changed. Despite the growing craze for beer, his wine remained in great demand. It was a time when it was difficult to see a young man training to tap palm wine. Walking long distances to climb twenty palm trees twice a day in addition to other tasks during the farming season no longer appealed to them. Besides, those that did were notorious for their smelly and sweaty bodies and ragged work clothes. 'Some like to go to where they can pay *penny, penny* and *half, half* to buy saccharine sweetened water which is passed off as palm wine.'

'Can the product of a son of the soil be compared with that of a stranger?' Okezie quipped. Uwakwe found such compliments gratifying. More migrant peasants from the hinterlands had taken up residence among them to work. A number of them were into palm wine tapping. They had approached it completely from the commercial point of view, diluting it with too much water and left with no choice but to salvage the taste with sweeteners. Of course, they sold at lower prices to swing the market in their favour. 'These jars have lasted well,' he said, admiring the two demijohns that Uwakwe brought out. One of the transparent ceramic jars was covered with wicker to protect it from breaking and the second was without cover and gleamed like new. Such products were no longer available.

'Iroegbulem brought them,' Uwakwe told him, pouring wine into the first jar.

'Aaah, the high and mighty.'

'That takes care of his order.' Uwakwe ignored the remark, pouring wine into a third container, a plastic jar of equal size. 'This is yours,' he said, standing up to ease the strain.

'How much is it again? Is it not one and eight?' Okezie haggled, feigning ignorance of the current price.

'Even Nwaneto won't sell for one shilling and eight. I will let you have it for two shillings, as I know you.'

'Let me have it for one nine, I beg you,' he urged Uwakwe.

Uwakwe accepted his money but made it clear that it was not the right price. He invited Ozurumba who had just come into the compound to have a taste. Okwudiri brought the pineapple-shaped plastic jug, which Uwakwe filled up. 'Are you hosting a meeting?' Ozurumba asked as Okezie lifted the plastic jar off the ground.

'I'm visiting my in-laws, today is their *okonko* day,' he replied, hurrying away.

Uwakwe completed the second round of his wine tapping earlier than usual that afternoon. A patient who came for a routine massage of his dislocated ankle was awaiting his return. After attending to him, he proceeded to the ancestral shrine to tidy it up, changing the white muslin tied round the *oha* tree. He was expecting Iheyinwa and her husband, Osuagwu, who had to worship there before setting food in the marketplace at the dead of the night to appease the spirits of unborn children.

The worship began with a purification exercise. Uwakwe circled the hen round Iheyinwa's head several times, transferring her misfortunes to the fowl. As the fire singed the feathers, the shrine was filled with sweet aroma. He had barely begun the invocation before the mild breeze gathered strength; the *tunja* illuminating the utter darkness flickered furiously before going out. Little glowing sparks from the dried fronds flew up, dying almost immediately. Osuagwu lit the *tunja* again, cupping his hand around it. Clouds billowed across the sky, hiding the twinkling stars. 'I hope it does not rain,' Iheyinwa muttered with concern.

'The weather has been like this for some time,' Uwakwe noted. 'It may stay dry.'

'If only the rain could keep away for this night,' Osuagwu wished as they left the shrine to wait for midnight. At Uwakwe's instruction, Okwudiri gutted the carcass of the hen used for the peace offering that worshippers had to partake in and it would make the yam pepper soup tastier. He went to take the kitchen knife and bowl to cut the carcass.

Nwakego would not let him. 'Mama said you should not touch any of her utensils, do you hear me?'

'Why?' he asked, trying to be headstrong.

'If you think your ears are tough enough, touch it. You know how she will deal with you.'

The veiled threat was enough to make him reconsider his intention to defy his sister. He went to Nwugo's kitchen and was about to take their knife and a bowl. 'What do you think you are doing?' Nkechi barked at him, her tiny eyes boring holes at him. 'Were you told we are idol worshippers whose utensils can be used? Don't touch anything in our kitchen, please.'

Okwudiri stood at the entrance to Nwulari's inner compound to report to Uwakwe that they would not allow him use the kitchen utensils he needed. Uwakwe concluded it must be the happy-go-lucky lot who wanted to make heaven. He became disturbed when he learnt that Okwudiri was also refused access to Nwugo's kitchen. Iheyinwa equally came out at that point, ready to plead with the women if necessary.

'What do we call that? Is anybody forcing them to eat the food?' Uwakwe asked, his tone becoming sullen. The implication of their objection dawned on him. 'Ok, using it will contaminate the utensils, right? Are the utensils going to be permanently stuck with the meal? Won't they be washed after use?'

'What is the problem?' Nwulari asked as she came out of her inner compound. Iheyinwa was about explaining the situation to her but Nwulari told her not to worry. She went in to get all that Okwudiri would need. On a second thought, she granted him full access to her kitchen. As one who refused to give up her traditional religion to convert to Christianity, Nwulari did not find it difficult making the offer. She did not see what was wrong allowing the use of such utensils. 'If it is Nwulari, they will call me a wicked woman that has a covenant with the devil. Being inconsiderate to the plight of others: is that true religion?

'Good fellow,' Nwakego jibed as Okwudiri went past her to throw away dirty water. 'Do you realise what you are doing?' she continued as he was closing the picket gate on his way back to the compound. 'See,' she called, running her hand from chin to her neck. '*Akpiri, akpiri*—uncontrolled appetite—is not good, if you don't know. I don't know if you have not tasted chicken before.'

'Let it,' Okwudiri scoffed. 'Are you judging me? Have you cast out the log in your own eyes?'

'The same woman that was heaping curses on you barely a fortnight ago is the person you are cooking in her kitchen,' Nwakego reminded him. 'And when you are done participating in idol worship, you will join us in the choir to sing croaking bass.'

Okwudiri ignored her and returned to Nwulari's kitchen which was in one end of her veranda in the rainy season or open area in her small inner compound when there was no threat of rain. He knew his sister was eager to heed the vicar's admonition but he did not consider himself as idol worshipper.

*   *   *

Ozurumba stopped up the opening through which water flowed into the pond. Ijuolachi stood in the water with her bucket; Okwudiri and Nwakego were equally ready to scoop out water. Ozurumba joined them when he was sure that the drain was blocked. As they bailed out the pool with their buckets, the water level slowly sank. The evergreen ferns with dense clumps of fronds and other perennials growing close to the pond were at the receiving end. Completely overwhelmed by the deluge of water, they lost their normal posture, dripping the water that threatened to knock them out. Ijuolachi spent more time resting and talking than working. 'I told you to stay at home today but you insisted on coming,' Ozurumba reprimanded her, breathing fast from the exercise. 'I will flog you very soon if you don't keep that mouth shut. Do you want the whole world to know we are here?'

'A leech!' Nwakego cried out, at the sight of a dark and slimy object clinging to Ozurumba's calf.

He pulled it off effortlessly. Ijuolachi clambered out of the water as fast as she could. She could not stand the thought of a leech sucking her blood. 'Why are you running?' Okwudiri teased her.

'You want it to drain my blood?' she retorted.

'See it there on your thigh!' Okwudiri teased.

'Papa!' she cried, running towards her father.

'Stop it,' Ozurumba snarled. 'All you will say is "sorry" if she gets hurt.'

'So you love life this much?' Nwakego taunted, joining in the teasing.

'You want me dead while you remain alive to enjoy mama's food, isn't it?' Ijuolachi shot back.

'Have you ever heard of a leech killing anybody?' Okwudiri asked, climbing out of the water. His shorts looked dirtier than ever, with mud spattered across them. 'This pond is big.'

'You're right,' Nwakego agreed. 'If it was the Onyogwe pond, the level of the water would have gone down a lot more by now. Am I lying, papa?'

'Is this why we are here?' he countered. 'Stop all the *ochochoricho*. We're here to drain the water and catch all the fish.'

They worked at it patiently until the water in the pond was reduced to a muddy rivulet which was not even ankle-deep except at the centre. Fish that were unstoppable in water became defenceless, floundering in the mud. A number of tilapia and croakers flapped their tails listlessly while others lay quietly, all eventually falling prey to the eager hands of the children who picked them up and threw them into the basket.

Ozurumba removed the barks one after the other. The barks, removed from fallen tree trunks, were purposively arranged to provide sanctuary for the fish. This was the rewarding part of fish farming in the village. The ponds dug in raffia palm plantation served two purposes. They were a false haven for the fish migrating from the ocean into the creeks at the time of spawning and some of them roamed away from Imo River during tidal overflow. Such fish would remain trapped in the ponds if they failed to return with the ebbing tide. The ponds also met the watering needs of the raffia palms, keeping the fronds perpetually green until they were cut down for thatching.

'This fish has shocked me,' Nwakego squealed as she dropped a fish involuntarily.

'It must be *eruru*, the electric fish,' Okwudiri said, coming to her aid.

'Be careful,' Ozurumba warned them. 'I will still go home if any spiny fish stings any of you. You know that the pain can bring anyone down with fever.'

'See, see, I have seen a barracuda. See how big it is,' Ijuolachi announced gleefully on sighting what looked like a big stick.

'Where is it?' Nwakego asked.

'There,' she pointed. 'Look, look.'

'That is true!' Nwakego exclaimed on sighting the fish but Okwudiri disputed the name.

'That cannot be *agueze* but *araghira*—a catfish. So you don't know the difference,' he went to pick it up. It slipped out of his grip; he only succeeded at the second attempt. 'See, this is what is called barracuda,' he told them, picking out a species of the *agueze* fish. Nwakego was about disputing it but Ozurumba confirmed Okwudiri's position.

'Papa, snake!' Ijuolachi exclaimed as she saw something slithering into one of the remaining barks. 'Where is it?' Ozurumba grabbed his machete, alert.

'Under that bark,' she pointed from a distance. Nwakego scrambled out of the pond, frightened.

Ozurumba used a long stick to remove the bark carefully, holding his machete aloft and ready to strike. He sighed when he saw what it was. 'Is this what you call a snake?'

'Is it not?' Ijuolachi was confused.

'So you can't tell the difference between an eel and a snake?' Okwudiri snorted.

They gathered more fish with every bark that was lifted. Ijuolachi was lifting aside smaller fish to get a look at their biggest catch when she suddenly snatched back her hand, wringing it in pain. She suppressed a cry but her father noticed. 'I knew you'd get stung. If you were a goat, I wouldn't eat your ears.'

The *nsala* soup that night was exceptional. Dissolved fish strands helped to thicken it, and everyone ate *utara* with relish except Kperechi. Fresh fish made her nauseous. She preferred them slightly smoked, at least.

'These children, they won't let me listen to the radio!' Kperechi shouted, faintly exasperated. *Nkwa Umunwanyi* was one of the IBS programmes she did not like to miss. Every week, it featured one hour of traditional music and dance composed and performed by women from different communities. Many communities, especially Nkwerre Imenyi, became famous because their women's voices delighted the listening public.

'That woman's voice rings like *ogele*—a metal gong,' Nwugo spoke up from where she was having dinner with Nkechi and Akudo. Though Uwakwe had a transistor, he was scarcely at home, so his family was used to listening in to Ozurumba's radio.

'There's no gainsaying that,' Kperechi agreed. The lyrics of the song captured the rhythm of their life. Like most women, Kperechi treasured their message, which often reinforced ecclesiastical teachings as well as their communal ethos. One of their songs urged women not to hate their husbands even in the face of unrequited love. Where a husband failed to clothe the wife, such a woman could count on her children for such love and support. Scared of widowhood, another songwriter prayed against lone parenting. No woman wanted to be saddled with the unenviable task of raising her children all by herself. Any woman constrained to do so could tell what a heart-breaking experience it could be. The parable of the white woman asking the songwriter to 'work before pleasure' really struck a chord. 'That is quite true, my fellow woman,' Kperechi agreed.

'Whoever pursues pleasure before work is inviting hunger,' Ehichanya opined.

'Do you know what? I saw Mmereole this evening,' Kperechi said at the end of the program.

'She came back this afternoon,' Ehichanya told them. 'She looked quite healthy.'

'Truly, we have really lost a gem in Ofoegbu, her father,' Nwugo remembered him fondly. 'He was one of the pioneers that brought the Catholic Church to our village, isn't it?' Kperechi recalled. 'May this night hold him,' she added as a prophylactic against any unpleasant experience which could occur as a result of mentioning his name that night. There was no Catholic church in Mboha before the war but some men got together to form one. It became easier getting relief materials distributed by the church.

'How we survived that war is a miracle,' Nwugo thought aloud. The mere mention of the war evoked strong memories. She recounted her experience in the '*ahia* attack'. She had travelled with other women far beyond Obowo, behind enemy lines, to trade in Ubulu salt and smoked fish in the riverside settlements. Sometimes it took more than two days to travel each leg of the journey. Kind-hearted people allowed them spend the night in their villages. To reciprocate, they would give their host something from their wares. On a particular night, their hostess tried to turn four of them over to some cannibals.

'Cannibals?' There was fright in Nkechi's voice. She asked her mother how she escaped.

'God used her son that came back from the warfront to save us,' Nwugo told them. Kperechi was shocked to hear that a fellow woman was privy to such wicked scheme. Nwugo confirmed it was not only a terrible night but the longest night ever. They went down memory lane, recounting a number of things that happened during the war. Their children could not believe some of the things they ate just to stay alive. They could not imagine anybody eating some of the leaves they ate as vegetables during the war. All the wandering in the bush without snakebites or some other calamity filled them with gratitude towards God. 'Truly, the God that made us survive that war is great!'

Ozurumba recalled vividly how he escaped death at the end of the war. Soldiers had occupied Mboha after Umuahia was finally overrun. Virtually everyone in the village fled to Ofeimo. They could not return immediately as identified Biafran combatants were shot indiscriminately. Very early one morning, he followed Ofoegbu to find out if the infantry brigade had withdrawn from their village. They made it before sunrise and parted ways as they approached the village. Ozurumba kept away from the footpath and places where he could be noticed until he got to a vantage position. From there, he saw the village and the soldiers. He was so tempted to walk up to them and explain himself but he resisted the urge. He turned to go and was moving from tree to tree when a voice rang out. 'Halt! Who goes there?' Ozurumba froze; then his legs began to wobble. 'What are you doing there?' asked the soldier.

'What is your name?' demanded a second soldier when Ozurumba failed to answer.

'I am from. . .' he attempted an answer.

'Na enemy. Abi make I blow 'im head?' asked the second soldier in Pidgin English.

'No try am ooo! Oga go court-martial us. Make we carry am go meet am,' the first soldier advised. 'You be soldier. No be so?' he asked Ozurumba.

He shook his head. 'No.'

They inspected his feet for any corn as a result of wearing military boots. It would have confirmed he was one of the soldiers that overstretched them. There was none. Military boots were not available at the time of his conscription even when he became a combatant. 'I for blow the bastard,' said the second soldier.

He was told to frog jump. It required him leaping from his squatting position. Noticing it was delaying their movement, he was asked to walk along in front of them with his hands raised. 'On the double! Bloody civilian.'

Major Yohana was eating when they arrived. He had enlisted in the army as a volunteer to stop the secession, suspending his career as a young teacher fresh from the college of education. Everyone was told that it would take only a few months to overrun the rebels. For him, the whole war was one hair-raising adventure after another. From the Fall of Nsukka to the Fall of Owerri and their incursion into Umuahia, time after time, he only narrowly escaped death. He was greatly relieved when the end of the war was announced, but the victory brought him only fleeting joy. He was still waiting to withdraw his troops. He returned the salute of the sergeant. 'Any problems?' he asked.

'Yes. We caught a man very close to the village.'

He ordered them to bring him. 'Did you beat him?' Yohana asked.

'No, sir. Yes, sir.'

'Kai,' he berated them, in Hausa language. 'Did I ask to you to beat anyone?'

'No sir. Sorry sir.'

'Any other problem?'

'No, sir. All correct, sir.'

Ozurumba was still expecting the worst. He was surprised when food was ordered for him. 'Rice of all things!' he thought. He hoped it would not be his last meal. He took five spoonsful before he stood up.

'What do you want?' Yohana asked.

'I want cocoyam leaves to tie food for my family.'

'Where are they?'

'Across the river.'

'Don't worry. We will give you something for them.' Yohana kept his word. A big bowl was filled with rice and beans and tinned fish. He urged Ozurumba to bring his family back and inform his kinsmen that the war was over.

Meanwhile, Ozurumba's kinsmen were mourning his capture and possible death when he returned to them with his bounty. When most of them returned to Mboha the next day, Yohana opened the army food store for them. Mboha could not believe it, but it happened. On the fourth day they were forced to bid Yohana farewell after his battalion was given the withdrawal order.

15.

Imo Broadcasting Service played a cocktail of music known as the presenter's delight. Hearing 'Fat, Fat as a Cow', Nwakego went back to the room to raise the volume. 'Landlady', the music of Joe Nez, was quite popular. Ozurumba asked Nwakego to bring the radio out but Kperechi quickly raised a protest. 'Nwakego to carry your radio? What if she drops it?'

'Ah, don't worry please. I don't want any hassles now,' Ozurumba changed his mind, getting up. 'That is my window to the outside world.'

Nwakego paused in her chores again and again, swaying to the rhythm, singing along with Nkechi, her cousin. They took a break as the presenter came on air, taking time to talk about the landlady, imagining how big she must have been. They had barely finished dancing to Boney M's 'Hooray! Hooray!' when 'Sucu Sucu', another favourite, segued in. It was the English version, and the male singer had a funny accent. 'I didn't know this music had an English version,' Nkechi observed.

As it did for many listeners, such programmes had developed an eclectic taste for music in Ozurumba and his household. They were at home with a broad range of music, from the high-pitched guitar strumming of Congolese soukous to the rhythmic samba, calypso, salsa, rumba, soca, and conga of both South and North America. Even though they did not understand the lyrics, they all had their favourites. Beside the pop stars and country music legends, they derived great pleasure from the works of Harry Belafonte, Alberto Cortez, and the dreamy and rich pastorals of Music Havana, which were peculiarly calming. It was a measure of their popularity, that a number of the foreign tunes were used in advertising jingles.

'But do you think they play our music in their country too?' Nwakego wondered.

'I will not be surprised if they do,' Nkechi surmised. 'Music cuts across boundaries.'

Placing the radio on his lap and pulling up the antenna, Ozurumba turned the dial, searching the waveband, stopping when a station spoke a language he understood. One of them spoke fast-paced English with an accent he could hardly follow. He paused, waiting to identify the station. But some of the words were not totally strange to him: Pearl Harbour, D-Day, the atomic bomb, Hiroshima, Nagasaki, Auschwitz. . . From his repertoire of knowledge, Ozurumba could tell they were all words connected to World War II. He concluded it must be about the war, maybe an anniversary. He was about moving on when the anchor mentioned the Voice of America. With his torch, he checked the wavelength on which the station was transmitting.

Okwudiri interrupted his father to remind him about the money he needed to start his bread business. The new bakery in Umuagu offered trading opportunities to many. He had not given Ozurumba any rest. 'I still don't have any ready cash on me,' Ozurumba told him for the umpteenth time.

'But papa, you promised. What about the jobs we did together?' demanded Okwudiri.

'Do I have to vomit money because you want to trade?' Ozurumba asked, irritated. 'Okay, I can advance two naira to you from the public money in my custody on the condition you pay it back it by next week.'

'I promise.' Okwudiri had calculated the profit he could make. By his fourth trip, he would make enough to repay the borrowed capital. He would hawk the bread morning and evening, and then watch his capital grow.

The following morning, Ozurumba continued the brick and mortar work at the oil mill shed. The pillars were made of blocks, and work on the store for the operator's tools was almost completed. The roof was also taking shape with the rafters and purlins in place. Work on the zinc roofing sheets could have started that day but Akwakanti was one of those in the hunting expedition taking place in Mboha. 'Papa, we are ready to go,' said Okwudiri, reminding his father about the money.

Ozurumba wished him luck and handed the money to him. He was amused at his son's eagerness to make money. 'Children, they think the sweet tongue used to borrow money is the same sweet tongue used to repay it,' he muttered.

'Papa, don't worry, I will make money from this business,' Okwudiri declared joyfully, racing off to the square with his tray, carton, and polythene covering, to join others in the trip.

Mboha witnessed the arrival of more hunters with dane guns and machetes safely sheathed in scabbards tied to their waists. Only Okpukpukaraka had a double-barrelled gun. Their layers of clothes meant to keep thorns and prickly bushes from tearing their skin were dirty and ripped, making them cut a perfect picture of a ragtag assembly. Old canvas shoes, military boots with peelings, rubber shoes commonly worn by nomads—all had been pressed into service to keep the notorious thorns such as *anamiri* from lacerating their feet. Shortly after, they left for the bush.

Virtually all the hunters came with a dog or two of various sizes, shapes, and colours. Those with bobtails looked fatter and healthier. The small bells dangling around their necks tinkled to ensure they were not mistaken for the games the hunters were out to catch.

The weather was kind that day. The sun refused to scorch with terrible intensity as it usually did at that time of the year. It withdrew behind the clouds again and again, allowing cooling shadows to fall across the landscape. Gusty mild breezes blew softly, ameliorating the heat even before the approach of eventide. 'Your son has jumped on the bandwagon of bread sellers,' Ogbuka noted as Okwudiri approached them announcing his ware.

'Buy sweet bread! Ten. . .ten kobo bread! Buy Sonye's Special Buttered Loaf, ten. . .ten kobo, bread!' Okwudiri called. Ozurumba told them that he started that day. George was surprised at the eagerness of children to make money at that time. He remembered that his mother owned the kerosene he hawked around in the village as a boy. But the children wanted to own the business.

'This is a passion for making money,' Ikwuako agreed, momentarily taking his eyes off the hoe handle he was carving. 'The earlier the better, isn't it?'

'But they have to make it with clean hands,' Amos said energetically, his voice rising, his mouth was open baring his teeth and pink gums. As usual, he was picking his teeth. His thickset frame was dressed only in a loincloth; his hair and beard were completely grey. 'Can't you see? It's leading them into trouble. See what it did to Obioma, an only son.'

'When you're telling them to keep their hands clean, it seems you are asking too much from them,' Josiah sighed. The village had been shocked by the condition of the young man, a wheelbarrow pusher in the city, who was brought back in chains. The fact that he was an only child made the pain of his condition more difficult for the villagers. To account for his condition, it was said that he outsmarted a woman and made away with her luggage. She must have taken his name to a sorcerer to bewitch and destroy him. 'Imagine, such a handsome boy. Where it starts is that they can't tell simple truth.'

It reminded George of the David Milgaard story aired over the CBC Radio the previous night. The young man had been sentenced to life imprisonment for rape and murder. 'His mother has been rallying public support for a retrial. Imagine if his mother did not believe him, he would spend the rest of his life behind bars.'

'What mother would admit that her son was capable of such heinous crime?' Ozurumba contested.

'Where did this happen?' Amos asked, curious to know the legal system which would not hand down a death sentence to a man that was guilty of rape and murder.

'That can only happen in the white man's land,' Ozurumba was sure. 'Whoever tries such a thing here will be hanged.'

'Is your radio different?' Amos asked. He was one of those who believed that George liked to tell stories of a distant world that was far removed from their reality.

'There's no death sentence in their country,' George said.

'What?' Ikwuako could not believe that. 'That's a licence to kill.'

The return of the hunters cut short any further discussion. Okwudiri seemed to have been timing them, as he came back to the square immediately with his bread. Some of the hunters bought a loaf from Ehichanya, Okwudiri, Ijuolachi, and Chimezie. They returned with lots of game. There were two antelopes, three hares, five monkeys, beavers, squirrels, and others. Some were butchered for sharing, so that no hunter went home empty-handed whether he caught anything or not. It was also a profitable day for Okwudiri. His strategy worked as he made enough money for another trip to Umuagu the following day.

As Ozurumba followed Ikwuako to his house to check the *iyagha*—the species of big yam—he wanted to acquire from him, they stumbled on a quarrel between Ure and Uluotuwe. Ure babbled furiously and incoherently, demonstrating with her fingers how much she was given. 'What have you done to her?' Ozurumba wondered.

'What did I do?' Uluotuwe asked. 'I paid her in full for the chair but she's denying it.' Ure shook her head vigorously, her busty bosom quivering, her index finger wagging in protest. Her hair, though plaited, was loose, old, and bushy, full of dirty flecks and crumbs making her look completely dishevelled. She stuck out her fingers, telling them how much she had before collecting Uluotuwe's money. 'I gave her two shillings and four kobo,' Uluotuwe persisted. The coins had become mixed up together, making it difficult to ascertain the truth. Unable to express herself, Ure was ready to fight, picking up a chair. 'I dare you to strike me!' Uluotuwe fumed. 'Did I make you deaf and dumb? How can you deny the money I gave you just a short while ago?'

'You know she's handicapped,' Ashivuka reproved.

Both men continued on their way after bringing the situation under control, but they were piqued by Uluotuwe's less than straightforward attitude. 'Ure may be deaf and dumb but that does not make her stupid,' Ikwuako opined. 'She does not take kindly to people taking advantage of her. Uluotuwe is lucky that people were around to stop her. She would have been nursing an injury by now.'

16.

Chief Ogbudu's 504SR glided to a stop in front of his palace. The caramel-coloured pebbles crunched underneath his shoes as he crossed them with regal stride. The brilliantly golden morning sun was nature's way of rejoicing with him. A year had slowly crept by but he was still alive! He imagined what the story could have been if things had gone awry. David's lamentation for King Saul readily came to his mind. 'How have the mighty fallen and the instruments of war perished? Tell it not in Gath and proclaim it not in the street of Ashkelon!' He would have been silenced forever.

Ekwuribe filled the seventh *nkponala* with gunpowder, positioned them and laid lines of more gunpowder between them. Some boys hovered around giving assistance that was not asked for. 'Nobody should get too close,' he warned, as he stopped to exchange greetings with guests arriving Mboha.

'Your handiwork is echoing far and wide,' a guest commended.

'Yes, everybody has to know that Mboha is celebrating,' he declared, unable to shake the guests' hands because his own were dirty. After a while, he lit the trail of gunpowder, making the flame snake towards the *nkponala* as he hurried away to a safe distance. A woman who saw what was going on froze in her track, preparing herself for the earth-shattering explosion. A boy, realising what was about to happen, ran away as fast as his legs could carry him. The other two watched from a distance as the cannons went off, forefingers stuck into each ear to protect their eardrums as the deafening sound reverberated like hundreds of thunderclaps rolled into a single explosion.

'Ekwuribe, you are terrifying us with your *nkponala*,' Egobeke complained as he entered Chief Ogbudu's palace. 'It makes my heart skip.'

'Would you prefer it to crawl?' he asked, traces of mucus darkened by tobacco hung on his greying and unkempt moustache. His dirty and worn-out blue safari top contrasted with his oxblood trousers which had not seen water for a long while; the drooping hems swept the floor as he crossed it in quick short strides. Wiry as a result of regular alcohol intake, his handsome looks were spoilt by his untidy appearance.

'It is not funny,' Nwanyibunwa added. 'Can't you move it further away or do you want it to ruin our hearing?'

Well-wishers continued to pour into Mboha to celebrate the survival of Chief Ogbudu. Ceramic and plastic demijohns of palm wine followed them. Guests from Abadaba were among the early callers, eager to felicitate with Mboha and her people. They harboured no ill-will towards their neighbour. Their demand for the swearing was meant to settle the matter for all time and to foster lasting peace. They had watched the time creep by with genuine apprehension. History must not record them as an example of a village that caused the annihilation of another. The chief's survival was an extraordinary relief. He could drop dead any time after that one year; no accusing finger would point at them. 'The king shall live forever!' some visitors greeted him as they met him at the door.

'And those who made him king!' he answered genially, ushering them into the parlour. Sycophants started that salutation to curry favour from him. It had gained ground with time and had become a standard way of paying him homage. Some villagers kicked against it, insisting it was too obsequious. Many of them adopted it with time even if they did not mean it. He turned to Ekwuribe after the greeting. 'Yes, how is it going?'

Ekwuribe repeated the salutation perfunctorily, saluting in military fashion before presenting his request. 'We need more gunpowder.'

'Won't you share a kola with us?' Ejike, one of the visitors, asked Ekwuribe as Chief Ogbudu handed him some money. Ekwuribe dipped a lobe of previously broken kola nut into the disc, scooping up the hot sauce. As he chewed, he downed a shot of schnapps to soothe the stinging sensation. He cleared his throat loudly. 'I have to run along. Who'd stack up stones on a shelf and lay a child to sleep underneath it?'

The celebration gathered momentum as the day wore on. The market awaited the arrival of the chief celebrant and his train. Those still buying and selling hastened to conclude their transactions as the celebrations took centre stage. As the herald made their way to the square, the undulating sound of the drumbeat gave way to a pulsating rhythm, heightening the glee and anticipation. A procession led by Chief Ogbudu and his *lolo* approached the square bedecked in finery. Another salvo of *nkponala* pealed off.

'Truth shines like moon,' Uwakwe remarked, gulping down what was left in his *nkuku*. He handed one naira note to the treasurer as his contribution to the monthly savings club for their age group. It was the turn of Clarke to collect that week's contribution.

'It goes without saying,' Ayozie added, handing a fifty kobo note to Clarke.

'Any other business?' asked Ejiogu standing up. 'I want to join the merriment.'

'We can't visit Ezeagwula today, can we?' asked Isaiah.

'Who prefers a house of mourning to a coronation party?' asked Ayozie as the market square came alive. Different dance troupes took turn at the centre of the square. Women sang and danced to old tunes. Their special number for the occasion elicited clapping and cheering. Odumodu and Abigbo cultural dancers entertained the crowd. The *ikpirikpe* war troupe kept barging into people to scare them. The merriment continued at Chief Ogbudu's palace where guests were received until the first signs of twilight, when guests began to leave with their empty jars.

*   *   *

Joshua uncorked the bottle of Golden Guinea lager for Ozurumba and Star lager for Albert. A bottle of Aromatic Schnapps and a shot were set on the stool beside George. 'Did you hear about the woman that flew an aeroplane today?' Joshua asked. His provision store, the biggest of the three in the village, served alcoholic beverages, a reason for quarrelling in many homes as husbands, the only customers allowed to drink in his compound, frittered away meagre resources in the name of relaxation and pleasure.

Ozurumba brightened up, leaning on the backrest. 'Since I was born, I've not heard of such a spectacular achievement. It is an event I would have loved to witness personally, true.'

'That woman is exceptional,' Albert concurred, his taut face and high cheekbones unable to express his pleasure properly. He shoved a thumb full of tobacco into his nose as two kid goats, sighting their mother, sped off, grabbing the teat of her udders, pulling and tugging, suckling with every sense of urgency. The mother goat, sensing they deserved the milk, stopped and stood aloof, chewing cud. The kid goats squatted beneath her and sucked eagerly.

Shortly after, she moved away, leaving them snorting and licking their mouths, all dispersing to pursue various interests except one that remain rooted on the same spot bleating. Apparently, she had not been given a fair chance to feed. The mother goat returned to give her a chance. 'She's a child worth having,' he sneezed loudly, turning aside to blow his nose, making sure the spattering brown mucus did not touch anyone.

Imo State Government celebrated the achievement, rolling out the drums to give Chinyere Onyenucheya a red carpet reception. She had brought glory and honour to her fatherland. IBS aired the ceremony that afternoon with accolades pouring in from every quarter. To prove her mettle, she piloted an aircraft with Governor Mbakwe and some dignitaries on board. There was wild jubilation as it touched down. 'She must be the first woman to do so,' Ozurumba imagined.

'There is no doubt about that, at least in Africa,' George beamed, taking personal pride in the achievement. 'We have brilliant minds; you know?' He took a sip of Aromatic Schnapps and exhaled contentedly. 'What is good is good.'

'That is a daughter any man would be proud to have,' Ozurumba added.

Joshua went to attend to some children that wanted to buy tablets of orange tango and goody-goody chocolate bar. The provision store he set up on his return from Kaduna had stood the test of time. 'Chimezie, come down, it's enough,' he called to his son who was plucking guavas in their little orchard. He also grew some exotic fruit trees usually considered the white man's version of their own fruit, like avocado pears, sour sop which they called *chop chop*, *ukwa beke*—nuts that looked like chestnuts but believed was a species of breadfruit—and paw-paw. 'Wash that knife,' he snarled at Chimezie who had brought a dirty knife for peeling the oranges.

'Joshua the British,' George hailed. The whole of Mboha knew how fussy Joshua could be about neatness. It was not unusual to find him sweeping, weeding, or gardening, things considered as residue for women and children. 'I don't know why you didn't follow them back to England.'

'The British lifestyle runs in your blood,' Ozurumba added.

Joshua kept a straight face, picking one of the few hairs that grew on his hairless chin. 'Cleanliness is next to godliness. That is what my master used to say.' His voice still conveyed the deep respect and affection he had for them.

'The money spent on this woman's education is not a waste,' George noted, continuing their conversation.

'Who is not happy sending his daughter to school? It is only the lack of means,' Ozurumba pointed out. 'In the Western Region, where education is free, who talks about giving the male or female child preference?'

George was so happy with the point that he stretched out his arm to shake Ozurumba's hand. 'Education is the best gift Awolowo gave to his people,' he stated with satisfaction. 'To keep the children in education and to encourage others to join, he made sure pupils were fed during school hours—while our government was busy sending children away from school for failure to pay tuition fees.'

'*Eeeeee?*' Albert queried as if it was news to him. 'If he likes, he can bring heaven down for them.' He was not excited hearing about the elder statesman's name. He was one of those who considered such open admiration for him a *faux pas*, given his perceived role during the civil war. 'If kwashiorkor had wiped us out, would I be here to hear how great he was?' he asked; his long disfigured tooth equally seemed agitated.

'What about the money our people had in the banks? The accounts were all frozen and they handed only twenty pounds to the account holders irrespective of the actual book balance,' Ozurumba added to the list of grudges.

'I don't want us to dwell on such things forever. Even at that, it wasn't just him. What about the properties our people owned that were declared abandoned in Port Harcourt and other places, did he do that?' asked George. 'Even if we hate him from now till thy kingdom come, it would make no difference. Having lost the war, we cannot run away from a number of consequences. Another question is: were we totally blameless? We must search ourselves closely,' he stated.

He ran through different accounts of what sparked off the ire of the northerners, culminating in the mass killings. It was a fact that the pogrom did not start immediately after the death of the Sardauna. From what he heard, the coup plotters found him a hard nut to crack. After several shots could not fell him, a grenade was thrown at him but they heard his crackling laughter from the wall where he vanished into. Overcoming his resistance was not easy. Perhaps, this story was the basis of a number of political cartoons in the media shortly after his death.

One of the cartoons depicted a cockerel crowing out in victory. There was also the musical band that played in Kano which was interpreted to mock the northern leader who was in the throes of death. Such indiscretions made the northerners to become acutely aware of their loss. It was like rubbing salt to a fresh wound which sustained the allegation of insensitivity and lack of humility. In vengeance, his brother-in-law and many others were slaughtered by the northerners. His sister, Matilda, was not only forced to watch the killing of her husband but had to hold a bucket to collect the blood.

Though he was not expecting it but he appeared to be persuading them as the strong dissent appeared to be vacating their faces. His respect for Awolowo had grown stronger when he got to know that virtually every compound in Ondo State could boast of a professor. Such good report was a credit to his political thinking built on freedom from ignorance, disease and want. It was aimed at making life more abundant for all. The educational policies he pursued were meant to lead to mental emancipation of his people. He did not only work hard to see children go to school but provided them with necessaries. In addition to getting books and school uniforms, the children were readily fed while they were in school. Effectively, he fought against any excuse which could keep the children away from school. He was a man that promised to implement a full regime of insurance in the country if he became the president.

His thinking which centred on conferring benefits on others and enhancing their lots was certainly praiseworthy. When he became the Premier of Western Region, he demonstrated it beyond cavil that the ideals articulated as his political manifestos were not mere eloquent declarations or rhetoric. Without a doubt, he showed the level of importance he attached to his fellow men. It was not difficult to discern the source of his inspiration. Perhaps, it was probably true that the first set of coup plotters in the country truly wanted to arrest the country's drift into anarchy, release him from prison and hand the reins of power over to him.

Those who were well-aware of the leadership challenges which the country was facing at the time knew his worth. Frustrated that he did not become the president of the country, the same Emeka Odimegwu Ojukwu that led Biafra paid him tribute at his death. He was the best president Nigeria never had. Presuming he was a sworn enemy of the sage, the immediate kinsmen of Awolowo saw the tribute as a Greek gift and failed to accept it as a remark made in good faith. All these attested to how much he was venerated. He demonstrated such level of awareness that qualified him as the best to lead the country. But those that were interested in perpetuating neo-colonial hegemony were afraid of him and became the mountains before Zerubbabel. According to them, he was too independent minded to be trusted. It made them uncomfortable.

But George could not dispute that there were a number of faulty policies he initiated or supported. It was particularly so in what he considered as politics of advantage. In his position of strength, he forgot to be fair to his perceived enemies. All the talk about all was fair in war had undoubtedly beclouded his mind and produced a result that nobody could be proud of. If he had given fair thought to it, it would have occurred to him that using starvation as a strategy of warfare was bound to cause slow and traumatic death. The concerted efforts of the Catholic priest, Fr. Kevin Doheny and many others, led to the formation of the *African Concern*. While this charity was at the forefront of the humanitarian organisations making effort to get food and other reliefs to the dying in Biafra, there was a sustained blockade to weaken and crush resistance.

The slow and painful death was worse than death by bullets and shrapnel. Pictures of a people so malnourished and turned into living skeletons were available for all to see. The frail frames of children unable to cope with stomachs that were distended by kwashiorkor made the trauma more acute. The wiry veins on the swollen stomach, the heads that became oversized for their thin and weakened bodies, the eyes, totally sapped of energy and looking vacantly into space all told the story of their ordeal. The cruelty shocked the world and moved many to clamour for decisive steps to be taken to end the war. Offspring of the victims continued to wince at the sight of the pictures, finding it difficult to believe that their own people went through such suffering. The sight of it was a torture of its own. If love had ruled his heart and prevailed over the natural instinct to hurt those that hurt him, he would have remembered to practice the important precept of not only praying for his enemies but doing good to even those that wronged him. If he knew that such anger and animosity would possess the hearts of the victims of a strategy he must have thought was an ingenious way of gaining victory over adversary, perhaps different thoughts and actions would have prevailed.

It amplified the overwhelming responsibility which intellectuals owed humanity. Although he was not the head of government, it was apparent he was closely consulted and his counsel well sought after. Like a shadow director, he pulled the strings and called the shots from the background. Most of the policies and actions that took place must have been at his instance.

'War is not a good thing, true,' Joshua chipped in calmly, heaving his shoulders.

'More so when it is lost,' Ozurumba added.

'Even before the war, were we not paying fees?' Albert pointed out.

'Ohooo,' George enthused, spreading out his hands as if that point had vindicated his position. '"Education is expensive",' he mouthed contemptuously, repeating one of the most common reasons given by government officials for insisting on tuition fees. 'If education is expensive, try illiteracy. Is it not what Awolowo said?'

'Our people still tried their best,' said Albert.

'There's no doubt about that, but we could have done so much more,' George insisted. They mentioned names of well-lettered persons of their ethnic extraction that excelled in education and public service and how well they had performed after taking over from their colonial masters. 'Who could speak English like Dr Benjamin Nnamdi Azikiwe?' he asked, recalling his enthralling and electrifying speeches. He could still visualise Zik speaking before a mammoth crowd at a campaign rally. Many attended rallies just to hear the unprecedented and unusual vocabulary of the Great Zik of Africa. He remembered a particular instance how ululation swept through the crowd as he mounted the podium. 'Ziiiiiiiiik, Ziiii. . .' the crowd continued to hail him. Seeking to disabuse their minds, Zik started with a brief preamble. 'Today. . .' He spoke with that enthralling elocution, pausing, allowing the words ring out resonantly, leaving them floating for a while before sinking in with maximum impact. 'I say, today, I have not come to *zikify* my *zikism*!' he pronounced, annunciating each consonant and vowel, stretching and enlongating the word zikify, giving it the maximum weight possible. The crowd momentarily went berserk. The howl of 'Ziiiiiiiiiik' flared up again and again. He had uttered a word they had not heard before. Yes, Zik had a complete mastery of the language that he could coin new words. Having received the needed tonic, they listened rapturously thereafter, hanging on every word, every argument why they should prefer him as the leader. That was the charismatic Zik, the epitome of learning, a model to the innumerable masses that wanted to speak like him.

'*Nna anyi*—our father—Zik was exceptional,' Joshua commented.

'Is that not why I left everything else to follow him?' George recalled, animated.

Education was the most admired part of all the process put in place for the acculturation of the British system. Being the backbone of public administration, his ethnic group, as goal-oriented people, embraced it with unstinting zeal, winning scholarships, travelling abroad to study, and returning distinguished in learning and in character. It moved from being a passion to an obsession: the route to success. Nobody wanted to be denied the opportunity. Not even traders escaped the lust for reading. Bookstores were stocked with Onitsha Market literary books, a number of the authors captured the essence of education from different perspectives: the difficulty of acquiring it, the cost it involves, the honour it bestows, and the mind it enriches. The folly of those who had opportunity to acquire it but failed to do so, the opportunity they were bound to lose in their lifetime could not be quantified. Musicians went lyrical, waxing vinyl, extolling its virtues. An enchanted poet, in his ode to learning, delighted abecedarians and adults alike with a rhyme that became a classic:

Akwukwo n'ato uto
Ona ara ahu na mmuta
Onye nwere nkasi obi
Oga amuta akwukwu
Oburu na nne gi na nna gi nwe ego!
Oburu na nne gi na nna gi nwe ego!

Mgbe m di na ntakiri
Buru akpa n'isi n'agba oso
Gbabata n'ulo akwukwu
Achirim ochi hahahahaha ewooo!
Achirim ochi hahahahaha ewooo!

'I have to be on my way,' Albert said, standing up. He dipped his hand into his brown khaki shorts and paid for his drink.

Akwakanti joined them. '*Dee* Albert, won't you buy a bottle for me?'

'For doing what?' he asked, bringing out more coins to cover another bottle.

'For being your kinsman at least,' Akwakanti spoke, his voice rising above his usual whisper. As the uncorked bottle was handed to him, he lifted the bottle, downing successive gulps, the content halved by the time he paused, belching noisily. 'It's a good thing I didn't die during the war,' he remarked.

'The dead do not praise Jah,' George quipped.

'I want battery for my radio,' Akwakanti told Joshua.

'Flash is eight kobo. Tigerhead is still seven kobo,' Joshua replied.

'Was it not only last week I bought Flash for seven kobo?' Akwakanti contested. 'Is it every day that you increase the price?'

'I went to market two days ago. The price has gone up. I couldn't believe it myself. A carton that used to sell for one pound less twenty-five kobo now sells for one pound. They refused to reduce anything,' he explained.

'Let me have the Tigerhead then,' Akwakanti said. 'I don't want to get into debt.'

'They are the same thing,' Ozurumba said. 'That's what I'm using. What should I do with my goat? It has been shivering with cold and its droppings are so watery.'

'Maybe it ate something that the system does not like,' pondered Joshua. 'Tetracycline may calm the stomach?'

'Add APC, maybe,' George suggested, passing his hand across his face. 'It could bring the feverish condition down.'

'It is not a human being,' Akwakanti pointed out.

'Does it make a difference? It is the same breath,' Joshua replied.

'In that case, Cafenol should be better. It's only a kid goat,' Ozurumba explained. At home, he pulverised the tablets in a spoon and made the goat drink it.

17.

Launching! Launching! Launching!' the radio announced. 'The clergy and laity of St John's Anglican Church Mboha cordially invite members of the general public to the fundraising ceremony of their modern church auditorium under the distinguished chairmanship of. . .'

Nwakego was ecstatic at the mention of Mboha. 'Listen, listen,' she called excitedly, clapping her hands to get everybody's attention as the announcement continued. 'The radio is talking about our village.' They listened incredulously, doubting her statement until they heard the name of Nwakanma, their vicar, Chief Ogbudu, chairman of the building committee, and Josiah, the secretary, as signatories to the invitation. It was too good to be true. Their humble and remote village, Mboha, was in the news! Those who did not hear it on that occasion were not disappointed; the announcer repeated it on five different occasions before the great day came.

Mboha was abuzz with the news. 'Haven't I said so? Chief Ogbudu is extraordinary!' Egobeke was very excited.

'What a sweet surprise,' Kperechi beamed. 'I salute his effort. Nobody knew it was going to be on air.'

'Watch and see what will happen that day,' Ashivuka predicted. 'I'm sure he'll pull a big crowd to the fundraiser.'

'Let it be,' Kperechi prayed. 'It will lighten the financial burden on us.'

The image of Chief Ogbudu continued to loom larger than life as the village looked forward to the event with great expectation. As chairman of the building committee, he had forged ahead with the church auditorium, and some parts were already at the lintel level. Having attended events at the instance of his friends where he donated generously, the launching would be a good opportunity for them to reciprocate the gesture. One of the events he attended was the investiture of Ukelonu as Knight of St Mulumba in Ikeduru.

Ukelonu's citation was very rich and attracted one of the longest ovations he had heard. A community project like the church would certainly receive such ululation during his knighthood.

As the event drew near, the church youth organised themselves to clean up the church and school premises. Some went to get the materials for the canopy including forked sticks, bamboos and ropes. The girls particularly did a lot of weeding. 'Emevo, what's happening?' asked Anna, the assistant youth leader. Emevo's plot was still covered with the weeds she was meant to clear. Emevo simply pointed at her midriff, indicating a stomach upset.

'Stop malingering, my friend,' Mercy teased. 'You have been talking and playing all the while, haven't you?'

'Who knows if a goal has been scored?' Adanma winked, smiling.

'What did you just say?' Emevo asked, springing up in a fit of rage. The smile on Adanma's face froze. 'If you think you're funny, it's no fun to me. Let this be the first and last time you say that to me!' she cried, her finger wagging in Adanma's face. Any suggestion of pregnancy had to be stoutly repelled as it was capable of casting doubt on a young girl's chastity. No maiden took such a thing lightly, lest tongues began to wag.

'What is the matter? Is it not people that get pregnant?' Adanma asked, trying to make light of her remark and defuse the tension. She was surprised at how Emevo took the joke.

'I've not been sleeping around with men, if that is what you do!' Emevo was vehement. 'I can't put up with such jokes.' The assistant leader, Anna, intervened and apologised to her, assuring her it was truly meant as a joke. 'It is a costly joke, isn't it?' she asked, simmering down. Nwakego and Mercy lent their voices to bring the situation under control.

Work continued peacefully with the usual banter until Ajuzie sighted Chinedu from a distance. 'Very good,' he muttered. 'I need to teach this boy a lesson.' Okwudiri challenged him if he was not part of the mission work but he promised to join them as soon as he finished running an errand. He did not notice Ajuzie in good time before he got hold of him. He demanded to know why he was holding him. 'An antelope that escapes on *afo* day forgets that another *afo* day is a hunting date,' Ajuzie said, tightening his grip. 'Who did you abuse the other day?'

'Won't you leave that boy alone?' David challenged. 'Is he your age mate?'

'Leave me alone ooo! *Hiii, hiii,* who is not hearing me warn you,' Chinedu pulled his own ear, a gesture conveying a warning.

As Ajuzie raised his hand to slap him, Chinedu head-butted him. Ajuzie recoiled, clutching his jaw in pain. 'I'm dead ooo! My teeth ooo!' Chinedu fled before Ajuzie could catch him. 'Are you not coming to this mission work today? Let my hands get hold of you, I. . .'

'Come back Ajuzie, that little boy has beaten you,' Amalambu derided.

It attracted the attention of Onyinye, the youth leader. 'What is all that about?' he frowned, asking them to call off the jibes. The task was completed a little after noon. They marched to the houses of the absentees to demand fines. The first defaulter was down with high fever.

'Nnaoma come and pay them ooo,' screamed the mother of the second defaulter. 'Come out from your hiding, Sampson, the man of valour! It's time to show your might.' She offered them his box of clothes. Bartholomew asked why he did not attend. 'I neither sent him to the river to fetch water nor to the bush for firewood. It is better he explains himself. I can't cover up for his bad behaviour.'

Onyinye consulted some members before he spoke. 'We know what to do to him. Tell him to wait for us. We shall visit him again.' The crowd turned to Chinedu's house. He refused to open the door however loud they knocked. The voice of his mother who came back from farm did not move him to open the door. 'What type of child do I have in this boy?' Ochiabuto lamented.

'You attend church but won't participate in mission work, you!' David cried through the door.

'I will not attend that church again. I'm no longer a member of that church from today,' Chinedu's voice retorted.

'Yet you call yourself "Chinedu"?' Amalambu jeered.

'Don't call me Chinedu anymore. Henceforth my name is Ekwensunedu. Do you hear me? I say, call me Ekwensunedu. Let me see anybody who will call me Chinedu again,' he threatened. They banged on the door again. But a sharp metallic bang on a stone warned them that he was armed with machete. 'Blood will flow if anyone takes me on this afternoon!'

A number of them took to their heels. 'Chinedu will attack anyone who forces that door open,' Nwakego warned, keeping her distance.

'Is it that easy? If he kills anybody, will he live to tell the tale?' Ajuzie countered, dismissing it as empty threat.

'It seems you have forgotten what he did to you this morning,' Nkechi reminded him.

'If he is Sampson the valiant, why didn't he wait?' he retorted. 'He's simply pretending to be deranged. He has not met anyone who is acutely mad.'

'We know how to handle him,' Onyinye promised as a face-saving measure before leading the other youth members out.

*   *   *

With a machete and a disused wrapper for a head pad, Nwakego joined her friends to make another trip to the forest to fetch firewood for the Christmas celebrations. The old rumpled gown she wore was somewhat tight, unintentionally accentuating her curves except at the waist where it was flared and bouncy. She carried her slightly fleshy body with admirable poise, her waistline moving rhythmically with jaunty gait. A scarf covered her cornrow braid to keep debris from her hair. Stepping off the path, she stopped to cut a palm frond bud, which she needed to pleat into a strong twine for tying her firewood. 'The concert this year promises to be lots of fun,' said Serechi in a happy mood.

'Nwakego, you always start off sounding nervous,' Ngaleze pointed out.

'With all those eyes staring at me, what do you expect?' Nwakego admitted.

'It can be unsettling,' Adanma agreed with her. 'Ebereonu, did you choose Ovim Girls' High School?'

'My father said it has to be Adanma Girls, Afougiri,' Ebereonu answered.

'When is the common entrance examination?' Nwakego asked.

'It's still far away. Isn't it in March?' Emevo asked. 'But what is the need for all the hard study when we are meant to end up in the kitchen.' They were quite familiar with the word 'WEEK' when used as an acronym. It had been drummed into them that 'Women's Education Ends in Kitchen'.

'It's no longer like that in this modern world,' Adanma argued. 'Didn't you hear about the woman who piloted an aircraft? What a man can do a woman can do better.'

However, a number of the girls had accepted they would not be going beyond primary school. 'My father said he does not have the money to send a woman to college,' Udodirim stated, her tone unquestioning. She had come to terms with the priority given to the male child. 'I will be learning sewing at Nduaka's place. It is good for a woman to acquire a skill to complement her husband's earnings.' A seamstress, Nduaka was quite popular in the village. She made the school uniforms for most of the female pupils in the village and was even busier from October when many of them started to plan for Christmas by asking her to make dresses for the festive season. Sewing school uniforms was another busy and hectic time. She was one of the few skilled women in the village that earned an income and did not depend on her husband to provide everything.

'If I have my way, I will only accept marriage proposal from a suitor that lives in the township. I'm not ready for all the drudgery of working in the farm from morning till night each day,' Nwakego declared.

'You spoke my mind,' nodded Ngaleze. 'Marry a man because his family owns large tracts of farmland, innumerable palm trees, and raffia palms where I have to work and work until I age and ache or drop dead?' She shook her head. 'Count me out. That is not for me.' There was still a tradition of a young bride having to prove her strength. She had to impress everyone with the amount of work she could do and the level of inconvenience she was prepared to put up with in order to impress putative in-laws.

Their attention was caught by a song borne on the crest of the waves echoing unsteadily in the distance. The voice rose and fell with each gust of fresh air. The sound modulation got steadier and the lyrics became clearer as the girls went deeper into the forest and got closer to the audio range.

> *'I have decided to follow Jesus*
> *I have decided to follow Jesus Christ*
> *I have decided to follow Jesus*
> *No going back! No going back!*
>
> *The world refuse me*
> *Yet will I follow*
> *The world refuse me*
> *Yet will I follow*
> *No going back! No going back!'*

'A revival crusade is probably going on in Ofeimo,' Adanma guessed.

Nwakego was happy picking up the lyrics. 'The song sounds so nice. I simply love it.'

'They need it,' Ebereonu did not mince words. 'I hope it will make their people repent and turn away from their evil ways.'

The story of a man from Ofeimo who died as a cultist was still circulating fast. People believed he was being punished in the hereafter for all his atrocities on earth. Sapling of iroko tree was seen growing on his grave. A concerned family member, noticing the first sprout, uprooted it before another two came up. Five saplings were on the grave before a relative of the deceased claimed he saw their dead kinsman pleading with the person uprooting them to stop. Each time the saplings were uprooted, one more tree was added to the number of trees he had to cut with a razor blade. The dream caused no little stir in Ofeimo and beyond. 'Who knows if that's the fate awaiting Romanus,' Ngaleze wondered aloud.

'Isn't it,' Adanma was quick to agree with her. 'People are told to take it easy with the pursuit of earthly wealth but they won't listen.'

'What shall a man give in exchange for his soul; is it not what the Bible said?' Nwakego asked, alluding to Romanus' bad eye, which caused him to wear shades. As a successful produce merchant that bought cocoa seeds and palm kernel, many believed that Romanus was a member of secret society. 'As I heard, the Ofeimo man was always wearing a hat because a part of his head was rotten. Those who went close to him said he smelled like a corpse while he was alive.'

'Those stories are not worth telling,' Ebereonu said as they got busy.

Once in the forest, the thumping sound of machetes chopping dried woods from branches became the dominant sound of activity in the forest. Each girl hewed the firewood with the best of her ability. Ordinarily, girls did not work with very sharp machetes due to fear of injuring themselves. They were forced to strike the woods severally to sever each stick. Ngaleze cried out after working for more than two hours. The edge of the wood she cleaved fell on the bridge of her left foot which left her with a bleeding cut. 'Oooooo!' Ngaleze cried, gritting her teeth. 'What do I call this?'

'What happened?' asked Nwakego who got to her first.

'After cutting, I tried to detangle it from other branches but the sharp edge fell straight on my leg,' she said.

'What is it,' Emevo asked as she came around.

'She has a cut,' Nwakego answered, plucking some siam weed from a nearby shrub. She rubbed her palms speedily, squashing the leaves into pulp.

With her hand hovering over the wound, she squeezed the leaves to extract the juice. Ngaleze winced, her eyes tightly shut as she tried putting up with the pain. 'That would stop the bleeding for now.'

'Put the leaves on it,' Adanma suggested, tearing out a piece of her head pad to tie and keep the leaves in place. 'It will help to keep infection away.'

'*Chai*, Ngaleze, the enemy has tempted you,' Emevo said. 'It appears they don't want you to enjoy this Christmas.'

'Can you imagine? Whatever it is, I know that the devil is a liar. I have already celebrated this Christmas,' Ngaleze declared. 'Nothing will stop it.'

'This is not a time to nurse injury,' Udodirim said. At that time of the year, they did all they could to avoid such injuries which could affect their free movement.

'It doesn't appear deep,' Ebereonu said. 'Once it is massaged with hot water, that will keep infection away.'

'If you were still in Chief Ogbudu's house, this will not be happening,' Nkechi pointed out. Ngaleze's mother was friendly with Chief Ogbudu's wife, Uzoma. When her mother learnt that Uzoma needed a young girl to help her run errands, she volunteered to send Ngaleze. Barely a year after, Ngaleze returned back to her parents' house complaining that she was overworked and treated like a slave. Chief Ogbudu's house was one of the few houses where girls did not have to go to the forest to fetch firewood. Most of the time, when he was coming back from the town, his car boot was filled with cleaved woods. In addition, there was a standing kerosene stove which his wife often used when she cooked in the kitchen. A number of the girls had envied her for the rare privilege to live with the rich and mighty. They were surprised to learn of her dissatisfaction.

'It doesn't matter. I'm happier in my parents' house where I feel at home,' Ngaleze replied.

Late in the afternoon when they finished, everyone had put together two big faggots. Each of them carried a bundle home but left it within the vicinity of their house. In building a reserve of firewood for each family, three or four of such bundles were left leaning against a tree within the neighbourhood. Stones were placed on them to ward off anyone who might be tempted to remove any part thereof without permission. Nobody cherished the idea of wandering off into the bush in search of firewood at the thick of Christmas and New Year celebrations.

At home, Kperechi had successfully given their mud wall a facelift. Most of the walls in the village were smoothened and painted with *shimmanu*, in preparation for Christmas. If a wall was already smooth and painted, another coat of oil was applied to make it glow anew. For aesthetics, chalk and charcoal dissolved in water were used to draw different designs on the walls.

The following day was the Ekeikpa market day. It was the last opportunity to trade in a big market before Christmas Day. The normal village markets only boasted of ordinary slippers or plastic shoes and *okrika*, the second-hand clothes discarded by city dwellers. At Christmas, many were able to close their eyes to the cost and buy new, good-quality items of clothing and footwear.

On their way to the market that morning, Emevo and Ngaleze lent a hand to help Nwakego set her load of cassava down. She became free to help them set their loads down. Kperechi and other women met them at the bank of the river, just as the canoe man anchored his boat. He took on only twelve passengers before he rowed away slowly and carefully. Cassavas, bananas, palm kernels, and a goat were among the other things in the canoe. The earlier they got to the market, the better price they might fetch. Reaching the far side of the river, they paid the boatman and resumed their long walk.

'Mama, I thought we're getting a bus after crossing the river?' Ijuolachi asked, frustration creeping into her voice as they mustered energy to walk up the slope that characterised the bank of the river.

'We still have a way to go before we get to where they are parked,' Kperechi told her.

'It's such a distance,' Ijuolachi complained, labouring to keep pace with them.

'You want to go to Ekeikpa, isn't it?' Nwakego taunted, quickening her stride. 'You're lucky we had a rest at the riverbank.'

'I would have thrown it down,' Ijuolachi replied. 'You know what I can do.'

'Your mouth sounds like *ugbakala*, the oil bean,' Emevo said, overtaking her. After climbing a fairly steep hill, they caught sight of buses and open-backed pickup trucks popularly called *azuanuka*.

'At last we are there!' There was relief and triumph in Ijuolachi's voice. Taking a bus or truck was the pinnacle of excitement for any child who went with their parents to Ekeikpa. Ijuolachi's friends had regaled her with stories of their own ride. She had eagerly looked forward to it when a vehicle would transport her to a destination without her exerting her energy of walking the distance. The fairy tale experience was about to happen! They joined the queue for the *azuanuka* as their loads fitted better in a pickup than in a bus. The morning sun shone brightly with the gusty breeze drying their sweat.

Many buyers invaded Ekeikpa that morning. Some hung about on the paths leading to the market, keeping an eye out for arriving sellers who had what they wanted. The market was nearly in full swing when they arrived. Those who came with plantain and bananas had a good day with high demand driving up the price. But the steady stream of basins and long baskets filled with cassava flooded the market with cassava resulting in a glut. Buyers were offering ridiculously low prices, far lower than the offer sellers got earlier in the morning. The single head of banana which Ijuolachi brought to the market fetched more money than all the cassava that Kperechi and Nwakego brought to the market. They were forced to sell it all the same. They could not entertain the thought of carrying it back.

'*Leeee* woman!' a voice called.

'Someone is calling you!' A different woman drew Kperechi's attention.

Kperechi turned. 'Oh, Ochiabuto, it's you. How is it?'

'Prices are shooting through the roof,' Ochiabuto said. 'Imagine, Abakaliki rice that sold twelve cups for ten shillings is eleven cups today.'

'What about the tomatoes and onions?' Kperechi nodded. 'Their prices are scary.'

'How much did you pay for this rooster?' asked Ochiabuto, weighing the bird in her hand.

'Just over a pound,' Kperechi answered.

'It's a good bargain. It's quite heavy.'

'Let's hope it's not just feathers,' smiled Kperechi, as they parted company.

When they passed the shed of a confectioner selling *agidi* and *moi-moi*, she acceded to Ijuolachi's request to stop. They sat on one of the improvised benches vacated by those who had just eaten and she ordered two wraps of *agidi* and *moi-moi*.

18.

Igboajuchi's return made sense of all their festive preparations. Eating and drinking was not the only thing about Christmas. It was also a time for the villagers to behold the faces that were away from them for a long time. Returnees renewed ties with friends and families, breathed in the pure fresh air in the village and wordlessly declared allegiance to the land of their birth, the place where their umbilical cords were buried. It brought unspeakable joy to the Christmas season and a feverish ecstasy, unlike any other time of the year.

In Mboha and other villages, the city dwellers strutted and paraded themselves. They brought with them treasures of the city, giving the village folks a taste of modernity and civilisation—things they craved for with all their hearts and souls.

'*Alahaji ba Mecca!*' Ahamba called as he entered the compound. The place was rocking with music, the volume tuned up very high. Three of his friends were already there, talking, sharing experiences of their travel and catching up with one another, an especial pleasure for those living in different cities.

'*Walahi talahi Mallam Nagudu. . .*' Igboajuchi replied in Hausa, mesmerising the un-travelled onlookers before turning down the volume of the new Sanyo GhettoBlaster he brought home. 'Long live the Federal Republic of Nigeria. . .'

'*Eeeee eeh Nigeria in Africa!*' they chorused boisterously.

'Go. . .go. . .go Slow 1980!' Jerry chanted a slogan from the album, brimming with joy.

'*Lem lee motorcycle!*' Eric added, repeating the cliché that was in vogue. 'Who forbids good things?'

'Tell me, who?' Ahamba asked, sitting beside Jerry and James on a bench in the open compound. *Onwere onye ihe oma so nso* – is there anyone who forbids good things? It was one of the many catchphrases in the music of Oriental Brothers International Band. There was something different about their music which made it widely acceptable. For a people who had just come out of a war that ravaged them physically, emotionally and otherwise, their music was a breath of fresh air. Torn between gratitude to God for surviving the war and grieving the loss of loved ones, their conducts and the words of their mouths were considerably pensive and sober, reflecting their mood. Most of their songs were soft and gentle ballads and dirges probing into different issues of life including the nature of their existence. This sombre mood made the air thick with gloom and despondence.

The music of Oriental Brothers succeeded in bringing a change. It was out to bring back the joy of living which the war stole from them. Life lessons abstracted from happenings around them and other realities of life were condensed into one liner catchphrases which people easily related to. The band sang with gusto, making joyful music that buoyed the spirit of their people. The bell-wielding Sir Warrior, their lead vocalist, was the embodiment of this joyful renaissance. The energy with which he sang was infectious, his bell jangling at intervals to heighten euphoria. The fingers of Kabaaka, the guitar virtuoso, went on the overdrive, strumming with uncommon dexterity to awaken dormant feelings, however deeply buried. Local acoustic instruments worked together with others to create a fusion of sound and rhythm from the array of local and foreign musical instruments. It was no surprise that feet moved nimbly, waists wriggled provocatively with bodies swaying, sweating, dancing to the delightful performance of these music makers. 'Your train must have arrived quite early this morning,' Ahamba continued.

Igboajuchi told them how the engine of their train was unhitched at Enugu for repairs. As a result, they spent more than two hours waiting for its return. Ubadire smiled on hearing this. It was exactly what happened to them while they were returning two days earlier. 'The engine might be in perfect condition. The station master and his cohorts deliberately delayed trains to allow their wives and hangers-on sell all their food to the passengers.'

'Youuuu . . . you . . . don't mean it?' Jerry stammered, his trademark smile fading with incredulity.

Ozurumba was equally astonished. 'How can they do that?'

'They are such a terrible lot,' Ubadire spoke. 'Some guys were on the verge of shouting "*boys oh yeah!*" before the radio man announced the return of our engine. . .'

'You trust our boys,' said Ahamba, remembering the wild revolt that greeted such flagrant abuse of office in the past. Public officers dreaded such rabblerousing calls which led to wanton destruction of properties. They knew that members of the public who were often taken for granted could express their frustration with unpleasant consequences. Igboajuchi wished they had the slightest inkling of what was happening. Surely, they would have gone after the station master to teach him a lesson.

'Certainly, the station manager would have lost his job,' Ozurumba said. 'How can they do such a thing?'

'It's so terrible. Many Ovim passengers disembarked at the station and opted to complete their journey by road,' Ahamba told them.

'That must be additional expenses,' James pointed out. 'The day the engine would be truly faulty nobody will believe them.'

'Since the white men left this country, nothing has been the same again,' Kperechi rued. Although she was busy cooking, she heard enough of the conversation. She was surprised Igboajuchi could bare his body in the harmattan cold after removing the dirty top he wore for three days, the duration of the train journey. They made light of her concern.

'Do you call this cold?' asked Ahamba. 'You have lived in the north—you don't have to be told when you see the full rigours of harmattan.'

'*Olooo m*, my husband's children,' was all Kperechi could say, her face radiant. 'I'm not surprised. Full-blooded young men with good health and vitality cannot be prone to cold like those of us in the village.'

'*Daa* Kperechi, JMJ is taking good care of you,' Ubadire complimented, his face broadening with a smile. 'He must have dipped deep into his pocket to pay for this intricate hairdo.'

'You see how I spend my money?' Ozurumba was quick to take the credit, a mischievous smile playing across his face. 'Would my kinsmen blame me for spending it so well?'

'Ah papa, you are saying you paid for mama's hairdo?' Nwakego protested. The unexpected objection left them rocking with laughter. 'Don't mind my father ooo. He knew nothing about it.'

'What type of a child are you?' Ozurumba feigned anger before the frown began to thaw with a grin.

'If *Dee* did not pay for it, I will,' Ubadire said, dipping his hand into his pocket. He brought out one naira note. Ozurumba stretched out his hand to collect it but Nwakego was quick enough. She claimed the prize with a triumphant dance and took it to her mother.

Still in a convivial mood, Nwakego set a tray before them with teacups and a big loaf of bread. They poured hot chocolate from the plastic jug and dipped chunks of bread into the cups for a delicious snack. Ozurumba munched with delight. 'This is what I call bread, not that yeast-bloated chaff we buy as *Sonye's Family Buttered Bread*.'

Kperechi cleared her throat suggestively, subtly reproving him. 'I know it: the old wife is relegated or completely discarded once the new one arrives.' But she knew they would go back to the old loaves when the more delicious Onitsha and Enugu loaves were finished. She had made a big effort to impress the city savvy young men who had gathered in her house to share a breakfast with them. Happily, her house could boast of some imported porcelain and other chinaware.

'Your husband is not wrong, you know,' Leriakawa supported Ozurumba, taking a sip from the plastic cup in her hand before wrapping up the chunk of bread in a piece of nylon to take away with her. 'In my opinion, I prefer *Alaoma Special Bread*. Anyway, so none of you saw Emma?'

'Emma will come back,' Igboajuchi reassured her. 'Agbisi saw him at the Kaduna railway station looking for space. Everywhere was rowdy, so he did not hear Agbisi's call.'

'Who is Agbisi?' Leriakawa asked, surprised that a human being could share a name with the stinging black ant.

It was difficult to come home at that time of the year. A number of the returnees incurred the double expense of travelling from Kaduna to Kano where they could secure a seat at the terminus. Every seat was occupied in Kano, and by the time they left Zaria, there was little or no standing room; the aisles were crammed with passengers and goods. The extra paid by first class passengers turned out to be a complete waste. Travellers shoved and pushed their way into any available space in every carriage. Most of the young returnees wanted to be part of the carol singing youths moving from one household to another on Christmas Eve. 'You need to see how we packed ourselves like sardines; some even rode on top of the carriage or hung by the door railings, not minding the risks. That is how much everyone wanted to be home for Christmas,' Eric told her.

Leriakawa consoled herself. 'Oh well, I will expect Emma at some point then. There's life after Christmas.'

'That's true, my fellow woman,' Kperechi concurred.

Ijuolachi rushed into the compound, excited. 'Nwokocha is here with his water tanker,' she announced cheerily, picking up buckets and the big plastic containers, hurrying off to get a good position in what promised to be a long queue. Nwakego ran to join her with two big enamel basins. The tanker's arrival would spare them several trips to the stream.

'Please be very careful!' Kperechi called. 'Make sure you don't drop those!' The basins had never been chipped, and numbered among Kperechi's most treasured possessions.

*   *   *

Igboajuchi did not disappoint the expectations of Ozurumba's household. Each of his siblings got Christmas clothes and his mother, Intorica George, the wrapper in vogue. Nwakego's shoes were not the usual high heels but platforms, the latest fad of their time. Her dress was a mini that stopped very much above the knees with embossed side pleating, and a short slit on either side. A string dangled from each side of the slit as laces, which the wearer could tie to keep her steps short. To cap it off, he had given her an afro wig which will make her look like Simbi Jones, the dashing beauty on the cover page of one of the magazines he brought home. Nwakego tried them on, beaming and blushing, parading around with an unaccustomed swagger, her tight-fitting garment accentuating her curves.

'It is too revealing,' Kperechi objected, her brow furrowed uneasily and her arms folded across her chest while making a mental assessment of the dress. She was quite happy at how it had fittingly enhanced Nwakego's statistics but vacillated between admiration and concern that the outfit might be adjudged immoral. She could not help imagining how men's roving eyes would ogle at Nwakego while she strutted about in the village. By such indiscretion she would be inviting unholy schemes against herself. 'Can't you see? It exposes a lot of your flesh and. . .'

'Village people, what do you know?' Igboajuchi dismissed her objection. 'This is what they wear in the city where light shines from the rooftops!'

'*Ooololorom*, city dwellers, we are still in darkness here in the village,' she conceded. 'Maybe, times are really changing.' She was not ready to offend him at that point but she was certain there was no way she would allow Nwakego to wear it and go beyond the confines of their compound.

Igboajuchi had also brought a lot of foodstuff: one bag of rice and another bag containing beans, onions, and beverages. Kperechi scooped out a big bowl of the rice for Nwugo, together with some onions. She sneaked some to Egobeke and Ashivuka, making sure Ozurumba, unpredictable on such matters, did not know about it. She was not ready to put up with his tongue-lashing.

After a long siesta, Igboajuchi had his lunch and dressed up. His *bongo* pants, tight at the waist and thigh but widely flared from the knee, matched the colour of his top, which was made of a stretchy material that hugged his flat stomach and broad shoulders. His Afro hair was rich in volume and length. His platform shoes, adding to his height, made him look like an American musician pictured on a record sleeve. He stepped out to join Agbisi and Ahamba dressed in safari clothing with the hats to match. They left for the traditional marriage ceremony in Abadaba.

Later in the night, the village gathered in the school hall to witness the Christmas Eve concert. Thereafter, the church youth were ready to go round Mboha singing Christmas carols. Most of the children wanted to go with them. 'Leave them to enjoy themselves a little,' Nkechi pleaded with Amalambu who was trying to disperse them.

'Don't forget what they did last year, sleeping at every compound we went to,' David reminded her as he joined Amalambu in the effort to send the children home. It did not work as they made their way back when they noticed that Amalambu and David had given up the chase. They reached a compromise after a while. No child would follow them beyond his or her compound. 'Do you agree?'

'Yes!' came the enthusiastic response.

Bartholomew started a song with a powerful baritone. '*Umu Youth nyem olu*' he intoned. Some cleared their throats and organised themselves, ready to go. Chidinma started the next song with an enchanting voice.

> *'Maaaaama mama mama mama mama ma! Mama!*
> *Oooo ooo yah!*
> *Paaaaapa papa papa papa papa papa pa! Papa!*
> *Oooo ooo yah!*
> *Ee!*
> *Akpafurum n'ozara n'awaghari na nmehie*
> *Ugbua alotawom Chukwu nuru olum!*

Akpafurum n'ozara n'awaghari na nmehie
Ugbua alotawom Chukwu nuru olum!'

The vicarage was their first port of call. Nwakanma's wife joined them, pressing a coin to Chidinma's forehead. In return, the youth cheered and applauded her for dancing to the drumbeat. After watching their performance, the vicar gave some money to Onyinye. They thanked him again and again before singing a valedictory song to mark their departure.

Chief Ogbudu gave them ten naira. This was greeted with jubilation when the figure was announced. They visited selected homes in the neighbouring villages, and by the third cockcrow, they were five villages away. The first signs of daylight caught them in the outskirts of Mboha on their homebound journey. Their tired legs barely carried them to their various homes before they succumbed to deep, blissful sleep. But a few with croaking voices sang on gallantly, resisting fatigue. They were the veterans of Christmas carols who insisted on returning to the church with a song just as they left it with one.

'*Obu gini wetara anyi onwu n'uwa?*
Obu nmehie nke Adam
Adam lee Adam lee
Obu nmehie nke Adam

Obu gini wetara anyi oria n'uwa
Obu nmehie nke Adam
Adam lee Adam lee
Obu nmehie nke Adam.'

*   *   *

The cassette deck which Igboajuchi brought home was different from Ozurumba's transistor radio. It was possible to listen to good music from it without the interference of adverts or boring chatter. They listened to several tracks from Voice of the Cross and their songs were quite uplifting like *Nri Nkpurobi* on a Sunday morning. It challenged them to show commitment to the faith they professed. Indeed, they had heard a number of the tracks over the radio but listening to a number of them at a stretch was a welcome change.

Ikoli Harcourt-Whyte's choral anthems and commentaries were the most astonishing of his collections. They were compelling arguments presented in sobering songs. A number of his commentaries were not only heart-wrenching but took his listeners through different difficult life experiences.

Picturing himself at a warfront, he was quick to declare that he did not hate his enemies but hated their actions and conducts. Constrained to fight a war he would rather not, he repeated a native aphorism that a snake does not strike a child in the presence of the mother. He could not idly stand by to watch the enemies take away the people he had treasured all his life. Addressing the concerns of his loved ones, he confirmed he had taken to the forest of his own accord and volition to become a hunter that hunted his fellow human beings!

He likened the sustained sound of gunfire to the continuous strumming of a stringed instrument, the unenviable reality he was part of. After each session, he lifted his head to look only to find dead bodies littered around him. A number of the bodies were his friends who had shared breakfast with him earlier in the day. One day it would be his turn. He would no longer have the opportunity to kiss the beautiful damsel he had desired to marry.

'*Chai*, things really happened during the war,' Kperechi whimpered melancholically.

'*Mhhh*, the stories of the war, can it ever be completely told?' Ozurumba reflected, adjusting his position to relax better. For a people who had survived a bitter war, his commentaries were quite evocative and captured their painful experiences and emotions. Thoughtfully, he delved into issues that barely crossed the mind of many soldiers. 'Who has the time to think of a beautiful damsel at the warfront?' he critiqued, smiling and becoming more interested in the discourse. 'All you want is how you can escape with your life, isn't it? Okwudiri, please turn the cassette,' he instructed when one of the sides reeled to an end.

Harcourt-Whyte was heartbroken by the political debacles and bloodletting ravaging the nascent African nations. The senseless killing of Patrice Lumumba, a leader that stood up against imperialism, grieved him. He could not understand the failure of Africans to rally behind Kwame Nkrumah, a true hero of Pan Africanism.

While bemoaning the fate that befell Africa, he condemned in no uncertain terms the hatred behind the fratricidal wars decimating African population. Completely gutted and disenchanted, he announced his intention to reincarnate as stone in his next life, or if he must return as a living being, he would come back as a vulture, the only animal that was not hunted and was free to perch on the rooftops of friends and foes alike.

'*Eleooo*, this man is really running his mouth!' Kperechi exclaimed in utter wonderment that night, her mind unable to come to terms with the thought of reincarnating as carrion-eating vulture, a bird many considered loathsome.

'How did he get to dwell on things few give scant thought to?' Nwugo also mused. 'Certainly, there are deep thinkers.'

'He lived most of his life in the Uzoakoli leper colony,' Igboajuchi told them, interrupting their rapturous attention to the deep vocals of the all-male back up, the only accompaniment to his flawless rendition. 'He died from injuries he sustained when he fell from a moving car.' It drew painful gasps from his listeners who never imagined that a leper could be such a great songwriter.

'That must be where Mary Slessor cared for lepers until she became a leper herself?' Nkechi thought aloud, remembering the Scottish missionary.

'Who was she?' asked Nwugo.

'Mary Slessor was the missionary to the Calabar people who stopped the killing of twins and cared for lepers,' answered Nwakego.

'Was she a leper?' Igboajuchi asked. He was full of doubt as he never heard it. Recalling a story about her culled from a foreign magazine, he narrated what she meant to the Ekenge people. 'Help, Ma, help!' was a call she never ignored, regardless of any danger to her life. She responded to such distress call regardless the distance and time of the day.

'I salute the dedication of those missionaries,' Kperechi declared thoughtfully.

'There's no gainsaying that,' Ozurumba agreed. 'I've never seen a people so determined. Death does not deter them.'

The following day was Nkwo Mboha, their special Christmas day. Virtually every home in Mboha had visitors that came to celebrate it with them. Igboajuchi took his visitors through the pack of snapshots in his Kodak photo album. There was a picture of him and a friend wearing safari gear and posing for a snapshot with a huge stretch of water in the background. 'What a big lake,' Joy commented.

'It's a dam,' Igboajuchi corrected her. 'It supplies water to everyone in Zaria.'

'*Alahaji ba Mecca!*' Ahamba called from a distance. Igboajuchi answered him, asking him and Emma, who had finally arrived, to come over.

'This is the Kaduna show, isn't it?' Agbisi asked, referring to another photograph.

'It was a terrific show,' Igboajuchi asserted with a tinge of pride. Emma and Ahamba also had a lot to say about Sir Warrior, Kabaaka, Dansatch, Alaribe who were members of the Oriental Brothers International Band.

'*Kimmon!*' James exclaimed, beaming, snapping his fingers as he looked at the picture. 'You were really having the time of your life.'

'I missed it,' Agbisi sighed. 'That is the day we rushed Goddy's wife to hospital.'

'Since I was born I've not seen such a magnificent show,' Emma swore.

'It was the talk of the town for a long time,' Ahamba boasted.

Chikwendu was gazing at another photo with incredulity, grinning widely, imagining how electrifying the atmosphere must have been. 'Sir Warrior himself!' he gasped. Here were his own village men hobnobbing with the musician, posing for a snapshot! 'I tell you, nothing compares to city life,' he declared happily. Their attention was distracted by a number of young girls milling around the entrance door, each struggling to enter first.

'Careful!' Nwakego called, going over to usher them in. Moving with dainty steps, they formed a circle around Ijuolachi, their lead singer, who deftly introduced a soulful number: '*Dim le abum oyoyo. . .*' She sang several questions to which the troupe members chorused an answer. Changing their steps, they danced vigorously to her whistles, drawing loud applause from the audience. In appreciation, they were rewarded with coins of various denominations before Igboajuchi gave them a fifty-kobo note. It brought them much joy. In addition, he took a group snapshot with his Polaroid camera and gave them the print.

Like many other returnees, Igboajuchi received an invitation to the fundraising scheduled to be held on their special Christmas day. Before they left for the venue, they sat down to a special sumptuous meal which Kperechi prepared. She was pleased to see how well they ate. 'My husband's children, you have really gladdened my heart.'

'You washed your hands thoroughly to prepare this food,' Agbisi complimented her.

'That is why today is our Christmas,' she responded, thanking those that gave her various sums as Christmas gifts.

'I feel good, *tararara rararam!*' Igboajuchi sang, mimicking James Brown.

'We have the energy to participate well in this merriment,' Agbisi said.

Igboajuchi towelled his perspiring body before going inside to dress up. He came out wearing *babariga*, the overflowing garment that was popular with the northerners, and *fula*, the tall, brimless hand-made hat. It was a thing of pride to dress like the president, Alhaji Shehu Shagari even if they had no Concord, the long Mercedes-Benz car, to go with it.

'*Alahaji ba Mecca!*' Ahamba hailed him.

'*Lem lee motorcycle,*' Igboajuchi returned the salutation. 'Tell me, who says no to good thing?'

'Who?' Emma asked, joining them to pose for a snapshot. 'Let's go and tell them that the owners of the village have arrived.'

The master of ceremonies announced their arrival, saluting each of them before they were ushered to their seats. The microphone was handed over to the master of ceremony after the chairman's opening remarks. Chief Ogbudu used his connections to get several dignitaries to the occasion. In his ceremonial dress, Chief Igbokwe looked every inch distinguished and rich. The car he came in was sparkling clean. Sheer ecstasy greeted his donation of five hundred naira. He gave a cash sum of two hundred naira, promising to forward the balance.

Other important guests who needed to leave early made their donations before the master of ceremonies invited most of the returnees to the microphone to publicly announce their own donations. The level of clapping depended on the amount announced.

As the Odumodu group took the centre stage, Ojigwe was at his best, singing the praises of donors. His voice grew stronger as he saw Igboajuchi and his friends join the other dancers. Even his withered left leg, tucked away under his burly frame, seemed perfect for the occasion. His palms and fingers, nimbly stroking the drum, raised the tempo of the beat, sustaining it for a while before breaking off suddenly. Effortlessly he made music with the names of selected individuals, flavouring it all with a smattering of his pidgin English. Picking out Ubadire and his brother Nathaniel, he sang their praises: 'Worthy sons of Iweha, are you hearing my voice?'

'*Lem lee motorcycle!*' Nathaniel's voice rose above others.

'Igboajuchi, alias *Alahaji ba Mecca*, I greet you. . .' Ojigwe's voice yodelled.

'*Ebe ooo! Ebe ooo!* Let the music play on!' Igboajuchi responded enthusiastically, joining others to shower him with money in appreciation. Ojigwe's voice rose in sustained tempo as he continued to sing song after song, all full of wise sayings.

BOOK TWO

THE RULE OF MONEY:
A PAINFUL HARVEST

19.

Okwudiri took long brisk strides, leaping and hopping, hurrying to catch a bus to Main Market. It was almost rush hour when most of the buses, filled with passengers, would zoom past commuters at the bus stop. The fourth bus he flagged down stopped. The conductor collapsed the seat in the middle to let him sit in the back with other passengers. He pushed a finger across his forehead, sweeping aside his perspiration before opening the side window to get some fresh air.

Azuka joined him to unlock the shop, the heavy padlocks clattering against the bars and reinforced burglar-proof grills. While Okwudiri did the stocktaking with Obiora, Arinze and Azuka cleaned the shelves and dusted the entire shop. 'Come, what are you fellows doing? Won't you hurry up and clean our frontage?' Obiora called to other trainees raking out the papers, nylon, and other muck from the gutter. The rubbish impeded the free flow of water, and the resulting stagnant pool was a breeding ground for mosquitoes. OMATA—the umbrella body of the various associations trading in Onitsha market—had set aside Thursday for the weekly sanitation.

At ten o'clock that morning, the door was thrown open and the shop was ready to do business. Okwudiri attended to one of the customers: '*Emzor* Paracetamol, Procaine Penicillin, Butazolle, Feldene, Fair & White, Egovin. . .' he recited, listing and punching the Casio calculator in front of him, adding up the prices. 'Fourteen thousand, eight hundred and fifty naira,' he announced, stacking them in a box with efficient haste, mindful of other waiting customers. Picking up each bundle, he rapidly flipped each currency note in-between his thumb and forefinger like a human machine, spitting on his fingers at intervals to moisten them and enhance grip of the notes. Running each bundle through the mercury light, he detected a counterfeit fifty naira note which the customer replaced without complaint. 'Where's the invoice book?' he asked, opening the third drawer. Arinze lifted it down from the shelf.

The droning ring of the analogue phone rose above the noise. Obiora picked up the receiver. 'Elloo, elloo . . . No, ehm, hold on. . .' He had noticed Okwudiri signalling that Silvanus had arrived. The deep sound of the Mercedes-Benz 230E door slamming to a close was too familiar to be mistaken. 'Elloo, hold on for him.'

'Hallo!' Silvanus spoke into the receiver. 'Yes, I am Silvanus Oragwusi, the chairman, MD, and CEO of Able-God Chemist Ltd. And who are you? Polycarp? Where are you calling from? Oh, Kano? . . . Yes, I just came back from Europe. My container is still on the high seas . . . Yes, your number, 064-368-55 . . . Yes, when it comes in, I will let you know . . . Bye-bye. . .' He counted the numbers and realised the digits were not complete. Okwudiri approached him.

'*Oga*, this customer here is short of money.' Okwudiri had found two counterfeit notes.

Silvanus stepped forward to address the situation. 'I suggest you come back with the right amount,' he said, looking at the customer with calm composure, his penetrating eyes trying to discern the type of character he was dealing with. He needed to make up his mind on how to deal with the situation. 'As you can see, it is not our policy to sell on. . .' He did not complete the sentence. He expected the customer to follow his gaze and his pouting lips pointing to the framed cursive writing hanging conspicuously behind the payment counter declaring that: MR CREDIT IS DEAD AND BURIED. The pencil artist had illustrated it with the drawing of a merchant whose business was in apparent ruins as a result of giving credit facilities. The shelves were practically empty, his elbows resting on the counter while his hands supported his chin. The message of the picture was quite clear. Even the customer who must have been used to asking for credit, on seeing the ruinous end of the businessman, was crestfallen when there were no more goods to get on credit.

'I came all the way from Port Harcourt,' replied the customer calmly. 'All I have here is my fare home. I'll bring it with me the next time.'

'Has he bought from us before?' Silvanus asked Okwudiri.

'This is the second time.'

'Well, I will take your word for it. Let him have it,' Silvanus yielded reluctantly. He had seen different types of customers over the years; many made promises they never kept. As he often told his trainees, the little sums the customers wanted to walk away with were the mark-ups that sustained the business. Inevitably, he was constrained to give credit to those he was not sure would honour their word. It was part of the risks in trading.

He was on his way out when a DHL despatch rider arrived with a message for him. He picked up the army green French rotary telephone and waited for the dialling tone and as soon as it started, he punched the numbers. 'Hallo, is that Pius?. . . Silvanus from Onitsha. . . Yes, I just got the bill of lading. . . Yes, you will get it on Tuesday. . . Yes. . . Bye-bye.'

Customers continued to stream into the shop. The whirring sound of a ceiling fan, oscillating at top speed, drowned out the steady buzz from the fluorescent tube. Coal City FM supplied the music. The shelves, fully packed, displayed the drugs, cosmetics, and provisions available at wholesale price for both retailers and wholesalers alike.

The atmosphere outside was rowdy as usual—the intermittent banging from a nearby workshop, the loud music far above permissible decibel levels from a record shop, the vulcanizer's machine blasting away noisily whenever he had to inflate pneumatic tubes and tyres were all part of their business environment. There were the quieter figures like the restaurateurs, different women that got footholds on tiny spaces to roast corn, sell soft drinks, cook hot *moi-moi*, *okpa* and other snacks, the *Mallam* displaying sweets, cigarettes, *gworo*, and few other articles for sale. The flurry of vehicles with their incessant and petulant honks; the business people with their hasty strides, the cart pusher, his body glistening with sweat, laboriously pushing and balancing his load; the occasional cyclist pedalling at leisure, the hawkers offering their wares, the aimless pedestrians trudging along—all fused together into a cacophony of sights and sounds.

Tito Santana, one of the touts that brought a customer to the shop earlier, came back for his commission. '*Nw' Onye Igbo*, what is this?' he asked, his cold shifty eyes narrowing with ominous calm as he studied the money in his palm. He oozed with the acrid smell of a cigarette stubbed out just before he entered the shop. From the blackness of his lips, it was evident his system had been saturated with tobacco smoke. The crescent cleft on his left cheek and a gash above his brow were not scratches on the face of a peaceful man.

Okwudiri returned his intimidating gaze with a scowl. '*Nwoke m*, how much do you want me to give you? What do you think you can do? Get out of here before I lose my temper,' he snapped, calling his bluff. The touts did not understand civility. Threats or even actual violence commanded more respect.

The tout backed off a little, but muttered menacingly, 'All you strangers that have no respect for the home boys. . .'

'What did you say, Tito?' Obiora barked at him in unmistakable Onitsha accent.

'I was telling your man to give me a little more, but he's stubborn. . .'

'I don't ever want to hear you make such threat again in this shop. Never! You understand? Otherwise, I will make you disappear from this Onitsha. Ask around about me, Obiora,' he growled, thumping his chest for emphasis.

'But ask him to give me a little more, my guy,' the man said stubbornly, although clearly cowed. Obiora conferred with Okwudiri before adding one naira.

'Tito Santana!' Azuka hailed, calling him by the wrestler's name he adopted as his own.

'*Enu uwa ma nma*!' He repeated his favourite refrain from Celestine Ukwu's music, crossing his wrists and clenched fists in homage, a broad smile thawing his hardened face. What touts got from dealers complemented anything wheedled out of the customer after helping him navigate the market for his purchases. It was sometimes frustrating for them that they were treated as nothing more than scum, despite their facilitating role.

'*Osikapa oyoyo!* I'm here now!' shouted a food vendor, stopping her cart outside the row of shops. Her mobile restaurant was the ready answer to many *nwaboy*—the trainees—who could not afford a break time for lunch at Mama Okondo or Madam Kodo, the popular restaurants.

'I hope you're not selling leftovers today?' Arinze asked.

'How can I serve leftovers to my dear son-in-law?' asked Mama-Eliza, busy dishing out a plate of rice. The steam and aroma filled the air as she opened a pot of stew filled with assorted meat and boiled eggs. 'As you can see, it is very hot and tasty.' She added beans at his instruction and three pieces of meat.

'Is this fifty-kobo food? Give me more rice,' Arinze cajoled. 'Don't you know I have to feed well before I can take good care of your daughter?'

'If you want more, I can dish it,' Mama-Eliza answered, her tone suggesting that he must pay more money to have more food.

'Arinze, you want her to give you the whole lot?' Amaechi jibed. 'Hasn't she given you enough for two already?'

'Am I Yokozuna?' Arinze asked jokingly, trying to make the jibe sound ridiculous. He was not the Japanese sumo wrestler who could tear any type of tyre into pieces with his bare hands except Bridgestone Tyre. Such strength could only come from consuming so much food. 'Okwy loves assorted meat. So, add beef, tongue, and *kpomo*,' he told her.

Silvanus' wife, Ukamaka, had organised the day's takings to lodge in the bank by the time Silvanus returned to the shop. The sack of money was put inside a box to disguise it as goods. She was mindful of the threat of armed robbery in Onitsha which had reached a dangerous proportion. Silvanus asked Okwudiri to follow him.

Arriving at the bank, Okwudiri proceeded straight to the 'bulk cash confirmation room'. He was there for close to thirty minutes before the teller attended to him. 'How much do you have?' she asked, completing the pay-in slip.

'Three hundred and fifty thousand naira,' answered Okwudiri.

As the counting machine ran through each bundle, she bound it in wrapping paper bearing the elephant logo of First Bank. Some of the notes, damp and worn out, clung together, making the bundle fall short of the figure. After two attempts, she was forced to count them manually before wrapping them again, placing them with the other bundle of notes which would be picked up by the cash officer for safe keeping in the vault.

From the open plan office, he sighted Silvanus sitting with one of the bank staff as he returned to the banking hall. He took a seat there waiting for him. Some, having already spoken to an official, sat down patiently with their tally number, waiting for the transaction to be concluded. The bank had devised the tally numbering system as an answer to the allegation of favouritism. Among the anxious or vacant faces, he could not tell who was there to take note of any customer leaving the building with a huge amount of cash. The *Carrier* air conditioners, two horsepower each, were inadequate for the size of the banking hall. He stood up briskly, ready to go as Silvanus stepped into the banking hall.

*   *   *

Onitsha was different in many ways from what Okwudiri had imagined. The type of Igbo widely spoken was different, making his dialect noticeable. This was the reason his mates initially called him *Nw' Onye Igbo*. It was a term adopted by the riverine Igbo who needed a different identity to dissociate them from the hinterland Igbo that fought the civil war. At the time of Okwudiri, it had become a friendly insult, implying that a person like him was too trusting—a simple-minded and faithful country boy with an overdose of conscience. Such a person lacked the smartness or acumen to ensure that no money-making opportunity slipped through his fingers just because his scruples would not let him con a customer.

As usual, Nwanyi Obosi's beer parlour was packed with all kinds of patrons when Okwudiri and his friends got there that Sunday. They took unoccupied chairs from other tables over to where Obiora was sitting in the midst of other OMATA boys.

'What will you take?' asked Patricia, the waiter.

'Whose money have you been walloping that makes you this beautiful?' Okwudiri threw a compliment at her.

'*Oga* Okwy, keep that one aside,' she replied, trying to remain business-like, making sure her focus was not distracted by getting involved in any intimate private conversation. She was aware that Nwanyi Obosi must be watching with the corner of her eyes.

Okwudiri ignored her objection. 'I hope all this your beauty is radiating only for Obiora. If I see anybody around you, you know that my people know how to carry machete,' he continued moving his head in a manner that suggested he would do the same thing.

Patricia knew he was not from a community where farming men were known to carry a cutlass and used it easily in a fight. '*Ooooh oga* Okwy, tell me what you will take. Time na money ooo,' she said smiling.

'Give me *nkwobi* and small bottle of Guinness Stout,' Okwudiri told her. 'Remember, it is for special customer.' It was a request to be generous in what would be dished into the bowl he would be served.

'How much is all of that?' Obiora asked the waitress who was waiting to get paid before going to get their orders. 'I'm paying for my guys today.'

'*Oga* Obiora, it is one hundred and forty-five naira,' Patricia answered after making a mental calculation of all the orders with the aid of her fingers. She brightened up at the sight of a bundle of naira notes Obiora pulled out of his jeans pocket. 'You are really wadded. As you know *otinkpu nwere* share—a praise singer has a stake,' she added the familiar line. Obiora beckoned to her to come within whispering distance. He whispered something into her ear when she bent her head. A coy smile broke forth on her face at what was obviously an amorous advance. 'We'll talk about that later,' she answered, hurrying off to the kitchen.

'Obiora, every bit of you has been smelling money, money, money since you came back. You must have hit the jackpot on this last business trip.'

'*Nna*, forget what is written on the vehicle and enter the vehicle,' Obiora quipped. He was looking smart in his new bleached jeans suit with marbled navy-blue streaks and whisker fades. The bold brown double stitches on the sides made it quite attractive. City Jeans were regarded as top of the range in the fashion vogue of their time and a bold statement of taste and class by those who chose them. They were more expensive than all the other jeans in the market. The brown belt he was wearing was big and bold and a good version of the tough well-cured leather worn by American cowboys. His feet were covered with thick sports socks and white runners and he wore a crested polo top designed after the football jersey of the conquering German team of the 1990 World Cup.

'You have to show me the way ooo,' Okwudiri teased. He was looking forward to becoming senior *nwaboy* like Obiora with the impending settlement of Achike. For the past six months, he followed Achike to Lagos to understudy him in the purchases of pharmaceuticals, cosmetics, and selected groceries.

'Don't worry, when the time comes you will get to know the tricks,' Obiora assured him.

'Is Achike's departure quite imminent?' Tagbo asked.

Obiora nodded. 'He will be settled by next month.'

'See this Okwy ooo, do you know you are such a lucky chap?' Tagbo teased. 'Are you not the boy who just came to Onitsha the other day? Your progress has been quite rapid.'

'Four years is just the other day, right?' Okwudiri countered.

'What would you say about those of us that it took almost six years to become senior *nwaboy*?' Anayo asked.

'B . . . b . . . b . . . but you started yu . . . yu . . . your training as a shop rat, isn't it?' Ekene stammered, getting involved in the conversation. Anayo was a victim of new thinking in the business circle. In the effort to overcome the high turnover of *umuboy* and the endowment paid upon their freedom at the conclusion of their training, the traders preferred to take in young boys plucked away from schools. They were given long training contracts of up to seven years or more. They made more economic sense when compared to the young adults who were eager to start off their own businesses.

'Don't mind Anayo, he is talking as if he is not aware of that fact,' Okwudiri added.

'Come to think of it Okwy, if I had remembered your slumber during the week, there is no way I would be paying for your drinks including the spices that are touching your tongue,' Obiora stated before telling others how Okwudiri submitted more than one thousand naira to Silvanus as overpayment made by a customer.

'That cannot be true,' Anayo expressed shock and surprise.

'Don't say so,' cried Cletus, another apprentice at Ogbogwu. Dropping his bunch of keys on the table, he tried to scratch his private parts but the thickness of his Bugle Boys Jeans made it difficult. 'When did Okwy become such a *mumu?*'

'Do you think it is everybody that will make this *mirrion mirrion* we are hunting for in this Onitsha?' asked Anayo who preferred to be called *Ichie Mirrion*. He was always going on and on about wanting to be a millionaire, like his role model who became a millionaire at the age of nineteen. As a result of the mother tongue interference in his speech, he pronounced million as *mirrion*, like many others who hailed from his part of Igbo land. 'You did not say it in good time. Definitely no spice would have touched his tongue today.'

Okwudiri disregarded the scathing remarks and continued to enjoy his *nkwobi* and pepper soup. He took a sip directly from the small bottle and pulled out a hanky to mop his face and took his time before answering. '*Gbo Nwoke m*, do you help yourself with every sort of money you come across?' he challenged. 'You must know what to keep and what you must not touch. That's the secret to survival.'

'All that is Mike Ejeagha's story,' said Udoka, scoffing at the idea of restraint. 'Change your name to *nwa father*—the son of a priest,' he derided, causing more rambunctious laughter.

'Didn't you know all along? Do you think it is only the altar boys that qualify as *nwa father*? I have been doing what the priest has been preaching to us.'

'Listen to *Nw' Onye Igbo*,' Udoka sneered. 'He wants to make *mirrion mirrion* but tell him what is involved; he sprints off as if the deuce is after him. Do you think money making is for the timorous soul?'

Okwudiri was not perturbed by *njakiri*—the teases and taunts aimed at unsettling the target. The only antidote was to ignore them or pretend to take them in good humour. Anger would only invite more acerbic jokes which could result in a fight or social exclusion from his peers. Like storytelling, teasing was a form of entertainment common to the trainees and young traders. More importantly, it served the useful purpose of peer review. The thoughts expressed on an issue and the general reaction to actions and omissions were the approval or disapproval of such conducts. They provided a guide to behaviour that was acceptable to the group.

It allowed them recount everyday events with humour and provided them with comic relief from what would have been a boring time waiting for customers. A skilled talker could keep his audience reeling with laughter. It was not so much about what was said but how it was said. Whoever failed to hone the skill was at the mercy of others and might be called a boring introvert. 'Oh oh!' Okwudiri exclaimed in pretentious surprise. 'Who told you I want my body redesigned with a horsewhip?' he asked, calling to mind the ordeal Udoka suffered at the hands of his master for getting smart with part of his business capital.

'That's the mind frame required for moneymaking,' Udoka bragged boldly, thumping his chest as one who had the guts to do the unthinkable, the daring spirit required to make money. 'If such cash is to come my way again, I tell you I will *die* it,' he declared, showing he did not regret his action. He had denied responsibility for the twenty-thousand-naira shortfall in his master's business account. Unable to pry the truth out of him, the master had used horsewhip and *Izal*, a strong disinfectant, on his body before he cracked and owned up to it. By the time the balance was retrieved, it was less than eight thousand naira.

'*Bia nwoke m*—come my friend—you really know how to spoil yourself. You mean you frittered more than twelve thousand naira within one week?' Cletus asked.

'Money you did not toil for, it is not difficult to whack,' Anayo stated. 'Haven't you seen where robbers are enjoying themselves?'

'What is there?' asked Udoka. 'Have you not heard it? There is a mind-set for making money and a different mind-set is required to spend it. If you don't have the mind-set, you can't blow it,' he maintained without a tinge of scruples.

'Do I have to be a prodigal before *ora obodo*—all and sundry—would know I know how to enjoy wealth?' Okwudiri argued. He doubted that his boss would use only *Izal* when Udoka got smart another time. His boss must be thinking of something more terrible like raw acid. It provoked some boisterous laughter and protest in equal measure. Obiora protested it as an extremely wicked scheme. He asked if Okwudiri would use raw acid on a person just because of money. Tagbo shook his head and wagged his finger at him. He was afraid that such thought could even cross his mind. He turned to Udoka and asked between him and Okwudiri, who had more liver? Okwudiri maintained that knowing what to take and what not to touch was a secret to survival. 'What if the owner of the one thousand naira had returned for the money?'

'I . . . I . . . I . . . would d . . . d . . . deny he gave it to me. It is his word against mine. Is it not?' Ekene stammered a response as quickly as he could, waving his hand to decline the general customers' towel which Cletus was passing to him after wiping his own hand. He pulled out a hanky from his pocket to clean his mouth and hand. '*Muuuuu. . .mugu* fall, guy man *whack*. That's life.'

'*Akwara anu!*' Obiora hailed him, thrilled by the witticism.

'Who is declaring today?' Victor asked after getting a chair to sit with his friends. 'It appears someone has slaughtered a carcass on the high seas,' he joked, smiling and making his boyish oval face look guileless. Tapping the seat Victor brought, Onochie urged him to sit down and enjoy himself. He had to forget what was written on a vehicle and just enter the vehicle. It was a local cliché deriding those who, out of due diligence, asked many questions as background check before getting involved. 'You can say that again. Is it every type of vehicle that you will enter?' Victor disputed. 'In this time and age, you look before you leap.'

'It is not what is written on the vehicle that is important. Will it take you to where you are going? That is the important question. *Gbo di anyi*, is it not so?' Udoka asked his friends.

Onochie did not hesitate in coming up with an agreeable view. 'If you like, travel by Brazil or by Concord. What matters is getting to your destination.' This swayed the argument in their favour for a while. Truly, most of them preferred the luxury buses known as *akpuruka* or Brazil for their business travels. It helped them to make extra savings as a result of the low fare.

'Don't mind Victor, let him keep arguing. Maybe he's going to be a lawyer. Hey!' Udoka signalled to the nearest waitress. 'Ask Victor what he will take. He is my guy.'

'D . . . d . . . did you wa . . . wa . . . watch *Fist of Fury* last night?' Ekene asked Victor, scratching his spiky sideburns. Victor shook his head to say nay. 'There was power outage in my area last night. Did it say what killed Bruce Lee?

'Iiii . . . it . . . it did not,' Ekene enthused, unbuttoning the second button in his royal yellow shirt which displayed a hairy and muscular chest. 'Tha . . . tha . . . that guy is s . . . s . . . something else.' He had argued with Victor on what actually killed the *kung fu* star.

'American Ninja is the ultimate action film now,' Okwudiri countered, taking a gulp directly from the Guinness Stout bottle.

'Only Ninja can kill Ninja,' Udoka quoted a popular catchphrase. The video home system developed by Japan Victor Company had gradually revolutionised their access to films. They did not have to wait for the television stations to show films such as *Agatha Christie, James Bond, Charlie's Angels*. As long as there was no power outage, they were free to watch enchanting voices that cried for love in *Sonita*, an Indian film, or the heroism of Sylvester Stallone in *Rambo*. '*Gbo di anyi*, have you contracted venereal disease?' he picked on Cletus who could no longer resist the urge to scratch his itchy private parts.

'I've not recovered from our escapades of the other day,' Cletus confessed.

'What escapade, the one of last weekend?' Obiora asked.

'Is there another one?'

'Something you barely spent a minute on?' Obiora derided.

'Was I supposed to sleep there?' Cletus asked, surprised at the question. 'What am I supposed to be doing after discharging my bullets?' he asked, looking askance and his veiled ribaldry provoking more laughter. His frank but blunt way of speaking often endeared him to his listeners. Like many other trainees, he had little or no time for wooing girls. Their times were mostly spent in the shop and at the end of the business day, there were chores waiting for them in the house of their masters. Like the last time when he felt quite randy, he had visited one of the nearby slums in some of the red light hotspots in the company of his friends. 'Let me know if it was meant to be a marathon?'

'It means you can't satisfy a woman,' Anayo teased.

'Time na money,' Cletus parroted a musical catchphrase. 'If you spend the whole day on top of a woman, what time do you have to make money, eeh? I'm not the one to listen to that,' he recoiled, heaving his shoulders.

'Ddd . . . do . . . do you know the meaning of what you are saying?' Ekene asked, pointing at him knowingly. 'Your wo . . . wo . . . woman would look outside and if she comes to me for service, yu . . . yu . . . yu . . . you know I won't say no.'

'I will simply chop off your testicles,' Cletus threatened, causing more uproarious laughter from their circle.

'What you won't eat, won't you let others eat?' asked Okwudiri.

'You are not serious Okwy. Will you give out your woman for another to service?' Cletus shot back.

'A . . . a . . . anyway, you are now a man,' Ekene stated. 'Yu . . . yu . . . yu . . . youuuuou can't say you're a complete man un . . . un . . . until you've contracted go . . . go . . . gonorrhoea. Have you taken antibiotics?'

'I will have to,' Cletus agreed without argument.

'The safest way is to use condom,' Victor opined. 'You don't have to worry about venereal disease or pregnancy.'

Without realising it, the way knowledge was acquired had changed in their time. They relied more and more on opinion passed from one mouth to another. The time when information came from a serious book which could be factually reproduced was gone. The story of the lady in an aircraft who was gushing with *'Chai, Zik ekwue ncha!'* while holding a newspaper would not happen in their time. A fellow passenger that caught sight of the newspaper in her hand swore that she held it upside down. She pretended to be reading newspaper just like other passengers. Time had changed and reading had ceased to be an esteemed culture. It was a time when mammon was in the driving seat and books were left by the side of the road.

20.

Onitsha had not looked back since a trading post was established in the commercial city with the coming of the Royal Niger Company. With arms wide open, she welcomed people from all walks of life trying to make their fortune. The cash crops—cocoa, rubber, palm oil, and kernel—all went to Europe. Lorries and boats dutifully evacuated them to Port Harcourt where the ships were anchored. Later it changed from being a mere market for raw materials into the trading hub for merchandise brought in from Europe and other parts of the world. Expectedly, many came to trade there and a significant number of them were people with little or no education or skill but who were ready to do anything, hoping that by happenstance fortune would smile on them.

Silvanus, whose youngest brother married Ekwutosi, built on the foundation his late father laid. Oragwusi fled Minna as a result of the war, abandoning his work as a hospital ward attendant. The pain of starting from scratch as a family man was hard to swallow. He was not among the easterners that had their savings confiscated, leaving them with a maximum of twenty pounds apiece regardless of the book balance before the war. He had had no credit at all.

Partitioning the store he rented, he used the outer part as Able-God Chemist. Silvanus still remembered the signage—a legible chalk scrawling on a slate that hung above the double-panelled door, directly under the electric bulb; the crude shelves sparsely stocked with a few simple analgesics and other nonprescriptive drugs, and cosmetics. The family was very poor. His father scrimped and saved, ploughing every bit of profit back into the store.

His father would leave him to mind the shop while he looked around for other ways of making money. The most trying thing was waiting for customers. Sometimes nearly the whole afternoon passed without a sale. The waiting occasionally stretched to the point of desperation and when anyone showed up at the store, he would use every trick to get them to buy from him. A little wheedling, some sweet talk, maybe a little lie stating why a particular drug was the perfect substitute to what was specifically prescribed. Some, refusing to be cajoled, went off to find another drugstore who might have exactly what they were looking for. At such a time, his frustration and failure to disguise his hurt could lead to a harsh exchange of words. The desperate significance of every sale had become ingrained into his soul.

The country, still in the glorious days of post-colonial administration, maintained the discipline and control imparted by the departing British. The inspectorate division in each local government office frequently swooped on market men and women, enforcing hygiene, licensing regimes and a host of other regulatory and ethical issues. With time, other drugs, most of them made in England, began to grace the shelves: silver tins for white tablets and gold-plated tins containing the deep yellow Camoquin, vitamin B complex, and other drugs usually dispensed by the pharmacies of public hospitals. Most of them were hospital supplies 'diverted' by workers on to the open market. Eventually, Oragwusi got his break, not from the chemist shop but from property.

Taking over his father's chemist business, Silvanus moved the drugstore to a strategic location on the ever busy Bright Street. Before long, his shop came under the hammer of a task force set up by the pharmaceutical council in a bid to clean up the drug market throughout the country. He engaged Adimora Enemuo Esquire to represent him at the Miscellaneous Offences Tribunal sitting in Enugu. 'I don't see how the tribunal chairman can rule against us,' Enemuo reassured him, confident he made a good case considering his submissions on the rules of natural justice, equity, and good conscience which he felt the council breached.

Silvanus sincerely hoped his barrister was right. It had not crossed his mind that his business premises could be closed for more than a week. Yet he dared not risk opening it, because the council had surveillance teams disguised as customers. 'Barrister, if they knew how much we are losing, they won't do this to me,' he sighed. He felt he could not cope with all the regulations demanded by the council.

'And at the end of the day, it is the big timers like you that will benefit from the rules,' Enemuo pointed out. 'If all chemists are forced to display their certificates, the ones dealing in fake medicines will be driven out of business.'

'But they are making it compulsory for us to employ pharmacists,' Silvanus pointed out with discontent. 'They are just creating jobs for themselves, isn't it?'

Enemuo smiled, reclining on his swivel chair, hands clasped behind his head. 'Don't forget you're dealing with public health and safety. You and I know the danger of quackery.'

'You are not lying,' Silvanus conceded the point with a nod, his handsome face more agreeable. He looked well-to-do in his short-sleeved grey flannel suit with a mandarin collar, his Omega wristwatch with the gold chain and made-in-Spain leather shoes. 'Barrister, you didn't go to court today?' he asked, having noticed that Enemuo was wearing ordinary trousers, a blue Van Heusen shirt, new and well ironed, and a red tie instead of the striped trousers and collarless shirts that Silvanus had come to know as lawyers' garb.

'No, I didn't,' he answered, making a note in his diary. 'I was in Asaba for a meeting. As I told you some time ago, when a business is incorporated as a company, it acquires a different status in the eye of the law.' He tried to sell the idea to him once more.

'How much did you say it would cost?' Silvanus asked.

'As a favoured client, you can pay twenty-five thousand naira.'

'We'll do it as soon as I put this case behind me,' Silvanus promised. The thought of Able-God Chemist acquiring a separate and distinct legal personality able to sue and be sued did not really appeal to him. Worse of all was the thought that the enterprise he had worked so hard to build could go into liquidation.

'You will be at the tribunal tomorrow?' Enemuo asked.

'Yes, I have to,' he answered, dipping hand into his inner breast pocket for crisp twenty naira notes. He handed ten pieces to him as the usual 'expenses' for the lawyer travelling to court, although in fact they would be going together in his Mercedes-Benz. 'We shall be out of there in no time,' Silvanus hoped, standing up.

Silvanus had put those days of struggle behind him. He instructed Enemuo to incorporate his company when he had to jump on to the bandwagon of importers and exporters. The bank facilities and foreign exchange available to him as an individual or sole trader did not compare to what a limited liability company had access to.

*   *   *

People's Club of Nigeria, Oliver de Coque's music, was playing in the background as the club hummed with people. Members and their guests packed the tables, and a spirit of camaraderie pervaded the atmosphere as captains of commerce and industries retired to unwind after another hectic day of moneymaking. Many had grey or dyed hair and sported protuberant bellies under their kaftans. Others were still shapely and vigorous especially the younger generation seeking to supplant and outdo their elders. Chike pulled up a chair to join his friends at a table. 'This is where Oliver played his best music,' he remarked, stretching out his arm to greet Nwankwo with the traditional salute of backslapping of hands. As a sign of reverence, he greeted with two hands. 'Eze Udo!' he intoned. 'Are you hearing Ogene sound?'

'*Akuchinyelunwata*,' Nwankwo, an elderly man, returned his greeting. 'The music is *igba*—excellent!'

Chike was not the only one who loved that piece of music dedicated to their club. *Ezi afa ka ego*—a good name is better than money—the chorus of the song captured a core essence of how they run business in Onitsha. But the flocking together of birds of very different feathers in Onitsha was sending a wrong signal to the outside world that it was a commercial city where anything goes in the name of moneymaking. On the contrary, a number of them maintained the strong ethical orientation of their upbringing. The scruples in their native mores in addition to the religious instructions which they received regularly had ingrained the importance of good behaviour into their souls. Oliver De Coque and other musicians infused such precepts into the lyrics of their music.

'Nobody saw you at the meeting. What happened?' Silvanus asked Chike, bringing out a hard-shell case for his silver-rimmed lenses.

'*Aaah!*' Chike exclaimed, mouth agape before holding his chin in his hand for a moment. 'You won't believe it; it skipped my mind completely. A number of us joined Osita to pay condolence visit to his brother-in-law in Ukpoo. You know Iloka Onwuteaka?' he asked. Rufus nodded his head in agreement. 'His younger brother and his family perished in Iru River. We went to commiserate with him.'

'What a tragedy!' Silvanus exclaimed. 'What happened?'

'No one can explain it. They fled the north because of the riot only for their vehicle to plunge into the river,' Chike shook his head, his teeth gripping his lower lips to check the grief welling up in him. 'Truly, I don't want to recount it.'

'*Mhhh,*' groaned the elderly Nwankwo. 'What would be would be,' he quipped, heaving his shoulder in revulsion.

'That bridge has been in a deplorable condition for a long time,' Ndukwe remembered. 'All the while, Ukpoo has been pleading with the state government to fix it,' he told them. Ukpoo was a neighbouring community that was separated by a river from his native homeland, Igbo Eze. He knew that the area was virtually cut off from the rest of the world. As a result, farmers found it difficult to evacuate their produce to the market. 'Perhaps, this loss of lives would force them to do something.'

'If only they knew, they would not have bothered,' Silvanus was quite sad.

'Religious disturbances all the time; so it has become a yearly thing, isn't it?' Nwankwo wondered.

'What can one say?' Rufus asked with resignation. They had lost count of the number of religious riots that took place in the north which sent their people fleeing for safety. 'Is it up to a year that the last riot happened?' he asked, scanning his memory to remember how many months ago it happened last.

'Permit me to ask, is it all the time they have to kill our people?' Silvanus asked, his brow furrowing with a frown. 'All the time they make our people run from pillar to post. Is it...'

'If a people say they don't want you in their midst, why must you remain with them?' Ndukwe interjected. He was of the strong view that all their people must leave the north. It was the most effective way of stemming the tide of such frequent killings. Whether actively discussed or not, the implication of the frequent riots bothered them. Just for bragging rights, a sect or school of fundamentalists could make a sport of their people's lives. Baying for the blood of resident infidels appeared to be the highest credit to different brands of violent extremism. However, it was such a surprise to see these assailants flee the scene of their murderous gatherings when security operatives were eventually called in to quell such riots. Crying *wayoo Allah nah*—oh my Allah—they ran as fast as their legs could carry them to escape the *bulala*—horsewhip—batons and, in extreme cases, live bullets of security operatives.

Ironically, the people who were out to mete out death to others were scared of corporal pain and death. Perhaps the only time they counted more than a year of relative peace when they did not have to flee any part of the north was during the regime of Sani Abacha, the army general who ruled the country with maximum powers. His men did not hesitate to take a renowned preacher into indefinite custody for being a threat to national security and good governance.

'Have I not always said so? Our journey with these northerners; I don't know the direction it is headed,' Chike said, shaking his head. He picked up the glass placed before him to inspect it. Noticing water marks, he poured a bit of Guinness Stout and swilled around to rinse it. He stretched his hand to pour it into a bowl on a nearby table. 'Anyway, how did the meeting go?'

'The commissioner of police travelled to Lagos on short notice. That is what the DPO told us,' Rufus answered.

'So, it did not hold?' Chike asked.

'The commissioner wants to be at the meeting,' Silvanus told him.

'*Aaah, arinze Chukwu,*' Chike repeated a phrase, thanking God for little mercies. 'It's an opportunity for me to make amends.'

They were members of a select committee set up by their trading associations to meet with the commissioner of police on how to resolve the lingering crisis between the traders and policemen. Many traders did not want any policeman to set foot in the market again. They were fed up with what their lawyer described as frequent molestation, harassment and intimidation. One of the traders, Igboanugo, started the trouble. He lodged a complaint against Ufere at the police station for alleged infringement of his product. Policemen swooped on Ufere's shop for searches and seizure. It led to a serious face-off between the traders and the policemen, resulting in a fatal injury to one of the trainee traders.

In the lawsuit that followed, the court made it clear that policemen were not permitted to enter any business premises to search and take away any product without a court order. Most of the traders disapproved the steps taken by Igboanugo. Usually, such complaint was lodged with the umbrella body. As a self-regulating organisation, they all knew that OMATA had a long history of combating counterfeits in the market. Unscrupulous traders cloned products that sold very fast in the market and tried to pass them off as originals. Realising the question of integrity it raised, the associations made it uncomfortable for such traders to remain in their midst. In discouraging such intellectual property infringement, members assisted younger businessmen that were grappling with the realities of starting off in business. Like sharecropping in the village, many young traders built their business by taking products on credit, sell above the importer's price and kept the difference.

'That is how sanity was restored to the main market,' Nwankwo told them. 'Knowing they cannot thrive in Onitsha, such traders relocated to markets in neighbouring towns. Such markets became the hotbed of imitation and quackery.' As the sole distributor of baking yeast powder for a Japanese manufacturer in the whole of Africa, he built his business on integrity. As he later became aware, a different trader met the manufacturer to be appointed distributor in another West African country. The Japanese company refused, knowing that the yeast would end up in Nigeria. It would be a clear case of parallel or grey import. As Nwankwo got to know, they decided to stick with him because he was not only faithful in remitting their moneys but worked assiduously to create a huge market for their product. As a people who did not trifle with integrity and trustworthiness, the Japanese company was happy to retain him as their sole distributor in the whole of Africa.

'Silva, did you get to speak with Pius?' Rufus asked. He had recommended Pius who was his customs clearance agent that cleared his goods from the ports.

'Yes, I did,' Silvanus answered, wiping his glasses carefully with an off-white lint-free cloth before placing them in the casing. 'I will forward the bill of lading to him next week.'

'You have seen Holland with your eyes,' Rufus stated, pouring more of the Satzenbrau beer for himself.

'What part of Europe is not wonderful?' asked Silvanus, making himself comfortable. He had made two business trips to Spain previously. 'It's good to travel to Europe once in a while, if for nothing else, to feast your eyes. Amsterdam is beautiful!'

'What about Germany?' Chike asked. As a dealer in auto parts, he had made three business trips to Germany, buying and shipping second-hand cars. They sold so well that several car showrooms that sold new cars were put out of business. Chike was impressed with German ultra-cleanliness. 'You can't litter anywhere. Cameras, cameras everywhere and their Polizei . . .' he rolled his eyes, suggesting they were police officers one could not mess around with.

'As soon as you step out of the plane at Schiphol, you notice how clean and sparkling everything is. You start wondering if you are meant to walk on such clean floor,' Silvanus told them while pouring Gulder lager beer into a glass which had the brand name 'Gulder' inscribed on the side with Lucida calligraphy.

'I know that kind of feelings,' Chike agreed. 'In such situation, I just do what others are doing.'

'That is exactly what I did,' Silvanus agreed.

'How times have changed,' the elderly Nwankwo noted. After a successful career as a businessman in Onitsha, Nwankwo retired to become the ruler of his autonomous community in Adazi but occasionally came to Onitsha. 'In our time, it was the white merchants that imported the goods: UAC, Lever Brothers, John Holt, GBO, Leventis, and many others. We bought from them whenever they imported from the manufacturers and they used to treat us well. We didn't take the trouble of going to seek out the manufacturers in their countries.'

The attendants served them with the wooden bowl of *isi-ewu*—goat head— which Silvanus ordered for each person on their table. '*Ogbuefi Nnanyelugo!*' Rufus hailed Silvanus by his praise name. 'Once again, you've done as you usually do.'

'Is that not why we call him *Ogbuefi*?' Ndukwe added.

'Are you saying we should enjoy ourselves?' Rufus asked.

'Eat and be merry,' Silvanus gave him the go-ahead, washing his hand. He took a chunk of the chevon and his taste buds were quite pleased with the spicy flavour of *uziza* and the minty taste of *nchuanwu* laced with a modicum of *utaziri*. They blended well with the chilli sauce for more palatable effect. It was not only the delight of munching the goat meat that made the dish popular. Whenever the native dish was prepared by anyone with good culinary skills, each bite was a double delight of savouring a recipe of well-prepared goat meat and nutritious herbs and spices. He took a sip of beer to assuage the hot sensation.

'You know how we wash plates?' Chike asked, pretending to be scouring a plate with sponge and soap. 'That's how they wash the roads people walk on.'

'Unbeknownst to me, what I thought was a small armoured tanker in Madrid turned out to be street sweepers sucking in dirt like a vacuum cleaner,' Rufus told them, agreeing with the point made by Chike. 'For the two weeks I was there I didn't polish my shoes.'

'The white man lives in a different world,' Ndukwe concluded after hearing them talk more about Europe. '*Ehee* Silva, I noticed that the work on your building is progressing rapidly. I told you that Chukwujekwu is really good.'

'Good, indeed,' Rufus countered, his lips pouting, scoffing at the thought of giving credit to the contractor. 'So you don't know when money is speaking? Ok, ask him to do it without money.'

'What are you saying? Is money everything?' Ndukwe asked.

'You know this thing called money?' Chike asked, supporting what Rufus said, his thumb flicking rapidly against his index and middle fingers as if counting currency notes. 'It is powerful. It answers all questions.'

'It's not a lie. That is what the bible says,' Rufus agreed. 'It is not about what one is doing that is important. The all-important question is: how much does it translate to?' It was a deft answer to an argument about the importance of traders in their time. Compared to those working in the more organised private sector or government officials in the civil service, they felt that traders did not receive the recognition they deserved. Their growing financial power gave them the confidence to challenge the status quo that accorded more respect and recognition to those with much learning. After all, the young traders were building houses that were better than what civil servants could build after several years of service. At different fundraising events, such officials were known to speak what was termed as '*big*' and '*long*' grammar. The paltry figures they usually announced as donations to the proposed community projects did not correspond with their grandiloquence. Yet, they were the people often given the microphone to speak. To challenge this, some young businessmen who wanted their voices to be heard at such events readily donated significant sum, often in cash, to buy the opportunity to address their kinsmen. Such opportunity was usually devoted to blowing personal trumpets, telling all and sundry how important such a trader was and why he must not be ignored in the scheme of things.

'What do they do that the traders are not doing?' Silvanus asked, sharing the view.

'Ii it is about those that drive the best cars, is it not traders?' Rufus asked.

As far as they were concerned, the traders were more dominant in terms of financial firepower. From the middle of the 1980s when different cars were in vogue, it was mainly traders that drove and flaunted such cars. From Peugeot's 505 Evolution and Volkswagen's Santana to Mercedes Benz 190 and different versions of V-Boots, the traders drove most of them in the country. To keep pace with mainstream workers, they printed their own business cards, letter-headed papers, acquired fax machines, telephones including the 090 cellular phones and other office or business accessories. Depending on their financial power, traders replicated many things done in official circles to enhance the ergonomics of their business offices or lock-up shops.

'My father said it all,' Rufus remarked. 'The priest can speak all the Latin in the whole world but he knows where to wait for him.'

'And where is that?' asked Silvanus.

'Where else?' asked Rufus. 'Is it not at the point where everyone will chorus "Amen"? Whether you are Chike Obi or . . . what is her name? That woman in Benin, Alele-Williams . . . what everyone is looking for is money. Isn't it?'

The elderly Nwankwo smiled at what he considered a faulty argument. 'If that is so, where is Sir Louis Ojukwu, the richest man in all of black Africa?'

'*Mba nu*, death is not part of it,' Chike countered quickly to the hilarity of everyone.

'But you said all questions,' Silvanus noted, hesitating to share in what he considered extreme views. 'Anyway, Ndukwe how did you resolve the issue of your *nwaboy*?'

'*Ohhhh*, now you can see the point, isn't it?' asked Nwankwo, looking quite happy that the issue was being put beyond reasonable doubt. He could not comprehend how a young trader would want to equate himself with Chike Obi, the renowned mathematician and the first person in their country to hold a doctoral degree in mathematics. It was also absurd to compare themselves to Alele-Williams, the iconic academic and professor of mathematics to become the first female university vice chancellor in their country. Those of them who were of the old order did not lose respect for learning. Quite a number of them did not take to trading out of sheer volition. If they had the choice, they would have acquired more satisfactory level of education before immersing themselves in the pursuit of wealth. As a result, those of them that made the money did not fail to send their children and other wards to school to acquire the education that eluded them.

'I disengaged him,' Ndukwe answered. 'I used him to set example for others.'

'*Umuboy* these days are a different kettle of fish,' Chike noted. 'They want to become millionaires while in another man's shop.'

'As if you know what I'm battling with in my shop,' Rufus told them about his running battle with his boys. 'There is no system I have not devised to check them stealing from me but they have always beaten me to it.'

'Don't you think you are giving yourself unnecessary high blood pressure?' Nwankwo counselled. 'The small cash squirreled away by trainees to buy themselves some fun does not ruin a businessman,' he told them. 'You need to allow them some latitude.'

'*Eze Udo*,' Rufus addressed the elderly Nwankwo with reverence. 'What we never thought of doing at our time, the *umuboy* of today will do it without batting eyelids. I don't understand how they muster the guts to do what they do.'

With both hands, the elderly Nwankwo motioned to him to calm down. 'You must make allowances for them,' he opined. He had heard stories of *umuboy* being unfairly dismissed at an advanced stage of their training contract. A number of the excuses given for such termination were ridiculous and untenable. Such excuses were used to deny trainees the sum usually endowed on them as start-up capital. He could tell that the younger generation of entrepreneurs were running aground the humane considerations which helped them overlook certain excesses of trainees, blunt out their rough edges and still went ahead to set them up. 'All these things were still there in our own time.'

Money was fast assuming the central focus of everything that the younger generation of traders did. They cared little about the diminishing character of the people making the money. The emphasis was more about how much of it was made. Little thought was given to the benefits it was meant to deliver to their fellow men. Without knowing it, the younger generation seemed to be losing sight of the higher purpose which valued human beings far above bags of money. In their time, it was more about the number of lives that were positively impacted. As traders who took delight in the mass training of apprentices, they took pride in praise names such as *ochiri ozuo* or similar sobriquets. Trainees that served their masters very well did not only get sums of money as their endowment.

In a particular case, Nwankwo endured the bad behaviour of a trainee for most of the period of his apprenticeship. When he settled him with a sum of money that was considered quite substantial, many were surprised. At the gathering to mark his disengagement, Nwankwo told him that others would serve him as he served his master. In contrast, he settled a loyal and industrious trainee in the same period with a sum of money considered less than modest but blessed him. The trainee that went with his blessing prospered, becoming an established businessman. Such was the conundrum of faithful service and reward in their time. In singing their praise, Oliver De Coque recognised them as the businessmen who planted wealth and riches in different parts of Igboland. Each person trained, endowed, and set up as a businessman became a tree of wealth planted in other fields and lands that grew to bear their own fruits.

'The ease with which some people make this money leaves me wondering if I'm doing the right kind of business, true,' Ndukwe stated as he told them about a young man that built a mansion in his village within a record time of one year and bought 25KVA generator to power it. 'It is so magnificent that people stop to stare at it as if they are watching cinema. The boy I'm talking about, how old is he? He is not more than thirty-four.'

'He must be into international business,' Silvanus guessed, knowing the type of money many traders made from merchandising and distributorship.

'Nothing special about his business,' Ndukwe said. 'He owns a shop or two in Lagos but travels abroad regularly. Is it up to four years *Ochiriozuo* settled him?' The uncertainty about time clearly showed that the fellow could not have legitimately acquired such wealth within such a short time.

'Perhaps he is into oil,' Rufus thought aloud.

'Who knows?' Ndukwe answered. 'And how he spends money leaves me wondering how he makes it. Everybody calls him *Omelora* — a philanthropist and champion of public cause.'

'Look closely,' Silvanus said. 'There must be something vomiting money for him,' he said, implying it must be blood money.

Chike smiled at their naivety. 'Are you not in this town? What else could generate such sudden wealth but trading in ashes and powdery substances?' he asked, using the euphemism for narcotics to describe the subject matter. He was aware that a number of their people had joined the rat race to make money from trading in narcotics following the trail blazed by men and women in high places. Their country had been turned into a transit route given the level of security in more advanced airports. Even traders joined in the free for all effort to make quick money. As a result, drugs were cleverly concealed in some goods imported into the country before using people to courier them to Europe.

He remembered a case in which an ancient city was thrown into mourning because a son of the soil was arrested in USA for drug trafficking. The screening machine had detected the presence of the substance and security operatives were immediately alerted. After picking the luggage from the carousel, the man confirmed ownership of the bag to the airport officials. He was a popular socialite that was known for his generosity, helping his people in different ways. Remarkably, the monarch of the town did not turn his back on him in his time of trouble but called for corporate prayers for God to intervene in his situation. 'It means you don't know how people are making fast money?' Chike continued.

'*Oh oh ho ya hoo!*' Ndukwe exclaimed in wonderment. 'Oh, so it is co. . .'

'Co... what!' Chike interposed as fast as he could, hushing him before he could complete the word. 'Whatever troubles you get yourself into, I'm not a party to it. I'm not here. Nobody mentions it by name.'

'*Ekwuzina!*' Ndukwe exclaimed, urging him to say no more as his curiosity and doubt melted away. What he had just heard could only be the answer to a jigsaw he was trying to fix all the while.

'By the way, when are you travelling to Lagos for the visa appointment?' Silvanus asked, changing the subject.

'It is next week,' Ndukwe answered. 'They should give me the visa to let me know what I'm doing with myself. I want to go to that Europe to feast my eyes, if for nothing else.' He wanted to see the glorious Europe that his friends spoke so much about.

Europe had been a distant fairyland to them but was getting demystified with time. It became accessible to more and more people who did not win scholarships to study in her universities. Many travelled to behold the massive factories occupying acres of expansive lands; the planned and uncluttered cities with their manicured parks; the sky-rise office blocks; the well-laid-out residential buildings, most of them based on the same architectural designs. The incredible land where a skilled artisan could earn enough to allow him live next door to highly educated professionals. Everything he heard about Europe gave a hue of reality to what was considered utopia in their own land. Human minds conceived them and human hands built them.

Cornucopia began to make more practical meaning in countries where foods which could feed forty million people or more were thrashed in a single year. But for Charles Dickens' *Oliver Twist*, it would have been difficult to believe there was a time when asking for more porridge meant serious trouble for a hungry child. Returning travellers testified that these countries were fulfilling prophesies long foretold: they beckoned to the thirsty to come to the waters, and even those without money could hasten to buy milk and wine. People were granted dignity irrespective of learning or social status. To the amazement of these travellers, it was not every European they met that studied until their hair went grey. Just as it was in the land of their birth, there were those who did not burden themselves with high ambition. Yet, they were not dehumanised or made the wretched of the earth. They were not employed to build the opulent parts of the cities but sentenced to live in festering slums riddled with squalor and disease. No one had to salt away a fortune before building a decent place to live in. It was possible to live in a nice house while payment for acquiring it was spread throughout a lifetime.

Their system did not leave them so vulnerable, making one a tenant for so many years without equity. Even when rent was not affordable, different housing policies and schemes did not allow the roof over the person's head to be taken away. The only few that slept rough in the streets were mostly addicts that their societies were fighting hard to regularise as normal human beings. All the same, making money and becoming rich was not strange in those societies. The rich did not have unfettered power to exploit the public to grow their wealth. Most activities, if not all, were highly regulated. Delivering service to the people and clothing them with dignity predominated their thinking. Their societies were designed to ease the pressure of acquiring the basic necessities of life. The rewards were bountiful.

Living a crime-free life was not too high a standard to ask of the citizens and residents alike. Truth became a common virtue. Why tell a lie when the truth, however ugly, would not deny the person compassionate and sympathetic considerations? Even when it was undeserving, human rights law was there to stay the hands of enforcement from excessive and disproportionate force. Without the threat of sanctions or unending homilies, conducts and behaviours consistent with biblical precepts became the core of their values. To cap it all, they elected the rule of law to govern them.

'Did you find time to relax?' Rufus asked Silvanus, mischief was quite obvious in his voice as he tried to convey his message.

'Of course, did I go just to look only at their skyscrapers? I drank a pint of beer now and then,' Silvanus answered, ignoring the true motive behind the question.

'So you did not see those exquisitely sculptured em. . .em. . .you understand what I mean,' Rufus laboured to clarify the point without getting explicit.

'Leave that aside,' Silvanus grinned. 'Is it the glass cubicles?'

'*Aaahaaaa!* You saw them?' Rufus exclaimed. They all laughed at the covert admission.

'Victor, a chap from Ukpoo took me to Kilimanjaro, a restaurant that served African cuisine. I ate pounded yam and egusi soup. I saw quite a number of our boys in Bijlmer.'

'That's the only blemish you'll. . .' Chike was speaking when Rufus burst into a song.

'*Afo muo afo muo inine emenuanu m aluuuuuuu!*' Rufus sang along, the music playing in the background, his body swaying to the dominant sound of the saxophone. *Agadi Nwanyi Na Inine*, a ballad of Chief Stephen Osita Osadebe, was difficult to resist. The saxophonist, working patiently at his instrument, sustained the tempo, producing staccatos of pulsating rhythm while Osadebe told his story. At the opportune time, gradually but consistently, the undulating sounds rose in pitch, his fingers working dexterously, his cheeks and veins bulging as he pumped the sax. His listeners, pleasantly inebriated, were caught up by the engaging rhythm—heads nodding, feet tapping, and bodies swaying, following the music to its cathartic soul-satisfying ending.

'*Obu ya,*' Chike, also enjoying the music, rose from his chair, miming, a hand on his head and another rubbing his stomach like a discomfited old woman, swaying from the waist, lost in the rhythm. The story of *Agadi Nwanyi* and *Inine* was intriguing as it was interesting. *Inine*—green leaves, the local equivalent of spinach—made a compelling argument against *Agadi Nwanyi*—the old woman. Daily the old woman plucked *inine* to make her food that enabled her to live. Unhappy that she was plucking them out of existence, the green leaves queried why she should live at their expense. After all, the God that created her was the same God that created them. On that fateful day, she plucked them as usual. While the pot was cooking the *inine*, the old woman, happy that nourishment was in the pot, waited with joyful anticipation. Without knowing it, *inine* had plotted their revenge and shortly after the meal, they afflicted her with stomach upset. Her discomfiture was a lesson at "live and let others live".

'Osadebe's music is *igba*,' the elderly Nwankwo enthused, his head nodding and foot tapping. Like a philosopher king, Osadebe frequently transported himself to different settings and locations, be it human minds or the world of animals and plants to bring back instructive lessons that were woven into his music. Easily, they captured the essence of life; teaching and reinforcing the lessons that made them unique as a people. Those who considered themselves to have mature taste in music maintained that Osadebe was the best of the highlife maestri. Celestine Ukwu or Oliver de Coque had their support base, but Osadebe lived long and kept releasing one record after another, drawing deep on his knowledge of life and human experiences to delight his fans.

21.

Albert brought his rickety bicycle to a stop in the village square—its original black paint had turned into mud red; the headlamp was gone; the chain casing was weather-beaten; the tyres patched in several places; the hand pump tied with a strip of old inner tube. He tucked his sharp machete carefully between the seat and chain supports, making sure it did not touch the spokes or hurt his leg. Sheathed in brown paper and dangling from the headlamp hook was the file to sharpen his machete. They were his tools as an outdoor worker with PWD—public works department—that was responsible for road maintenance. 'Ahamba, you came home?' he asked, dismounting from the saddle.

'Yes.' Ahamba stood up to shake hands with him. 'I came to see how you fellows are faring.'

'You have seen how we are. What about our people in the North—how are they?'

'They are fine. They sent their greetings,' Ahamba told him. 'Actually, I came to take my family to the north for my boy to receive medical attention.'

'Is that so?' Albert asked, his head bowed momentarily in thought. Knowing that the religious riots that displaced his people from the north were more frequent, it was strange to hear Ahamba thinking of taking his family to the restive north. 'You think it is a wise thing to do?'

'I gave careful thought to it before making the decision,' Ahamba assured him.

'I ask because of the frequent attacks on our people. Only God knows when they will stop?'

'I took that into account. There are so many of our people who still live in the north with their families.'

'What do they do when a riot starts?'

'We all run into the army barracks. That is what we do these days.'

'Please make sure you come around and let us chat further on this, okay,' Albert requested.

'Surely, I will,' Ahamba assured him. 'You're hale and hearty, I suppose?'

'You have seen us as we are, except those happy-go-lucky fellows at the local government who don't want to live up to their responsibilities,' he replied.

'Albert, have you fellows called off your strike?' George asked, taking a break from the newspaper he was reading. Albert was one of the outdoor workers with the local government that embarked on industrial action over the failure to pay their wages for four months running.

'They only paid us a month's wage but they have promised to clear the outstanding debt,' Albert answered.

'This caretaker administration is a huge joke,' George said, unable to disguise the contempt he had for them. Since the ousting of the previous civilian administration, the activities of the local government had practically collapsed. Most of the chairmen, appointed by the military governors, acted as if they owed no duty to the public. The basic services that tier of government had to provide were completely disregarded. Some of the chairmen were heard saying that the public had not appointed them and that the only way to protect themselves from being booted out of office was to please those with the power to hire and fire. Of course, such stories were only rumours. Yet the public were left no choice but to believe them, as no amount of petitions or complaints seemed to bother the chairmen, who were quick to label the whistle blowers as disgruntled elements who, driven by parochial interests, were determined to pull them down. 'Public service delivery has become history in this country.'

'What can you do when a person holds the yam and the knife? Is it not what he gives that you take?' Albert quipped.

'Well, they won't be there forever. A day is coming when a whirlwind will sweep them away,' Ozurumba stated. They had watched a number of workers lose their jobs, some of them giving them up out of frustration. The wages were never fantastic, but the jobs made a difference in the lives of those lucky enough to have them. The eighty or one hundred naira per month could not be plucked off a tree. 'With this attitude, will they pay your pensions at all?' he wondered.

Albert sighed wistfully. 'Who is talking of pensions when they can't pay wages?' he asked, walking away with his bicycle. Pausing, he added. 'Go to the secretariat, you'll see old people with sunken cheeks and pallid faces like mine whiling away their time in the name of waiting to receive pension. They keep telling them to come tomorrow, come tomorrow. . .' he waved his hand in disgust, before moving on.

'That is it,' Ahamba sighed—he also was familiar with the attitude of public office holders under the military regime. 'The handwriting is clear. Quit, if you're not happy. They don't give a hoot.'

'Let's talk about more important things,' urged Ozurumba. 'Did you say you're taking your family back with you?'

'What else can I do? If I'd thought about it, we could have run into the military barracks the last time, instead of jumping into the train,' Ahamba told them. 'I've just secured a room in Sabon Geri, in the same yard with Nathaniel. The military barracks is just a stone throw away.'

'Once you sense trouble, all you will have to do is run there,' Anosike said, happy to know what appears to be a solution to the frequent flights taken by their people.

'If I may ask, are they still taking vengeance for the death of the Sardauna of Sokoto?' Ozurumba wondered, repeating the perceived raison d'être for the frequent killings. The coup d'etat that resulted in the death of the Sardauna was tagged Igbo coup. It was particularly so when prominent politicians from the north and the west were killed while those of the east escaped before the putsch. However, those who held such opinion failed to take into account that General Aguiyi Ironsi in the west and Lt. Colonel Emeka Odimegwu-Ojukwu in the north that halted the coup were Igbo men.

'I agree that it has been more frequent and widespread since then,' George said. But he knew that the Igbos had been exposed to such killings in the past. He read about how his people were killed and their properties looted in 1945 in the city of Jos. It was the same story in 1953 when Akintola was to visit Kano. 'Sir Ahmadu Bello had he been killed by then? Yet to punish ordinary jeering and booing by Lagos crowd, who did they massacre? Was it not our people?'

'What can I say?' Ozurumba capitulated. 'Since his murder, the frequency with which they kill our people is beyond comprehension. Have you noticed? For the past five years or more, no year has passed without riots in one or more cities of the north.'

Akwakanti blamed it on his kinsmen. 'If they say you are not wanted, the best thing is it not to leave?'

'That is easier said than done,' George countered. 'If we are not wanted, why the civil war against our secession in the first place?'

It was common knowledge that their people did not lead a sedentary lifestyle. From the time of Omenuko to his generation, they had always moved from their geographical point of origin, looking for what life had in store for them beyond their immediate environment. With each person charting his own course towards personal success, wherever naira and kobo could be found, people of his ethnic extraction were there, diligently applying themselves. But their outstanding success as individuals did not translate to collective strength. That was what he found most disturbing—their vulnerability. Unfortunately, they did not see it from that perspective. Plagued by a mindset that accepted a plight that weighed heavier than albatross, all that seemed to matter to them was commerce and moneymaking, with the vast majority unable to imagine life without their lockup shops for a day.

'Well. . .' Akwakanti did not seem convinced but he knew it would be difficult to win such an argument against George. 'What is so special about the north?'

'You can't compare this place with the north,' Ahamba interjected. 'Schooling is free, medical care is free. Food is plentiful.'

'Nobody can dispute that,' Ozurumba agreed. 'Is it meat that you want? You can have as much as you please. Beef, goat, lamb, chicken, name it; they are all there in abundance.'

'Have you ever tried their *fura de nono* which their women hawk?' Ahamba asked. He had enjoyed the steamed balls of blended millet with the pasteurised full cream milk. 'All you need is to churn the *kindirmo*—the full cream milk— to get cheese or process it for yoghurt. They are really nutritious.'

Anosike pulled a wry face, looking as if he would throw up. 'How can anyone drink animal's milk?'

'What about the tinned milk you drink? Where do you think it comes from? Once it is pasteurised, it is safe to drink,' Ozurumba explained. 'What I miss is their guinea fowl. With eighty kobo, you can buy up to three of them for a pot of soup. I've not seen meat that tastes so delicious in *egusi* and *ukazi*. . .'

'Okoko Ndem!' Akwakanti called in mock admiration. 'A child that eats *akara* forgets he eats his money,' he said, repeating a local saying.

'The description alone can make anyone salivate,' Anosike said. 'Your mouth has really tasted different kinds of broth.'

'During the harmattan, we patronised *Mai Shai* up to two or three times a day to keep warm,' Ozurumba continued, dismissing the mockery with a wave of hand.

'Who is *Mai Shai*?' Akwakanti asked.

'The men that run the local cafe,' Ahamba answered.

'I wonder how we could have coped with the terrible cold without them. They are still there, isn't it?' Ozurumba asked, feeling nostalgic.

'They are there. No leave, no transfer,' Ahamba answered, looking quite cheerful. 'Their cold has no comparison.'

'In the morning before we start our labourer's work, we used to sit round his table for at least one cup of *Bongo* coffee. Two people could share a big fried egg sandwich,' Ozurumba remembered.

'But for the riots and killings, the north is a good place to be,' Ahamba confirmed. 'They're such a nice people. Is any of them here?' he asked, implying he was not saying it to please them. 'I've not met better fellows like them.'

'What? The same people that butcher our people?' Akwakanti looked astonished, finding it difficult to reconcile the friendly image painted of the northerners with the horrific tales that came from there.

'Ask anyone. Am I lying?' Ahamba turned to Ozurumba for support.

'Is it all of them that like the killing?' asked Ozurumba.

'You know Marcus, the building contractor from Aguebi? He would have been a dead man long ago but for the Alhaji he was working for. He was working in the man's house in Tudunwada when the last riot broke out. The man hid him for more than five days and personally drove him back home after the riot was quelled.'

'There is one thing I like about them. They take things easy. Everything is *ba kwomi*—no problem. You only see their ugly side when anything has to do with their religion,' Ozurumba stated.

'Papa, we want to go to Abadaba to grate cassava,' Enyioma called as he got closer. 'Mama is not at home to give us money.'

'How much do you need?' Akwakanti asked.

'So there's a cassava grating machine in Abadaba now?' Ahamba asked.

'Since when?' Anosike replied, suggesting it had existed for quite a while.

'That's good,' Ahamba was delighted. 'Is this not the development we're all talking about? Gradually they will all get to us one after the other,' he said, remembering what an arduous task it was to grate a basin of cassava manually.

'Certainly,' Ozurumba concurred. 'As you can see, we have joined the league of villages that boast of storey buildings.' The country home built by Iroegbulem's children turned out to be the harbinger of good tidings in Mboha. It opened the floodgate of storey buildings with three others springing up in quick succession. But Iroegbulemville remained the most remarkable structure which was patterned after an American edifice. According to one of his sons, as it was done in America, so it was done in Mboha. Anyone that was desperate to travel abroad but lacks the wherewithal was told to step on Iroegbulemville. It was the American soil where the green-white-green and the star-spangled flags were hoisted. It was not only Mboha indigenes that called it America house. 'Eventually, all the good things of life will. . .' He was still speaking when a yellow Mercedes Benz 220 D/8 pulled to a stop. They noticed it was David, their kinsman. He came out of the car to greet them.

'Aa aa, David, when did you learn to drive?' Ahamba was surprised as they shook hands.

'What is there in driving a car?' David asked. 'It's a skill anyone can acquire in little or no time.'

'Eehm, who do you drive?' Anosike asked. He had not imagined that David could own such car. It was not up to two years he left the village and he was not known to have a job with high paying income or a thriving business.

'What type of question is that? Is there any curse that says David can only be a chauffer instead of car owner?' asked George, pretending to be scandalised by the question. Being of the same lineage with David, he took it upon himself to protect him. 'Who is it that forbids good fortune? Instead of rejoicing at the sight of good fortune, we are throwing questions at him. Allow him to get home first and you can come with your questions later.'

'How can we rejoice over what we don't know?' asked Ahamba. 'David, you have to confirm it is yours before we can put our dancing shoes on.'

'Unless you want me to produce the purchase receipt,' David stated and made for the door of the car before Ahamba drew him back, shaking his hand heartily in congratulations.

'*Chei*, David the great son of Amaechi, the chip off the old block. Dried meat that fills the mouth, the animal that keeps grazing while hunters waste their bullets in vain, *akwaa akwuru, odogwu nwoke*, you're the true son of your father! Give me five!' George shook his hand while showering him with accolades.

David was delighted by the encomiums from his kinsmen. 'Don't worry, we have to get together to savour some broth and spices,' he promised, looking confident in the brown well-tailored and expensive short-sleeved suit. The brown snakeskin shoes and red brimless hat conflated into a carefully chosen outfit. He looked well fed with his natural fair and hairy skin, looking more toned up as a result of the body cream he used. His hand which they shook was not the common bony hand with lean flesh. It was quite fleshy and soft. 'I have to go,' he said, excusing himself as George joined him to take a ride in the car. 'I will send out a message to let you know when we shall gather as kinsmen.'

*   *   *

Ozurumba found Kperechi washing the goat neck and leg he brought back from *Afo* market. He was disappointed that the meat has not been cooked. 'I wonder at the kind of people I have in this house,' Ozurumba complained. 'All they are good at is eat and eat. Simple things, they can't do. How will the meat be properly cooked and still be ready for the kindred meeting this evening?'

Kperechi would rather blame her husband. 'I just got back from the market. You could have asked Ijuolachi or Akachi to start the cooking as soon as you got back from the market.'

'Of what benefit are all of you to me in this house?' he retorted.

'I don't know what it would have taken from you,' Kperechi replied calmly. 'Anyway, there is sufficient time to boil it. By the way, the kindred meeting for oil mill accounts is late in the evening when everyone is back from the market, isn't it?'

'Mama, you came back early,' said Ijuolachi as she entered dressed in green and white checkers, her school compound wear with her left arm laden with biology textbooks in addition to the hardcover notebook. At her time, the fact of a child progressing to secondary school was no longer a question regarding the sex of the child. With the secondary school brought closer home, most of the village children went to school as day students.

'The market was quite good today. My fish went like hot cakes,' Kperechi answered. 'How did your examination go?'

'It went well. It is one more paper to go.' She was writing her third term examination of her second year.

'Perhaps, you didn't go with enough fish,' Ozurumba thought.

'I bought two cartons of mackerel as usual,' Kperechi said. 'I can't believe they sold so fast.'

'They were not tiny like those we had two weeks ago. And you know I smoked them properly,' Ijuolachi said.

'There's no denying it, my daughter,' Kperechi agreed. 'We owe it to your father, though. The logs of firewood he brought home helped a lot.'

'Guess who I saw in the market today? Finecountry, the fellow from Aguebi, your village,' Ozurumba told her.

'He bought fish from me.'

'Is it true your kinsmen want to get a wife for him? I keep wondering the woman that will marry a bohemian like him.'

Kperechi placed a stool before him on which to serve his lunch. 'Akachi, get your father's spoon. He's not as mad as people take him to be. He's merely a recluse.'

'No, he's certainly unstable,' Ozurumba disagreed. 'His behaviour is not that of normal person. How can one build his house in the middle of nowhere and you tell me he is normal? He lives all by himself, is that normal?' He gave up the subject when he caught sight of the yellow Mercedes-Benz as it drove past. 'Is that not David's car?'

'It is,' Ijuolachi confirmed. She equally caught a glimpse of it before it went out of sight.

'Wherever fortune steps into, let it remain and may mine get to me,' Kperechi prayed. 'Is it not the same David that was in this village a couple of years ago? Who could have believed he would be a car owner today?'

'Lagos is truly the place to be,' Ozurumba opined.

'Is there something that breeds money for them in that city?' Kperechi wondered. 'What does he do to make the money to buy such a rich man's car?'

'He's into business. There are a lot of business opportunities in Lagos. Imagine, he bought the car from the proceeds of one deal.' Ozurumba told them.

Kperechi momentarily stopped the *odudu* she was unwrapping to gaze at her husband with incredulity. 'He made all that money in a single transaction and you believe it is genuine?'

'What are you insinuating?' he asked.

'Well, who am I to doubt him? Anyone who wakes up from sleep to say he wrestled with the spirits, why would I argue? Did I journey to the land of the dead with him?' she asked resuming the task at hand. While it was acceptable to admire anyone for achieving something significant at their time, it was increasingly important to ensure that the money came from a legitimate source. When it was obvious that the project was beyond the person's income, tongues began to wag. Hiding behind the tag of businessman to cover-up unexplained income sources was no longer working. There was no denying it that a businessman could come by sudden fortune and great wealth. However, a growing list of men who claimed to be businessmen had been unravelled. From radio and other sources, they had heard news of how some businessmen had been nabbed while carrying on nefarious activities. The owner of a supermarket was identified as an armed robber! It was a good reason why questions must be asked about the sources of a person's wealth. 'Anyway, he must not forget that good name is better than silver and gold.'

'Ahamba almost changed his mind about returning to the North. He wanted to follow him to Lagos but he said he had many businesses to attend to in Port Harcourt,' Ozurumba told her. For the first time, doubt crept into his mind. 'Anyway, he may do whatever business he likes in so far as he does not waylay people on the road with a gun.'

'The only wealth that endures is one made with a clean mind,' Kperechi maintained.

Ozurumba took the spoon, ready to eat. 'Is there no fish to go with this food?' he asked.

'I have sold them. There's no more,' Kperechi answered.

'Let me have some fish, my friend. Otherwise take away your food,' he ordered.

'You are saying you can no longer eat a meal without fish?' Kperechi asked, annoyed. 'You're looking for how to ruin my business.'

'Mama, give your husband fish to eat,' Ijuolachi cajoled, supporting her father.

'Don't let me shut that mouth for you,' Kperechi reprimanded.

'You see the type of mother you have? Okay, I will pay. Just debit my account,' Ozurumba promised.

'You have seen *tata* who doesn't know when you're kidding. How much do you owe me? And as for you, Ijuolachi, I will make sure your tongue does not touch it. You are goading him on so you can have some,' Kperechi reproved.

'Woman, what your husband earns is money, not sand,' Ijuolachi declared jocularly before trotting off to get the metal basket.

'I was keeping it for soup tomorrow,' Kperechi muttered as she took the basket. She frowned when she opened it. 'This is not how I left this fish,' she complained. 'Who touched the fish?'

'It's not me,' Akachi denied immediately.

'Count me out. I know nothing about it,' Ijuolachi was adamant.

'Did you touch the fish?' Kperechi directed the question at her husband.

'While I was at the market or in the forest?' he retorted.

'Did my ancestors rise from their graves to eat the fish?' asked Kperechi. 'If I don't get the truth, none of your mouths will touch this fish.'

'Akachi tell the truth. What were you doing inside when I came back from the stream earlier today?' Ijuolachi asked.

'Nobody should mention my name ooo!' Akachi warned, the threat to fight his sister was quite obvious in his voice.

'You see? There he goes again. You have to castrate him to get simple truth from him,' Ozurumba berated.

'Akachi, will you tell the truth or not?' Kperechi asked.

'He was shocked to see me when I came in. He swallowed, and ran to take a drink of water,' Ijuolachi reported.

'How shameful,' Ozurumba tongue-lashed. 'How can you be breeding *gagwo* and all manners of armed robbers in my house?'

Kperechi dropped the basket and went for Akachi. She slapped him hard on the back before he could escape. 'It is not in this my house that you will learn to steal. Do you hear me? I'm going to tell all your friends and they will make a public show of you. A child that craves delicacies that are not given to him is learning to steal.'

'Stealing is bound to destroy anybody's reputation,' Ozurumba added.

'You're the cause of all this!' Kperechi turned on her husband. 'This is the seed you have sown. "Will you eat bread or will you eat fish?"' she parodied. 'You see the result?'

'I know it. I know you will heap the blame on me. Did I make him take your fish?' he asked, in between mouthful of tapioca, *odudu* and *ugba*.

Suddenly, a few but large raindrops spattered on the ground but stopped immediately as if the sky had mistakenly allowed them to escape. The circle left on the floor made their size easily noticeable. Having come when the ground was still hot from the scorching sun, a dusty vapour rose from the ground filling the air with the tantalising but elusive *ono* aroma which easily aroused a craving for *nzu*, the edible clay that was freely available at houses where the birth of new born babies were recorded. Another sporadic shower that lasted longer than the first followed moments after. They had raced ahead of a low distant drone announcing the approaching downpour. It was followed by a gusty wind that made nearby trees sway helplessly, some of them letting go fluttering dead leaves from their branches. Everyone ran for cover.

It was not the usual wind that heralded a heavy rain; the rain had preceded it, coming without sign or warning, growing heavy even before the gathering clouds could dim the bright sky. It was truly in a hurry, the single drops became rivulets; the rivulets a flood; the waters surging across the land, seeking channels to flow into. Determined to turn everything upside down, the wind gathered strength, lashing at everything in sight. Thunderbolts clapped furiously, barely waiting for the lightning streaks to fade out of sight. The wind pushed misty waves of rain into houses again and again, forcing everyone to shut their doors. The force of the gusts increased, banging and slamming unfastened doors and windows, picking up anything light and hurling it around, sending the heavier objects squealing and squeaking across the floor as if dragged around by the scruff of their necks. Unsecured rooftops ripped away. Displaced thatched sheets fluttered to the ground, unable to fly, lay spread-eagled. 'What kind of rain is this?' Kperechi wondered as they remained indoors. 'Get the lantern, Akachi.'

'Is this a normal rain?' asked Ozurumba. 'There was no warning at all. Many will still be on their way from the market. They will be drenched.'

'I hope this wind does not hurt anybody. It's so strong it can uproot trees,' said Ijuolachi, running her hand over her face to swipe away rainwater. She crossed her hands over her chest, took an old wrapper to towel herself. She was almost wet through while setting out containers to collect rainwater with Akudo. It would save them a number of trips to the stream.

'Does it want to tear off our roof?' Kperechi asked, reacting to the ceaseless squeaking sound coming from the zinc roof.

'One of the nails must have come loose,' Ozurumba imagined.

The rain stopped as abruptly as it had started. The wind calmed; the sky grumbled gently as if apologising for its earlier fierceness. The brightness of the sky waned again with the approach of eventide. As the light faded, Ozurumba was alerted by the distant sound of a wooden gong. Its abrasive urgency disturbed him. A distressed voice called faintly from afar off. 'Stop all that *ochochoricho* and let me listen,' he barked.

'Every man in Mboha should come out ooo!' wailed another voice.

'What is happening?' asked Ozurumba, rushing out of the house. Everyone in the compound followed. 'What is happening?' His heart was beating hard.

'Something terrible has happened to Agbakuru!' Nwanyibunwa could not bring herself to break the news. 'Where is the mouth to tell the story?'

'What do you mean by that? What has happened to Agbakuru?' asked Albert as he also hurried towards the village square. 'What did you hear?'

'Get your machete! Whoever owns a gun should get it,' Okpukpukaraka spoke to the hearing of Ozurumba and other men. 'Agbakuru has been butchered!'

'It cannot be,' Akwakanti recoiled in disbelief.

Okpukpukaraka did not stop to convince him. He went into the old *ikoro* hut, retrieved the drumsticks, and began to beat. His troubled soul pumping energy to his sinewy hands. The sound of the *ikoro* was abrasive and urgent; deep, loud, and far-reaching. The call for help rang throughout Mboha and beyond. Men came out with all speed and haste. 'Why are you all empty-handed?' asked Okpukpukaraka as he came out of the hut. He shook his head. 'Times have changed. Many have forgotten our way of life.'

The death of Agbakuru shocked Mboha beyond speech. The question on all lips was: how could anyone be that dastardly? Many had seen him in the market that day. When he got back, he went in search of Amalambu that he sent to take a bunch of bamboo to the farm that morning. His family wondered where he was after the heavy rain had ceased. A woman that saw him on the farm path before the rain reported hearing him call Amalambu.

His neighbours and children immediately formed a search party when he was not found anywhere in the neighbourhood. His body was found butchered. His assailants had scattered his body parts around the place. His tongue and genitals could not be found. Mboha men rushed into the bush to hunt for his killers but did not continue the search for long. The rain had obliterated all footprints. The murderers had made good their escape.

'That must be the reason for the downpour,' Egobeke concluded, as they paid their condolences the following day in Agbakuru's homestead.

'I said it,' Kperechi remembered. 'That rain was not normal.'

'Rain that did not even get to Abadaba,' Nwugo stated. 'We did not notice any sign of rain until we got to the outskirts of Abadaba and their boundary with Mboha.'

'Our land has been desecrated!' Leriakawa lamented. 'What an end to a true warrior!'

'A man in every sense of the word—tall, erect, upright, and gentle,' Jenny bemoaned. 'How could anyone want to harm him? What did he do?'

'Mboha must get to the root of this matter. This is a big challenge to us as a people,' Ashivuka added. Everybody was aware that the men held a meeting to decide what to do and had determined to consult an oracle to uncover the perpetrators.

The village did not have to wait for long. The three men that set out to Ofeimo before the break of dawn returned while the sympathisers were still trooping to the house. Everyone besieged them, eager to hear the answer to the mystery. They kept their peace. The report could not be made public until the elders heard it and decided on the next course of action. But the information eventually leaked out. Agbakuru's protective charm was neutralised at an event where he shook hands with people. The conspirators lured him away from home. The plan could not have succeeded if there had been no insider to aid and abet the scheme. The oracle refused to mention names, otherwise more heads would roll.

Mboha was alarmed at the news. Who was the enemy within? Who in Mboha would be privy to the killing of a kinsman? Who could be that treacherous? Their problem was compounded by the refusal of the oracle to name names. 'Mboha *leeeeee*! Who are we to fear? Who could be in the company of his own *umunna* and still fear for his life?' Kperechi continued her lamentation.

'Terrible things do happen!' Akwakanti exclaimed.

'They will get to know what an important person they have killed,' Ezeagwula said. 'They have Ogwugwu and Igwekala to contend with.'

'A deaf-mute need not be told that the market is in uproar,' Anosike added.

'They could only have done it under the cover of the rain. If the dead are so brave, why do they sneak about at night?' Okoro asked.

Some wanted an oracle that would disclose the names of the killers to ensure they were brought to justice. They could not stand the thought that Agbakuru's death would not be avenged, otherwise it could happen again.

Others felt there was nothing Mboha could do which could compare to the wrath of the god Ogwugwu, whom Agbakuru had served until his death. They were sure that Ogwugwu would make mincemeat of his murderers, nor did they expect it to stop there. The punishment could extend to their wives and children. Mboha waited anxiously to hear of a sudden evil and calamity befalling a kinsman. Nothing happened.

Agbakuru was buried and mourned. Fewer men than usual participated in the funeral rites. The village did not witness the warriors' dance in the way it used to be. In every corner of the village, all faces were pale with mourning and lamentation. The sorrow thickened to despair. The able-bodied young people could no longer perform the traditional dances to mourn their famous kinsman and hero. Only the dead could mourn their dead. Those who failed to profess faith in the Lord were not worthy of the believers' adulation. The message was clear. It was not a few that took notice.

22.

Sigmund Pharmacy was relatively calm when Okwudiri got to the shop that morning. His friends were not there. 'Where is my boy?' he asked one of the junior *nwaboy* just before Tagbo walked in. 'My boy, don't tell me you just got here,' he started at him, trying to engage him in their usual battle of wits. 'Quick, quick, your boss is here,' he ordered, handing over his list. It was their usual practise to dash to a neighbourhood shop to augment stock in the event of shortfall.

'*Taa*, small boy,' Tagbo shushed him without taking offence. 'Do you want my boys to double you up?' Looking at the list, he asked Onochie to put the drugs together quickly. 'You don't have Dabsone too?'

'It appears the drug is scarce in the market,' said Okwudiri.

'Timoptol, England, or France?' Onochie asked.

'Ten each,' Okwudiri answered. Glancing around, his eyes took in all the features that made Sigmund Pharmacy the biggest in Ogbogwu Market, Bridge Head. It was the dream of many to grow that big. After years of dealing in patent medicine, the company expanded, employing pharmacists and becoming the biggest importer of prescription drugs in Onitsha. Hez, the owner, had more than twelve multi-storey buildings dotting different parts of the town. As Tagbo pointed out in one of their arguments, the sum total of all transactions in his numerous shops in Onitsha came to over two million naira a day.

'*Nna*, have you heard what happened to Cletus?' Tagbo asked.

'The girl he impregnated? That's old news, my boy,' Okwudiri said dismissively.

'Armed robbers shot him,' Tagbo broke the news.

'*Ewuu Chim ooo!*' he cried, both hands clutching his head. 'Onitsha has not become this bad, has it?' Okwudiri thought, remembering he often kept late nights.

'It happened after Ore. He travelled to Lagos and was coming back last night. Robbers attacked their bus. But after the robbery, he asked for receipt. They told him to run and one of them fired a shot at him,' Tagbo explained. Okwudiri was all the more puzzled—the idea of asking robbers for receipt did not make immediate sense. Seeing his confusion, Tagbo added, 'He did not want his boss to think he was lying.'

'But did he survive?'

'He is battling for his life in the hospital,' Tagbo told him, as Onochie brought out the drugs.

Okwudiri's head drooped for a moment. 'You mean he risked his life because of money? I wouldn't do that. The boss can keep his money. True to God,' he swore. It was the risk trainees ran, particularly towards the end of their apprenticeship. A minor mistake was enough to terminate his training contract. However, he did not believe that justified placing one's life on the line. 'How did Cletus come up with the idea of receipt?' he kept wondering.

Silvanus was berating his trainees for shortfall in stock when he got to the shop. 'What have you been doing in Ogbogwu all morning?' he rebuked. 'Common procaine penicillin is not in the shop. You want to chase my customers away, isn't it? What about Obiora? He's not back from Lagos?'

'*Oga*,' Okwudiri called him. 'Armed robbers attacked traders last night. They shot one of our boys.'

'What?' Silvanus was shocked, momentarily forgetting his foul mood.

Okwudiri narrated the brief details, without giving his opinion as to why Cletus asked for the receipt.

'*Chim ooo*, say no more,' Ukamaka cried, visibly frightened as if the robbers were lurking around. She had always dreaded the thought of travelling at night. Besides the risk of a breakdown and getting stranded on the road, the fear of robbers terrorising unarmed citizen was ever present in her mind. 'Anybody who values his life should not travel at night, true. Those *abali di egwu* are such a heartless lot,' she blurted out. *Abali di egwu*, the night is fearful, was another name for armed robbers.

'How terrible,' Silvanus sympathised, unable to understand the request for a receipt either. The reason suddenly dawned on him. 'Oh, oh, he does not want his *oga* to think he embezzled the money. That's crazy. What if he does not survive? Anyway, when is Obiora meant to be coming back?' They were still talking when the cart-pusher and Obiora arrived with the goods. 'Take Ukamaka to Toronto Hospital,' he told Okwudiri. 'I don't know what is wrong with Iloka. This is the second day he did not come to work. And at the end of the month he will expect me to pay him.'

Okwudiri, the only *nwaboy* who could drive, was often called upon to run important errands. It was the skill he acquired during his short apprenticeship as a motor mechanic trainee in Kaduna.

Okwudiri drove through the MCC Estate to get to Upper Niger Bridge Street. Once they were in Woliwo, the imposing edifice of Toronto Hospital came into view. At the honk of his horn, the gates swung slowly open. He dropped Ukamaka at the hospital entrance, before driving off to the parking lot. He turned off the ignition but left the radio on. He was enjoying Brenda Fasie's music coming from Coal City FM. He sang along, repeating the refrain, '*It's your wedding day . . . I do, I do. . .*' It was one of the music that made him love Brenda deeply. Her high octane voice had set his heart aglow. His mind automatically replayed the musical video where Brenda performed different roles. As a mother, she was in a celebratory mood, cooking and preparing to see her daughter get married. But in a conflict of emotion, she found herself crying that the daughter, the virtue that flowed from her, was about to embark on a lifelong journey. Just like many that watched it, he felt that her role as the priest was classic. At first, he did not realise it was Brenda officiating as a priest until somebody pointed it out. The best of the musical video was perhaps the little girl and boy chosen as the bride and groom. They offered a far more pleasant surprise. The groom and his oversized bowler hat dropping and covering his face; the joyous noise of a happy mother who was like any other woman in their native setting, making smile break forth on his happy face. Her energy and zest combined with her strong and flawless vocal to pleasurably imprint her image in the minds of the fans that simply adored her. She was the total package. He wished he would be rich enough to get her to perform at his wedding. But even if he could not afford her, her music must play at his wedding for his listening pleasure.

He had reason to agree that Coal City FM, Enugu had positively rivalled the Garden City FM, Port Harcourt in the quality of entertainment and information provided to the listening public. His thought drifted as the stonemasonry work of the building caught his attention. It made the hospital look sturdily built and it was quite obvious that a great deal of costs was incurred to build it. The statue of a man stretching out his arms, helping a child on crutches to stand up, called his mind to the passage in Acts of the Apostle where Peter asked the lame man at the beautiful gate to rise and walk, making his ankle receive strength.

Once again, all he heard about the owner came to his mind. Given the size and scale of the hospital, he had marvelled at the stupendous wealth required to build such edifice in the Seventies. In this regard, he heard a number of accounts. The owner came from a royal family and eventually occupied the throne. On this account, there was no question that he could attract the finance from banks and other sources to erect such structure. However, some believed that the community and city where HRH *Igwe* (Dr) Walter Eze studied had a hand in the project. It was their contribution to improving the medical infrastructure to a part of the country that suffered severe devastation as a result of civil war. Expectedly, it was named 'Toronto' after the Canadian city where the founder trained as a surgeon.

Okwudiri was more inclined to believe the latter account and he imagined what George, his kinsman, would say about the founder. It was the kind of thing George would love to hear, to illustrate his firm belief in the power of education. He would have praised *Igwe* Walter to the high heavens and, above all, credit him for being a worthy ambassador of his fatherland and people. His academic excellence and ability to apply himself with diligence to his work must have won the hearts of his hosts and made it an easy decision to invest in anything that would allow the brilliant doctor serve humanity amongst his people.

After a long wait, he was almost out of the car to look for Ukamaka when she emerged from the building. 'Sorry ooo *nna*, it was a long queue,' she apologised as she got into the seat at the owner's corner. 'Things are no longer the same. This is the second time I am made to waste time unnecessarily in that hospital. The death of the *Igwe* is beginning to tell in this hospital. One comes for a simple medical procedure but ends up spending the whole day waiting in the queue.'

What Ukamaka said reminded him about the obituary of the *Igwe*. Coal City FM aired the death notice severally and the lamentation eulogising the *Igwe* was the most profound he had ever heard on radio. Addressing him directly, the announcer intonated the title '*Igwe*' making it last far longer in his mouth. The grief laden voice chanted the name again and again, asking many questions as if it would arouse him to action. His academic excellence, dedication to duty, philanthropy, loyal service to God and country, and many other virtues were some of the many reasons his people were in mourning.

'A long queue has built up before the doctor came. If only *Igwe* knew, he would not have settled only Obosi people. It wouldn't have cost him an arm and a leg,' she muttered. He had no difficulty making sense of what Ukamaka said while venting her displeasure. As he heard, the parcel of land on which the hospital was built was subject to conflicting claims of ownership. Believing that the Obosi people were the owners of the land, *Igwe* settled the claimants from Obosi. The Onitsha family succeeded in the adverse claim filed in court. The judgment demanded that the *Igwe* paid a sum of money as annual rent to the Onitsha family. It was rumoured that the *Igwe* suffered from high blood pressure as a result of the case. Okwudiri wondered if it was the genesis of the well-known saying: *adighi ama ama, obodo gwara ibe ya*—you never can tell, that is what a people told another.

The music from the Coal City FM Radio stopped at the top of the hour as the anchor read news items from around the world. The most significant item to Okwudiri was about the US-trained Nigerian doctor that led a team of surgeons to successfully separate conjoined twins in Baltimore, Maryland. Okwudiri let out a scream of delight when he heard the name of Professor Leo Ogbuagu on the radio. '*Chai*, this must be my kinsman?' But he became less certain if professor was part of his name.

His excitement brightened Ukamaka up. 'Is there anybody from your place that goes by that name?'

'I'm sure it must be him,' he stated increasing the volume of the radio, hoping to hear more. But the radio turned to other news items. 'His father used to be a policeman. The doctor has taken most of his siblings abroad. *Chai*, I'm sure people in the village will hear the news.'

'Our people are doing well. If it is in this country, I doubt if he could record such a feat. That is why everybody wants to check out like Andy.'

'There will be so much joy in my village today,' Okwudiri enthused, switching to join the faster lane of the slow-moving traffic on Upper Iweka Road before it gradually came to a standstill. Interstate transporters, in their usual hurry, tried to force their way through the traffic. Some, seeing nothing coming from the opposite direction, entered the lane for oncoming vehicles only to end up blocking the lane as well. Others tried to make their way through every available gap between the vehicles. Car owners, fearing a scratch or dent honked petulantly, warning the offending drivers or raining abuses, reproachfully glaring at such driver, querying if the nuts in his brain had gone out of kilter.

The sweltering sun offered them no respite. Hawkers, always looking forward to such traffic jams, came out in droves, crowding around different vehicles with the hope of receiving patronage from the occupants. 'Buy Our Lady's Buttered Bread, the № 1 in town,' a young man offered, tapping the window to get her attention. From Ukamaka's disinterested look, the hawker concluded that she was not a traveller who needed to buy such loaves as a treat for those at home. Briskly, he moved on to the vehicle in front. Another hawker thrust a VHS cassette into the car, offering it for sale. '*Living in Bondage*, it's a great film.'

'Failure to follow the rules of the road is a terrible thing,' a bus driver sighed, shaking his head in frustration.

'Idiagbon wanted to clean up this country but you fellows wouldn't let him,' another driver called back. 'See, this is the terrible mess we always get ourselves into.'

'I want Gala,' Okwudiri told a boy that was offering him *aki n' ukwa*.

'Eloka, bring Gala,' the boy called. Two other boys came sprinting between the vehicles, arriving almost at the same time. Each tried to outdo the other, shoving the beef sausages close to his face.

'Stop!' Okwudiri snapped, glaring at them. 'Did any nut come loose in your skull?' he glared, tapping his head.

'Sorry sir,' both of them chorused without remorse. They were ready to do anything, as long as he would buy from them. He took a pack to check the expiry date. 'Na fresh Gala,' the boy reassured, feeling lucky. Okwudiri took two more from him before doing same for the second boy, passing four to Ukamaka at the back.

'Pure water! Cold pure water!' announced another hawker, thrusting a sachet into the car. Holding it, Okwudiri confirmed it was truly cold before buying two. After consuming the food and water, they tossed the empty packs out on to the road, leaving them to be crushed under feet and tyres. The rubbish mixed with the loose red earth from many potholes of different sizes and dimension all combined to ruin what must have been a smooth surface of a tarred road at some point in time. A number of passengers fed up with sitting in their vehicles walked down the line of traffic to find out what caused the gridlock.

'Turn the air conditioner on,' Ukamaka instructed spitting out the beef roll in her mouth as the stench of wastewater stung her nose. 'What type of traffic is this?' she complained as she noticed the source of the smell. A woman cooking a meal of beans by the roadside had poured away dirty water that stirred a stagnant pool. Partially lifting the sack covering the pot on fire she went for the wraps of moi-moi with her bare hand. Burnt by the hot and steaming wraps, she involuntarily withdrew her hand again and again to dip it in a bowl of water kept for the purpose. Her hand returned to the pot for another attempt until she succeeded in removing a number of them into a bowl which a girl promptly took away for hawking.

Close by, a blacksmith was busy with his hammer and anvil, knocking coarse metal into shape to fabricate a range of cheap household items on display. From his twisted fingers and stoop, it was easy to conclude that he had been at the trade for years. His perpetual exposure to the elements and the greasy particles and chippings from the articles of his trade gave his skin a blacker look. It was the same with the welder working on a cheap iron gate.

A little distance away, a vulcaniser tugged at a rope; his machine came alive, blasting away noisily, the stay shuddering, moving back and forth. He dragged the nozzle along, inserting it into the valve to inflate the tube he had just vulcanised. It reminded Okwudiri that the front tyre on the passenger side needed some air. With the consent of Ukamaka, Okwudiri called on him to pump it up before handing him thirty kobo coins.

The traders had converted the space between the road and the wall into ramshackle sheds. That they ran the risk of being crushed in the event of an accident seemed to weigh little on their minds. A man pushing a wooden cart stopped by the woman's stand to supply her with charcoal. Apparently, the woman did not have ready cash to pay him.

Ironically, they lived in the same city where transactions in some shops grossed over five million naira a day. Yet, they could barely survive despite the grit, toil, and labour. Without complaint, they invested all their time and effort but were rewarded with nothing more than hunger and thirst, rags for clothes, dirt, unfulfilled dreams, and privation in extreme. They worked in the trades that nobody else wanted anything to do with. It was a harsh way of surviving for the defeated, the simple-minded, the weaklings, the rejected, and all those locked out from the respectable circles of society whether it was their fault or not. With little or no education to work out an exit strategy, they remained trapped in a quagmire that was ready to consume them. Nevertheless, the will to carry on did not desert them. Hope was rooted in the stories of the past—fortune, without defining her beneficiary, had smiled on some in similar circumstances. It could happen to them or maybe their children. Okwudiri remembered all the mantra about the dignity of labour and earning honest living. Seeing the reward, he shuddered at what could have become of him as a mechanic.

The car engine continued to steam as the traffic remained in gridlock for over forty minutes. The fuel gauge had gone down a notch. 'The air conditioner is really consuming the fuel,' Okwudiri pointed out.

'Ewoo! Why did we take this way? *Chim egbuem!*' she said before instructing him to turn it off. There was a sudden flurry of activity—drivers and passengers hurrying back to their vehicles. On the horizon were soldiers from the 302 Military Cantonment dressed in their starched camouflage, wielding horsewhips, walking briskly, ready to restore sanity to the situation. Some errant drivers, particularly those in the wrong lane, did not escape some lashes which they endured without fighting back. 'That is the language we understand,' Ukamaka muttered. Many engines roared to life and those that refused to start got a push. The lines began to crawl forward. As they reached Moore Street, Okwudiri accelerated, fresh air gushing in as the car gained speed.

23.

The luxury bus came alive with passengers scrambling up to reach their hand luggage stowed in the overhead racks even before the driver came to a complete stop. They had all boarded the old bus at the Iddo Park in Lagos, and it was crammed with goods. Okwudiri was looking out for the boxes marked in red with his initial; he counted them as they were off-loaded. 'Ah *nna*, have you come back?' asked a brawny fellow, as a prelude to the more important question of whether he needed a truck.

'Bright Street,' Okwudiri answered. Quickly, he positioned his cart and was ready to load it up when Okwudiri interrupted him. 'How much?'

'Fifteen naira.'

Okwudiri was furious. '*Gbo di anyi*, drop those boxes,' he ordered, his disdain becoming stronger as if he suddenly became more aware of how scruffy the man looked.

Taken aback, the cart pusher stopped in his tracks, mouth agape and smile frozen on his face. Realising that there was no point in arguing when there were other cart pushers around who were ready to take his place, the man pulled a wry face. 'There's no need getting angry about it. Tell me what you can pay.'

'If you won't accept five naira, don't touch my load. You're asking for fifteen naira; how much did I pay from Lagos?' Okwudiri continued, taking the opportunity to drive a hard bargain. At a time and place where meekness and civility were seen as weakness, ruthlessness was the only answer.

'Make it eight naira,' the man requested. 'You know the distance between here and Eze Iweka Road before proceeding to Bright Street,' he contended, lifting a box.

'The best I can do is six naira,' Okwudiri countered, helping to load the cart.

'O! O!' shouted a fellow, slapping the bus, indicating to the bus driver to change direction. The bus moved forward before pulling out completely, the big tyres crushing the empty cans and other rubbish littering the wide wet expanse.

They had only taken few steps when a young man in his mid-twenties stopped them, thrusting his hand forward with two pieces of paper. 'Your ticket,' was all he said, his lips twisted, exhaling cigarette smoke and pushing it up. The truck pusher turned to Okwudiri who was already dipping hand into a small bag dangling from his neck, producing fifty kobo notes. The young man withdrew the ticket. 'One naira each,' he demanded, the scowl on his grimy face showing he was not ready to entertain any question or protest. His completely worn out sleeveless t-shirt, bearing MC Hammer's image, exposed a long scar on his arm in addition to those on the bridge of his nose and forehead. His middle and forefingers held the cigarette which Okwudiri could easily tell was Target, the brand Fela Anikulapo Kuti always advertised on radio. Like many motor park touts, he must have fought for his life at one time or the other.

'When did it become one naira each?' Okwudiri protested all the same.

'Hurry up, my friend,' he barked. 'I'm in a hurry. This one is for the chairman, the controller of the territory; this is for the park,' he explained each ticket. Okwudiri handed two naira to him without further argument; he knew quite well that his goods would be detained if he failed to pay.

Close by, a conductor was returning a marginal portion of the fare to four passengers who were not taken to their destination. They would need to buy more tickets to complete their journey. Thinking he could stand up to the conductor, one of the passengers was expressing his displeasure at being stopped halfway. 'But I told you I was going to Aba!' he protested.

'What is wrong with him?' asked the thickset driver walking past them, a nonchalant look on his face as he puffed cigarette smoke. He left them to sort it out with the conductor.

'How can you only take me halfway?' the passenger insisted.

The scowl on the conductor's face was enough to warn the passenger he would not get far with him. 'If you don't take this money and disappear from my sight, I'll get *agbero* to bite off your ears. You'll see it now now.' That seemed to do the magic. The news of Mike Tyson biting off the ear of his opponent in a boxing match was still fresh in their minds. Undoubtedly, the thugs would happily re-enact it. The troublesome passenger, looking deflated, accepted the money reluctantly. The conductor quickly beckoned to a wheelbarrow pusher to deal with the protest about his load. 'Take this load to the Relief Market Park,' he instructed, handing over a twenty-kobo coin to him.

Another man in his fifties, sitting at the exit, held out another set of two tickets. Okwudiri showed him the tickets in his hand. 'Those are for Bosco and his group. This is for the NURTW and local government,' the man stated. Mercifully, he accepted one naira for both before lowering the chain.

Gritting his teeth, the truck pusher leaned forward, pushing with all his body weight, muscles fully flexed and feet rolling inwards. The cart lunged forward, forcing him to quicken his pace as he guided it past the many potholes. His slippers, clapping noisily against his heels, and his worn-out woollen trousers that were rolled up above his calves were not spared the mud spattering. Okwudiri paid two more tolls imposed by other territorial bosses before getting to the shop. The cart pusher was full of thanks on getting an additional one naira.

After unpacking the load and taking inventory of what Okwudiri brought back, the shelves were stocked. 'I have to get to the yard,' Okwudiri announced, leaving for the compound to clean himself up. It was the second year since he started embarking on such business trips as a senior *nwaboy* in the shop. He alternated the trips with Obiora before Silvanus directed them to introduce Arinze and Phillip. He was to make the trip with Phillip but Arinze was down with malaria and Phillip stayed to cover for him. Though he was entitled to take the remainder of the day off, he hoped to return to the shop to join his friends to go to DMGS—Dennis Memorial Grammar School—football pitch for a fixture that promised to be a cracker.

At the compound, Okwudiri met Amobi his neighbour, loading up cartons of the locally distilled gin which he had poured into Brandy, Gordon Gin, or Scotch Whiskey bottles which, taken to the market, were passed off as the original beverages but at a reduced price.

Opening their door, Okwudiri noticed the room was in a mess. He could imagine what happened: Obiora must have woken up late and hurried off to the market, leaving the pap bowl and the piece of old newspaper used to wrap the *akara*—the beans cake—he must have eaten while taking the pap. There was sand on the black-and-white plastic carpet stretching from wall to wall. Clothes that ought to be on the hanger were on the bed. 'This Obiora knows how to mess things up, *eeh*?' he muttered, sighing loudly and unbolting the windows to let in fresh air.

'Anyone that comes here now will think this is a pigsty,' he said, tidying up the room. He contemplated mopping the floor after sweeping it but changed his mind. He brought the curtain down as the lachrymal voice of Sonny Okosun singing *Fire in Soweto*, floated from Coal City 92.8 FM Enugu. Though he did not follow the events in South Africa that much, he could tell that the international campaign against apartheid was gravitating towards a definite end. It was impossible to escape awareness of the events, with the legions of musicians lending their voices to the cry. The crooning voice of Onyeka Onwenu extolled Winnie Mandela, the soul of a nation crying to be free; The Mandators, Victor Eshiet and his wife cried for Mandela's release from prison; and the venerable Sonny Okosun, garbed like the Zulu warriors, rallied African soldiers, dead or alive, to rise to the challenges besetting Africa. From all indications, time seemed to be running out for P.W. Botha especially with the emergence of F. W. de Klerk.

Unrolling the two posters he bought in Lagos, he glued them to the wall. Lionel Richie, sporting Jheri curls, looked glamorously cool in his grey pullover with a gold Rolex watch on his wrist. Stevie Wonder, in sunshades and dreadlocks, stood with Marvin Gaye in his suit and bowtie.

Picking up a towel, he took the soap dish and water in a plastic bucket to head to the common bathroom. First, he opened the toilet door to see if he could use it. Although it was not in a terrible state, the enamel bowl of the squat toilet that was once white had become brown with encrusted dirt and the surroundings were sleazy with grime. In one corner stood the twenty-five-litre plastic can, its top slashed off, holding the usual dirty water kept for flushing. In the other corner, a broken plastic bucket held papers of various descriptions—cement bags, pages torn from exercise books, newspapers—all smudged with faeces. It was almost full. He wondered whose turn it was to keep the toilets and bathrooms clean that week. The bachelors contributed the money to buy the brooms and disinfectants but the married women in the compound took turns to keep them clean. The wall and doorframes were similarly besmirched. Some, maybe in extreme hurry and unable to lay their hands on any paper, decided to make do with them. It was possible to tell, from the height, which marks had been left by children and which by adults. The disgusting smell and sight meant a number of the tenants preferred to smoke while in the toilet.

Leaving the toilet, he took the bucket of water at the door into the bathroom to bathe. He was moisturising himself in the room when he heard a gentle tap. 'Yes?' he answered, wondering who it could be. As the curtain opened, he stood face to face with Rosemary. Happily, he gathered her into his warm embrace.

*   *   *

The traffic jam on New Market Road that evening was not unusual at the end of a business day. The bus transporting them had a cavalcade of motorcycles to contend with. Onitsha had caught the motorcycle bug that originated from Lagos. In their usual haste to beat the perennial traffic jam, the motor parts traders in Idumota and Balogun resorted to motorcycles as a means of transport. It was possible to meander and wind one's way through the narrow spaces between cars or between the cars and kerb. 'Oh ooo, I should be on one of those motorbikes,' Nonso wished, sighing with frustration at the sight of the traffic jam.

'There's no way DMGS can beat Metro this year,' argued Obiora, banking on the sensational striking force of Olunkwa and Pele.

'I have not seen a football talent like Olunkwa,' Okwudiri joined the fray. 'If Metro beats DMGS today, they'll surely carry the cup this year.' He was equally excited by Olunkwa's football skills. Metro's ouster from the Anambra State Academicals Cup the previous year had pained them all.

'You are not factoring the schools in Enugu zone, why?' the driver disputed. 'CIC, Nike Grammar School, St. Patrick Emene and Awkunanaw Boys are no pushovers, you know that.'

'Let's beat DMGS first,' Obiora insisted. He was passionate about Metro, his alma mater. 'The referee robbed us of victory last year. It won't be so this year.' Much was usually at stake in any fixture involving two of the Onitsha big three—DMGS, Christ the King College, and Metropolitan College—always producing a thriller that no football lover wanted to miss. However, it was not all about the schools in Onitsha. The College of Immaculate Conception, Nike Grammar School, St. Patrick Emene, and Awkunanaw Boys from the Enugu zone offered stiff opposition, with a string of victories to their names. It was also the joy and pride of the Enugu zone that it produced the remarkable school principal of Nike Grammar School, C.O.C Chiedozie and the exceptional soccer star, Jay Jay Okocha. Jay Jay was their gift to football both to their country and the global soccer scene.

'See, see,' cried the driver aghast, watching a young man on Honda CD 175—he was leaning dangerously on the corners, with only one buttock on the saddle. The silencer was gone and the Honda was roaring like banger, catching everybody's attention. 'Imagine this idiot playing with his life.'

The rider continued to rev the engine, bursting forward at top speed, bringing it to a sudden stop with cadence braking; allowing it to surge forward again, rearing to go before screeching to a halt. As if intent on wowing the onlookers, with one foot on the ground, he spun the bike 360 degrees before speeding off again. His audience of enthralled young men started clapping and cheering his name. 'Sankara! Sankara! Thomas Sankara!'

'Truly, no expert rider can beat Sankara,' Obiora enthused.

'This is nothing. Wait till you see his daredevil stunts,' Nonso added.

'It is not a lie, he looks every inch like Thomas Sankara,' said the driver reflectively, remembering the charismatic president of Burkina Faso whom they had so loved and admired. His death in a coup d'état was a terrible blow, which had saddened them all. Many of his admirers adopted his name.

'I don't even know why he is wasting his time trading,' a passenger commented.

'I'm sure he could be the number one escort rider to the governor if he is a Mopol or soldier,' Okwudiri agreed.

'This *nna-anyi* Zik is always rooted to the same place whether the sun is up in the sky or the rain is pouring down,' noted a maternal passenger ruefully, wondering why the Zik's statue in Onitsha was never spared the vagaries of the weather. The peeling paint gave it the rough appearance of a man poorly kept in threadbare and tattered clothing.

'It is only a lifeless statue. Does it know whether it is raining or shining?' asked a middle-aged male passenger.

Okwudiri was surprised at her thought processes that lavished concern on things many people ignored. She must have empathised with the statue for a long while before voicing it out. They turned into Uguta Road, off the roundabout, and the bus pulled off the road to let the boys disembark. They barely made it to the DMGS field when the tumultuous roar of 'G-O-A-L!' erupted in the air. 'Olu, kwa, kwa, kwa, Olunkwa!' sang a section of the spectators as their team celebrated the goal.

Obiora was smarting from the defeat that Metropolitan College had suffered at the hands of DMGS after a penalty shootout. It was Olunkwa who did not convert his penalty kick. 'That is foo . . . fo . . . football for you. . .' Ekene tried to cheer him up as they ate the *suya* that Okwudiri had bought at the barbeque spot in Awada Layout.

'I'm sure Rangers FC will snap him up as soon he finishes school,' Nonso predicted in between mouthfuls.

'Anyway, football is not mathematics,' Obiora admitted, gladly quoting Earnest Okonkwo, unarguably the best football commentator of their time. 'If great players like Zico and Socrates of Brazil could miss penalty, then. . .'

'You have slaughtered on the high sea,' Victor commented as he saw the amount of *suya* Okwudiri had bought. He shoved a chunk into his mouth.

'What else? Whoever joins *akpuruka*, at the end of the trip, he will taste spices and lick fingers, isn't it? Whoever plays ball is entitled to lick orange. Enjoy yourself,' Okwudiri told him, chewing the beef with the spicy granules, tomato portions, and onions. He looked good in his blue jeans suit and immaculate BYC vest, his half shoe was a quality product from Spain in shades of vanilla, grey, and blue. Most passengers preferred the modern coaches to the older models but they were all imported from Brazil. The operators of the old coaches counted on the faithful patronage of *umuboy*, the trainees, who in a bid to cut back on their expenses readily put up with discomforts like sitting on *obere-oche*, the extra seats conductors place in the aisle for those paying reduced fare. Delayed arrival was not much of a bother to them, since they knew that 'Anyhow, anyhow, *akpuruka* must come back'. Epigrams such as ARRIVAL IS ARRIVAL: NO CONTROVERSY and BETTER LATE THAN NEVER often appeared on the rear windscreens of such coaches.

'Let's go to my place to watch *Living in Bondage*,' Victor proposed. It was a welcome suggestion as they walked down the street. As they entered the courtyard, they saw a Peugeot 505 Evolution parked behind a Santana car, the Volkswagen product that was equally in vogue.

'Another new car,' Udoka noted with admiration as they inched their way through the narrow space between the cars and the wall. 'Who launched this *asampete*—beauty?'

'The same guy,' Victor answered, fishing out the union key from the bunch in his hand.

'The carcass your neighbour slaughtered on the high seas has no equal,' Obiora concluded. Slaughtering carcass on the high sea was their colloquial expression for any moneymaking tactics involving minimal effort within a short time. Such enterprise necessarily involved some form of positive dishonesty or illegitimate conduct contrived to dupe or fleece business associates. For many that were obsessed with achieving success by all means and all costs, making money ruled and dictated their lives. They despised the prudence and patience which led to gradual growth.

'These are merely tips of the iceberg,' said Victor. 'Who do you think owns that architectural masterpiece being constructed at Iwunze Crescent in Omoba Phase II?'

'He . . . he . . . heeeee cannot be the one,' Ekene blurted out. He could not see how a young man without a long history of making money could suddenly come into such wealth and fortune. Work went on at the site day and night to deck the storey building which looked like a family house. Most houses in Onitsha were four-storey buildings. While the landlord occupied the fourth floor, other flats were rented out which brought in income. But that commercial purpose was absent in the house they talked about. It was roofed after the first decking. The landscaping and other details showed that the owner had a taste for quality far above what was generally available at their time. It was strange that any moneybag in Onitsha would let the opportunity to make more money pass him by on the fanciful altar of building a family home. It meant that the man must have more than enough sources of income.

'*Money good o money good o my friend!*' Okwudiri sang one of Prince Nico Mbarga's famous tracks from the album, *Sweet Mother*. 'Where is he getting his money?'

'He also bought a house in this Awada. I'm sure he'll pull it down to build one, two, three, four. What if it were your yard?' asked Victor with mischievous grin. It meant his friends could have accommodation crisis soon. With Onitsha undergoing rapid transformation, there were only a few houses in Awada Layout that remained a bungalow. From the balcony of the fourth floor of his storey building, every landlord wanted to behold the sprawling city and its environs, including the splendour of River Niger flowing in its channel.

'If . . . if . . . if that happens, yu . . . yu . . . you guys will have problem,' Ekene surmised. He was certain that Silva would not allow them back under his roof.

'If it is you, will you allow it?' Victor asked, grinning. The story of the *nwaboy* that slept with the wife of his boss had taught many shop owners a lesson. Apparently tired after the day's hustle and bustle, the unsuspecting husband retired into his bedroom, leaving his wife and the *nwaboy* playing ludo in the parlour. The sound of *sikky* after *sikky* was not only too frequent but too loud that it was interrupting his attempt to sleep. After his call to stop was not heeded, he had walked back to the parlour to call them to order but found his *nwaboy* on top of his wife.

'I'm not scared,' Obiora rebuffed. 'Soon, *Ogbuefi*'s house will be ready. We'll move into one of the flats.'

'There is always a way,' Okwudiri remarked.

Victor's room in the family house was adorned with different posters— Michael Jackson in a dazzling white suit carrying a cub; the Musical Youth in jeans and t-shirts; the group photograph of American musicians that participated in the *USA for Africa* album; Donna Summer—which Jane, his regular girlfriend, had bought; and a young woman clad only in her briefs, her big luscious breasts bared invitingly beside his bed. He pushed a button to eject the video cartridge before inserting *Living in Bondage*.

'Is it not money? I will make it in this life. People will hear my name,' Udoka assured them, beating his chest.

'Do you think they are making all that money with clean eyes?' Okwudiri asked, bearing in mind the recent story of Ogundu who scandalously admitted that his wealth was satanic. After his several pleas for God to enrich him failed, Ogundu said he was left with no choice but to take some satanic steps. 'Is it not what Patty Obasi called a head for a head?'

'That is the same story as in *Living in Bondage*, is it not?' Victor speculated aloud. 'Money, money, money, that is what everybody is crying for but for me, it is not the ultimate. You see those overseas countries, my legs must get there and I'll live life like decent human being. You see all that rat race for money; I'm not cut out for it *chaa*. Whenever I lay my head on the pillow, I want to sleep deep without fear of offending God or man,' he articulated his dreams. He saw things differently from all those obsessed with crass materialism. For him, the pursuit of happiness was the ultimate goal.

24.

Nature appeared to be at peace with all men that Sunday. It was a brilliant day, the sun shining in the sky shared time with the clouds travelling across its face. The blazing sun withdrew at regular intervals for the clouds to cast shadows that calmed the atmosphere. This came with gentle breeze that took the edge off its intensity. Having worked for the last six days, Onitsha was observing the day of rest. The quest for money, the bedlam of activity, and the thunder of the rat race were all in abeyance, overtaken by other considerations. The gentle purr of an engine as the occasional car drove slowly up and down the streets; the neatly dressed figures clutching their Bibles, missals, and church bulletins on their way from church or on a visit became the dominant sights and sounds in the neighbourhood. Most people were indoors observing the day of rest, taking an unaccustomed siesta, hosting guests, or having a sumptuous meal before their social engagements later in the evening.

The cool breeze seeped through the blinds, like Noah's dove bringing news of a congenial world outside. The long curtains, hiding their heads in the curtain-board railings, were equally happy, gracefully fluttering up and down, draping the nearest sofa, satisfying their longing to touch and be one with the settees. The presenter of Music of the Masters at the Coal City FM came on air again as a piece of the sacred oratorio came to an end. It was a performance by the Philadelphia Philharmonic Orchestra. In a deliberately measured speech pattern, Pete Edochie unhurriedly told his listeners more about Charles Jennens, the librettist that collaborated with the great composer, George Friedrich Handel to produce the *Messiah*. He compiled different Bible passages from the King James Bible which he presented to Handel. At a time when the Bible was not freely available, Jennens had a strong urge for people to hear what the mouth of the Lord had spoken. He was equally driven by the urgency to counter the deists and their strange thinking that denied the core of the Christian faith. When a number of charities from Dublin called upon Handel to compose and perform at a public concert to raise money to free debtors from prison, he got the needed inspiration to use the Bible portions in his composition. It was first performed in Dublin in 1742.

Edochie's rich baritone flavoured the accounts he gave, every word like a golden drop of honey. Before concluding his presentation that afternoon, he acknowledged the greetings and compliments of ardent listeners, one of them, a judge of a high court sitting in Enugu in addition to two senior lawyers in Onitsha and Asaba. They appreciated him for the background he provided to most of the classical pieces. While signing off, he decided to repeat the *Halleluiah Chorus* due to popular demand.

Ndukwe recognised the name of the presenter. 'But he is the same man that acted as Okonkwo in the *Things Fall Apart* film, Isn't it?'

'You can see how beautiful English language sound in his mouth,' said Silvanus.

'The weather is so nice,' Rufus observed, wiping beer froth from his mouth. His little touch moved the lace blinds back to its position where the breeze blew it up and down.

'It's a welcome respite from the terrible heat,' Silvanus agreed, a bit absent-mindedly, poring over an address book and some papers. 'Where did I keep Alhaji's phone number?'

Akabueze, Nelly Uchendu's music came on air as the radio started a different program. The speakers drew Ndukwe's attention to the entertainment centre, an all-in-one brown lacquered wall unit with fine cabinetry. 'Nelly is something else,' Ndukwe enthused; his eyes did not miss the Sony twin-cam deck which was a new addition.

'*Elelebe eje olu* will remain a classic,' Rufus agreed.

'If I may ask, who is that Chinwude?' Ndukwe asked. 'She must be such a stunning beauty.'

Silvanus merely smiled. He believed she was describing herself. From her luxuriant hair to her deep necklines and folds, she could be the angel of any man's dream. Rufus tried to hush him, fearing that Ukamaka might hear them. 'But am I lying?' Silvanus continued above the boisterous laughter.

'She must be such a stunning beauty. It's not just her soothing voice that intoxicates but everything about her.'

'*Haaa!* Nnanyelugo, when did you become a poet?' Rufus interrupted.

'You heard me. If Ukamaka catches you, my hands, my legs are not party to this conversation.'

Her music appealed to anyone that grew up in the countryside. The purity of her piercing voice spoke of her raw talent. The folklores and true life experience captured by her songs transported her listeners back to life in their rustic settings. It was a sweet reminder of their upbringing which strengthened the bond between her and her fans. 'She's our Dolly Parton,' Silvanus told them.

'Where do you place Onyeka Onwenu or Christy Essien Igbokwe then?' Ndukwe asked.

'Our own Miriam Makeba, Mama Africa. Christy is our Diana Ross,' Silvanus's answer was spontaneous, causing more laughter. 'What I don't know is what Nelly was looking for in the murky waters of politics,' he rued. He was aware of the snippets circulating the grapevine about how she was used as cannon fodder by politicians. 'Ah, here it is,' he announced triumphantly, retrieving a business card from the cardholder. 'I used another card to cover it.'

'Thank God,' Ndukwe said, his face brightening with a smile. His hope of getting the import licence at a more reasonable price was suddenly revived. He was interested in the lucrative import and export business. For more than two weeks, Silvanus tried to locate the business card of Alhaji Sani. A different Alhaji that Rufus introduced Ndukwe to had demanded two hundred and fifty thousand naira but Ndukwe bulked at the cost. If he was to spend that much to get a licence, how much would he raise as capital for the international trade? '*Ogbuefi Nnanyelugo*, you don't know how grateful I will be if this works out.'

Silvanus cautioned against wild optimism. 'Let it work first,' he answered. Rufus was confident that no other source will quote such scary price. They bemoaned what officials of the ministry of commerce and industry did to them. Import licences were rarely issued to the traders that needed them. Instead they were issued to their friends and cronies who formed a cartel. Many of them argued that the traders themselves caused the problem. The middlemen were feeding off their desperation. They easily double-crossed one another by making irresistible offers. For the middlemen, disappointing one trader to make more money from another trader that offered more money was merely sharing from the profit the traders were making. 'Who spits out sugar or salt that is put in his mouth?' Silvanus asked. 'Anyway, Alhaji Sani is different. He is comfortable and principled. If he has it, he won't be outrageous in naming. . .' A knock on the door interrupted their conversation. 'Arinze!' he called. 'Please see who is at the door.'

'May the peace of God be unto this household,' Chike greeted, announcing himself as he stepped into the parlour. '*Ogbuefi Nnanyelugo!*' he called.

'*Oh oh ho yah ooo!* What is happening? *Akuchinyelunwata,*' Silvanus responded. He stood up for the traditional salutation of backslapping their hands before clasping them in warm handshake.

Chike greeted Rufus in similar fashion, calling him *Onwa 1* of *Abatete*. He called Ndukwe by his praise name also, '*Nwokedioranma*, the pride of Ichida.' They all expressed the great pleasure to see one another again.

'You look good *Akuchinyelunwata*. Nobody catches a glimpse of your brake light anymore,' Silvanus said, comparing him to a car that has raced out of sight.

'He's been globetrotting, trying to make money like you fellows,' Rufus volunteered an answer on behalf of Chike.

'*Ogbuefi Nnanyelugo*, did you hear that?' Ndukwe gushed with delight. 'While I'm still preparing, some people have been scooping the money freely. *Ogbuefi*, you fellows have to show me the way. Truly I have to belong.'

'Are you able to do what it takes?' Silvanus teased. 'Otherwise it is better you continue to count one before counting two and then three,' he said, re-echoing the philosophy in the music of Mike Ejeagha, the gentleman balladeer.

'What he said is the truth,' Rufus concurred, his deep baritone voice drawing attention to his burly build. His velveteen *isiagu* top with dominant red background sat comfortably on him, contrasting superbly with his cashmere black trousers. Their mood remained convivial as they discussed different issues until Rufus told them about the letter that armed robbers sent to Ofoka. 'They told him to expect them?'

'What?' asked Silvanus, surprised to hear what was fast becoming a pattern of armed robbery in Onitsha. The robbers wrote to their targets ahead of time to ensure there was substantial cash on the day of their visit. Targets must not continue to say they were taken unawares as an explanation for meagre cash available as ransom. Armed robbery was not an easy task which should meet with less than handsome reward. Otherwise, they would make blood flow during the attack. 'When will Onitsha overcome these villains? Is it not Okondo, Cross Country and their ilk?'

'Atinga and Bosco, too,' Chike added. 'It's only the day Onitsha shall get rid of them that this city will know peace again.'

'Have you heard?' Ndukwe asked. 'The mother of that dirty thing called Okondo can enter any shop, pick whatever she likes, and walk away without paying. The shopkeepers dare not ask her to pay.'

Silvanus listened with utmost incredulity, his mouth agape with surprise. '*Hia*, in this Onitsha or another place?' he asked. 'OMATA has to do something serious about these scourges.'

'At this rate, Onitsha must witness another "*boys oh yeah*" as it happened in 1979,' concluded Rufus. 'How can they hold us hostage like this?'

Ukamaka came out of the kitchen to greet them with Ogonna and Arinze following her with plates of jollof rice for each of them.

'Oh oh ho yah ooo! Ukamaka, it appears we timed our visit to coincide with your cooking,' Chike could not hide his pleasure. 'The food of the wealthy can be quite nourishing.'

'Not so much, please,' Ndukwe said, indicating that the quantity in the plate was more than what he would want to eat. 'If I fill my stomach, I won't be able to eat at home and I will have a query to answer.'

'*Nwokedioranma*, are you the one speaking?' Ukamaka protested. 'Tell Chidiogo you ate in my house. She can call me to confirm it if she wants.'

*   *   *

The decorations in the church mirrored the celebratory mood in the parish. Plantain trees, laden with bunches of elongated fruits with their fresh leaves, were tied to the doorposts on either side of the massive entrance to the vestibule. With their roots chopped off, the base of their trunks were wrapped up, to make sure the sap did not stain the terrazzo floor. Palm fronds, all lush and green, were pleated together above the doorway to form an archway; bouquets of flowers and leaves were tied with ribbons to the pillars in the nave to create a verdant atmosphere in the Metropolitan Archdiocese of Onitsha.

Piously, Obiora dipped his hand into the baptismal pool, touching his forehead, chest, and shoulders to make a sign of the cross. Okwudiri did the same, their carefree attitude deserting them as they entered the nave. He followed without protest, entering the fixed pew on the fourth row, careful not to walk on the kneelers. It gave them a good view of the sanctuary. Selected crops including big tubers of yam, cocoyam, baskets of oranges, pawpaw, and other fruits graced the foot of the chancery. A big turkey squatted calmly, its shanks tied, the wattle and caruncle easily catching the eyes. A giant rooster lay at another end, its eyes darting around quizzically, adjusting to the unfamiliar surroundings, surprised to still be alive and unharmed.

After the Eucharist, the announcer walked to the microphone and gave details of the harvest thanksgiving. Thereafter, row after row of the congregation filed out for the offertory. Once again, the images and symbols in the church caught Okwudiri's attention. He could tell the various Stations of the Cross captured by the frescoes on the wall and how they helped him recall the different passages of the scriptures. The stained glass windows accentuated the grandeur of the cathedral dwarfing his mental image of those in his Mboha church. The picture of Christ with a crosier and a flock was strikingly similar to the story of the Good Shepherd in *Help From Above*, the yellow pamphlet containing a collection of Bible passages written in English and Igbo. The Stations of the Cross and the tapestry of the triumphant Christ upon resurrection helped to keep all the crucifixion and resurrection of Christ in mind.

It took the congregation over thirty years to build the structure—a period of time that spoke volumes about patience and planning, focus and commitment—virtues which their generation was lacking seriously. He did not think that the pittance put into the offertory bag could fund the building. The names of Bishops Shanahan C.S.Sp, Heerey C.S.Sp, and Arinze rang bells at every turn. They built on no other foundation than the one laid by the Master Builder. Time had tested their works, and they came out refined like pure gold.

The various societies in the church took turns to give their special thanksgiving, and the Legion of Mary made the congregation jubilant with their new number:

> *We are honouring Mary, we are honouring.*
> *We are honouring Mary but we never worshipping.*
> *People say we worship her, Not at all!*
> *Everybody join the chorus honour her, honour Mary.*

After the benediction, the thurifer, leading the procession of altar boys and officiating priests, filed out of the church to bring the Mass to a close. The nave was abuzz with warm greetings and handshakes of members as they made their way out. Shortly after, the bazaar began.

25.

Ukamaka counted the naira notes and arranged them in various denominations before wrapping them together with First Bank paper bands. As usual, there were a number of dirty and worn-out notes that clung together. 'Who keeps receiving these terribly old notes, *gbo?*' she wondered aloud, her brow creasing at the musty notes. As the question was directed at nobody in particular, she got no response. 'They ought to take them to the bank instead of offloading them on us. Silva has to. . .'

Distracted by the sharp ring of the telephone, she picked up the receiver. 'Ellooo . . . ellooo, ellooo. . .' she spoke into the mouthpiece, raising her voice above the noise in the shop. Realising she was interrupting the person at the other end, she paused to let him speak. The other voice had also stopped speaking, waiting for her. Both of them were in a hurry to get off the phone, but they had wasted time talking over each other. Silvanus did not expect anyone to spend more than two or three minutes on the phone—anything more than that was handing NITEL a license to send a prohibitive bill at the end of each month. 'Who is talking?' she asked, her eyes glinting with frustration. 'Did you say Sebastian? . . . ooho . . .is that *Ochiriozuo* of Amichi? . . .fine. . .he is not around. . .you want how many cartons? . . .fifty cartons of each *SKB* product? . . . okay. . .you want it now, now? . . . tomorrow morning . . . that is okay . . . I will tell him.' She beamed as she replaced the receiver.

SKB, the label Silvanus introduced into the market, had turned out a huge success. It was a complete departure from the existing franchise and distribution arrangements between European manufacturers and the traders in terms of merchandising. Without owning a factory, the market was flooded with cosmetic products bearing his logo.

The commercial jingle was quite catchy—*SKB*, originating from Swiss laboratories, was specially formulated with the tropical weather in mind.

Enriched with vitamin E and Swiss collagen, the cream, lotion, moisturisers, and gel were specially designed to take care of different skin conditions, bringing out the natural essence and glow.

With the radio jingle playing on average of every thirty minutes, and with equally numerous slots on TV, the products became household names within three months and sold like hotcakes. The advertising agency organised beach parties and other fun activities to showcase the users of the products. The young and beautiful girls with fair, spotless and glamourous skins were all using *SKB* beauty and cosmetic products. *SKB* medicated soap dominated the market, taking over from Roberts and Tetmosol.

Victor came into the shop and sought audience with Okwudiri. 'Paulo, the snake we killed, how many pieces are they?' he asked Okwudiri. He needed to know the outcome of their discussion. Okwudiri had adopted Paulo as his name after one of the characters in *Living in Bondage.*

'He approved Dabsone but not promethazine,' he replied. 'It belongs to phenergan family and we have more than enough in stock. He said your price is too high, though I tried to persuade him otherwise. So let me have twenty of the Dabsone.'

'You are my man. I told you how I came by it.' Victor spoke a little above whisper, though his voice was steady. 'If I don't sell it, I'll be stuck with them. Look, I'll come back to you if you change your mind,' he said, ready to take his leave.

Okwudiri had to make a quick decision. 'Let me talk to *Oga*'s wife,' he said, going off to speak with Ukamaka. He came back. 'Let's have twenty of each. You confirm there is nothing shady about it, right?' he asked cautiously. They did not buy drugs from peddlers because of the risk of being in possession of stolen property.

'I have the receipt. If you like you can call to confirm. You know I don't involve myself in dodgy deals,' Victor reassured him. 'You know, a good name is. . .' he said, smiling. 'Meanwhile, did he say anything about *KILL IT*, the insecticide?' Victor was a freelancer, sourcing and marketing products that were scarce in the market or selling any product based on an agreed commission. When he was not so engaged, he turned to hustling, sweet-talking buyers and, like a cicerone, guiding them around the market. He was not ready to be tied down to any training contract after his five years of secondary school education.

'He's not interested in that,' Okwudiri lied. In fact, he hadn't even bothered Silvanus about it. 'Your best bet is talking to those hawkers. There is nothing they cannot sell.'

'No skin pain,' Victor said, strutting off with his head held high, each thumb in his jeans' pockets, his long-sleeved shirt rolled up just above his wrist and left flying over his belt.

'Okwy, can you please attend to this customer. He's asking for *oga*,' Amaechi called Okwudiri as the senior trainee in the shop. 'He said that armed robbers attacked them.'

Okwudiri listened to the customer as he told his story. 'Armed robbers attacked me and other passengers last Monday on our way to the market. I was robbed of over fifty-five thousand naira from. . .'

'*Eeeyaaa!*' Okwudiri agonised. 'Where did this happen?'

'Before Obolo-Afor.'

'These armed robbers are becoming such a menace. It happened to our Otukpo and Ankpa customers about three weeks ago,' Okwudiri recalled. 'The traders now travel in convoy with police escort.'

'Our escort escaped into the bush when he heard the gunshots.'

Okwudiri suppressed some laughter, imagining the fleeing policeman who must have feared being overpowered and possibly getting shot at. He heaved his shoulders as a natural sign of disapproval. 'So what do you want?' he asked, checking the time.

'I have a contract to supply drugs worth twenty thousand naira but I was only able to raise twelve thousand after the robbery. I'm wondering if *oga* can help me.'

'*Chai*,' Okwudiri sympathised. 'As you can see, the boss is not around. Hold on for a minute. . .' He went to confer with Ukamaka.

She came forward to meet the customer, commiserating with him before telling him there was nothing she could do. 'Unfortunately, *Ogbuefi* is not around and I don't have the power to grant such credit. Okwy, please give him special discount for what he would buy.'

The shout of the food vendor reminded them how fast the day had gone. It was easy to tell, at just a glance, that Bright Street was as busy as usual—the long line of vehicles queuing bumper to bumper with pedestrians walking to and fro. It never occurred to the local authorities to restrict vehicular access and make it a pedestrian-only zone within designated hours despite the heavy human traffic. Any driver that entered the street during its busiest hours had no choice but to be patient. Taxi and bus drivers stopped to pick up passengers. Commuters tried to cram into the buses at the head of the queue, to ensure they could leave as soon as possible.

Suddenly, two brawny men entered the shop, one bearing an all-metal rifle folded and strapped over his shoulder. The sight of the rifle terrified the trainees. At first, Okwudiri thought they were undercover policemen who had come to arrest them. It had happened in the early stage of his training when Achike sold menstrogen tablets to a girl with delayed menses. She haemorrhaged during the abortion and, before she bled to death, had managed to gasp out Able God Chemist as the place where she had bought the tablets that caused her bleeding. They were herded off to a police cell.

But these men looked mean and business-like. Their eyes, completely hidden behind reflective sunglasses, made it difficult to recognise them—hence the locals' aversion for dark shades. They were associated with men who, inclined to villainous activities, sought to hide their identities from inquisitive eyes. Also it meant no-one could look them directly in the eye lest the opium-induced courage needed for armed robbery operation desert them. A sudden pang of guilt or pity due to eye contact was enough to enervate them.

'Keep still everybody,' the man in front ordered. 'Bring out all the money you have,' he said, moving towards Ukamaka.

His partner was holding the automatic rifle in such an authoritative manner that passers-by glancing in would believe they were witnessing a lawful operation. 'Cooperate with him if you don't want blood to flow.' He spoke slowly but ominously, handling the rifle with accustomed skill like one who had always used it as a work tool.

Ukamaka melted with fright, kneeling and hiding her face on her seat, pointing to the drawer where the naira notes were stacked. 'Where are your bags?' he asked, looking around. He found a medium-sized sack and hurriedly stuffed the wad of notes into it.

Within five minutes, the operation was over. The robbers hastened to their powerful motorbike and zoomed off before the completely petrified Okwudiri and others were able to raise an alarm. The gangsters obviously encountered some obstruction on their way—two gunshots rang out. Everybody scampered for safety.

*   *   *

Obiora was locked in a game of draughts with Felix when Okwudiri got to the compound. The initial swift movements of eager fingers pushing a piece forward, jumping and capturing the opponent's pieces, had given way to slow and reflective movements. '*Zuo okwe*, play your game,' Obiora taunted Felix, tapping the draughtboard. 'Do you want to borrow my hand? You know how generous I can be. I'm not stingy. Take,' he offered, pushing his hand into his space.

'*Keziah № 1!*' Amobi called Obiora. It was a derogatory name for girls considered to be promiscuous and freely gave out their bosom to different boys. They were generous and free givers.

'Felix, you have a. . .' Okwudiri was drawing attention to a move available to Felix.

Obiora was quick to hush him. 'Paulo, not at all, Okwy! There's a stake in this game. No coaching. It is not allowed,' he insisted, his knuckles cracking as he flapped his hand. 'But he can borrow my hand F.O.C. Yes, free of charge! Okwy, ask him if he wants to do so. You heard Amobi. I am Keziah, the free giver.'

'*Nna*, be quiet. You're not allowing me to concentrate,' Felix protested. 'I don't know if I'm playing against your mouth or your hand.'

'That's Obiora for you,' Amobi added. 'Distraction is one of his game strategy.'

'A g . . . g . . . g . . . good footballer d . . . d . . . does not only pppp . . . play with his legs alone,' Ekene remarked.

'Oohoooo, Ekene, you see? You would have been a good lawyer,' said Obiora, scratching his unshaved chin. 'A footballer is free to use any part of his body—head ooo, chest ooo, back ooo, even your bum—so far the ball does not touch your hand. Is it not?'

'Have you heard? Another body was found floating in the river this morning,' Ignatius announced, joining those who sat on the long bench Okwudiri brought out.

'Minus one,' Amobi responded, quite sure it must be the body of an armed robber.

'Another salute to the Red Berets,' Felix spoke, the back of his right hand on his forehead in military salute.

'Amobi, do you know that Emeka eventually found that box of wrapper in this Onitsha?' Ignatius stated.

'It cannot be,' Amobi reacted with strong doubt. 'Where did he find it?'

'At the White House. I was with him when he recovered it,' Ignatius told them. Emeka was a trader dealing in textile materials and accessories like Ignatius. Two days after a business trip, he realised that one of the cartons of wrapper he brought from Lagos was missing. He returned to the office of the transport company but did not find it. He was redirected to the White House where lost but found items were kept. Amobi did not believe that Emeka would still find the box after the transport company denied having it. It was true that Onitsha had become more secure and peaceful after the Red Berets led the revolt against armed robbery and other unwholesome practices. However, expecting that the fear and awe that befell Onitsha would eliminate every form of vice was asking for too much. 'I was asking myself if this was truly happening in Onitsha.'

'That is a miracle,' Okwudiri stated as he heard the gist of the story. 'How did he identify himself as the owner?'

'They kept a careful inventory of what was brought to the centre and from where it came. In the first place, fear will not allow anybody to go there to claim what did not belong to him.'

'True repentance has come to Onitsha,' Obiora concluded. Stealing or robbery in any guise became an abomination in Onitsha. In their rage, the inhabitants had taken the war to the robbers, lynching as many as they could catch. The faceless Red Berets Squad took the war a step further. Powerful medicine men were engaged to bewitch the robbers to keep them from escaping and ensure the return of those that left town. The faceless taskforce picked them up one by one, killing them and dumping their bodies into the river.

The assault against armed robbery extended to petty thievery. There was serious doubt in a particular case, whether the person lynched was the actual thief. Some believed that the true felon fingered an innocent man who was mobbed without giving him the opportunity to speak. 'This must be the first killing after Cross Country?' Anayo thought aloud.

'Onitsha has become a holy land, true. Whoever comes to Onitsha now would not believe what it was six months ago,' Obiora concluded.

'The worst was those boys on motorbikes,' said Amobi. 'Opioro will never forget them.' Opioro was walking along the street carrying a dirty black nylon bag to disguise the sum of twenty thousand naira he was carrying when armed robbers chopped off his hand before picking up the bag and speeding off on powered motorbike. At that time, nobody carried a respectable bag along the street and when armed robbers realised money was carried around in dirty and crinkled nylon bags instead, anybody holding such bag became a target.

'If Onitsha remains like this, nobody will need burglar-proof barriers anymore,' said Okwudiri, referring to the measures taken by virtually every home to protect themselves from robbery. The amount of wealth in a home determined the size of barriers. Unable to penetrate one particular house, the armed robbers had set it ablaze, shooting the occupants when they tried to open the doors to escape from the inferno.

Eventually, Felix deftly moved a piece, leaving Obiora with no option but to capture two of his draughtsmen after which Felix jumped three pieces, ending up in the kings' row. Confidently tapping the board, he requested his piece to be crowned. '*Uwa mgbede ka nma, eee, eee, eee uwa mgbede ka nma. . .*' he sang along to Mike Ejeagha's music coming from his room.

'*Ekpe etiem utari!*—the masquerade has flogged me—the man with the innocent face has spanked me,' Obiora cried, recoiling as if in shock.

'The dog tha . . . tha . . . that doesn't b . . . b . . . bark bites the hardest,' Ekene enthused. 'That m . . . mmm . . . move was a . . . a . . . a . . . masterstroke. In sh . . . shh . . . short, the game is over,' he predicted.

'No, either of them can still win,' said Anayo.

'We can do side betting if you want,' Amobi challenged.

'My oh my!' Obiora cried, remembering his English teacher, Mr Chris, who was fond of making such exclamation whenever he was flabbergasted. '*Di, di, di,*' he muttered, his forefinger tapping his chin. 'Certainly, our land cannot allow the lizard to grow hair!' he blurted, picking up a piece and slamming it noisily on the draughts board. 'Play! *Zuo okwe*! The fear of death does not deter men from war! *Ana esi n'ani we liba enu, uwa mgbede ka nma!*' he sang, joining in singing Ejeagha's music, feeling exultant. '*Agusia mbu, ewe guba ibuo, agusia ibuo ewe guba ito. . .*' Obiora sang expressively, swaying his body slowly to the rhythm.

If there was a musician in their generation whose works illustrated the universality of values, of nature and its law, regardless of race, culture, and civilisation, Gentleman Mike Ejeagha, the great balladeer, occupied that pre-eminent position. Focusing mainly on *Omenani*, the customs and traditions of his people, Ejeagha consistently highlighted the strength of their values and lifestyle. It became evident even to the most cynical that the mores of his people were not so different to those of the Greco-Roman civilisation. Not even the British colonial administration could condemn all that the natives did as barbarous especially when it had to do with issues of natural justice, equity and good conscience.

That was why the younger generation who were unable to live up to the ideals his music espoused made derisive remarks about them. Such ideals were at best fairy tales, which did not take account of the realities of their time. Of what relevance was patience to a man who had to be a millionaire before he turned twenty so he could own houses in the village, the city where he carried on business and, if possible, overseas? What would happen to his dream of becoming a hero that would provide for his kith and kin? Whatever they could do to win must not be vilified. If killing, maiming, compromising all other interest that conflicted with his—if that was what it took to become a hero, it became justified. Yet as time rolled by, they found themselves victims of the success they sought.

Felix made a move without noticing the piece that would have captured Obiora's piece. To huff the piece, Obiora tapped the board close to it, to call attention to his error. 'As you can see, I'm not pinching you,' he said, abridging a local proverb that required a person checking a dog for fleas to show the dog what was picked, lest the dog think it was unfairly pinched. 'Mr Chris didn't ask me to show mercy to any *iti boribo*, ignoramus. *Zuo okwe!*' he cried, elated.

'Men! How did you make such mistake?' Amobi yelled.

'What! You got me cheap!' cried Felix. He poured the captured pieces back on to the draughtboard, declaring a draw. 'The money I thought was already in my pocket.'

'He who fights and run away, lives to fight another day,' Obiora sang like the legendary Bob Marley, collecting his one naira from Ignatius. Felix stood up as Amobi took over.

'You know what? I thought *Ogbuefi* is one of the powers to be reckoned with in this Onitsha,' Felix voiced his thought. 'I was surprised that robbers could go to his shop and escape unharmed. Maybe the man is naked.'

'Do . . . do . . . do you hear that?' Ekene exclaimed, happy to hear a different person re-echo the view he had previously expressed. As businessmen became more successful, many of them were known to take extra measures to protect themselves from attacks to their person and business. 'Yu . . . yu . . . yu . . . you see? D . . . d . . . didn't I say so?'

'What kind of clothes do you expect him to wear?' Obiora asked, feigning ignorance of the point that was made. Amobi maintained that if the robbery was attempted in certain shops in the same Onitsha, the robbers would not come out alive. The robbers would forget their mission to make themselves busy with different activities—sweeping the compound, playing games or fighting themselves—until the owners arrive to neutralise the spell and catch them. Okwudiri did not readily believe such stories. If such powerful spells existed, he queried why such shop owners still lock up their shops at the close of business each day? 'Thank you, Paulo, you suckled your mother's breast very well,' Obiora concurred, slamming down his piece. 'My mother told me not to play with fire!' he intoned. 'Fire will burn you. . .' he sang, nodding his head.

'Do they ha . . . ha . . . have to make it so obvious?' Ekene countered.

'That robbery was quite terrible,' Okwudiri said. '*Ogbuefi*'s wife has not recovered from the shock and trauma till date. She has not been to the shop since then.'

'That's some respite from the close monitoring and marking,' Felix pointed out.

'Let's go to Nwanyi Obosi,' Ekene suggested. 'You know Victor is in town.'

'I need to see the car he bought,' Obiora announced.

'Victor?' Amobi asked disbelievingly. 'Is it not the same Victor that comes here?'

'My, oh my, Victor *egbugo ozu*!' Obiora beamed with delight.

26.

Kperechi crossed the pedestrian gate to enter the family house that Iroegbulem's children built to honour him at his old age. She followed the walkway leading to the entrance of the house. Tumbled pebbles of red and caramel colour beautified the concrete slabs used to pave the walkway. As part of the optical enhancements, the flowerbed with topiary arts was at the centre of a mini roundabout surrounded by ixora flowers. One of the flowers was shaped into an eagle while the second was a galloping horse.

It was a classic case of what *omumu*—childbearing—could do. *Ma obughi omumu onye ga enyem*—but for children, who would give me? As a song, it celebrated the remarkable achievements and unusual feat of one's children for the benefits, honour, and pride they bestow on parents. For the family of Iroegbulem, the meaning of the song came alive and demonstrated what it meant to have useful children. At a glance, one could easily take in what made Iroegbulemville the most outstanding compound in Mboha. Mboha was so proud of the building that the villagers boasted that whoever set foot in the compound was as good as having been to *ala beke*. The grandeur of the landscaping alone was more than enough to convince them that the building was a replica of another structure in American.

The Bermuda grasses in the green lawn were not the regular grasses that grew locally. Conical conifers flourished in-between the raised flowerbeds running parallel to the walled fence. Four Italian cypress towered into space with junipers and yew in between. A golden yew stood on either side of the entrance to the main door. The backyard wall was hedged with the crowded shoots of creeping juniper. Climbing roses, a bit of wisteria and clematis combined to screen off the spaces in between the ornamental iron of the walled fence. Eyes outside the compound could not see through them except by peeping at a close range. A Californian nutmeg, pine, and cypress trees were part of the exotic plants at different positions in the compound. The villagers regarded them as special Christmas trees as they looked very beautiful at Yuletide when decorated with light.

Kperechi clapped her hand again. 'Is there nobody here?' she asked, looking up at the empty balcony. It was obvious that the traffic of well-wishers coming to welcome Jemima had calmed down after five days. Many came to say their greetings and have the chance to partake in the presents she brought from the USA. It was the second time Kperechi was visiting and hoped it would be a good time for a meaningful catching up with her. Alfred, the gardener, went to meet her and pushed the bell button. Egobeke came to the balcony to show her face. 'Oh, my fellow woman, you are here?'

'We just came back from Aguebi,' Egobeke told her.

Kperechi climbed the stairs laboriously, holding the railings with one hand and the other hand on her waist. 'Climbing these stairs is like going up the steep hill at the stream.'

'You better learn how to climb it very well,' Egobeke teased, surprised to hear any kind of complaint against storey building, the dream structure that everyone wanted and wished it could dot each compound. It was the latest craze for the young generation and they were outdoing one another on who would build the best in the village. 'Is it not what your children are building for you? What will you do when you move into it?'

'Let me be, Egobeke,' Kperechi protested as she got to the landing. 'Perhaps, my waist would be fit by then. What about Jemima?'

'She is in the shower.'

Jemima came out of the bath tying a big towel across her chest with globules of water all over her. She wanted a cool bath terribly was undressing herself right from the gate. 'Kperechi my fellow woman, you are welcome. Please take a seat while I quickly put on something.'

'*Ooolom*, American woman,' Kperechi called. 'You are really indulging yourself. A cool shower in this hot afternoon is the best way to calm the body down.' She walked to the veranda, dragging her footwear on the floor. 'And you Egobeke, you have not even gone home to change, *eh*? Are you not feeling hot?'

'You're asking me, what about you?'

'Once I get home, I doubt if I will come this way again. Is your body not itching for such bath, *eh*?'

'Kperechi, let me be. Were you told that I just came back from America? This skin has been toughened to withstand any kind of weather. Anyway, I will shower at night.'

Jemima came out wearing a very light material. '*Eheee* I feel fresh,' she said. It was quite obvious that she added weight. 'The heat here can drive one crazy.'

'Did you have to wet your hair?' Egobeke asked.

'I had to,' Jemima admitted, standing up. 'I feel like soaking myself in a pool for a while. Last night, I splashed water on myself twice before dawn.'

'The heat has been terrible for the past few days,' Kperechi agreed. 'It has to rain to placate the earth and ease our suffering.'

Jemima returned to the veranda shortly after with a small basket containing her drugs, some cream crackers, and cookies. Two photo albums were under her armpit. Obinwanne returned with bottled water. 'Is the water cool enough?' she asked, stretching her hand to feel the plastic bottle of Swan water. It was. She held her cup as Obinwanne filled it with water. She drank it all and exhaled contentedly. 'These happy-go-lucky lots did not supply electricity all night,' she mused, opening one of the plastic containers to get a tablet, which she placed on her tongue.

'Mama Ukwu, have you eaten?' Obinwanne asked, reminding her she was taking drugs on empty stomach. She reassured him that she was not making a mistake. It was some chewable multivitamins which could be taken without food.

'Were you not served refreshments at the official launch,' Kperechi asked.

'The food was quite salty for me,' Jemima answered. 'I managed to take only two spoons of *ugba*. It was so tempting I could not resist it. She asked Obinwanne to get some soft drinks for her guests but Kperechi who was staying off sugary stuff declined the offer. According to her, she did not have the strength to cope with the rigours of urine sickness. Her blood pressure was high and on medical advice, she was keeping away from anything that could add to her cholesterol or increase sugar level in her blood. Jemima changed the instruction and asked Obinwanne to get soda and a bottle of water for her. 'Where is Sabina? The food should be ready by now. Please tell her to hurry, I'm starving.' As he hurried off, she asked them to have a taste of the biscuits she brought out. 'Cream crackers are quite good. They are not sugary.'

Kperechi's face broadened with a smile on seeing the picture of Ebereonu with her twins. The straight bridge and curvy edge of her nose enhanced her silky beautiful face. Her black pupils gleamed calmly at the camera. 'See Ebereonu ooo,' she enthused. 'Motherhood fits her perfectly.'

'Do you have twins in your lineage?' Egobeke asked.

'No, but her husband has. Those boys are such a handful,' she said. 'Here is Celestine and his American wife.'

'What is her name again? Is it not Jessica?' Egobeke remembered how friendly the American lady was during Iroegbulem's burial. She joined the village women to do what they were doing. Many were happy to see her dress in wrappers and blouse and other native attire. 'That woman married your son with all her heart. I hope she will come home again for us to see her.'

'They will,' Jemima answered, taking another glass of water. 'I've told them to come again while I'm still alive. I heard that your boy, Okwudiri, got married to a German.'

'I equally heard so but I have not set my eyes on her,' Kperechi answered. 'We have asked him to bring his wife and son home for us to see. Ah ah, are these not our people?' she said, keeping the album some distance away from herself to get a clearer view of those posing in a group picture. She could identify Leo, Celestine, Edward, Emma Nwokocha, and her son, Akachi. 'So Akachi came to visit you?'

'Leo hosted our old Bende people in Texas in his Houston home,' she told them. 'I didn't know Akachi has grown that big. I don't know what makes children grow so fast these days.'

'That is wonderful,' Egobeke said. 'So we have such number of old Bende people in America?'

'What are you saying? This group picture is our Ohuhu chaps,' Jemima told them. They spent more time on that particular picture. She pointed out those she knew in the picture and the name of their communities. One of them was from Aguebi, the son of a man who rose to become a permanent secretary in the State Government.

Kperechi knew the Ukelonu family very well and was elated at the information. 'It appears that Akachi has really settled in,' Kperechi noticed how robust he looked with his fashionably coiffed hair glistening, his sideburns trimmed to the barest minimum, making him look trendy. 'I just hope he keeps his head cool to learn what took him there.'

'Who are you talking about? Is he a kid? You are talking about a person who has almost qualified as an aeronautic engineer,' Jemima boasted. 'He came to meet Leo three weeks ago to stand as his referee and guarantor for his aviator course.'

'What I like, may it be pleasing to my God also,' Kperechi prayed, before turning another page of the album. She noticed the layers of dresses Jemima was wearing—the thick pullovers, stockings, and gloves. 'How many clothes were you wearing at a time? Were you sick?'

Jemima smiled. 'Anyone who fails to dress like that during winter is asking for trouble. I didn't want cold to mess with me.'

The photographs gave the women a peek into what life in America looked like, a world that was different from their own in several ways. The well-fed, healthy, and happy-looking children; the opulent furnishings in the sitting rooms; the screed walls and the creamy vanilla paint which achieved smoothness that was calm, alluring and sublime; the rich creamy carpet on the floor with flowery designs were not merely items of luxury when compared to what they had in the village. They were part of utopia. 'See how everywhere is sparkling,' Kperechi gushed with delight.

'How would one step on this carpet?' Egobeke asked. 'It will get dirty so easily.'

'Over there, footwear is rarely dirty because everywhere is tarred. Whenever the children stain or make it dirty, their father vacuums it.'

'Ooooh America! This is simply living life at another level,' Kperechi remarked.

'That's why it is *ala beke*,' Egobeke concluded. 'Is this a toy or what?' she asked, surprised at the jumbo size of the plastic car inside the sitting room. Jemima confirmed that they were electric cars for kids. She even told them that a whole room was dedicated to toys. 'They really lavish money on children.'

'What you said is not a lie,' Jemima agreed. 'A place where you shop for pets as you shop for human beings.'

'What would you buy for a dog or pussycat?' Egobeke wondered, raising her eyebrows, her forehead furrowing, wondering why anyone would shop for pets when they were meant to be given leftovers after their owners had been well-fed. It occurred to her that a happy and generous owner could stop at the meat seller's stand to get some bones for their dogs. Perhaps, pet owners in America were more dutiful in doing that. The next page in the album seemed to answer her questions. A fat cat was lapping fresh milk from a bowl. A second cat was lying comfortably on the sofa with a white lady sitting by the side. 'See, the cat is lying on the sofa. How can they allow that?'

'That is nothing to them. A dog can lie on the bed of the owner. If I tell you the kind of trouble they take for those pets, you won't believe me. They groom them carefully and take them to veterinary clinics. You see this woman? Those cats are her companions. No children, no husband. I keep wondering what the problem is but they said that is what she wants. I wanted to ask why a beautiful woman like her won't get married and raise a family.'

'And what did she say was the problem?' Egobeke asked.

'Ebereonu wouldn't let me ask her. She said I would be invading her privacy.'

'That is quite strange,' Kperechi was surprised to hear that. 'So if you see a person on a wrong path, you have to turn a blind eye?'

'My sister, the law that governs them over there is strange in many ways,' Jemima told them. 'They are always careful to observe them. The worst of their laws I have seen is the one that forbids parents from beating a child. A child can mess around but if you lift a finger to beat the child, you have breached their law.'

'Oh, do they prefer to spoil the child?' asked Egobeke, her tone conveying strong disapproval. 'Don't they read the Bible anymore?'

'In my presence, social workers took custody of the children of an African family. Why? A mother spanked her children. She didn't know when a neighbour called the police. You won't believe it; it became a court matter.'

'Let their law remain with them,' was all Egobeke could say.

Jemima pulled out the side stool for Sabina to serve them food. The portion of jollof rice in her plate was small with vegetable, fried plantain, and steamed fresh fish. She only started eating after her friends were served.

'Can I get some salt?' Egobeke asked Obinwanne who had just brought a jug filled with water and another bottled water for Jemima.

'You want to eat uncooked salt?' Jemima asked, shaking her head to discourage it. 'That is not good for your health. As one advances in age, you have to cut down on some of those things. I've stopped adding salt to my food. There is enough salt in the seasoning.'

'*Okpokonti!*' Egobeke exclaimed in wonderment. 'Don't bother,' she said to the hearing of Obinwanne who was running down the stairs already. 'Your long stay in America has turned you to a white woman.'

'At a point I thought you have relocated permanently,' Kperechi added.

'Does one learn to be left-handed at old age? Home is home.'

'Were you gone for five years or more?' asked Kperechi.

'Five years? When did IG pass away? It will be five years in another two months. I travelled after the one-year anniversary. Remember?'

'Time really flies,' Egobeke remarked.

'Someone you are used to and suddenly, he's no more. It doesn't amuse,' Kperechi heaved her shoulders, simply afraid to contemplate widowhood.

'Kperechi, what your people in Aguebi witnessed today is not a little thing,' she said as the Christian mothers' uniform caught her attention. The wrapper, an English wax, was blue and white and her top was a white lace. The Umuhu women had worn it to add colour to the event.

'What is good is good, true,' she agreed.

'Udemezue really made your people proud with that factory,' Egobeke added. One of the immediate benefits of the factory to Aguebi was water. The giant borehole drilled to supply water to the factory equally supplied water to the whole village. Everyday, the taps ran for three hours in the morning and another three hours in the evening. As a result, Aguebi people stopped fetching water from streams and rivers.

'That is not all,' Kperechi added. 'A number of the factory workers have secured accommodation in Aguebi, paying rent to their landlords. It may not be much but it is a good source of income, isn't it?'

'The benefits will keep trickling down to the community one way or the other,' Egobeke agreed. The remarkable change the carpet factory brought to Aguebi made it the most important development in the whole of Umuhu. Local folks who had been farmers all their lives began to wake up in the morning to prepare for work at the factory. Those working in the office block had to take their bath in the morning. The landscaping was lush and green. The complex simplicity of the modern bungalows built as residential quarters for the expatriates were a sight to behold. They were comparable to the ALSCON Quarters in Ikot Abasi. The Italians that installed the machinery lived in Aguebi for more than a year, training local manpower.

'But it's not all about benefits,' Kperechi pointed out. 'Waste from the factory has been ravaging farmlands in Aguebi.'

'What waste?' asked Egobeke, surprised.

'My brother's wife complains about the effluent discharge from the factory. It has contaminated the soil. Tubers of yam and cassava planted on the impacted areas are not up to this size anymore,' she told them, sticking out her index finger.

'Those are the side effects. Rarely would you see such a good thing without any but,' Jemima stated.

'Jemima my fellow woman, I have to be on my way,' Kperechi said, putting away the album on her laps.

'What is the deadline for the community hall levy, if I may ask?' Egobeke directed her question at Kperechi.

'What community hall levy?' Jemima asked. 'I thought David promised to build a community hall for us?'

Egobeke could not hide her disdain at the mention of David. 'If we are looking for those who can do something for the community, will he be counted in the number? Even if he built one, I'm not sure my legs would step into it.'

'Why?' asked Jemima, surprised at the vehemence.

'If he has his way, he would turn everyone into sacks of money,' Egobeke continued. 'The time he will meet his waterloo is fast approaching.' She was one of those who did not want to hear anything about David. After the initial money David made had thinned out, he became pauperised to the point of begging food. His mother ate the bread he brought home after a visit and became mysteriously ill. She did not survive the sickness. Another surge of inexplicable money kept tongues wagging that his wealth was satanic.

'My fellow women, I must take my leave,' Kperechi announced, standing up. 'I need to see how Ozurumba is faring.'

*　　*　　*

The interdenominational thanksgiving service at St John's Anglican Church, Mboha, was brought to an end with the officiating vicar leading the congregation to say the benediction. The reception of guests and well-wishers followed immediately at Iroegbulem's compound. There was every reason to celebrate the appointment of Leo as the Honourable Minister of Health at the Federal cabinet. Having risen to the position of professor of medicine after studying in one of America's Ivy League schools, the new democratic regime had asked him to serve in the government. He was one of the technocrats invited to revamp the decaying medical infrastructure in the country.

A live band entertained at the venue and some of the guests joined the chief celebrant at the bandstand to dance and spray the lead vocalist with money. A band member brought names of the guests that appeared wealthy and distinguished at different intervals and handed them over to the lead vocalist who dutifully wove the names into songs and sang their praises. This was having the desired effect as more of them came to generously spray naira notes on him. Three band members were saddled with the task of picking up currency notes that fell on the floor and stuffing them into cellophane bags.

'I never knew a thing like this can happen in my lifetime,' Akwakanti said as Ozurumba took a seat close to him under the canopy.

'That is true. Goodness is in the land of the living. You have to be alive to experience it,' Ozurumba concurred.

'It's not a little thing,' Ekeleme concurred. 'Thanks be to *Obasi bi n'elu* – the God of heaven – that one survived the war. Isn't it a rare privilege to witness an occasion such as this?'

'IG should have been alive to witness such a momentous event with his own eyes,' George spoke up, taking a bite of the garden egg. As a form of special recognition, seats in one of the canopies were especially reserved for Mboha and they turned out in their numbers. Their indigenes living in various cities sent representatives. A similar canopy was reserved for guests that came from Ngor-Okpala, Jemima's maiden home.

'Do you think Iroegbulem is not aware of this event?' asked Ekeleme.

'Wherever he is, his spirit must be walking tall and proud. His labour was not in vain.' Instinctively, Ozurumba cast a glance at the part of the compound where Iroegbulem was buried.

'Have the spices touched your tongue yet?' asked George, his face brightening as he munched and crushed a mouthful of *ugbakala*. The self-imposed restraint of a model public figure was momentarily forgotten as he savoured every bite with approving nods. The parting in his usual wedge haircut had given way to the realities of an advanced bald head but the remnants were dutifully dyed to hide the grey hair.

It was quite a long time since such quality of *ugbakala* touched his mouth. *Okporoko*, the stock fish that was highly cherished by his people, had practically gone out of circulation. It had become the exclusive preserve of the very rich who could spare thousands of naira to buy it. Many homes, determined to enjoy it even if it was just the flavour, resorted to buying the *isi okporoko*, the head of *okporoko* that was known to be full of bones. The strength of the dish in his hand could easily be told. The smoked beef was properly seasoned and diced into tiny bits. The bits and pieces of *okporoko* must have come from cod, the best quality in the market. He could tell that the potash used was not *akanwa* but from burnt *ogbe* and *uziza, anara* leaves and local nutmeg, *ehiri*, were proportionally measured by skilful hands to get the best result in the dish.

'This is grade one,' Ozurumba declared after crushing the first spoonful he shoved into his mouth. 'Nothing can be more tasteful like *ugbakala* that is well-prepared.'

'*Oriri biawa ogu adala*,' Akwakanti intoned. '*Oriri biam biam n'onu!*' he stretched out his hand to have his cup filled with palm wine but midway, changed his mind and asked for a bottle of Star Lager Beer. 'Today, let us enjoy like the high and mighty.'

'George, you must be a happy man today,' Josiah noted. He was obviously referring to the church service earlier on. One of the important guests acknowledged him as one of his father's colleagues and commended him in his role as a lay leader in the church.

'Sir Hilary was such a great personality. We were together when Herbert Macaulay was the national leader of the NCNC. He worked more closely with Sir Francis Akanu Ibiam when he became the governor,' George told his kinsmen. 'He was an exceptional fellow.'

'What the earth has consumed is not a little,' Josiah said at the mention of their political leaders and heroes who were no more. 'Both the good and the bad are all consumed by the earth.'

'Who thought that the great Zik would one day be sought but not found?' Ozurumba asked, agreeing with Josiah.

'You ever thought so?' asked George, surprised. 'A sojourner must return from whence he came.'

'*Gbam*, that's a fact of life,' Akwakanti concurred.

One of the dignitaries was speaking when Okwudiri and two of his friends came into the compound. They were ushered to a table amongst the dignitaries to be entertained with food and drinks. 'Money has spoken eloquently here,' Anayo observed as they took their seat. On the table were assorted drinks including cans of Heineken and Becks beers, packs of Don Simon and other fruit juices. There were champagne, Jack Daniels, Campari, and other exotic drinks loaded on tables before dignitaries. They were all imports from different countries. Any event where such drinks were lavishly served was considered a big success.

'There is no gainsaying it,' Obiora agreed. 'How would you compare an event organised by the wealthy to our ordinary parties? Do you know what we are talking about? It is about a minister of the Federal Republic.' The power generator growling quietly close to the gate did not escape their attention. It explained why the drinks were properly chilled despite the epileptic power supply in the country. The granite marble used to cover the grave of Iroegbuelem gleamed from the sunrays. A number of slants etched into the head stone surrounded a cross. They represented shafts of light beamed on those in whom the Father, the God of all comfort, had lifted his countenance upon to grant them peace. Written in cursive, the epitaph on the tombstone contained his biographical data in addition to Christ's declaration: *I am the resurrection, and the life: he that believeth in me, though he were dead, yet shall he live.* His bust had been carved wearing colonial constabulary uniform, military hat and aiguillettes, all testifying to the remarkable features of a man of authority.

'This is how you know those who are well-read,' Anayo added.

'If it is about education, I give it to them,' Okwudiri told them. 'The man made Grade One in his school cert. His brother, Celestine, also made Grade One, including their sister, Ebereonu.'

'If they built something like this when they had no minister, what would happen now that they have one? Perhaps, a more beautiful structure will spring up very soon. Your village will continue to develop rapidly,' Obiora predicted, admiration and envy were evident in his voice.

Noticing that the chief celebrant was less engrossed with political heavyweights at a point, Okwudiri walked up to him to say his greetings. Leo was so pleased to see him, thanking him for taking the trouble to be present at the thanksgiving. He enquired about his family and other things. Okwudiri assured him he could not absent himself from such momentous occasion taking place in their dear Mboha. It was the development they had yearned for and he was happy to be there to celebrate it.

Okwudiri had more reasons to be present. It was another opportunity to build on the bond existing between them. In addition to the mutual obligation to help and support one another as member of the *umunna*, there was a special relationship existing between both families. There was clear intention to carry on the friendship that existed between their parents. It was not a surprise that

Leo agreed to stand as guardian to Akachi on his arrival to USA. And with Leo becoming a minister, it could be an opportunity to secure contracts such as medical supplies.

'I just came in with some friends. I told myself there's no way I could absent myself from this momentous occasion.' Okwudiri sounded confident, calm, and suave. He had taken after Ozurumba in height but broader in shoulder and thickness more as a result of bodybuilding and healthy appetite. His near black complexion was made more pronounced by his lustrous eyes, fashionable beard, and moustache, giving him a debonair look.

'Very nice of you,' Leo appreciated, fishing for something from his pocket. He handed a business call card to Okwudiri. 'You can reach me on this cellular number,' he said, scribbling the 090 cellular number for him. On a second thought, he added his Thuraya number in the event he was outside the cellular coverage area. He knew there would be no time for them to sit and talk for long as he would be leaving for Abuja the following day. 'I know we shall have a lot to do together. I have to be properly briefed at the Ministry and we see how to re-organise things in our hospitals. I know how good the Germans are.'

'Okay, then.' Okwudiri shook hands with him again before returning to his seat. Shortly after, they decided to leave the venue for the site of his new house under construction. 'The turnout is quite impressive,' he commented on their way out. There were many cars with the FGN number plates, pilot cars and expert rider bikes. The governor attended the church service but left shortly after the reception started.

'Paulo, you see these people in government, one should fear them. What they can do is incomparable.' The occasion was another confirmation that the growing number of Igbo moneybags in Onitsha, Lagos, Kano, Aba, and other cities were way behind what their counterparts in government service could do. After recording quick financial successes, most of the youth in business wrote off civil service workers for their lack of financial firepower. He told them about his maternal uncle who was regarded as a never-do-well and how that image was suddenly transformed. The man was in civil service for over twenty-five years. When he was made a director in one of the ministries, he completed a country home that was a wonder to behold. The whole of Abatete did not see a house that was comparable to it in sophistication. On the day one of his daughters got married, Abatete saw the crème de la crème of federal government functionaries.

Businessmen and traders made such a determined effort to meet up with the standards set by the mainstream workers in the civil service. They encouraged one another to attend events hosted by members of their business communities in large numbers to give strong presence just like when top government functionaries hosted events. At a point, they made sure they drove their cars in convoy with the pilot drivers blaring sirens, announcing their presence on the road or arrival at events. Like flag officers, some of them hoisted the national flags on their cars. Whenever they witnessed events such as this, they realised that all their money could not buy such finesse, and this made them feel that the gap had, once again, been widened.

Work was at an advanced stage in the new storey building under construction when Okwudiri and his friends called. Okwudiri had invested the substantial sums of money made at the early stages of his life as a businessman into building a house which his parents and siblings could move into. Shortly after, he travelled to Belgium but eventually settled in Germany after he got married to a German lady. He was actively engaged in the business of shipping secondhanded goods into the country. In his second year, he shipped over one hundred cars and lorries and the fortune he made from it he sunk into buying the adjacent land and erecting the tasteful storey building under construction. 'Oh oh ho yah ooo,' Anayo exclaimed with delight. 'Paulo, is this not the storey building you started the other day? It is almost complete. That was very fast.'

'You have set a new record. Completing a storey building within a year is no mean feat,' Obiora added. Okwudiri accepted the compliment, stating that good things had consumed his money. He left his kinsmen to carry on with the blame game. They inspected the plastering going on at the site. The work was satisfactory. Obiora noted that his friend really sank a lot of money into the building. He saw the architectural drawing and prototype when Okwudiri visited fourteen months earlier to start the project. Seeing the prototype translated into an edifice within a short time was simply awesome. Okwudiri wanted it to be ready before his family could visit.

Later that evening, Okwudiri sat with his parents to discuss. It was the only night he would be spending in the village. 'How is my grandson?' his mother asked.

'They are fine. Erika sent her greetings. There are some things she sent to you.'

'When will they come for our eyes to behold them?' Ozurumba asked.

'It has to be the coming year. Perhaps, during the holidays when I'm sure the building will be ready,' he told them. He was equally eager to bring his family to know where he came from. Ozurumba was happy to hear that and told him that Igboajuchi's wife had put to bed about two months earlier. Okwudiri confirmed he spoke with his elder brother after the childbirth. That could explain why he had not visited home to see them for more than three months. Kperechi told Okwudiri how his brother worked so hard supervising the building. 'He must have shown the contractor that he has experience.'

'A number of alterations were made at his instance. He really made good use of the skill,' Ozurumba agreed. At Kperechi's prodding, he told Okwudiri about their meeting with Ekeleme. 'His son, Michael, wants to travel abroad and they are looking for how to raise money to finance his journey. They are putting up that parcel of land near the school for sale.' Okwudiri mulled over it before agreeing to help them raise the money. 'You can go ahead to discuss with them. Let me know how much they want.'

27.

The gate swung open to allow the convoy of expensive cars drive into the compound. In a show of camaraderie, Okwudiri's friends had driven to Port Harcourt International Airport to receive him. Chauffeurs revved car engines to excite family members and relatives who had gathered to welcome them, opening and slamming car doors to show off. As a doting husband, Okwudiri hurried to the other side of the car to open the door for Erika. The compound became animated with loud greetings. Most of them were eager to greet Erika as Okwudiri unbuckled the seatbelt to get Charles and little Irina out.

'Erika, welcome, welcome,' Kperechi greeted, both women locked in warm embrace. 'Oh my daughter-in-law, you're a beautiful woman. *Asampete nwa* that is what you are.' Although she had seen Erika's pictures, she was delighted to see her person. They were about the same height and her curves were fairly well endowed.

'*Danke,*' she started in German before switching quickly to English. 'Thank you. You are fine?' asked Erika, picking her English words with much effort.

'Fine, fine, *nwam,*' Kperechi was all smiles. 'You are well?' she asked, also choosing from her limited words of English.

They went to greet Ozurumba who remained seated on his easy chair at the veranda of the older structure. His face beamed with joy as he welcomed them. 'How are you?' he asked Charles, stretching out his hand to shake him.

Erika was on her knees speaking with Charles to have him greet his grandfather properly. 'Grandpa, *der Opa,*' Erika spoke in German language. The puzzled look on his face showed the difficulty of reconciling the new figure he was seeing as his grandfather, given the person he knew as grandfather. He asked questions which Erika answered. Persuaded, Charles placed his hand in grandpa's hand and went for a hug.

'Good boy. So how are you?' Ozurumba asked.

'Fine,' Erika replied on his behalf, her blond curls tumbling with each nod. Besides the Pidgin English, she noticed everyone speaking to her raised their voices and gesticulated hoping this would convey their message and help her make sense of it. Ozurumba asked after her people but she could not make out his words.

'*Wie wäre es mit Ihren Mitarbeitern?*' Okwudiri interpreted.

'Fine, fine, thank you,' she answered, stretching her hand to take Irina who was sniffling and determined to get away from the strange faces and back to the arms of her mother. 'It's time to feed, isn't it?' Okwudiri signalled to her, asking them to go up after the euphoria of the initial meeting had died down. Their suitcases and other luggage were sent up.

'Charles, *kedu*, how are you?' Nwakego was asking as she lifted the young mulatto unto herself. Her toddler who felt displaced started crying, stretching his hand to be carried. She was constrained to carry two of them at the same. '*Chei*, it appears Ozurumba has reincarnated himself while alive,' she said, gazing into his face.

Ijuolachi hopped out of the car that brought her home. She took Charles from Nwakego and went upstairs to meet his parents in their room. 'Welcome! Welcome!' she cried loudly from the passage to announce herself before knocking at the door. Okwudiri opened the door whereupon Ijuolachi embraced him briefly before holding Erika in warm embrace. 'You're welcome to your country. I'm sure you will enjoy your stay here,' she said, picking up Irina.

'Sure, sure,' she answered, standing straight with her hand on her nape, or running it through her hair at intervals. 'This is Iju. . .' Erika guessed, attempting to pronounce her name with much difficulty.

'Yes, this is Ijuolachi,' Ijuolachi answered. 'I came after your husband,' she said pointing to Okwudiri who was shaking the feeding bottle of the milk he had just prepared for Irina.

'Okwy, is it not terribly cold,' Ijuolachi asked, making her way out of the room that was freezing cold from the air conditioner.

'If this is cold, will you survive winter if you come to Germany?' Okwudiri asked. Erika looked quizzical, making Okwudiri interpret what they said.

'This is good,' Erika answered, going to the window to draw back the curtain to let in light from the waning evening sun. 'Aaaa,' she gasped with delight beckoning at them to join her to see the verdant foliage a short distance from the house. 'Awesome!'

Curiously, Ijuolachi went to see the object of her pleasure. 'Forest, bush,' she said, unable to see what could excite her.

'Mother Nature!' she cried, delighted.

'Have you seen the type of thing *nwa beke* likes? If you allow her, we would be out there on an adventure to discover the plants and animals in our environment and their taxonomy.'

'What we are running away from?' Ijuolachi was surprised. How could she be excited at the sight of trees and bushes, the same thing that represented backwardness? They yearned for civilisation as the effective tool that would tear the thicket to make way for a new dawn characterised by tarred road and street lights.

'Her father is a reputable botanist and worked in different conservatories and botanical gardens until he retired two years ago. She likes exploring the jungle to discover various kinds of plant,' Okwudiri told her. He lapsed into German to have some conversation with his wife to which she nodded vigorously, sticking out her three fingers on her right hand, looking quite proud. 'Yes, her dad worked as a botanist and conservator for more than thirty years.'

'*Uwam la Chim bia rara ofe okwuru,*' Ijuolachi exclaimed in pleasant surprise, uttering the native invitation to her world and Maker to a sumptuous meal of okra soup. She could not understand why anyone would be happy and proud about working in a plant nursery for so long. 'Let me leave you two. I want to change my cloth.'

'Are you in the military? A soldier?' Erika asked.

'No,' said Ijuolachi, smiling. 'This is uniform for National Youths Service Corps,' she explained, expecting Okwudiri to explain it better.

'Please make sure my guests are properly served. I will be with them shortly,' he told Ijuolachi as she opened the door to leave the room.

The following day turned out to be sunny. Having rained that morning, the air was cool and pleasant to the skin. The refreshing atmosphere turned out to be a blessing in the absence of electricity to power the air conditioners. Charles was as happy as he could be, wearing his sleeveless top with New York Yankees inscription, smart brown khaki shorts and summer sandals while Irina was dressed in flowery Caribbean summer wear. Erika noticed that her children shared a number of physical attributes with those of Nwakego's children who were equally robust and well-nourished. She did not cringe from the overzealous relations or local folks who wanted to interact with them. Okwudiri excused himself to follow his friends out for some time. '*Ich werde nicht mehr lange dauern,*' he told her, promising he won't be long.

'*Erzähl Nwakego wohin du gehst zu,*' Erika replied, asking him to tell Nwakego where exactly. '*Wir kommen zu Ihnen holen, wenn man zu lange zu bleiben.*'

Okwudiri smiled at her threat of coming to fetch him. '*Wie viele Stunden? Fünt?*' he asked, showing three fingers to indicate how many hours he would be away.

For a fleeting moment, Erika shook her head vigorously. '*Du wagst es? Zwei max,*' she answered, holding up two fingers. Okwudiri gathered her into his arms and cuddled her for a while, giving her a kiss. 'Take care of her. If she's getting bored, you can take them out for a walk,' he told Nwakego.

'Make sure you don't stay too long, you know she is *nwa beke*, before she starts speaking what I don't understand,' Nwakego warned. She gave expression to the common notion that white people were delicate and sometimes difficult to please.

'Get the gas cylinder,' Okwudiri told Oliver who had just handed a list of grocery needs to him. Opening the car's pigeonhole, he locked away his wallet and an envelope filled with a bundle of crisp naira notes. He strapped on his seatbelt as the BMW 5-Series rolled out of the compound. The interior remained posh—a comfortable off-white leather seat, a dashboard with an array of dials with 'airbag' embossed on the passenger side. The roundel on the steering wheel gleamed calmly calling to mind all he knew about Bavaria Motor Works. The picture of a white aircraft propeller slicing through the blue sky crossed his mind fleetingly.

'*Nna*, this car is simply exquisite,' Chimezie remarked, raising the volume of the music. *Exodus* floated from the speakers. The unmistakable voice of Bob Marley filled the car with the positive force of the legend who had lived like a meteor. 'The Germans spent their time to build this car,' he enthused.

'That's German technology for you,' said Okwudiri, with a tinge of pride. 'It's a country that boasts of excellence in virtually everything they do, especially their technology.'

Chimezie drove the car into David's compound and tooted the horn expecting him to come out. He appeared on the veranda, wearing an inner vest and combing his hair. Okwudiri wound down his glass. 'You are not ready?'

'I am, but won't you come in? You have to break kola with me in accordance with tradition? Have you forgotten that I am a titled man?' he cajoled.

Chinyere, David's wife, came out to open the glass door. The parlour was spacious and uncluttered despite the big entertainment centre with the external speakers on the sides. The settee was designed in a semi-circle which could seat over ten persons and a circular centre-table took most of the space. A big native ottoman made from less refined leather occupied a position close to the room divider. The red and black colour with the artistic designs of a big calabash used by the nomadic Fulani women for selling fresh milk and steamed millet balls confirmed it was a product of Hausa artisans. Synthetic creeping flowers crawled out of various flower vases at different corners of the house. Some of them were suspended by antimacassars. Benin masks decorated the curtain pelmets. Water bubbled in a cheaper imitation of a locally fabricated aquarium that was covered with antimacassar. The plastic used lacked the transparency common with standard glass aquariums. A school of tiny goldfish swam in what was meant to be a coral reef with sandy waterbed, algae, plankton, and other aquatic livestock. A number of china figurines stood on the shelves.

'*Okwa Dike, Omere-Oha, Oshimiri Atata, Opi Dinta,*' Chimezie cried various praise names which David acknowledged with inebriated swagger and backslapping of hands in traditional greeting that was not common to their part of Igbo land. David returned the greetings, calling him *Onwa-Zuru Igbonile*—the moon that shone for the whole Igboland. The Jacquard brocade which sat comfortably on David was a top of the range Swiss voile, which contrasted with his black brimless hat. He set before them five-lobed kola nut, garden eggs and alligator pepper in the ceramic kola disk placed on the centre table.

'*Izuru ezu na nwoke*, you're a complete man,' Chimezie replied, pushing out his chest.

Okwudiri kept his cool by refusing to let the show of conviviality get the better of him. He shook hands with David. 'You know I'm not a titled man like you fellows,' he said as an excuse for not joining them in the exuberance. He drank the undiluted palm wine with relish as he ate garden egg with the flavoured groundnut paste. '*Chei* this *okpokiri* reminds me of my uncle, Uwakwe. I'm not sure anyone could tap palm wine like him.'

'He was exceptional,' Chimezie concurred. 'Palm wine is now a big treat,' he said, draining the contents of his glass.

'Who wants to be known as a palm wine tapper these days?' asked David. 'That is why a bottle of good palm wine cost more than a bottle of beer,' he said, shoving a pinch of alligator pepper into his mouth at intervals, quietly chanting incantations. Sometimes he held his *ofor* totem aloft, praising and pouring encomiums on what it represented, calling it by the names of various warriors. Okwudiri was amused and asked him when he became such an ardent idol worshipper. 'You don't understand,' David riposted. 'The white man started by giving our tradition bad names. You see, you call it idol worship. You give a dog a bad name to hang it. But some of us know better now. We have resolved to go back to our roots.'

'Are you no longer a Christian?' Okwudiri asked him.

'Who are the church leaders?' Chimezie asked.

Okwudiri merely smiled and allowed the issue to pass. He did not want to get into any unpleasant argument about the way another person chose to live his life. He knew that David's argument glossed over the true reason for those like him who went to hide behind the traditional religion which they had previously renounced. He was aware of the hideous things done in secret—the mediums that were consulted, sorcery, and other arcane practices undertaken—all done in the pursuit of wealth. Eventually, what they did in hiding became open secrets. There was a growing home movie industry that was bent on exposing the evil practices that was dismantling every form of social cohesion in their time. Driven by the curiosity of the people to know the secrets behind certain wealth in a society that was in the grip of cabals, the film industry did not cease to whet the appetite of a public that is a victim of ungodly practices.

David was aware of the heavy burden of observing the strict rules required to keep the wealth. Some lived in sheer torment, unable to sleep from day to day. Whenever they succumbed to sleep, horrifying nightmares with packs of demons tormenting them made their lives a living hell. A healthy man could be obliged to sleep with an insane woman for the money to flow. The rate at which mad women were getting pregnant confirmed it was no fiction. Some were constrained to shed the blood of their fellow human beings. Lives of family members were given; some gave themselves or mortgaged their soul to enjoy the wealth for a certain time. When the time was over, they must die even if it was untimely. Those were the definite prices paid for riches.

With the priest of each deity determining what was or was not acceptable to the god, the traditional religion provided a cover for those who had chosen this path. For a people who did not merely accept the gospel but were keen to uphold and advance its tenets to the point of purity in all spheres of life, mammon worship was a difficult challenge.

'Guess who I saw in town this morning? Ralph,' announced Chimezie, taking a bite from one of the kola nut lobes. 'So, it is true he was deported from Amsterdam?'

'Don't mind the idiot. Who knows if he voluntarily submitted himself to be deported?' David asked. 'I have not seen a lazy fellow like him. He cannot hustle like his mates. All he wants is to sit and consume what others have laboured for. Anyway, can he spend all the money his father has made?'

'That guy is a prodigal son. If you allow him, he will level that money in less than five years,' Chimezie was certain.

'More jobs are falling through by the day. *Mugu fall. . .*'

'*Guyman whack*,' Chimezie parroted, completing a local cliché for those that were totally devoted to moneymaking. So far money was being made; that was all that mattered. It did not matter whether it was made by swindling, obtaining by false pretences, couriering narcotics, manipulating and cooking account books. The only form of moneymaking that did not go down well with the devotees was robbers arming themselves with gun to waylay others on the road or attacking people in their homes.

From the way they were carrying on, Okwudiri believed they were not aware of the major incident in Amsterdam which led to the crackdown on immigrants. 'I don't think you know about the outrage that took place in Bijlmer.'

'What outrage?' David asked.

He narrated the story briefly. A drug courier was unable to excrete the package of drugs he swallowed despite all he took to induce them to come out. 'Suspecting foul play, the consignees lost their patience, slit his stomach open to get to the drugs and threw his human remains off a balcony.'

'Crazy world,' Chimezie said. 'They could have given him more time.'

Toughened by experience, David showed little or no emotions. 'That is the risk in this business. One thing or another is bound to kill a man.' He knew they were living dangerously and whenever one of them fell like the character in the story, they still had to soldier on. The fear of death did not deter men from going to war. Their generation had taken a difficult route in the search for wealth. It had paid off for some, resulting in a complete and sudden change in their environment. Their locality earned the appellation 'small London', an expression that celebrated their success. 'It must have provoked a massive manhunt,' he guessed.

'Such manhunts easily expose illegal immigrants in a country. Were the drug dealers arrested?' asked Chimezie. Okwudiri told them that the building was a condominium which made it difficult to identify the particular floor it fell from. As a result, police cracked down on immigrants in Bijlmer and all of Holland. Buildings housing people in the area were pulled down for redevelopment. They could not believe the extreme people could go for the sake of money.

'Any risk taker knows what he has signed up for. Death could come anytime anyhow,' David did not bother with the question of right or wrong. 'If it had been a successful trip, when he retires to enjoy the money people would call him names. That is why I don't blame those who enjoy this money whenever it gets into their hands. Whatever enters this stomach, that is all it gets, isn't it? Life is unpredictable and death could come at any time.'

'Do you still hear from Vanessa?' Okwudiri asked.

Chimezie smiled and shook his head. He was deported from Austria for drug offences. From all indication, Okwudiri could tell he was still into it. He did not hear from her for more than two years. Asked about the two boys born during the relationship, Chimezie said there was nothing he could do and hoped they would look for him when they grow up. Dwelling on the subject easily reminded him the story of his life. As one of those determined to get to Europe by all means and at all cost, he recollected the harrowing experiences he went through. He told them about the human traffickers that took them through the tortuous trip to North Africa. Stranded in Algiers for more than two years, he did all he could to survive. From there he moved to Tangier before he crossed over to Tarifa, Spain. His story was not different from that of Uche that was dumped in Turkey when he could not say ordinary 'come' in Turkish. To get to Greece, Uche trekked all the way from Turkey. A Good

Samaritan saw him lying exhausted at the railway station. That is where he met Hadassah, the woman that he eventually married.

Okwudiri stood up, ready to go. 'The palm wine tapper: can he really say all that he saw during his tapping exercise?' he asked as they left the parlour.

'If he does, ears will tingle,' David did not hesitate to agree with him.

*   *   *

Okwudiri went to the kitchen where Oliver was grilling fish and chicken. 'Do we have more ice cubes?' he asked, taking two stem glasses from the rack. With four cubes in each glass, he poured out shots of Malibu Rum with coconut. Wearing palm sandals, beach shorts, and a sleeveless T-shirt, Okwudiri took the drinks upstairs. He was on the veranda when the gate swung open for the entry of a metallic grey Mercedes-Benz S-Class and Cherokee Jeep. They rolled into the compound, the engine steaming silently. Victor and his family alighted from the Mercedes-Benz car that was still humming with air conditioners. Tagbo and his friends who came down from the Cherokee Jeep looked quite robust and well fed. Phillip had folds at the back of his head.

'Guess who we have here?' he asked Erika who was wearing shorts and spaghetti top.

She stubbed out her cigarette in the ashtray. '*Wer?*' she asked, in German. 'Victor!'

'*Amerikanisches*,' said Erika, smiling, her eyes behind big brown sunglasses. Okwudiri also smiled, remembering Victor's wife, Frieda, who thought that Victor was an American when their relationship started. They met at a club where Victor, with Stars-Spangled bandana tied round his head and American accent, carried himself like a shorter version of Hulk Hogan. She had been swept off her feet by his friendliness and charm. As Oliver ushered them into the inner parlour, Okwudiri and Erika came down to welcome them. They had lunch together after drinks.

Okwudiri pushed the sliding door back until it stopped at the same point as the collapsible burglar-proof screen. The exterior magnificence of the house was enhanced by the opulence of the parlour. Drawing open the curtains, which, like the embroidered valance, were made of taffeta, he tied them back to allow for more air. 'Where's Oliver?' he called, raising his voice.

'Yes sir,' answered Oliver, bearing a tray of washed glasses, which he placed on the counter of the home bar. '*Oga*, mosquitoes and houseflies, won't they come in?' he asked, mindful of the approach of eventide.

'Don't worry, I bought insecticide,' Okwudiri answered. 'The generator cannot run the air conditioners.'

'This house is well-built,' Phillip commended, admiring the interior décor. The floor was made of deep green and maroon marbles and black chips flattened into the polished terrazzo floor, giving it a glossy finish. The Styrofoam roses in the ceiling enhanced the beauty of the chandelier, and an exquisitely designed glass table stood on a fluffy carpet at the centre. 'Paulo, this is evidence of good taste.'

'My boy, this is simply classy. I'm glad you did not disappoint me,' said Tagbo, noticing that virtually everything in the house was imported. 'But the best thing about a house is the interior décor. You really followed my instructions on quality,' he boasted, taking a sip of beer from the glass.

'*Taa* nwoke m!' Okwudiri hushed Tagbo. 'It appears you've forgotten. . .'

'Forgotten what?' Tagbo challenged.

'Have you forgotten me, Okwy, Paulo *gburugburu*, isn't it?' asked Okwudiri, thumping his chest with pleasure. 'Anyway, I credit Erika with all these,' Okwudiri told them. They had shopped for the furniture and fittings and other household items, which he shipped down to Port Harcourt in a forty-foot container. From the look on Erika's face, she did not follow the conversation very well. '*Er will unsere Inneneinrichtung*,' Okwudiri told her.

Erika smiled at the obvious compliment before turning to have an animated conversation with Freida in German. 'European standards,' she said, sipping her soda on ice before adding, '*was uns felt, ist nur Schwimmbad.* Weather, hot, swim, swim. . .' She made a sign for swimming, shaking her head at what she considered sweltering heat. Okwudiri instructed Oliver to put the generator on.

'That's quite true,' Victor agreed as Erica and Frieda excused themselves so they could go upstairs to be with the children. 'Maybe, we'll consider heading to Port Harcourt. I'm sure the Presidential Hotel will have a good swimming pool.'

Okwudiri thought it was a brilliant idea. 'It's not a bad idea, you know.' Shortly after, the familiar sound of the alarm went off indicating that electric power had been restored. Oliver came in to switch off the air conditioners and other electrical appliances before going to turn off the generator. '*Arinze Chukwu*, God is gracious. Let's hope it can power the air conditioners.'

Surprised at how beautiful the women were, Tagbo could not resist the urge to put a question to his two friends. 'Paulo, you have not told us the secret of how you came about these beautiful damsels. Is it not the same Europe?' They had seen different types of European women—the obese, the old spinsters, the divorcees, midgets or those with health issues—brought home by young men to attend marriage registries. Since they were not able to attract the attentions of their compatriots, the status-seeking immigrants came in handy.

'Are you suggesting that I, Okwudiri Mbachu alias Paulo, can't get a good-looking woman anywhere, anytime?' Okwudiri asked. There was a mischievous smile on his face as he used a slice of tomato to dab spicy *Mai Suya* granules in the plate of grilled fish and mutton.

Victor threw his arms wide open to describe the size of the woman a fellow from his village brought home to marry. 'Do you know what a friend asked? What would happen if the woman finds herself on top of the man whether playing or fighting? There will be emergency. . .' he said, smiling. Pouring Campari into half a glass of Schweppes soda, he scooped some ice cubes into the glass. He took a sip and nodded his head at the taste. The mix was exactly what he wanted. 'It was one Osahon that opened our eyes to the idea of marrying the white ladies.'

'It appears you have perfected the art of mixing drinks,' Okwudiri teased.

'When you live with a white woman in a house, you must know the recipes for various cocktails. Otherwise you won't be able to maximise the pleasure of. . .' the mischievous grin breaking forth on Victor's face left his listeners to figure out the rest. 'While many of us were hiding from the police, Osahon brought home a woman who was old enough to be his grandmother. Before we knew what was happening, he became a Dutch citizen.'

'The truth is that my wife said she likes mulattoes,' Okwudiri told them. She did not hesitate when he came along. They both worked at Wertheim. Phillip had come to dislike them because of how easily they walked out of marriage anytime for any reason or no reason at all. He dated one that threw him out within six months. Victor expressed doubt that Phillip gave the woman what she wanted. 'Who has heard anything about Arinze?' Okwudiri asked.

'Nobody knows the whereabouts of Arinze anymore. The last I heard about him, he had left Taiwan and is now in Singapore,' Phillip answered. Victor welcomed the idea as he was aware that development was rapidly sweeping through the country. I heard that Azuka travelled to China?'

'That is the new destination for our businessmen. China business has no part two,' Phillip stated confidently. 'As your container is landing, that is how traders are queueing to buy wholesale from you.' Victor opened his arms wide to describe what the profit margin looked like. Okwudiri paid Phillip compliments for really doing well. The rings of flesh folds on his nape were easily noticeable. Like many young and successful businessmen of his time, he had taken time to spoil himself with gourmet meals, choice wines and fruit juice. When his bank account started to bulge, he had gone into seclusion in a good hotel where he ate well-prepared meals and getting a full blast of the air conditioners. It was a reward to his body for all the pains taken in the struggle to achieve success.

'Paulo, have you heard that Udoka is no more?' Obiora asked.

'What?' Okwudiri screamed, shocked. 'What happened?'

'He turned into a vulture but could not change back to human being,' Tagbo told him.

'Are you talking about the Udoka that I know or a different Udoka?' Okwudiri probed.

'It was Ekene your friend that misled him,' Obiora alleged before summarising the story. Ekene's business picked up very well after four years of trying to find his feet. Within a year he opened two additional shops and was building a house in Ochanja. Before many of them realised it, Ekene became a big shot in Onitsha.

'What kind of big shot?' Tagbo challenged, his frowning face showing his disdain. 'He has sold his soul to the devil just for the sake of money. Judgment Day is coming.'

'How did the sheep suffer tooth decay when it was the dog that consumed faeces?' Okwudiri asked, unable to piece the jigsaw together. Udoka went to the witch doctor that helped Ekene. Three of them had gone for the money-making talismans. They consented to be turned to vultures and would remain so for three days. Unfortunately for them, the native doctor was crushed to death while crossing a road. On the third day when they returned, the native doctor was not there with his antidote. The three vultures flew to their various shops and perched on the roof. People realised they were a different kind of vulture with human legs. Okwudiri had goose bumps. He snapped his fingers slowly in revulsion. 'May such evil not befall my kith and kin,' he said, heaving his shoulder. 'This is stranger than fiction.'

'It's no fiction. The calendars and almanacs that were made from it sold like hotcake. If you go to certain homes today, you'll see the pictures,' Tagbo said.

'This is what I saw long ago,' Victor stated, snapping his fingers to denote time. 'I said it. This rat race for money has never gone down well with me *chaa*.' His voice conveying his displeasure at the choice their friends had made.

Obiora, Tagbo, and Phillip could not be persuaded to spend the night with them. 'Owerri is just a stone's throw away,' Phillip reasoned. Obiora reassured that they would be back the next day to participate in the celebrations. As they drove out of Mboha, the promise of pomp and pageantry was evident on the eve of the fiesta. Different parts of the village were festooned with balloons, ribbons, tinsels, and incandescent ornaments in addition to the ceremonial costumes of various age groups with their insignias. There was a pervasive air of jubilation.

The following day, all roads led to Mboha as the *Iriji* ceremony got underway. Onyinye, the president-general of Mboha Progressive Union, assured everyone of nothing less than a carnival as part of the modernisation process. To allay the concerns of practising Christians, a number of them formed part of the local organising committee. They agreed to exclude anything like masquerades, pouring of libation, blood sacrifice to various pantheons and other forms of non-Christian rituals. Those were the practices that made the ceremony to be seen as heathen practices. It was purely a thanksgiving event similar to a harvest and bazaar, except that the village was organising it.

As the sons and daughters of Mboha gathered with their well-wishers to celebrate, the sprinkling of different skin colours—the initial evidence of a new diversity—did not go unnoticed. The success most of them yearned for seemed to have come to stay, but hearing the stories of what men did for the sake of money, Okwudiri wondered if it was what they bargained for. In the increasingly difficult economic environment, the number of those who could pursue their life ambitions without getting involved in one satanic scheme or another continued to shrink.

28.

Ozurumba switched on the light although the bathroom door was ajar. The voltage was so low that the dim light from the sixty-watt bulb did not light up the room well enough. Perhaps, the transformer that was recently installed was bad again. The light admitted by the translucent window louvers augmented it. Massaging his body with hot water, his mind drifted away, remembering how things used to be for his family in a past that was not too distant. He did not have to wait till late in the night anymore to take his bath under the cover of darkness. There was no need to avoid the enclosure that served as bathroom with its mucky water-logged floor and irritating earthworms. Eventually, he became a living testimony.

With Okwudiri doing well in business, the whole family was gradually lifted from poverty. Igboajuchi was a transporter working for a man that owned a fleet of vehicles but he became his own boss when he started driving one of the station wagons Okwudiri sent. He also took one of the trailer heads to start a haulage business, which was growing. Akachi his brother had left for the USA for further studies. Okwudiri had confirmed he was training to become a pilot after qualifying as aeronautic engineer. Ijuolachi had equally completed her university education. Nwakego's husband was doing well. One lighted candle was overpowering what was a looming darkness and strangulating poverty. From the overcrowded compound, he moved to a new homestead. Anyone who knew that parcel of scrubby land would be surprised at how it transformed into a home. Okwudiri had bought a bigger parcel of land adjacent to it. Akobundu had offered the land to them to raise money to fund the travelling expenses of his son, Uchechukwu, who wanted to travel to Europe.

If nothing else, it demonstrated that the lessons of the war did not go unheeded. Owning a building in the village was an essential, even if it was the most simple of structures. But Okwudiri's generation did not only go to Lagos,

Port Harcourt, Onitsha, Kano, and other business centres in the country. The soles of their feet had touched the grounds of other lands and climes and they returned with a new concept of what a family home should look like.

If there was any fly in his ointment at that time of great celebration, it was the absence of Igboajuchi. They had expected him to return with his family. Having worked tirelessly to ensure that the contractor maintained the quality of work and kept within the timeframe, his presence was necessary to enable the whole family celebrate together. Also it would have been a great opportunity for his grandchildren to meet themselves for the first time. Okwudiri had maintained they would not spend more than two weeks since it was an international flight. With only three more days to go, the hope that Igboajuchi and his family would come in time to meet Okwudiri's family began to fade. As the time continued to run, their disappointment gave way to anxiety.

'Maybe, his children are still in school,' Nwakego thought aloud while they talked about it the previous night.

'What kind of school?' Kperechi asked sourly. 'This opportunity does not come every day.' In the absence of riots, it was easy to imagine that the problem could be the schools. The frequent industrial actions by school teachers at the local and national levels had altered the school calendar. The long vacation period in July, August, and September was equally affected. Many school systems had to make up for lost time and could be found in session even in August.

'Should I proceed to Kaduna to find out what is wrong?' Ijuolachi volunteered.

Nwakego thought it was too late. She calculated the length of time the journey would take. 'It will take you a whole day before you get there unless you want to make a night trip.'

Kperechi would not hear of it. 'Make a night trip—from which house? Nobody is stepping out of this house on a night trip.' The story of violent armed robbery attacks along the northern route had sent shivers down the spines of all that heard it. It was not the usual attack of robbing passengers of moneys and possessions. The armed robbers were heartless and shot indiscriminately, nearly killing all the passengers. Such massacre in the name of armed robbery was so cruel and unusual. Armed robbers were known to kill one or two passengers to demonstrate intent and it was enough to frighten other passengers to comply with whatever they demanded. Investigations traced the violent robberies to a bandit from a neighbouring country on the northern borders.

'It will take you another day to come back. By that time, Okwudiri and his family will be on their way,' Nwakego concluded.

Ozurumba returned to his easy chair at the veranda after massaging his body with *ori* and *okwuma*. He ran a comb on his hair, which had lost volume but remained black with few strands of grey despite his age. He was unable to gobble down the venison set for him on the side stool despite the delicious aroma of *uziza*, one of his favourite spices, and hot chilli. The family cat, crouching on the windowsill, drooled at the sight of the covered plates, mewing loudly, her gaze fixed on Ozurumba. 'Are you hungry?' he asked. He was happier feeding the cat by spooning some of the pieces of meat on the floor. The pussycat must have found it hot for her palate. She coughed, shook her head vigorously. It occurred to Ozurumba that the cat needed water. With his walking stick, he drew a small bowl at the corner closer and poured some water from his cup. Gladly, the cat lapped some to quell the hot sensation before going back for more pieces of meat on the floor. After four more morsels, the cat went back to the plate to drink and refused to go back for more meat. 'Are you full?' Ozurumba asked. 'Or is it too peppery for you?' he asked without expecting an answer. He reclined back on his seat, his hand above his head.

As he looked out, the imposing mansion crept into his thoughts once more. The civilisation which they had pined for had really taken root in Mboha in his lifetime. While they rejoiced at the physical transformation, there was growing concern that the simplicity and innocence of rural life had been replaced with alienation. Money was all that mattered. A child could no longer fetch a bucket of water for an elderly person without naming his price. Maybe Ozurumba was one of the few who believed that Mboha was still a village. At the last count, the village alone could boast of more than fourteen two-storey buildings excluding those abandoned halfway, some of them sandwiched between less flattering structures. But a different voice argued from within: did he count those of Ajuzie, Young, Uchechukwu, and Chikodi? He started all over again, keeping count with his fingers but got different results after three attempts. He gave it up. Most importantly, the wheel of fortune had not passed his family by.

The village was producing a number of illustrious sons and daughters that were doing the country proud. Emma Nwokocha became a very important scientist in America and was doing amazing things with computers. He was known to draw a perfect circle without the aid of any mathematical sets. As the villagers heard, he worked in a place where they make spaceship that go to the moon. He made so much money from one of the patents he registered that he came home to build something similar to Iroegbulemville. Sunday Nwokocha, his father, travelled to USA. There was no hesitation in granting him USA citizenship and a number of his siblings had equally moved to America.

His thought strayed to the rabbit he saw earlier in the afternoon. He had watched out for any snake or other reptiles which could have chased it out of hiding but he saw none. Immediately, he began to mouth a number of verbal prophylactics to remonstrate against any form of evil it represented. 'Whoever harbours positive thoughts shall harvest the benefits of positive thinking. Goodness is the reward of those who do good. Is anything comparable to a clean heart and a clean spirit? Anyone whose thought is filled with evil, can he ever experience goodness? Never! Evil shall follow him in the daytime, at night-time, and all the time. Evil shall dot his steps at all times of his life and overwhelm him. The Maker of the Universe, see, my hands are clean. If I did not plan and did no evil against any one, why should I expect evil? He who has done no wrong has nothing to fear. Evil shall not befall me.'

Known as nocturnal creatures, sighting rabbit in the daytime when it was not fleeing from the hot pursuit of a predator was a bad omen. If there were times he was sorely tempted to consult an oracle for the divination of the unknown, this was one of such times. But at the instance of his father, he had never patronised sorcerers and necromancers to foretell the future. He was not going to start it in his old age. On a second thought, he asked what type of evil could seek to befall him at a time of unspeakable joy. He had lived to witness a complete transformation in the whole of Mboha, with his household benefiting from the abundant grace that God had generously dispensed towards them as a people.

That reminded him of his nightmare three days earlier. There was confusion in the former house as an irate and murderous mob invaded the homestead insisting they would kill the billy goat which had characteristically strayed out of the compound. But Uwakwe joined him to resist their demand on the ground that a goat that was not cut down outside the owner's compound could not be pursued home. While the argument dragged, they demanded to know why Akachi failed to turn up for community service. 'Which of you does not know that Akachi has travelled out of the country?' he had asked them. They insisted on searching every part of the house. Before they could be stopped, they found the goat hiding under the table where he always kept the transistor and other family stuff. Furiously, they rained blows on the goat, hitting him like a common criminal undergoing the torture of a public show. By the time the attack was stopped, their victim had dropped dead, the body completely mangled. It turned out to be the body of Uwakwe. Ozurumba had drawn *akparaja* from the scabbard to slice off their heads when a noise in the compound woke him.

He enquired about Akachi when Okwudiri and his family came back and was reassured that he was doing well in America. He was still enmeshed in those thoughts, but the arrival of George and Oriaku brought him back to the present. After they exchanged greetings, Ozurumba called the young boy living with them. 'Clement lee!' there was no answer. 'Clement lee!' Ijuolachi came to tell him that the boy went on errand for her. She curtsied to greet the visitors. While standing up to go into his parlour, her father requested that she get some liquor shots for him. He returned with a bottle of Gordon gin, the kola disc with lobes of kola and bitter kola. Moments later, Clement returned with the shot glasses dripping with water.

Nwakego and Erika came into the compound with the children. They stopped and chatted as the boys ran to Ozurumba. 'Hallo Opa,' Charles spoke in German, slapping Ozurumba's outstretched palm. Ozurumba also stretched out his hand to Chika for a handshake. He called Clement to get some drinks for the children. He returned with the two-litre green plastic bottle of Sprite and plastic cups. Erika came in just before the drinks were poured. She kicked against the idea of giving them the drinks at that time of the evening. 'No fizzy drinks by this time. He won't sleep,' she said picking up Irina. '*Jetzt im Obergeschoss*, upstairs now,' she spoke to Charles pointing to the new building. '*Sagen auf Wiedersehen Opa*, say bye to grandpa,' she instructed.

'Lucky generation,' Oriaku spoke with admiration, dipping a lobe of kola nut into the peppery sauce. 'The number of our boys who are getting married to white ladies is growing by the day,' he said, naming two other boys from Umuochoko that brought home two foreign ladies as wives. 'What is strange is that one of them does not understand the white man's language.'

'Oh, you thought that every white person speaks English?' George asked. 'It's like saying every black man speaks Igbo.'

'It's not a lie,' Oriaku agreed as the point dawned on him.

'The one you just saw does not speak English,' Ozurumba pointed out.

'Things have really changed,' Oriaku said reflectively. He was surprised that their own children were getting married to the children of white men. Nobody would have thought it was possible when they were young. George readily agreed that everything about the young generation was different. The size of house they built and the speed at which the house were completed; the big cars they drove to the huge figures they pronounced easily amazed him. Things he could not imagine in his own time were possible with them. How many could dream of owning one million pounds in their time? The person must own a transport company like Sir Louis Ojukwu. On that point, Oriaku observed that money had seriously lost value. 'In our time, a person building a simple house of three or four rooms could spend three or four years building it. But this imposing edifice was completed at the blink of an eyelid.'

'It fills me with wonderment,' George admitted.

'The pace at which Mboha has developed in recent times is bound to surprise anyone who has been away in the last ten to fifteen years.'

'What would you say about Umuochoko, your village? Haven't you seen the structure Anselm is putting up? It has almost challenged what Iroegbulem children built,' Ozurumba countered, making way for the pepper soup Clement came to serve them. As George noted, Anselm was one of those that went overseas while the world was still asleep. He expected such a good building from Anselm given the fact that he was a professor in England. They were more surprised at what the sons of Ibe were doing. Their success was a glowing testimony to the power of unity. They recouped what their family spent to send them abroad many times over. Oriaku believed if they could do like Okwudiri poverty would be completely banished from their family.

'Daniel, is it not the name of the first son? He's the one that sent his two brothers abroad, isn't it?' asked George.

Oriaku confirmed it, telling that in less than a year, the one called John shipped many cars home in addition to other things. 'I must be on my way,' he said after polishing off the bowl of pepper soup. 'We have just concluded the committee meeting at the church. We decided to stop over to say hello.'

Kperechi came in to meet them on the veranda as they were about to leave. Exchanging pleasantries with her, George teased her a little. 'I know you fellows will be offering us something special for the church service tomorrow.'

'Yes ooo, George, my good husband. You must be prepared for us. Make sure your pocket is filled with naira,' Kperechi teased him also. The male members of the church committee had left after their usual deliberations but the women continued to conclude their plans about their charity walks the following day. She excused herself and hurried into her room. She returned shortly after and handed some money to Nkemakolam. 'My fellow woman, use the extra on top to get some goodies for the children.'

'Thank you very much Mama-ukwu. God will replenish where this has come from,' the young lady thanked her profusely when she opened her palm and saw the denomination of the naira note. It was far more than the pay for the job done. The difference was completely gratuitous. She had led a team of three women to weed Kperechi's farm.

'It was an excellent job that you did. Thank you my fellow woman,' Kperechi said.

'I have to run along to make sure that dinner is ready. I have a full house,' Nkemakolam said, bidding everyone goodnight and hastening away. 'So it is true that Chikwendu and his family returned this evening?' Ozurumba expressed no little surprise at that turn of event. None of their kinsmen had fled from the north in recent times. 'Didn't they see the soldiers' barracks to run to?'

'Didn't you hear that the soldiers were taking sides this time?' George asked. 'Some of the people that ran to the barracks were shot at night.'

Oriaku heaved his shoulders in revulsion. 'When will these people stop the incessant wasting of human lives?'

'Is it not since last week that we heard about this riot?' Kperechi asked. 'They should have quelled it by now.'

'Ok ooo, let everybody sleep and wake up well,' Oriaku said as he bade everybody goodnight.

'Sleep well,' Kperechi responded to his goodnight wishes.

*   *   *

The centenary anniversary celebration of the Umuhu Archdeaconry was a huge success. As part of their Christian service, mothers in the church decided to raise funds for the various charitable homes in addition to their continual prayers. In encouraging the members to support the noble cause, the vicar continued to remind them of the teachings of Christ: For I was hungry, and you fed me. I was thirsty, and you gave me to drink. I was a stranger, and you invited me into your homes. They had decided to visit the Motherless Babies' Home in Umuahia and the Uzoakoli Leprosy Centre.

Much of the deliberation by the Christian mothers centred on how to combine the need of raising fund for charities and praying for their communities. In their time, the women had witnessed or heard about a number of atrocities that made their ears tingle. While many continued to hunger and thirst for righteousness, an increasing number of their own were caught in the obsession of making money by hook or crook to survive the economic hardship in the country or to live their dreams of success. A village evangelist said it all: if Prophet Amos had lived in their time, he would have moved from one city to the other to cry out against their generation and deliver different messages of doom one after another.

If a fraction of those atrocities had taken place in the past, the chief priests of various villages would have called for purification to appease the gods. But Christianity had become the mainstream of their lives, the precept that righteousness exalts a nation and sin is a reproach to any people had gained ground. Their women in the cities returned to the village to join others to pray for their various communities. It became known as the August Meeting and it was quite popular. The women turned to the Bible for direction and were persuaded to heed the divine promise in the Book of Chronicles: If my people, who are called by my name, will humble themselves and pray and seek my face and turn from their wicked ways, then will I hear from heaven and will forgive their sin and will heal their land.

After the church service that Sunday, Ozurumba returned home with his children and grandchildren. He settled into his easy chair barely able to eat the lunch he was served. He had not been able to explain the foul mood which the nightmare had thrown him into. The sight of the rabbit had also aggravated it. In wishing the mothers happy celebration, a member of the public who was aware of the women's activities in the Umuhu Circuit sent out a request card on radio asking for Onyeka Onwenu's music *Ochie Dike* for his listening pleasure. His anxious mind experienced some soothing relief on hearing the song. His mind was transported back to his childhood days and his face lit up at the warm memory of Ehichanya.

His reverie was interrupted by the song of the approaching Christian mothers visiting his neighbourhood to pray. The women were clad in their uniform of blue and white wrapper and white top and most of them had another piece of the wrapper as head tie. It was reminiscent of Mothering Sunday.

Anyi n'agaghari n'obodo
Anyi n'agaghari n'obodo
Anyi n'agaghari n'obodo
Irio aririo n'ikpe ekpere

Okwuchi prayed as they got close to Ozurumba's compound. 'Lift up your heads O ye gates. Be lifted up O ye ancient doors that the King of glory may come in. Who then is this King of glory? He is the Lord Almighty; he is the King of glory. Who will ascend the holy mount of the Lord but those whose hearts are pure? Create in us a pure heart oh Lord, a heart for the less privileged. Bless the homesteads in this area. Bless our husband and our children . . . in Jesus's name we pray.'

'Amen!' chorused the other women. Two or three women entered each homestead to receive donations. Ozurumba gave what he had after a brief banter with the women that came to him.

They were still in the neighbourhood when three rickety cars drove into the village, bringing home the effect of the ill-wind blowing in the north. Nathaniel, Emma, and Ahamba were there. Chiadikobi, Igboajuchi's wife, and her children were in the second vehicle. She came out of the vehicle and threw herself down wailing, something that shocked Mboha. Many hurried to know the reason for the tears.

Though the radio had reported the religious disturbances in the north, yet nothing had prepared them for their return. It was common knowledge that travelling usually came to a halt during periods of riot. Experience had taught the private coach operators to withdraw their buses from the road once the riots started. They had lost so many of their buses through wanton destruction and burning. The trains had become grounded over the years. Instead of improvement, all the rail tracks and their coaches had fallen into desuetude.

Having become more irascible and impassioned, the blood of their hosts easily boiled over at any perceived offence. Homogeneity was all that mattered and bloodletting was the only thing to quench the stirring and put the offending group in their rightful place. It overshadowed every other argument and justified the elimination of any individual or group with a different view, regardless of where they came from. Blood flowed horrendously from Zangon

Kataf to Bauchi. The streets of Kaduna to Kano, Zaria, Maiduguri, and Potiskum all turned into macabre theatres. The military barracks became the best option for those hiding from the violence like frightened rabbits. But there was a story that the soldiers had taken sides to secretly kill those who ran to them for refuge; such horror was beyond comprehension.

Mboha heard what brought them home. Igboajuchi and Ubadire were still missing since the riot took place. Both had gone out in Igboajuchi's Peugeot 505 station wagon. Their worst fears were confirmed when a car with Igboajuchi's plate number was discovered burnt beyond recognition. Traces of charred human remains were removed from the vehicle by the time it was found.

'*Owoworom m ooo! Owoworom m ooo!*' cried Okwuchi, shrieking, taking uncalculated and unrehearsed dance steps, celebrating what was at best a pyrrhic victory. 'Two heads from the same womb, where's the mouth to tell the tragic tale? At least one head is back. Mboha lee! Who would not say it is recompense for my sins? *Chineke m leeeeee! Chineke m leeeeee! Eleooo*, the sun had set at dawn,' she broke down and sobbed. Her fellow women got hold of her, stopping her frenzied and demented dance. They made her sit down. 'Will the world not ask where my God is?' she asked, standing up. 'I want to go home.' As they led her away, she stopped and clung to Nathaniel, looking closely into his face, searching for the faintest sign of a hoax, her tears flowing freely. '*Nna dim*, tell me, it is not true,' she requested, shaking her head gently, wishing she could wake up from the nightmare.

Seeing his mother's tears, Nathaniel's manliness deserted him, his sad face dissolving into tears, wailing. Others pulled him from her hold. 'What are you doing, eh? If you, a man, are crying, what do you expect of your mother and his wife?'

'That's what we've been telling him right from Kaduna,' Emma added. 'You're the one to comfort your mother. Gather yourself together.'

'*Eleoo! Eleoo! Eleeeoooo!* Goats have eaten fronds off my head ooo!' Nathaniel yelled, refusing to heed their advice of restraint, sobbing like a baby. 'So, Chioma and Dede have become fatherless!'

'Don't go on and on,' Akwakanti pleaded with him. 'You are there for them, aren't you?'

'Won't you be a father to them?' Anosike demanded.

A number of sympathisers had gathered in Ozurumba's house. Ahamba told them more about the riots. It was about the peaceful demonstration demanding the implementation of the Sharia code in Kaduna, the remonstration against it and the roadblock that resulted in open confrontation between the Muslims and Christians that led to the killing of more than fifty people. 'When peace seemed to have been restored, that was the evening Igboajuchi and Ubadire went out. We didn't know there had been silent killings all the while. That night, there was full-scale riot and killings in Tudunwada and Angwar Sunday.'

'When will they stop killing our people like this?' George mused.

'We are always their victims even when they fight their fellow northerners. That is the most annoying part of it,' Ahamba said.

'So they fight their own people too?' Akwakanti was surprised.

'Some of them are Christians. So when they fight them, we are not spared,' Ahamba answered. 'They burnt our church and knifed our priest. Whether he will survive it, I don't know.'

'Imagine,' George was surprised that religion was balkanising the north despite the cohesion that the Sardauna, Sir Ahmadu Bello worked so hard to build. 'Is it not a case of one turning round to say his brother smells like the ghost they are out to hunt?'

'The sickle they used to behead others has turned against their own people,' reasoned Okpukpukaraka.

'Blood has entered their eyes,' Ozurumba concluded, speaking for the first time since the sad news was broken. He had been staring vacantly into space, his mind far away from the turmoil around him. 'They had been killing without cleansing themselves; now human lives mean nothing to them. Kperechi always feared this uncertain end. If only we listened to her, our people would have left the north long ago.'

'He's been planning to relocate,' Okwudiri spoke, sniffling, his eyes puffy and his nose running. Erika handed him some tissues and went to hold him.

'What a way to end his journey. Is this how a warrior is sent to the grave?' Anosike lamented, his hands clasped over his head in grief.

'For the first time, our people carried out reprisal attacks on the northerners in Aba and Onitsha. What made our people to take vengeance; don't you think it is really imperative?' George asked. The import of what George said was not lost on them. Their people had shown restraint in the face of incessant attack. Killing a handful of the northerners in their midst would arm their assailants with reasons for more massacre. Their imperfections as adherents of Christianity notwithstanding, spilling human blood was not in their character. 'That tells you how bad it is. We must hope it does not result in another war.'

'If war will break out, so be it. How many times does one die? What is it?' Akwakanti added, exasperated. 'All the time they butcher our people up north, they should count themselves lucky this is not Umuahia Township where they have *Ama Awusa*. We would have laid hands on their people so they know what it feels like.'

Faced with the recurrent danger to life, they shed the garb of docility to fight for their space and gain a foothold wherever they lived. Kano witnessed the resistance—petrol bombs flew from one side against the other without their people calling retreat. It could have been worse if the coaches filled with barrel-chested *akpu obi* boys with arms and munitions heading for the warfront had not been intercepted by the intelligence agency. At the end, Sabon-Geri and No Man's Land bought some peace. Their people had shown resolve that they would no longer be cowed. But it was not until the Yuletide when most of their people travelled to the eastern part of the country for Christmas that their hosts struck again. Gideon Akaluka became their victim: his decapitated head was hoisted on a spike and taken round Kano city in a victory lap.

Kperechi's agony was visible. 'Imagine, a child that suffered all his life, working hard to support the family. See, when things were getting better that is when death came to snatch my son. *Eleooo, uwa m lee! uwa m lee!*' she cried, starting another round of wailing and grieving, her hands clasped over her head. 'If only I had been taken seriously, they wouldn't have seen my son to kill ooo! *Eleooo, eleooo*, death why didn't you come for me? Chiadikobi my daughter widowed so early in her marriage, her children suddenly fatherless. *Ewooo* what did he do? What did Igboajuchi, my son, do? *Eleooo. . .*' Kperechi refused to be consoled.

Most of them could not hold back their tears which flowed freely from reddened eyes. '*Ozuola*, it is enough. It is enough, *ndo*, my fellow woman.' Jemima held her closely, dabbing her eyes with the end of her wrapper.

'*Ozuola*, enough,' Egobeke called consolingly, holding her on the other side. '*Ebezina, nwanyi ibem Chukwu no nso*—enough, stop the tears my fellow woman, God is nigh.'

'If it is his time to go, nothing would have stopped it even if he was here in the village,' Nwugo lent her voice.

The attempt to rationalise his death and talk her out of her grief did not assuage the pain of losing him. It did not answer the questions that troubled her soul. If he had died at home, they would have seen his body to bury at least. 'Would they have crossed all the frontiers to kill him?' Kperechi asked in between her wails.

ACKNOWLEDGEMENTS

This work benefited from conversations with different persons, reading and listening to documents and materials about events and information within and outside the personal knowledge of the author. This acknowledgment recognises, *Dee* Udenze Nwachukwu and *Dee* Chinonye Nwoko for readily answering questions about traditional beliefs and practices. Edward Onyemata, Pedro Azuogu, Rev. E.O. Inyang, Alex Alino, Ndubuisi Onunze, Victor Ilo, Jossy Akwuobi, Richard Okafor, Raphael Odukwe, Oliver Orji and many others too numerous to list are equally acknowledged for different perspectives that enriched the narrative. Your good works were not forgotten.

Helen Falconer, Uduma Kalu and Viola Okoli deserve a lot of credit for editing the manuscript and calling attention to different areas that received attention and enhancements. The author takes responsibility for whatever imperfection(s) that remain. Also many thanks go to the publishing consultant and the production team. Officials of Fingal County Libraries, Blanchardstown and Central Catholic Library, Dublin were immensely helpful.

Aunty Nnenne deserves a special mention for the earliest novels meant to keep the author busy. It is natural to return thanks at this point for seeds that were unwittingly sown which is yielding good harvest. For Kelechi Nnadi, this mention acknowledges several interruptions to school homework to join in hunting for words and expressions that best convey certain thoughts. May you continue to increase in stature and wisdom. Ngozi, the Ada of Nnadiegbu was a wonderful sister. Her limited education notwithstanding, she read voraciously and had a vast collection of novels. From this fountain the author drank deeply and like the Chinese wine, it made him sober. Again, Eric Donaldson's music from her sound box was oracular. It deposited the seed that was incubated leading to the birth of this piece. That evergreen piece from Eric Donaldson *the land of my birth* inspired this voyage to discover how Mboha fared in the quest for modernity.